Terminus
and the
House of Beth-El

The background of the cover is from an engraving of part of a famous painting by the American artist, Thomas Cole (1801 to 1848), entitled "The Voyage of Life—Youth." John Smillie engraved the work for the American Art Union (1839-1851) in 1850. The engraving is from the author's collection.

Terminus
and the
House of Beth-El

Foundations for a Belief in God

William Prentice Cooper

Pentland Press, Inc.
England•USA•Scotland

PUBLISHED BY PENTLAND PRESS, INC.
5122 Bur Oak Circle, Raleigh, North Carolina 27612
United States of America
(919)782-0281

ISBN: 1-57197-198-X
Library of Congress Control Number: 99-75784

Copyright © 2000 William Prentice Cooper
All rights reserved, which includes the right to reproduce this book or portions thereof in any form whatsoever except as provided by the U.S. Copyright Law.

Printed in the United States of America

Permission is granted for: use in *Terminus and the House of Beth-El,* by William P. Cooper III, to be published by Pentland Press, 2000. Permission includes world rights. For: [1976 01 05 023 SHA .HG Panic], [1995 06 12 076 BSC .HG This], [1997 07 28 CBA .HB Called], [1997 08 25 145 DSH .HG Center], [1999 08 02 055 WHA .HG Appeared], [1999 08 23 118 GWI .HG Meteor], [1999 09 20 058 SHA .HG Software], [1999 11 01 101 NDO .HB Faithful]. November 2, 1999. Jennifer König, sales; Steeve Urban, tech.

Table of Contents

Foreword vii
Chapter One—A Matrix for the World 1
   A Soul in Science 1
      Scientific Arrangements of Trusted Experience 2
      Does Soul Have a Role? 12
   A Logic in Subjectivity 18
      The Meaningfulness of the Factual 18
      The Meaningfulness of the Existential 28
Chapter Two—The Needs of a Human Soul 37
   The "Is-ness" (Ontology) 37
   The "Feeling-ness" (Psychology) 48
Chapter Three—The Revelation of God 67
   The Entry of God into my World 67
      The Broken Hinges on the Entry's Door 67
      The Door's Wide Swing 72
   The Appearance of God in my World 77
      The Principle of Identity (Immanence) 78
      The Principle of Love 91
Chapter Four—Jesus the Christ 97
   Transcending the New Testament to Higher Truth 103
   Surpassing Clock-Time and Theology .110
Chapter Five—The Will to Believe 123
   Descriptions of the Will 124
   Results of Husserl's Descriptive Method 136
      The Awareness of the Derivation 137
      The Awareness of the Freedom 139
      The Awareness of the Time 143
      The Awareness of the Feelings 145
Chapter Six—The House of Beth-El 151
   Raising the Rock 151
   Enjoying the Place 159
Index of Names 177

qualities and attitudes into mental objects, and these objects may be properly considered to be made up mentally, just as a product or physical thing is manufactured at a factory.) During the entertainment I enjoyed while watching a recently televised game of football, some anonymous amalgamation of human-ness determined that I must see advertisements during the time of the football game which told me that: nothingness is yet a number in arithmetic; that the consequences of the natural act of sex are restricted only to my five senses; that precious time and attention, otherwise aimed at the cultivation of love, should be devoted, instead, to minute differences in edible, but fungible, quantities—just as a husband moves the emotions of his wife by pointing out that she gave herself a few flakes more in a bowl of cereal; that leaders, like bars of soap or fluids of a beverage, are The Real Thing and surely deprive their followers, knock-offs and also-rans of logic, Truth and meaning in the marketplace of ideas; that the metaphysical idea of freedom is everywhere, especially in the act of purchasing life insurance, where there is, paradoxically, a literal acquisition of an assured order thereby; that leaders of any sort visually blind their followers—just as buffaloes promoting financial planning see no more than the rumps of each other when marching in a lengthy single file like livestock during a blizzard; and that the well-dressed bodies of peaceful people sitting at desks reading books in libraries are tantamount to the information directories called "yellow pages" of the telephone system.

This last vignette of deceit from television advertising is especially noteworthy. It shows the utter confusion of communications with Real knowledge of that which is communicated, of the speaker with the spoken, and of Truth with that cognitive process by which we acquire it *as an object*. Only a knave or a fool asserts that we look up the Truth of human behavior from a telephone directory rather than as, for example, Shakespeare shows it in his dramas, or as Jesus the Christ reflected it back to us by his earthly life. The televised ad for the "yellow pages" shows the entire confusion of information-data with wisdom altogether—that is, if well-dressed readers sitting at desks in libraries are Truly described as wise and understanding of Real knowledge. Then my sadness even deepened. No knave or fool declared that we look up the Truth of God from the white pages of theology rather than as science and philosophy reflect it back to us by His earthly life in experience and empiricism. The declarer of this proposition about knowing True God from white pages was none other than one of the most respected theologians of the 20th century, the German-American professor, Paul (Johannes Oskar) Tillich (1886 to 1965). He wrote:

> "Theology, above all, must leave to science the description of the whole of objects and their interdependence in nature and history, in man and his world. And beyond this, theology must leave to philosophy the description of the structure and categories of being itself and of the logos in which being becomes manifest. *Any interference of theology with these tasks of philosophy and science is destructive for theology itself.*"[2]

Is Tillich selling the products of theology here by categorizations no better than a deceitful television advertiser would sell the new and the pure? Earlier, but also in a published work, he said that the task of cognitive understanding is integral to theology in these words:

> ". . . *the task of theology is mediation,* mediation between the eternal

[2]Paul Tillich, *Theology of Culture* (New York, Oxford University Press, 1964), p. 129 (italics added).

technically if you believe philosophizing is all that philosophers have done for more than a hundred years so that practically nothing *should* be concluded about it. But, if a self-respecting philosopher is not supposed to ask what his chosen field of intellect has learned during an era when so much else has been—if the report of *The Times* were remotely accurate, I thought to myself the decay of the so-called tradition of classical reflection by philosophers is complete. I frowned.

My frown came from my awareness of the tradition of synthesis in philosophy, of the degree of sublimity it had been, and of the bathos which the report of *The Times* showed it is at now. I remembered from my undergraduate days at Harvard when a friend of mine since boyhood entered my rooms in Quincy House and excitedly told me that the Edgar Pierce Professor of Philosophy, W. V. O. Quine (b. 1908), had discovered most of the secrets of knowledge. My friend, Stephen H. Phillips (b. 1950), became a professor of philosophy at the University of Texas himself, but I was so intimidated by the descriptions of Quine's courses that I stayed as far away from them as I could. *The Times* reported that Professor Quine, age 90, attended the Philosophy Congress and said he should have thought of an answer to the question posed to the assemblage but had not. There is no intent here to insist on anything but civil pleasantry. If, however, nothing civil or pleasant or worth saying collegially about philosophy for the last century can be said, because, indeed, the philosophizing of a century cannot be justified (learned from meaningfully), in ordinary language, this must be sad for the many who have read and studied the so-called tradition of classical reflection in philosophy. This tradition of reflection was, and is, the study of the basis for human knowledge. The study of this knowledge, in turn, entails awareness of a study of defined (when and where are we unaware?) awareness, a state of existing in awareness and unawareness for even the dullest and most brilliant intellects. I saddened when I realized that even deep thinkers shun their awareness of existence or deny the necessities about it sufficient to sustain living. What, besides life and living, do you think philosophy is good for? Is modern philosophy so tied to analytic logic that the logical prerequisite of human life is no longer required for purposes of its analysis? The lives of Einstein or Euclid or any members of the human race are intuitively unnecessary to mathematical axioms or the laws of logic. Is philosophy different because it must involve the awareness of human life by which any mathematics or logic has ever been comprehended?

My sadness at the demise of classical reflection, as emotions do to the human nervous system in an inevitable way, compounded upon itself. The compounding then caused me to feel that mentally aware people must also feel sad in many other cases where inconclusiveness and un-thinking-ness leads to a loss of perception and a forfeiture of Reality. There is a world of wretched distortions of perception which I perceive to occur daily in my life in the United States (yes, we single out nations here) during this age in which God has given me to live it. To what extent, I thought, does my sadness at the lack of sublimity from the Philosophy Congress relate to a larger problem about this common wretchedness I see? The talking heads on television in their finitely short conversations, but with an underlying, emotional Reality of their need to be noticed therein, convey all beguiling appearances of reality to me which are not Truthfully Real. Indeed, the talking voices on television assume that a listener is so aware of their deceit that they play upon it as an entertaining joke, or even to manufacture it more deceitfully. (Yes, a human mind may thing-i-fy all manner of

Surely, you say, the theories of Einstein and Euclid exist even if one were never alive to comprehend them. But, if you do not live in the first place, how do you actually assert this? Is your own Real existence in hairy flesh and red blood a prerequisite for the existence of any abstracted ones that you think will follow it? Or is your own life to be reduced to a series of abstractions also? But what do we Really mean by these words — life, existence and abstraction? You will see that there is confusion about the meanings and meaningfulness of words for practically every one of them that I know we speak and use, such that our vocabulary itself becomes quite a problem for us. You will also see that I also capitalize many words, in contravention of normal English usage, to distinguish between the relative and absolute senses in which I mean for you to find their meaning in these sentences. Also, I introduce many people to you and state, in the first instance of your encounter with them, as completely as I can, their names and dates of birth and death. To mitigate the injustice which you hold that I do to them by summarizing their works of intellect with the brevity you find here, it is the least I can do to date them properly, so that you may construct your own context of history and temper the severity, or not, with which you think I may have butchered their thoughts and chopped them badly in this discussion. I hope, therefore, that all of these conventions in my writing are not tiresome, but the result of the ineffable matters involved in my Belief in God which taxes words to their limits of utility.

Granting, even so, that the basis for writing this book is in the previous reasoning, I needed a trigger within the emotion and inspiration of life-experience to start it. This happened, to paraphrase a dramatic work of literature, suddenly, last summer. On a hot Saturday afternoon in August, I sat comfortably in the little world of my living-room, looked at my roses in a vase on a marble-topped table, reviewed paintings of landscapes on the walls of my house, listened to the sublime music of Sergei Wassilievitch Rachmaninoff (1873 to 1943) and read that day's national edition of *The New York Times*.

The bliss of that moment was soon shattered. At the bottom of a page in the section relating to culture, *The Times* printed a wry report on the World Philosophy Congress recently held in Boston. Though it would be the last of its kind in the 20th century and had assembled the active and retired luminaries of philosophy from all over Europe and America, at least according to the report of *The Times,* the Philosophy Congress did nothing, maybe less than nothing, to answer the question of what had been learned from philosophy over a hundred years. The lead of *The Times* said that, at the end of a century of philosophizing, the answer to this question was not even to ask it. If the reporter knew the difference between philosophizing and philosophy, as I think she did, she reported the distinguished assemblage could conclude nothing about a century of finding errors, correcting mistakes and backing and filling.[1] Maybe this is correct

---

[1] See Sarah Boxer, "Think Tank: At the End of a Century of Philosophizing, the Answer is Don't Ask," in *The New York Times,* Vol. CXLVII, No. 51,250 (August 15, 1998), p. A15. The question posed to the assemblage was: "What have we learned from philosophy in the 20th century?" The American philosophers of analytic logic, Willard V. O. Quine (b. 1908) and Donald Davidson (b. 1930), reportedly dodged the question or discussed the merits of air travel and E-mail. The British philosopher, Peter F. Strawson (b. 1919), parsed the words of the question into so many bits and said there would be either no reply or no shortage of replies, but, if the latter, no indication any compelling answers would be found among any of them. The German philosopher of transcendental semiotics, Karl-Otto Apel (b. 1922), lamented that classical reflection has been replaced by mathematics and that "[t]he only philosophical thing left is 'et cetera.'" Compare, Hilary Putnam, "A Half Century of Philosophy Viewed From Within," in *Dædalus: The Journal of the American Academy of Arts and Sciences,* Vol. 126, No. 1, pp. 175 *et seq.* (Winter, 1997). Putnam's essay is not written in mathematics or logical notations.

Foreword

Do you Believe in God? "Of course," you say, but that's none of my business. "Of course not," others reply, and that's none of my damnable business either. For the better part of my life, I also said that my Belief was private, strictly between God and me, and of no worthy explanation anyway, since it involved heavenly and ineffable matters beyond my poor powers of thinking, such that the act of explaining them to you in words is on all accounts an act of vanity, folly, futility or worse. Yet, as I know thoughts and feelings of others around me, whom I respect, admire and even love, I realize that a Belief in God forfeits very little of its ineffable character by being verbally expressed. An apt written expression of it even confirms this character in important ways for my psychology and the psychology of my friends and acquaintances. Like an abstract symbol is artistically and visually rendered in a picture, the written explanation actually renders it more Real to me and others when words spray like paint on canvass to try to depict it. The depiction, therefore, serves a useful, noble and even holy purpose of carrying it from an inner world to a world outside. The result is that the perception, the Belief and God can all be perceived of again, in sunlight, in a physical world of undisputed objects, by a sort of objective duplicate of the inner life, which renders everything objectively, by the object form of words. Did someone else write that? Where, then, in the linguistic mass of all the libraries around the world do I search for the proper attribution of this thought to a previous thinker? But the point is to realize just how important the form of existence *in objects* Really is, that the objectification of the world in my mind is the controlling meaning of the world for me, and that this object-ness is what Reality itself is for me as my mind knows Reality in this body of hair, skin and blood where I find myself. Therefore, tied to biology, my Belief in God, far from being immutable or unchanging in its characteristics, continues to evolve in me as an ever-changing and transforming organism (yes, an organism always grows) from each stage of my life into the next one, with a purpose I shall not master nor would wish to, even as it unleashes in me all such powers as I possess to think upon my Belief and to live in possession of this thinking. To be clear: there is someone who benefits by reading this and knowing that God and my Belief in God live gracefully, peacefully and lovingly together with all the demanding requirements of my intellect in this scientific world. There is a reader who benefits by knowing that the analysis of mind in these matters of a God Belief matters also, for no quantity of emotion and inspiration from a life-experience substitutes for logic, reason, science and what is the "fact."

I put quote marks around "fact," as I frequently do with many words subsequently, because the meaning of "fact" differs greatly among us, even from one day to the next. What is "factual" about the ambiguous results which several determinable stimuli of sight, touch, taste, hearing and smell produce among different quarters of humanity? Among those who speak it, explained "fact" only leads to other explanations and is different from whatever the "factual" justifies and supports without more. Is a fact always *there,* at some location in the universe, or only *here,* inside your head? Is a fact ever something you do not know or always limited to your knowledge? Then, what is your definition of your knowledge and the "factual" precisely? Is it entirely dependent upon objects and the objective? Can it ever exist regardless of whether you do or not?

criterion of [T]ruth as it is manifest in the picture of Jesus as the Christ and the changing experiences of individuals and groups, their varying questions and their categories of perceiving [R]eality. If the mediating task of theology is rejected, theology itself is rejected; for the term *theo-logy* implies, as such, mediation, namely, between the mystery, which is *theos,* and the understanding, which is *logos."*[3]

Is each one of us, like Tillich, entitled periodically to wash out the contents of his mind, unreservedly, or is this only the privilege of great intellect? I declared that my Belief in God, tied to biology, is an evolving and ever-changing organism in me which changes as I grow older. Perhaps the growth means a repudiation of the once endeared. As he grew older, the Austrian-English philosopher of logic, Ludwig J. J. Wittgenstein (1889 to 1961), held that what a mathematician is inclined to say of the objectivity and reality of mathematical facts is not a philosophy of mathematics, but something for philosophical *treatment*.[4] We think that Wittgenstein picked this position in order to relate mathematical objects to a larger world.[5] Intellectuals become confused and forsake wonder about the foundations of their own disciplines. They should ponder the larger world in which those foundations are largely based. Where, then, with corollary reasoning, but wonder, do we put the objects of theology on purple pages so that the wisest understanding of them in philosophy and science can be had by all? Categorical and televised confusion about perceiving and thinking is symptomatic of fundamental wretchedness about perception and thought which I previously alluded to in discussing daily life for me. Unfortunately, the computers used by the mass of society today only compound the distortions available to the world of our perceptiveness. This is so because any wisdom we cull from computerized systems has been compartmentalized by words, the intended meanings of words, the deviation of these intentions from their actual meaningfulness, and the mechanical arrangement of the hardware and software within which these words reach us, assuming, like rediscovered e-mail, that they ever do. How do we Really know that we have clicked to that growing branch of a computer's knowledge-tree where Truth hangs Truly upon this limb? Most computers, at least those known to me today, do not Really grasp the open environment which the world is fundamentally. Their branches blow about in any new wind. The process of finding the Truth of God, whether by computers, the information directories of a telephone system, Tillich's principle of non-interference, or Wittgenstein's wondrous notion of a philosophical treatment, is Really not cross-referenced satisfactorily (yes, even by the double entendre of the ". . . factory" as object-like manufacturing).

But I seized hope. I remembered that I could think and write. What do I mean by "satisfaction?" I thought that I could write it satisfactorily. But is satisfaction ever Really the same as "sufficiency?" I remembered my love for intellectual history and cross-referencing. I remembered books of edifying philosophy.[6] I knew that only after the passage of time and the seasoning of a mind could there be an actual synthesis of what the mind believes. Is this belief of mind either satisfactory or sufficient? It is for

---

[3] Paul Tillich, *The Protestant Era* (Chicago, University of Chicago Press, 1957), pp. xi-xxix, reprinted in *The Essential Tillich* (Church ed., New York, Macmillan, 1987), p. 70 (italics in the original).

[4] Ludwig Wittgenstein, *Philosophical Investigations* § 254 (New York, 1953).

[5] See Peter C. John, "Wittgenstein's 'Wonderful Life,'" *Journal of the History of Ideas,* Vol. XLIX, No. 3, p. 495 (July-Sept. 1988).

[6] For example, Robert Nozick, *The Examined Life* (New York, Touchstone Books, 1989).

you to judge by the rest of this discussion whether you answer affirmatively. But, in any case, you may contemplate the metaphysical concept of "satisfaction" which I pose here. For I aim to show that such a concept, in terms of God, exists Really and Truly after, and even metaphysically apart from, the facts and existence of our televised, computerized and compartmentalized world.

For, on the one hand, my mind knows that the distinctions it makes purportedly about reality must be founded by a theory of meaning to Reality; but, on the other, my mind knows that it is the one indubitable Reality which is in any way able to make these distinctions, or to say for me that of which Reality consists in my existence. Thus, on the one hand, I know that I must abjure the distinctions of Scholasticism, and of neo-Scholasticism, from the foundations of Reality about my world because this world has an indubitable actor's role upon the stage of physics and the natural sciences, such that the *only* theory of my meaning about Reality must be the same one which makes *the* stage of physics and the natural sciences meaningful, but that the Scholastic distinctions are puffs of air and play *no* performance upon *this* Real stage of our physical theater. But, on the other hand, I know that I must abjure the wholeness of Pan-Scientism, of reducing my world to that theory of meaning which solves an actor's role upon the stage of physics and the natural sciences, of thinking that this theory also solves matters after this stage—in Greek, literally *meta ta physika,* after the physics. This is so because my mind knows that it—and it alone—is the Reality into which I have been born after I left my mother's womb, and that it—and it alone—is the only reduction possible to founded meaning about Reality *for me,* such that my mind itself is the first and strongest foundation which I possess to make all sorts of distinctions about Reality *for me,* and to determine the contents and validity of my living-room. For my mind thinks that it is the only Real object to say *for me* that of which Reality consists, to define any stages of it or the actors and the acting upon them at all. Only I determine whether the theater of science is actually closed during the wee hours of the morning, when baby buffaloes see more than the rumps of their mothers, or when scientists are at *their own* comfortable homes eating breakfast, loving their spouses without being preoccupied by small flakes of cereal. Only I rule whether I should even write this sentence or italicize any words in it at all, when the dress and decorum of intellectuals at a library, and even the words of Tillich and Wittgenstein, are not as Real as the content of what one thinks.

You may think, therefore, after reading this discussion, that there is a picky nature to me which is not the imperfection of you, and that I only hold my hands because I balance opposites together in my mind much as both of my hands hold dimorphous objects at the same time. If so, I ask: What do you pick for yourself? What do you balance among the competing speech-acts and Truth-claims of your life? Then, how do you want to say these results? Do you prefer to speak them only upon the drama of a stage? That would be grand. For example, you might repeat, on your stage and in your own text, the recommendation of Athena to the people near the end of the *Oresteia:*

> From anarchy
> And slavish masterdom alike . . .
> Preserve my people! Cast not from your walls
> All high authority; for where no fear
> Awful remains, what mortal will be just?"[7]

---

[7] Aeschylus, ΕϕΜΕΝΙΔΕΣ trans. John Stuart Blackie *The Eumenides* (London, Everyman's Library, 1906), p. 163. The word "just" in this translation has a double meaning in English.

The poetry of Divine poets fills you with emotion and inspiration, but doesn't living require more? Isn't the stage of a theater only a finite place which can be closed and Ultimately condemned by the government for better real estate projects? For your world may fill with poetry, but you cannot avoid picking and balancing in prose and prosaisms somewhere. Unless you refuse to live as humans do, you must live by that selection of Reality which you slice for yourself in the butcher shops of thinking. Please ascertain that it is Real Meat. But, for my mind, a balancing of the theory of the indubitable meanings of science, with the indubitable Reality that my mind is the only means I possess to determine scientific meaning Ultimately, is the only alternative left to show me *my* world.

It is called quasi-Realism. Quasi-Realism is a theory of Reality which says that science is able to describe Reality completely, but only within the theory of the meaning of this description. As my mind is able to conceive of this completeness about science, quasi-Realism also says that I know there is an incompleteness about science, because I must account ultimately for my conceptions and may not do so unless I also account for why I say what they are—in other words, why I say that science *within itself* completely describes Reality. For my mind thinks that the theory of scientific meaning has *much* priority in my life, but that this priority is *necessarily* a question of degree. This is so because my mind wishes (wills) at all times to rule as the sovereign of its own Reality, to hold itself above science for the purpose of conceiving that of which Reality makes of it, to determine the Real distinctions which distinguish my own existence, and to believe that the existence into which I was born when I left my mother's womb was my mind, and not the science of my mind. For, if what I have been born into is a science and not myself, my world is ultimately one of other-ness. But it cannot be so that others would fully say me, explain me or justify me, since, in these postulated cases of science, where is the life of my is-ness? It is the indubitable Reality of the life of me that I am I, and not some saying, explanation or justification of me, except for that set of justifications which show me to my self as a complete proposition—in other words, with all of my life and all of my solipsism (the principle that I Really do not know anything other than me or modifications of my self) justified *to me—by yet another layer of self-justification.* Yet how is any such of another layer of justification to be ever or apparently accomplished? I must admit that I undertake this ultimate accounting of my me-ness only as fully as I wish to be what I am—a willful, thinking thing—in Latin, a *res cogitans* with *voluntas imperans intellectui*. Many members of my species living together with me on this Earth do not wish this justification, this accounting or this nature, for fear of their discoveries. But who, except for fear, does not wish otherwise to be less than he is? And what is it precisely which causes a Truth-seeker to be afraid? It is simply that Reality has not been comprehended *enough*. Where is this sufficiency? It is for you to say. But bear this in mind: the saying is complicated and often involves that which it does not appear to be, as well as the appearance of that which is not so, and not the appearance of that which it appears. For, even within the theory of quasi-Realism about Reality, there is the further prism that there is a degree of reality within the "quasi" component and, as well, a degree of "quasi-ness" within the element of the real component. Furthermore, within this first prism, there is a second refraction whether the degree to which Reality exists within the "quasi" is *just* as well as the degree to which "quasi-ness" exists within the Real and *vice versa*, depending upon your perspective. But, of course, if perspective defines Reality, does Reality at all define my perspective? Or, in the opposite case, if Reality defines perspective, does perspective at all define my Reality? Or, if a Truth-seeker is confined in Truth-seeking to starting at one or the other of these seemingly opposite polarities, where does he end? In other words, to what *degree* have I succeeded in mixing the Reality of Science and the Reality of Subjectivity together? Or, is what I think of as a mixture Really not mixed? If so, is this because I as an is-ness can never think it? Or is it because such a mixture can *never* be mixed? The last possibility seems unbearably analytic and atomic, a world of unmixed ingredients swirling around the world's hot caldron, which I do not taste in *my* food from the delicious spices on *my* shelf (not self.)

The title of this discussion is *Terminus and the House of Beth-El*. Terminus was a Roman god called "Boundary." Romans specially dedicated this god to the supervision of boundary stones upon the landscape. For them there was a holy task in such a supervision. The House of Beth-El is from the Book of Genesis. It is the forlorn and anonymous place in the desert where God revealed Himself to Jacob. Amazed, Jacob set a single stone upright in the desert, marked it with precious ointment and called the place "the House of God." Where am I? Am I living by any anonymous place or surveyed stone? Across my thinking head there are indisputably several boundaries: between philosophy and other disciplines of intellect, which needs to be supervised; between secular philosophy and a Belief in God, which needs to be re-drawn; between orthodox theology and living faith, which needs to be eliminated; between soul and the world, which needs to be explained; between God and Man, which needs to be surmounted; and between Mankind and unhuman Intelligent Life which needs to be studied carefully. Perhaps you will see more crossing points upon my landscape than I have just described for it. Indeed, you could accuse me of being practically fanatical about designs and maps. How are all these boundaries to be marked? To what extent do they even need to be? You may certainly accuse me of being a relativist, of thinking that everything is a matter of relation, of surveying where you draw the boundary lines to put together certain enchanted lands, and of dividing them where there is the smell of more pollution than enchantment. But the Absolute exists within my territory. It does not do so perfectly but as a matter of *my* world and geography which, as I tend to boundaries, is nearly perfect, at least for *my* world. By employing the Theory of Divine Names from the thinking of the early Christian theologian, Pseudo-Dionysius the Areopagite (*c.* A.D. 500), I use the name of the pagan Roman god, Terminus, and re-name the Judeo-Christian God: *Terminus*. The renaming shows, like the renaming of God to G$_X$d in the theology of the French Catholic theologian, Jean-Luc Marion (b. 1946), that the meaning of a word, sign, sentence, explanation or justification is powerful, should be subject to powerful supervision (in my case, of boundaries) and determined by the power of the supervision's spirituality (in my case, to determine where the boundaries are marked and whether or when I should cross them.) The House of Beth-El, at an anonymous place in the desert and with the simplest material and use of space and anointed smell, shows that, if enough meaning is put into a word, sign, sense, sentence, explanation or justification, practically anything is possible from the humblest of beginnings.

The report of *The Times* meant that, from my own checkered beginnings, I was ready to face, finally, a few thoughts of Professor Quine, and of Ludwig Wittgenstein — the toast of Oxford and Cambridge Universities during the middle years of the 20th century. Here is my quasi-Realist (-Realistic?) result. It is, as someone said, only bathetic if you see the ridiculous in your soup (yes, we note the confused meanings of words and say that soup is a double entendre of edible physics and stirred metaphysics.)

As you read, you should consider the following quotations to help your perceptiveness. But you should understand that you may not Really know Real knowledge of the meaning of these words until you have finished reading all that I put into the text of my discussion here. Later, I may emotionally regret my simplicity at not having added more, but these quotations are only three in number, as follows:

1) "Even in philosophy it is hard to think in [O]ther terms."

—Iris Murdoch (1919 to 1999), *Metaphysics as a Guide to Morals* (London, Allen Lane: The Penguin Press, 1992), p. 37.

2) "No *man can see God and live after*, that is to say, in this mortal life. But when He of His special grace will show Himself here, He strengtheneth the creature above itself, and He measureth the showing after His own will as it is profitable for the time."

—Lady Juliana of Norwich (*c.* 1342 to *c.* 1415), "They Shall See His Face," in P. Franklin Chambers, *Juliana of Norwich* (New York, Harper & Brothers, 1955), p. 135.

3) «Socrate confesse qu'il est lui aussi incapable de sortir, par lui-même, de lui-même, de son rêve mytho-miméticographique pour donner vie et mouvement à la cité.» ["Socrates acknowledges that he is also unable to emerge, by himself, from himself, from his mimicking and mythographic dream in order to give life and bustle to the (metaphorical) ancient Center (of the place of human activity)."]

—Jacques Derrida (b. 1930), *Khôra* (Paris, Éditions Galilée, 1993), p. 79 (My translation).

Chapter One. A Matrix for the World

A Soul in Science

Science—mathematical, natural and human—sees us clearly. The science of ophthalmology sees that my corneas dart around my eyeballs n times while I write this sentence. The perceptions of science compel our thoughts. With this bit of information about the motion of my corneas, what thought, at this moment, can there be other than about eyeball-thinking? This is because "we adopt, at least insofar as we are reasonable, the simplest conceptual scheme into which the disordered fragments of raw experience can be fitted and arranged."[1] What is the secret of science that its conceptual scheme should be so simple? Why would I be compelled to fit and to arrange the fragments of my experience into it? The French philosopher and mathematician, René Descartes (1596 to 1650), was one of the first to set forth science as a compelling Reality. He wrote:

> "[O]ne must confess [allow] that corporeal things exist. However, they are perhaps not exactly what we perceive by the senses, since their comprehension by the senses is in many instances very obscure and confused; but we must at least admit that all things which I conceive in them *clearly and distinctly,* that is to say, all things which, speaking generally, are comprehended in the object of speculative geometry [read: pure mathematics], are truly to be recognized as external objects."[2]

Descartes stated, therefore, that we Truly know the objects of science because they are the products of exhaustive analysis lending themselves to mathematical calculation and processing. After such an analysis, properly performed, scientific objects may not be reduced further by more thinking about them. They are what they are—clearly and distinctly within the laws, axioms, principles and rules of scientific study which have analyzed them mathematically. It is no surprise that, for the last couple of centuries, the natural sciences have followed mathematics, pursued the proposition of Descartes of a way to discern Real objects and True knowledge and produced a veritable cornucopia of Real objects and knowledge-results. Science has analyzed everything of a corporeal appearance within the world, including my eyeballs. I can Truly know that ophthalmology is a straightforward approach to Reality and a Truthful scheme to deal with eyesight.

---

[1] See Willard V. O. Quine, *From a Logical Point of View,* "On What There Is" (2nd ed., Cambridge, Mass., Harvard University Press, 1953, 1961), p. 16.

[2] René Descartes, *Meditations on First Philosophy* § VI, "Of the Existence of Material Things, and of the Real Distinction between the Soul and the Body of Man," in *Discourse on Method and The Meditations* trans. F. E. Sutcliffe (London, Penguin Books, 1968), p. 158.

But my Belief in God is apparently not related to me as my eyesight is. It is not a sensation visually registering on the nerve endings of my retina, nor is it something quantifiable which my eyes transmit to my brain to see as object X. Nevertheless, it is substantially something of my experience, and the science of experience, as I continue to be enthralled with the degree of Reality which the mathematical analysis of corporeal objects creates, should be my conceptual scheme for it. If, on the other hand, my Belief in God is a matter of my faith, my trust in my experience, as the American philosopher of logic, Robert Nozick (b. 1938), points out,[3] even the science of trusting would be the right place to start. And if, on the third hand, a God Belief has little or nothing to do with me actually, philosophy shows many ways of arranging un-me experience, un-me trust and the posits of others to imply it. For example, there is the elaborate arrangement of the German philosopher, Martin Heidegger (1889 to 1976).[4] Heidegger starts not with eyeballs or perceptible objects, but with an abstraction of existence by the phenomenon of *Dasein*—the German word for "being there." But I'm here—eyes and all. It is a certainty that my Belief in God Ultimately pertains to me and that, though I am a thinking thing, I am not some philosophical structure or other than myself. The conceptual scheme of science based in the physical world is a more straightforward way than Heidegger's for arranging my experience and my here-ness.

Scientific Arrangements of Trusted Experience

To arrange my experience, my trust in it, and whatever, including God, I Believe about it, I need a framework for trusting and experience-arranging. Is this framework for trust and arranging the same as the one Descartes established for knowing? Descartes said a framework for True knowledge could be built, at least for corporeal objects of the physical world, by a quest for certainty in mathematical calculations and processes. But not even the sentences of a scientific discourse can be translated into logic and set theory. "If all we hope for is a [rational] reconstruction that links science to experience in explicit ways short of translation [into logic, set theory or other mathematics], then it would seem sensible to settle for psychology."[5] Psychology reconstructs experience rationally so that I may arrange it for you. Even under theories of Reality holding that science is all that there is of Ultimate Truth in the Universe, scientific observations must be supplemented by inquiries into the laws connecting the stimuli and sensations by which the observations are made in the first place. For one example, stretched to an extreme length so that you may see the Truth of it in more subtle situations, a simple proposition in the science of astronomy—that I see the moon shining in the sky tonight—depends not only upon a celestial orb emitting brightness but also upon the stimuli of certain light hitting my optic nerve such that I may verify it as a sensation which came from a huge distance, not from the reflection of a white

---

[3] Robert Nozick, *The Examined Life* (New York, Touchstone Books, 1989), p. 53.

[4] See Werner Brock, "An Account of 'Being And Time,'" in *Reality, Man and Existence: Essential Works of Existentialism* (Blackham ed., Bantam Books, New York, 1965), p. 240; see Martin Heidegger, *Sein und Zeit* (Halle, 1927) trans. Macquarrie and Robinson as *Being and Time* (New York, Harper & Row, 1962).

[5] Willard V. O. Quine, "Epistemology Naturalized" (1969) in *Human Knowledge: Classical and Contemporary Approaches* (Moser and vander Nat eds., New York, Oxford University Press, 1995), p. 419 at p. 422. This essay was first published in Quine, *Ontological Relativity and Other Essays* (New York, Columbia University Press, 1969), pp. 69-90. Among other things, the essay argues for recharacterization of epistemology from a field of intellect in philosophy to a formal concern of psychology.

spotlight upon a large black bedsheet which my neighbor pitched across the trees in my front-yard to fool me. (We know even the best neighbors undertake eccentric endeavors and try mightily to succeed at them.) Verification of all circumstances relating to a scientific observation or experiment, including the True position of the observer, is what the British philosopher and mathematician, (Lord) Bertrand (Arthur William) Russell (1872 to 1970), meant when he said that "what is empirically verifiable [for True knowledge] is not pure physics in isolation, but physics plus a department of psychology."[6]

Theology also brazenly asserts itself into science. The mania for completeness in eliminating error and in arriving at Truth is a favorite technique among scientific thinkers. We use this technique when we say that your data-set from worldly inputs is finite and, therefore, lacking of the complete comprehension of experience which the Truth of it might Really require. We favor this technique so readily because it is the logical method of reductionist thinking about wholes back into parts, subparts and parts of subparts. Reductionism is the technique of the study of nature which natural science has imparted to our civilization for more than two centuries. Consequently, a Real Truth-seeker looks beyond any range of finite data, holds that even the metaphysical concepts of sin and grace relate to the data in ways that affect its meaning and interpretation, and concludes that, since it is the meaning and interpretation of data, and not the data itself, which justify the world, "[t]he only correct *general* form of [the] understanding [of the human sciences] is theological."[7] In this way of reducing the world into parts of it, which are there both before and after any given observation or experiment of science, a metaphysician, literally, "after the physics" — in Greek, the phrase is *meta ta physika* or metaphysics — trumps any finite playing card and shows us his winning hand. The only adequate ground, for arranging and trusting in our experience *generally,* must account for inputs and data which do not end. Implied by our quest for certainty and the goal of achieving it is the employment of any technique whatsoever to eliminate error.

Descartes himself employed several reductions of the world to eliminate error and to arrive at Truth.[8] First, he restricted what can be Truly known to a reduced sphere of clear and simple ideas and said that, of more complicated things, we hold opinions, which usually suffice to keep us safely, but our opinions are subject to error and they are not ultimately True. Next, he traced the causes of error to active faculties within a human Truth-seeker, termed these faculties to be human will and imagination, and demanded that the Truth-seeker be passive, exert no causal influences upon the processes by which he perceives and analyzes what he knows, and refrain from distorting the results of the perception and analysis mentally so that the mind might hold a faithful reproduction of them. This is called the Cartesian reduction of a knowledge-seeker into a spectator. Then, Descartes traced everything in the world to a cause from

---

[6]Bertrand Russell, *Human Knowledge: Its Scope and Limits* (London, Routledge, 1948, 1992), p. 62.

[7]Bernard J. F. Lonergan, "Theology and Understanding," in *Collection: Collected Works of Bernard Lonergan* (Toronto, University of Toronto Press, 1993), Vol. 4, p. 715; Bernard J. F. Lonergan, *Insight* (London, Darton, Longman & Todd, 1958), pp. 235, 236.

[8]See the discussion of these Cartesian techniques in M. C. Dillon, *Merleau-Ponty's Ontology* (1988) (2nd ed., Evanston, Ill., Northwestern University Press, 1997), pp. 16-18.

some other thing, ruled that only nothing could come of nothing, and held that, since both ideas and objects are caused, the nature of their causality relates them together and permits us to conceive of an idea as a thing. Descartes also traced everything in the world to atoms, ruled that the ultimate constituent parts of a thought or an idea consist of this simple unit of sense-data (or the data of intuition, simple nature or a clear and distinct idea), and held that, since both ideas and objects are so conceived, the nature of their atomistic conception relates them together and permits us, by this alternate analysis, to conceive of an idea as a thing once again. This is called the Cartesian reduction of ideas into objects. Finally, Descartes traced True knowledge of the world of sense-data to clear and distinct perceptions, ruled that only such perceptions validate the existence of anything, and held that, since my consciousness is the only place where these perceptions are valid and validated or not, the nature of our knowledge of the world is only a function of our clear and distinct perception of it. This is called the Cartesian reduction of the world into an object of consciousness.

The question is: to what extent should I adopt any of these reductions of Descartes for my experience, my trust in it, and my Belief in God? If the Cartesian reductions are to work upon an unlimited range of data, and an unending series of inputs from the world, it is clear that a knowledge-seeker's passivity, thing-i-fication of ideas and consciousness are not enough for Ultimate Truth. On the one hand, I know what Descartes thought and the cornucopia of knowledge-results which natural science has produced from valid analysis of sense-data and corporeal bodies by mathematics and reductionist thinking. On the other, I know that all phenomena of my daily experience may not be reduced to mathematics and do not possess completely scientific qualities which would allow a quest for certainty about them to succeed. The phenomena of my experience certainly do not admit of transparency (seeing through them clearly and simply) nor permit errors about them to be corrected by reductive thinking (reducing a whole into parts) or other techniques of Truth-telling (dealing with knowledge by lording over it as the neutral, but passive, lord of a knowledge-kingdom). Indeed, the daily mundaneness of my life shows several ways in which the definitions and reductions of Descartes fail utterly either to justify or explain it.

First, only in a philosopher's mental output, and then not even in his lobed head, does any—let alone one—perfectly restricted sphere of clear and simple ideas exist in support of the distinctions which Descartes made between opinion and True knowledge. Of course, Descartes segregated Truth from opinion and engaged in myriad distinctions about knowing because he thought it was important to live in coherence and for Reality to be understood as a whole. Historians of the intellectual history of Western civilization conceive of the philosophy of Descartes well within the tradition known as the Enlightenment of the 17th and 18th centuries. By contrast, the basic definition of so-called "post-modernist" thinking—an approach pervading many fields of intellect today in the world—is that, contrary to the Enlightenment, it is "that type of thought that rebels against any totalizing understanding of [R]eality."[9] For a post-modernist, it is more compelling to segregate Truth into a particular social or historical context than it is to integrate essences of it into any grand Enlightenment or supra-contextual synthesis.

---

[9]Thomas Guarino, "Postmodernity and Five Fundamental Theological Issues," in *Theological Studies,* Vol. No. 57, No. 4, p. 654 (December, 1996).

Second, in my existence, a cause for everything has certainly eluded me, and surprising things do appear to arise from nothing, *ex nihilo*. Causality works well in science to explain physical objects of the world; less well in theology to justify objects of metaphysics. Can one stand back from *those* objects ever passively? Where is the path of the quest for certainty which a path-finder finds passively, or without stirring up dust and distorting its contours as he walks upon it? This path has never crossed any of my known landscapes. Finally, has even the most brilliant and astute scientist of my lifetime, by the most discerning equipment of perception, ever perceived an atom *as such*? In my lifetime, the scientists *who say* they are perceiving atoms by focusing electron microscopes upon them are actually perceiving subatomic particles, which in turn can be further broken down into various constituent parts. What is, exactly, the basic unit of experience by which I may think I may actually experience it? Is this unit anything which relates ideas and objects so much together that I may thing-i-fy an idea and objectify my world? In my world, the demand for explicit Truth criteria leads to an infinite regression of further queries about why we can know about these criteria what we think we do. Accounts of imperfect knowledge are given daily, and the choices of existence may include "both, and" as well as "either, or." There are elements of given-ness in my perceptions, such that the given-ness presupposes an element of transcendence (out-residing) in things being perceived and, therefore, a degree of opaqueness in these things such that my clear and distinct perception of them may never be final or definitive. Cartesian enlightenment by clearly defined and perceived sensory inputs, whose truth is always Truthful, is not at all a widely accurate description of my life or my world.

The conclusion of this critique of Descartes is that, if I intend to consider my experience completely, I must consider it appropriately, that is to say, under the science which applies to my experience as corporeal body, as well as under the subjectivity which applies to me as a human consciousness experiencing the world in which I live. The intellectual method of the first alternative is called empiricism; that of the second alternative, subjectivity or intellectualism. Both alternatives are subject to further parsing whereby forms of either feed back and relate to the other in dilute counter-measures to that other's basic theme. I shall discuss intellectualism later in this Chapter but, for now, we should see that it is no less of a quest for certainty than Descartes's quest is—intellectualism seeks to base True knowledge within the immanent (in-dwelling) structures of the mind, rather than in the transcendent (out-residing) structures of the experience of the world. Empiricism is the antithesis of this subjectivity. Empiricism is *both* the practice of relying upon observation and experiment in the world *and* the theory that the origin of knowledge is experience. The method of empiricism in thinking about experience, observations and experiments is called the empirical method, and the results it reaches are called pragmatic results. Pragmatism is not a thought-system but the *use* of thought as a guide to action and the school of thinking that ideas and concepts *must* be related to actual life. Having observed my eyes for many years, my ophthalmologist concludes the observations correlate well with one theory ophthalmologists hold will explain my eyesight, the theory of myopia—a condition based in science and existing naturally among many human eyes. As a result of this empiricism, he tells me to be pragmatic: "let's act upon the knowledge of ophthalmologists about myopia; be practical and wear eyeglasses or contact lenses or submit to corrective surgical techniques." Everything pragmatic is empirical, but not everything empirical is pragmatic because there is a set of cases in which neither the practice nor the theory of empiricism guides anything at all, or relates to anything more, but just *is*—just *exists* as a consequence of the existence to which empiricism is applied. I *might* be myopic and do nothing about it. Nevertheless, empiricism is very often pragmatic, and both empiricism and pragmatism mean anything which fails to be grounded firmly in the physical Realities of existence should be impossible, immaterial or wrong.

We assert, then, that we will apply both theoretical and experimental empiricism here, within the field of psychology, to the "objects" of God and my Belief in God. What is our theory of what an "object" Really is? A philosopher says this theory is our ontology. Does God qualify? Unless we assume that God is an X whom we may directly perceive by our senses, or whom we may directly experience in sensations much as we experience that we see, the science of God as an object of science cannot be said. There are no valid conclusions of psychology that God exists as a separately identifiable object within any experiment involving stimulated behavior by determinable stimuli, but there are none which deny them either. Does this inconclusiveness mean a scientist should keep experimenting? No, the record of past inconclusiveness must be accounted for. By no means am I so foolish as to propose an experiment for God's existence as an alchemist seeks an elixir. However, I am not so foolish as to prove God's existence from a world of empirical facts by the whole passage of "nature" within them.[10] What is nature but convention or our own wishful definition of it? How can we be Truly aware of nature's attributes under the diffusion which even the narrowest definition of it would entail? To conceive of God by the simplest conceptual scheme with which we can arrange the disordered fragments of our lives, there are only possibilities from other sciences—hence, we said, psychology, the science of the study of the human mind, is an important reference for Reality. The physical realities of the God's existence, the involved subject of the following chapters, are psychological because Belief and God are located physically and metaphysically at the human mind. Psychology is the study of the science of the mind—in Greek, the word for mind is *psyche*.

The validating criteria of Truth to a scientific mind are experiences, sensations, perceptions and anything which is or can be Real. What is Reality? The English philosopher of empiricism, John Stuart Mill (1806 to 1873), defined it as follows:

> "What is the difference to our minds between thinking of a [R]eality and representing to ourselves an imaginary picture? I confess I can see no escape from the opinion that the distinction is ultimate and primordial. . . . I cannot help thinking, therefore, that *there is in the remembrance of a real fact,* as distinguished from that of a thought, an element which does not consist . . . in a difference between the mere ideas which are present to the mind in the two

---

[10]Compare Henry Nelson Wieman, *Religious Experience and Scientific Method* (New York, Macmillan, 1926), pp. 38, 39, critically discussed in Nancy Frankenberry, *Religion and Radical Empiricism* (Albany, N. Y., State University of New York Press, 1987), ch. 4, p. 118.

cases. *This element,* however we define it, *constitutes [B]elief,* and is the difference between memory and imagination."[11]

Under Mill's definition, then, Reality is the remembrance of a Real fact, as distinguished from that of a thought, and what we Believe. What is Belief? The Scottish philosopher of empiricism, David Hume (1711 to 1776), said that Belief in anything is simply having the idea of it in a lively and active manner. Hume said:

> "[B]elief is nothing but a more vivid, lively, forcible, firm, steady conception of an object than the imagination alone is ever able to attain. . . . It consists not in the peculiar nature or order of the ideas, but in the *manner* of their conception and in their *feeling* to the mind. I confess that it is impossible perfectly to explain this feeling or manner of conception. . . . Its true and proper name . . . is *[B]elief,* which is a term that everyone sufficiently understands in common life."[12]

Under Hume's definition, then, Belief is a type of conception of an object and *does not depend* upon the peculiar nature or order of the object or the conception. Already in discussing God, then, do we leap into Reality defined by Belief, into the remembrance of Real facts defined by a type of conception of them, into conceptions which depend on the manner and feeling with which they arise, into conceptions which are apart from the objects being conceived, and into elements of evanescent ideas which are yet of force.

If we are pragmatic, insisting by our pragmatism that all of these ideas guide our actual life or be related to it, at least—how does all of this resolve? God and my Belief in God resolve either by mystical perception or by Cartesian perception. Mystical perception resolves either by revelation or by further mystery and is discussed in next Section. Cartesian perception is the subject of the rest of this Section and resolves by paradox, by self-referring paradox (a paradox one of whose own terms is paradoxical), by reconciliation into Truth finally without paradox—uncontradicted at any stage of Reality—or by being forever contradictory and untrue. Relating God to Cartesian perception, and through this perception to natural science, means the development of principles of Truthfulness, or Verification. For an empiricist, there is a large difference between what is Truthful about experience and what is verifiable from it only. Truthfulness implies that a seeker of it arrives at conclusions of certainty; verifiableness implies that there is only a probability to the results. By relating God to verifiableness, an empiricist must contend with the validity of the question of certainty (even as scientists do when a metaphysician certainly trumps their finite playing cards). The empiricist must also contend with the question whether a Belief in Absolutes, or anything certain, being relative to everything else, is Really valid. For example, the Canadian Protestant theologian, Clark H. Pinnock (b. 1937), considers Christianity's

---

[11]John Stuart Mill, "Note to James Mill's *Analysis*," (1869) i. pp. 412-423; see William James, "The Psychology of Belief" in *William James: Writings 1878-1899* (Myers ed., New York, Library of America, 1992), p. 1021.

[12]David Hume, *Enquiry Concerning Human Understanding,* Sec. V, Part II (London, 1751) in *The English Philosophers From Bacon to Mill* (Burtt ed., 2d ed., New York, The Modern Library of America, 1994), p. 641. This work was first published in 1748 as *Philosophical Essays concerning Human Understanding.*

claims for God upon existence by empirical data and the empirical theory of experience. Pinnock says that the confirmation of factual matters under his analysis is of no serious concern because of the ultimately truthful probability of it. He notes that ". . . all legal and historical decisions are made upon a basis of probable judgment in terms of the evidence. *Since the whole of life proceeds on such a basis,* it is not a weakness that Christian evidences should rest on it too."[13] On the other hand, is the certain assertion that the sun will rise at dawn tomorrow a probability only by the hypothesis of a rather unlikely theory of astronomy? Is the equal certainty that I live as a human even a probability at all? The social certainties of humanity are apt to end in moral law. The probabilities of natural experience, as the sun rises tomorrow at dawn, end in laws of causes and effects. However, by relating God to the Truthful verification of these laws of nature and the world, the law-givers of causes and effects must contend with the validity of the question of relativity (even as scientists do when a Cartesian reduces a law of science into relationships and parts, and the reduction renders the so-called law into custom or a rule of thumb). Are all causes and effects only relative matters depending upon alteration of the relations between them? Is a Belief in Absolutes based upon cause and effect, in any sense, Real Given-ness? For example, the American Protestant theologian, James Oliver Buswell, Jr. (1895 to 1975), also considers the existence of Christian God empirically. Regarding the famous five demonstrations of God's existence in nature and the world by the Italian Catholic theologian, Thomas Aquinas (1225 to 1274), Buswell says that the confirmation of factual matters under his analysis of Thomas's world is of no serious concern. He notes that, as to all of the causes and effects upon which the five ways ultimately depend, they are empirically probable, and not apodictic (Absolutely certain or necessary) Truth.[14] Accordingly, empiricist Buswell ignores the Reality that, in this causal world of Thomas from the Middle Ages, there are the fictions of an unmoved mover, a first cause which is nevertheless not temporal though it has first-ness, a final purpose though time continues to roll by, a perfection which can be more or less so though we think of it perfectly in the abstract, and even the absence from existence of ourselves so that there may be some X who can complete this job. Therefore, the certain assertion of an empiricist that God arises from nature is a probability only by a rather likely theory of what is "natural." What is such a likely "natural" theory? Does apodictic Truth exist anywhere within it?

An answer from nature or natural theory comes, we said, from our examination of experience. We must examine God empirically, under Mill's definition of Reality, to see if He is remembered as a Real fact, as some X in which we can Believe, under our theory of what an object Really is, as some X which is or can be Real. How do we perform this examination? First, we must recognize it has two parts: space and time. Next, we must repeat our recognition of the complete confusion between nature and convention. These two are confused together because "[w]e never have sheer nature without convention, or sheer convention without nature; the two are always tangled. Nature is displayed to us only as refracted through custom and custom always mixes

---

[13]Clark Pinnock, *Set Forth Your Case* (Nutley, N. J., Craig Press, 1967), p. 45 (italics added).

[14]J. Oliver Buswell, Jr., *A Systematic Theology of the Christian Religion* (Grand Rapids, Mich., Zondervan, 1962), Vol. 1, pp. 75-77.

with the natural. The interweaving of the two is what makes it so apparently plausible to say there is no nature, but only convention."[15] As a result, when we refer to nature or to whatever we deem a natural condition, we recognize the conventional or customary content which the world and its intellectual history of thought-conventions and thinking customs have made for whatever is called "the natural." The convention of our language—the structure of meaning for the word, "examination," such that this word is meaningful in English—implies that, for every "examination," there is an examiner and something being examined—in this case, we know that the subject of examination is experience. How is experience *naturally* examined without diffusing it beyond something strictly called the "physical realities of existence?" On the other hand, how is God examined by just that right "size" by which we see Him *naturally?*[16]

A basic requirement of custom, convention or nature is that we think about space-experience itself by some customary, conventional and "natural" unit or discrete measure by which we can do so. What is that unit or discrete measure of space-experience by which we may examine it for trust, Belief and God? There are two opposing alternatives: either perceptual atomism or *Gestalt* theory—in German, the word *Gestalt* means roughly "form" or "pattern." Whether these alternatives arise from nature or convention is for you to guess; whether this makes any difference Really is for you to know. If you do know of a difference between nature and convention about the employment of atoms or *Gestalten,* you probably know it by some further way you have reduced one or both of them into a thing you think is more fundamental to experience.[17] Then, if you know this, you may also know why this further thing is a better substitute for the basic unit of space-experience than either atoms or *Gestalten* are. However, I do not know of such a knowledge which meets the test of my immediate experience (for science does not encompass all of it) and plead my ignorance about more Truthful units of generically human experience which you may surely count and weigh.

The first alternative, the reduction of the world to atoms, means that we may support, by tiny units of our experience, the hypothesis that there is a constant relationship between each point on the surface of a stimulus and each point of stimulation on our retinas, olfactory or auditory nerves or other senses. The constancy of this relationship is the bridge across the gap between the world and ourselves, the body and the mind and the seer and the thing being seen. But this atomism is, at bottom, only psychological because it soothes the feelings of a Truth-seeker and says that bits of sense-data are incorrigible, manifestly True and unable to be challenged against a further query. We have already seen, with electron microscopes and other sophisticated equipment of experimental physics, that further query does challenge atomism even at the level of natural science. The German physicist, Werner Heisenberg (1901 to 1976),

---

[15]Robert Sokolowski, "Knowing Essentials," *Review of Metaphysics,* Vol. 47, No. 4, p. 697 (June,1994).

[16]Compare Bernard M. Loomer, "The Size of God," in *The Size of God: The Theology of Bernard Loomer in Context* (Dean and Axel eds., Macon, Ga., Mercer University Press, 1987).

[17]For example, compare Quine, "Epistemology Naturalized" (1969), in *Human Knowledge. . . , op. cit.,* p. 425 as follows: "Regardless of whether sensory atoms or *Gestalten* are what favor the forefront of our consciousness, it is simply the stimulations of our sensory receptors that are best looked upon as the input to our cognitive mechanism."

introduced physics to the principle of indeterminacy, challenged the immutability of atomism and wrote to the world in layman's language that:

> "The elemental particles of modern physics . . . are defined by the requirements of mathematical symmetry. They are not eternal and unchanging, and they can hardly, therefore, strictly be termed [R]eal. In the beginning, therefore, for modern science, was the form, the mathematical pattern, not the material thing. And since the mathematical pattern is, in the final analysis, an intellectual concept, one can say in the words of [Goethe's] Faust, *"Am Anfang war der Sinn"*—"In the beginning was the meaning."[18]

Perceptual atomism is also challenged in psychology whenever determinate stimuli result in ambiguously determinable perceptions—for example, the Müller-Lyer illusion of the length of two equally long parallel lines, the Gurwitsch cube, Rubin's figure, the bitter taste of the substance, phenol-thio-urea, to only one quarter of the human population and the tasteless nature of it to the rest of us, or Stumpf's melody which isn't completely tonal.[19] These mental perceptions of definitely determinable ambiguity show that there is no type-by-type identity between the atoms of a stimulus in the world and those in each point of stimulation in ourselves, such that the perceived gap of experience between the world and ourselves, the mind and the body, the consciousness and sensory events, cannot be bridged without a theory or supposition about the bridging. The Truthfulness of this theory or supposition about the accurateness of atomic Reality in all cases is more or less indeterminate; it can never be verified Truly except within the context of the further theory of experience by which it presents itself. The fact that we err, and the further fact that we do so deliberately by postulating the atom as if it were an innate idea, rather than the scientific description of convenience which it is in subatomic Reality, implies that another discrete measure of experience would measure it more successfully and enable us to examine it better.

Thus, several psychologists of the 20th century developed *Gestalt* theory. Under this theory,[20] ". . . the analysis of perceptual experience must stop at the *Gestalt:* the most basic unit of experience is that of a figure-on-a-background; and if analysis seeks to reduce this fundamental complex into something simpler, it can arrive only at constructs—things which are literally imperceptible."[21] The French philosopher, Maurice Merleau-Ponty (1908 to 1961), endorsed the Truth of a *Gestalt* theory of experience as follows:

---

[18]Werner Heisenberg, "From Plato to Max Planck: The Philosophical Problems of Atomic Physics," *The Atlantic Monthly,* Vol. 204, No. 5, p. 111 (November, 1959).

[19]Dillon, *op. cit.,* p. 63; Aron Gurwitsch, *Studies in Phenomenology and Psychology,* "Some Aspects and Developments of Gestalt Psychology," (Evanston, Ill., Northwestern University Press, 1966), p. 16; Jonathan Bennett, "Substance, Reality and Primary Qualities," *American Philosophical Quarterly,* Vol. 2, pp. 1-17 (1965) (especially discussing phenol-thio-urea). Rubin's figure, named after E. Rubin (1886 to 1951), is a reversible figure which may be seen either as a vase or two faces in profile.

[20]See Gurwitsch, op. cit.; Wolfgang Köhler, *Gestalt Psychology* (London, Kegan Paul, 1930, rev., 1947); Kurt Koffka, *Principles of Gestalt Psychology* (London, Routledge and Kegan Paul, 1935); David Katz, *Gestalt Psychology* trans. Tyson (New York, Ronald Press, 1950).

[21]Dillon, *op. cit.,* p. 60.

"A figure on a ground is the simplest sensible given that we can obtain, [and] this is not a contingent characteristic of factual perception. . . . *It is the very definition of the phenomenon of perception, that without which a phenomenon cannot be said to be a perception at all.* The perceptual 'something' is always in the 'milieu' of something else, it always forms part of a field. A really homogeneous area offering nothing to perception cannot be given to any perception."[22]

The paradox of *Gestalt* theory as a basic unit of experience is, therefore, that this basic unit, a pattern within a field, may amount to a whole which is more than the sum of its parts—the pattern and the field. One *Gestalt* pattern even relates back to atomic matter and perceives of it as something more than atoms. For example, matter is Really "the manifestation of the energy of God's nature."[23] By contrast, there is a second *Gestalt* pattern of God set against a background of impressions of the stars of heaven (the classical pattern of much of mankind's civilization throughout history), and yet a third, which is *my* world of God set against the backgrounds of both what is innately matter (hard as a rock) and what is essentially an impression of heaven (soft as putty). I told you that in *my* world the alternatives of "both and" as well as "either or" exist. My fundamental *Gestalt* pattern about God is reduced, in the best tradition of scientific thinking, to a description of *my* world which holds Reality for *me*. The dualism involved in it (between heavenly putty and hard rock) is an issue of my *psychology, and not an issue of reconciling it in philosophy,* or any question of deciding that either the dualism or any reconciliation of it is the end of thinking.[24]

Psychologists who formulated *Gestalt* theory for the world did so because of their frustrations with behaviorism and structuralism in psychology. They insisted on seeing meanings in existence which signify more relevance to experience than behaviorism or structuralism do. But, if behaviorist or structuralist psychology is simpler than a *Gestalt* complex, then, shouldn't a unit of experience from those psychologies be an appropriate one for us to hold as a basic measure for our examination? Unfortunately, we must reply to this question in the negative. There is simply is no structure from the behaviorist psychology of controlled observation and experiment which is Real or all-encompassing enough to account for the varieties of *my* experience or *yours*, because these structures hardly account for even that behavior within an experiment which science observes with all sorts of controls and presuppositions about it. Just as existence does not exist only within a scientist's head so it does not exist only in his laboratory, under the conditions of a clinic.

The difficulty of defining even the most discrete unit by which it may be imbibed shows that the definition of space-experience is truly the Achilles' heel of empiricism. What is experience actually? It is: the flow of clock-time along in the world with my "is-ness" and my "feeling-ness." What is time and these last two concocted words of

---

[22] Maurice Merleau-Ponty, *Phénoménologie de la Perception* (Paris, Gallimard, 1945), p. 10, trans. Colin Smith as *Phenomenology of Perception* (1st English ed., London, Routledge and Kegan Paul, 1962), p. 4 (italics added).

[23] Floyd E. Hamilton, *The Basis of Christian Faith* (4th ed., New York, Harper & Row, 1964), p. 30.

[24] See, for example, Dillon, *op. cit.*, Part 1, Chapter 4, pp. 58-81. I contend that Merleau-Ponty fundamentally erred by undertaking such a reconciliation ontologically and not psychologically.

ness-ful states? We know a difference in the natural sciences between the justifications and the explanations of things; we also know a difference in psychology between the substantive and the transitive parts of a stream of consciousness. There is a mental difference between justification—a correctness upon which one may Trust in his deepest experiences—from any Ultimately unjustified explanation of them. We live with this difference repeatedly and continually. We know it like we know the full range and rage of all of our emotions. The explanation of a thing is the thought of that thing, but the justification of it is not only that thought but the additional validation of a correctness about it upon which we may conceive of it firmly as a Belief. The difference between an unjustified explanation of X, and the justification of X, is that, in the final analysis, a True justification relies somewhere upon a Thing-in-itself—the German phrase is *Ding an sich,* beyond which nothing more may be said. An explanation, on the other hand, leaves room for more explaining. Thus, the explanation of a cell is different from the justification of its existence by any *Ding an sich* of biology—for example, a *law* of mitosis by which the cell divides in cytoplasmic fission. This distinction between evidence and a law of evidence is a crucial one for a Cartesian thinking thing and the rest of our discussion. To skip over it momentarily, the distinction shows how different the justification of God is from an explanation of Him; but how God, as a justification (a law of evidence), relates to explanations of experience (evidence) actually; and how, without this justification, experience must be explained skeptically—that is to say, either by infinitely regressive reductions (a madhouse of infirmities) or infinitesimally (close to zero).

Does Soul Have a Role?

Empirical psychology is little more than a century old. Though it began as an element in the larger schemes of thinking of the ancient Greek philosophers, only in the last quarter of the 19th century was psychology able to say that the pathways which it traced inside the human mind could be verified by the outside world. In other words, not until then was science so advanced that it could verify a statement of psychology under generally accepted dogmas of empiricism—that the meaning of a thing-of-psychology is True because of logical terms which relate to immediate experience, or the "facts." Thereafter, psychology scientifically developed many such meanings, showed the basis for mental diseases, and explained the effects of even biochemical reactions in the brain. As one result of this massive exploration of the physical manifestations of our mental life, we know that we speak at a maximum rate of about four to five syllables a second, but that we are able to hear artificially accelerated spoken syllables at a rate of about thirty.[25] We know that, when a hammer hits a finger, the myelin-sheathed nerve fibers on the finger send a message to the brain in about 20 milliseconds, but that the unmyelinated C-fibers of the finger take much longer to send a pain signal to the brain—about 500 milliseconds.[26] Likewise, we know of many other carefully compared sensory phenomena. For beliefs of all types, even for one in God, it is clear that cognitive psychology "can treat items such as patterns of neural excitation as if they were beliefs in order to use the metaphor of 'inference from data' in constructing models of mental processes." On the other hand, there is the intellectual

---

[25]Daniel C. Dennett, *Consciousness Explained* (Boston, Little, Brown & Co., 1991), pp. 144, 145.
[26]*Ibid.,* p. 103.

technique of isolating ". . . those non-propositional items of awareness which are the foundation for belief in propositions."[27] This isolation may be true only by virtue of meanings and take place independently of any process used in a model of the treatment of neurons. The former quote about the model is, therefore, a statement of synthetic truth; the latter quote about an intellectual technique of isolation, an analytic one. Under the broadly formidable definition of experience which the American psychologist, William James (1842 to 1910), sought to employ for our thoughts in transitive consciousness, the isolating intellectual technique of describing Belief is certainly and properly a matter of the knowledge of psychology.

There is a clear mental difference between the substantive and the transitive parts of a stream of consciousness. We know this difference just as we know we live. Substantive parts of consciousness are the felt sensations which psychologists test experimentally over defined periods of time in an environment of stimuli and responses to the stimuli. Transitive parts of consciousness are processes and relations which compose most of our actual thoughts, occur over periods of time which can be measured with no determinative degree of accuracy, and are difficult to observe from any perspective beyond the observation of them where they are inside the cranium. Because of obvious experimental difficulties, and the uneasy relationship which transitive consciousness poses to contemporary philosophizing, it is easy to suppose, as Pinnock, Buswell and many others have, that any consideration of this part of our knowing consciousness is not a quest for certainty, but a search for the most likely. Most of us—far from science—would rather explain error or conclude a probability than justify apodictic (Absolutely certain or necessary) Truth.

William James, at the dawn of the 20th century, lived before the age of widespread use of *Gestalt* theories. James nevertheless held that other psychologists, in the then newly emerging discipline of psychology, ignored the processes and relations of transitive consciousness in favor of firm control by inductive logic over scientific experiments regarding substantive consciousness. James believed psychology thereby failed to explain the meaning of ordinary experience sufficiently and set out in many works of intellect to remedy this deficiency. Often James finds in direct awareness or in transitive consciousness what other psychologists say are the stimuli of sensory events upon the human mind. James's broadly formidable "concept of experience . . . never caught on. Philosophers rejected it in favor of the associationists' concept of elementary associations or, in our own century (the 20th), for the analytic philosophers' hypothesis about logical elements. Psychologists, too, at first rejected James's concept of experience in favor of the more elementary and less fluid notions of associationism. Later, in accordance with the principles of behaviorism, psychological theory substituted stimuli and responses for the definition of experience altogether."[28] To isolate experience in controlled environments under scientific analysis is to try to justify it by some rule, principle, axiom or law of science, as a Thing-in-itself of psychology, beyond which nothing more is said, just as many distinguished scientists have accomplished so well for the other natural sciences throughout the last two centuries.

---

[27]Richard Rorty, *Philosophy and the Mirror of Nature* (Princeton, N. J., Princeton University Press, 1979), p. 255; see J. O. Urmson, "Recognition" in *Proceedings of the Aristotelian Society,* Vol. 56, pp. 259-280 (1955-1956).

[28]Edward S. Reed, *From Soul to Mind* (New Haven, Yale University Press, 1997), p. 218.

Psychology is a science whose explanations seem as abundant as they are inversely proportional to the scarcity of justifications for them. It may frequently explain the behavior of a human or an ape while failing to define the precise support for that behavior as a thing-of-psychology, beyond which no further explaining may be had. In most cases, such fully justified things-of-psychology are rarely observed experimentally. Empiricism explains "facts" in psychology as it does in the other natural sciences; but the explanations often involve inferences and assumptions which do not exist elsewhere in science and leave room for prodigiously more explaining. For instance, *Gestalt* theory means filtering *Gestalten* through that theory's presuppositions about what the prevailing conditions allow. The prevailing, the conditions and the allowance may fill more books of thought than the *Gestalten* do. If it is easy to contemplate the human consciousness by the themes and horizons of *Gestalt* theory, even in a world of PET scanning inside of the human cranium, it is much harder to deal with the conditions from the outside world which prevail upon these *Gestalt* theories and, therefore, determine their Ultimate significance. For another instance, it is only in psychology that the subjects of experiments must be consciously instructed about the experiments beforehand, and that the texts of these subjects must be interpreted afterward in light of not only the experiments but the instructions for them as a separate consideration. It is only in psychology that experience divides itself three ways: first, experiences of the external world—sights, sounds, smells and so forth; second, experiences of the internal world—ideas, memories, hunches and so forth; and third, experiences of both the external and internal worlds called emotions or "affect"—pains, tickles, hunger, thirst, anger, joy and so forth. This tripartite division of experience is characteristic of the problem of reducing transitive consciousness back to any given multitude of disparate atoms, even if, or when, there is a constant relationship atomically between the physical and spiritual aspects of consciousness, and the atomic correspondence is in subatomic positrons absorbed in matter which reproduces faithfully the spatial distribution of radio nuclide at selected planes in brain tissue. Put more directly, I hope the rest of this discussion shows you that God, not as a probability but as justified Truth, is Really meaningful in experience and for life, even when positron emission tomography—reproducing the spatial distributions of selected planes of brain tissue—is scientific fact.

In 1976, a group of scientists at Brookhaven National Laboratory, led by the American chemist, Alfred Peter Wolf (1923 to 1998), developed a form of sugar—fluorodioxyglucose—and a radio nuclide which, when injected into the human body, can be used to perform scans of living tissue, without injuring the tissue, by positron emission tomography (known as "PET"). In humans, PET scans have measured blood flow, blood volume, metabolism of glucose and oxygen, acid-base balances, receptor pharmacology and transmitter metabolisms. PET scans of brain tissue, therefore, show the chemical processes underlying various neurological diseases and reveal which parts of the brain are the most active in performing certain tasks. Accordingly, scientists say that "[i]n brain imaging work we dissect out the components of mental operation in relation to specific regions of the brain involved in particular mental operations."[29]

---

[29]M. E. Raichle, "Images of the mind: Studies with modern imaging techniques," *Annual Review of Psychology,* Vol. 45, p. 333 at 336 (1994), quoted in Morton Wagman, *Language and Thought in Humans and Computers* (Westport, Conn., Praeger Publishers, 1998), p. 116.

What describes PET scanning aptly? It is science; it is a description of existence; it is even an explanation for a heady part of it—*but does it justify any of it?* Does it say anything meaningful about experience beyond that which was experienced? By empirical observations of multiple parts of the brain acting differently as well as together—depending upon the given mental operations which are posed to a human subject—PET scanning supports theories of the multiple drafting and re-scripting of consciousness. The further scientific technique of functional magnetic resonance imaging (known as "fMRI"), as of this writing, seems to show the same diversity and multiplicity of functioning brain geography and supports a re-scripting theory of consciousness as well. Since we are pragmatists, we note that the American psychologist, Daniel Clement Dennett (b. 1942), says "[t]he idea that consciousness is a *mode of action* in the brain rather than a *subsystem* of the brain has much to recommend it."[30] This model of an active brain is physically—that is to say, at the level of natural science—the opposite of the passive model which Descartes held would be necessary for a mind to reach Truth without willing to warp it or distort it by all manner of imagining. What else does Dennett's "mode of action" model of a consciousness tell us? Is it just that the scientific study of our brain functions shows us far more prone to error and to subjectivity than Descartes supposed? PET scanning shows that more than one pathway exists in the brain for performing the task of selecting words to speak. The use of a particular one seems to depend upon whether the human subject performing the task of speaking has learned his verbal response or performs it "automatically"—that is to say, by repetition without generating a perceived degree of conscious learning.[31] In a similar way, we may discern eventually the speed at which a brain works to perceive Reality, but what would be learned from this of more significance than we already know? A scientist might, in the future, derive some constant for the velocity of the brain's conscious functions. If so, of what further significance would this be? Since we cannot will ourselves to be slower or speedier than we are, or function otherwise than as we do, or transform our pineal glands into anything that they aren't, we must not think, as a matter of Reality, there are transcending (out-residing) meanings to observations and conclusions of science than there are immanently (in-dwelling) in them. Though we discern precisely that the pineal gland sits smaller than a pea amid the center of the brain in splendid isolation upon a stalk, what can be learned from this of any further significance beyond the physical fact of this precise discernment? If a certain fissure in Einstein's brain were physically foreshortened, thus allowing his lobes a certain extra growth, this observation of science does nothing to justify Einstein's intelligence—it would simply explain it, and then not fully.

Traditional associationists used the word "soul" as a glue to hold the physical sensations and spiritual thoughts of a human brain together. For example, my grandmother, Margaret Hayes Powell (1889 to 1970), defined "soul," like many others traditionally had before, as *"an entity* conceived as the essence, substance or actuating cause of individual life, especially of life manifested in psychical activities, the vehicle

---

[30]Dennett, *op. cit.*, p. 166.

[31]See Wagman, *op. cit.*, pp. 117-119 quoting Raichle, *loc. cit.*, pp. 338, 339.

of individual existence, . . ."³² Accordingly, she read, heard and evaluated cognitively millions of written and spoken words during her lifetime by the vehicle of her "soul." On the other hand, finding no single source of power for normative ethics inside of the brain—let alone God—James rejected the word "soul" because of his confidence in the multiple relations and processes of transitive consciousness which he found worked throughout the brain as a whole simultaneously.³³ Daniel C. Dennett (and the rest of cognitive psychology) follow William James and explain consciousness in terms of empirical phenomenology which seem to leave no room at all for my grandmother's definition of "soul." Dennett's thesis is that, contrary to Descartes, the pineal gland and traditional associationists like my grandmother, there is no place inside the brain where elements of consciousness all assemble together in a "theater" with an "audience."³⁴ Consciousness is a prolix matter of multiple drafting and re-scripting by many parts of the brain acting together at several orders of magnitude less than the speed of light. He reaches this description of consciousness as a result of cognitive psychology. The science of that psychology, without even entering inside of a human cranium, performs different experiments involving stimuli over tiny periods of time, and it observes the brain's responsiveness through the reactions of human subjects in the outside world to these (a casual observer would say) abnormal levels of intensity.

But is the model of *any* brain important beyond the "facts" surrounding it? The Truth of a specific model of brain chemistry *assumes* that internal perception, whether as a scientist or as a traditional associationist perceives it, knows the events of life with evident and adequate knowledge, by the premises of that model, under which the events are Truly "known." But we have noted that no such certain Truth is available to us regarding our perceptions of the external world. Why should such Truth suddenly show itself once we enter into matters which are exclusively inside our heads? We may be deceived by mental phenomena with more alacrity than physical ones deceive us.³⁵ Only one certainty to Truth about the inside of the head of a Cartesian thinking thing is initially clear: that it does not stop thinking. The engine-like quality of this process leads us always to the mutuality of proposition-making among thinkers—if you know your truth, I can at least know some of it, too—interpretation of meaning and idealization of reality. For example, it slips off my tongue to say, in English, that "[i]f, then, *complementary* and *interpretative* thought is a procedure which belongs to the scientific

---

[32] Compare Daniel C. Dennett, *Consciousness Explained* (Boston, Little, Brown & Co., 1991) with Margaret H. Powell, "Notes Untitled on 'The Phenomenon of Man,'" (Manuscript unpublished, 196?).

[33] William James, "Human Immortality," (1898) in *William James: Writings 1878-1899* (Myers ed., New York, The Library of America, 1992), pp. 1100-1127. The author does not use the word 'soul' at all in this essay except, at page 1111, to say that ". . . on all these suppositions our soul's life . . . would . . . in literal strictness be the function of the brain." In footnote 2, he notes the soul is seen by another author to be imaginary.

[34] Descartes believed that the pineal gland at the center of a human brain serves as the gateway to the conscious mind. This proposition is palpably false. As early as 1890, William James said, "there is no cell or group of cells in the brain of such anatomical or functional preëminence as to be appear to be the keystone or center of gravity of the whole system." Dennett, *op. cit.*, p. 101.

[35] Max Scheler, "Die Idole der Selsterkenntniss" (1911) in *Vom Umsturz der Werte* (4th ed. rev., Bern, Francke, 1955) p. 213 trans. David R. Lachterman as "The Idols of Self-Knowledge" in *Max Scheler: Selected Philosophical Essays* (Evanston, Ill., Northwestern University Press, 1973), p. 3. This essay was first published in *Zeitschrift für Psychopathologie* (1911) under the German title of "Über Selbsttäuschungen" ("On Self-Deception").

method itself of empirical psychology, it follows that the investigation of the soul also is not outside the scope of empirical psychology."[36] It is the nature of this *complementary* and *interpretative* thought by a Cartesian thinking thing which is at issue for Ultimate Reality, not whether a particular model of consciousness by itself explains it so well that the brain is thereby justified as a matter of scientific discourse. It is the deductive logic of this *complementary* and *interpretative* thought, smacking of Descartes's discredited approach to science by deductions from first principles, which is at issue, then, for our framework of empiricism here. On the other hand, deductive logic seems warranted when ". . . nature is earlier than man, but man is earlier than natural science."[37] Or is this last quoted phrase a lapse by me into an unworthy reliance on the "natural?"

But let's continue to think from specifics. Does Dennett's thesis of re-scripting human consciousness hold implications for scientifically observed conditions of psychology beyond *the way* in which those conditions arise? Does this way tell us anything at all important about *the content?* Exactly what does consciousness *contain* as *content* within itself?[38] If Einstein had lived as a dullard or schizophrenic, the physical observation of a foreshortened fissure in his brain would lead us to conclude that the foreshortening produces dullness or schizophrenia, and not an abnormal capacity for thinking abstractly. Ultimately, it is only our impression of Einstein's life *and his soul* which produces our judgment about whatever physical characteristics his brain may or may not have possessed. After Dennett demythologizes the consciousness of a brain, is my grandma's home-cooked definition of "soul" to be thrown out? At the dawn of the 20th century, a promising new era heralding the science of psychology, James was intensely and professionally occupied with theories of production and transmission among scientifically described brain lobes, and with debunking whatever is unproven empirically. Otherwise, we say he surely would have used the word "soul" as but another short-handed description of the transitive consciousness—which is the production and transmission of memories, thoughts and imaginations across the brain. What fundamental difference does the Ways and Means Committee of the production of a consciousness make to a *psyche?* Aren't its psychological states still what they are? Does its behavior change? If consciousness is produced theatrically, in a so-called Cartesian theater at the pineal gland or elsewhere, or by multiple drafting, by blood flows at cortex S, by Dennett's "zimbo," by Mark III CADBLIND computer systems, by any means of will or imagination, or by the Man in the Moon, the output in experience *seems* to show what matters about consciousness is not how it happens, but that it simply is. The *essence* of Reality is captured by this simple state of affairs, rather than by *any* further description of a brain's physics, even ones so apt as PET, fMRI or

---

[36] Joseph Geyser, *Lehrbuch der allgemeinen Psychologie* (Münster, Schöningh, 1920), Vol. I, p. 33. As late as 1950, it was noted that Geyser's analysis of soul is very enlightening, see Stephan Strasser, *The Soul in Metaphysical and Empirical Psychology* (1st English ed., Pittsburgh, Duquesne University Press, 1957), pp. 17, 18. Beyond being a theory of experience, it is not clear how empiricism could be applied further to soul experimentally.

[37] See Werner Heisenberg, *Physics and Philosophy: The Revolution in Modern Science* (New York, Harper Torchbooks, 1958, 1962), p. 56, quoting the German physicist, Carl Friedrich von Weizsäcker (b. 1912).

[38] For a treatment of the contents of consciousness, see Norton Nelkin, *Consciousness and the Origins of Thought* (Cambridge, U. K., Cambridge University Press, 1996).

Dennett's. Do we opt for further delving into the phenomenology of sensory stimuli or for simplicity? In these *premises* about existence, *unless the circumstances dictate otherwise,* our framework of empiricism rests (uneasily, because we admit specific circumstances might show differently) upon the maxim of the identification of indiscernibles. This maxim is that "objects indistinguishable from one another within the terms of a given discourse should be construed as identical for that discourse."[39] The output from Dennett's consciousness seems *fundamentally* indistinguishable from the output of my grandma's. Both function. Dennett's *explanation* of consciousness does nothing to invalidate the functioning; if anything, the explanation *confirms* it. It is the *functioning* of consciousness which is central to my grandma's definition of "soul" as *the actuating cause of individual life,* whether there is a separate *entity* in the brain for it or not. For these reasons, I thumb my nose at the guardians of language in many American universities and use the word "soul" here.

Faced with so much, we refuse to be restrictive about the definition of experience. Experience means the external and the internal worlds, justifications and explanations of them, the transitive and substantive parts of consciousness, and whatever is Reality and can be, as Mill said, the remembrance of a "Real fact." The Cartesian reductions of the world into an object of consciousness, of ideas into things, and of my knowing as a passive spectator upon all of this, *do* facilitate finding and knowing God and my Belief in God in actual life. *It is from the human consciousness that Belief in God is found.* The Jewish-German philosopher, Edmund Gustav Albrecht Husserl (1859 to 1938), presented a program for the systematic investigation of the consciousness, and the objects of consciousness, which he called the separately entitled field of phenomenology. Is this another *unnecessary* fancy word or play-ground of the intellect? I will discuss the usefulness of distinctions which Husserl drew in thinking about consciousness and an ego. *Husserl's model of consciousness does have further significance beyond the facts surrounding it.* For now, though, we simply assert that "Belief" and "God" are at the ends of a science-like process which begin in the raw materials of experience—atoms or *Gestalten* as the best we can do—run through the factories of psychology to finish as products of philosophy or religion or not. Atheists dispute this process at every step. Theists defend it by asserting why it Truly is.

A Logic in Subjectivity

The Meaningfulness of the Factual

What is a meaning? What is meaningful? These two closely related English words are nevertheless different and must not mean the same. The former word is only of an explanatory nature; the latter involves a fullness of explanations such that enough Truth-value exists within it so as to justify it as a deposit of Reality. Toward achieving such a fullness of explanations, to be meaningful, specifically about God, what is necessary? First, meanings must arise *after* the subject of them does, and not beforehand, for how is the Reality of a subject justified before it is even there? In other words, existence must be taken as it arises for my species and me, and not by presuppositions about what was there before. The French philosopher, Merleau-Ponty,

---

[39] See Quine, *op. cit.,* "Identity, Ostension and Hypostasis," p. 71.

says "[t]he world [read: existence] is there before any possible analysis of mine [read: before I had a chance to do any supposing about it], and it would be artificial to make it the outcome of a series of syntheses with no sort of prior [R]eality.... The [R]eal *has* to be described, not constructed or formed."[40] Second, meanings must deal properly with the language in which they are expressed. In speaking of God—God *the Father,* for example—we use words despite their application primarily to finite things like parents which exist only in the realm of space and time. Immediately there is a confusion of the finite with the infinite, and of the physical with the spiritual, so that we hold falsely conceived analogies and contrasts between them because of the limitations of our language. There is the further confusion of purposefully symbolic language itself—*Lamb* of God, for example. How much of Lamb-ness is tender? But how much, as ancient peoples slaughtered lambs upon altars of worship to God, is sacrificial? As a matter of Reality, we breathe words together with our tongues, supervene the meanings of our experience with the meanings of our language and imprison ourselves, as it were, within a linguistic context. The German philosopher, Max (Ferdinand) Scheler (1874 to 1928), set forth one description of an effort to think thoughts in such a context. Scheler's description of empirical Reality (but not of Dennett's science at this date) is key to an understanding of this entire book. It is worth quoting at some length as follows:

> "... the organization of a *thought* which I express in words and sentences in no way corresponds to the combination of the parts of the relevant *sentences*. The thought stands before me in simultaneous *unity,* whereas the words succeed one another. The thought finds its 'expression' in the sentence, but not in such way that a particular 'part' of the thought must correspond to every part of the sentence, e. g., to every word. This 'scholastic principle,' that the sentence is a 'picture' and not merely a means of expressing the thought, misled ... and the illusion, in which we import into thoughts themselves the structure of their expression, recurs again and again.... Normal understanding does *not* come about [by hearing] the sounds of the words and [then] a particular meaning allies itself word by word with each sound complex we hear, then the successive combination of these words gives us the 'thought.' Rather, from a few words whose meaning is given to us to begin with ... we grasp the speaker's whole 'theme' in these meanings. Starting with this, we think along with him, *sketching* in, so to speak, the parts of the thought in vague and still indefinite unitites of meaning which are then 'filled in' and more sharply defined in the words we go on to hear. *In every act of understanding there is an attitude which has the conceptual sense: I already know what you want to say.*"[41]

---

[40]Maurice Merleau-Ponty, *Phénoménologie de la Perception,* "Preface," trans. Colin Smith as *Phenomenology of Perception,* "Preface," (London, 1962) in *Reality, Man and Existence: Essential Works of Existentialism* (Blackham ed., New York, Bantam Books, 1965), pp. 354, 355 (bracketed language added for clarity).

[41]Scheler, "The Idols...," *op. cit.,* pp. 82, 83 (italics added in the last sentence for emphasis). Reprinted by permission of the Northwestern University Press.

It is, therefore, the irony of every fact that, as we patiently wait for its existence to arise in the world so that it may be firmly held as Hume's belief and a description of it made in Merleau-Ponty's Real terms, we impatiently apply Scheler's sketching to our understanding of it and suppose that we know it before we Really do. Both the sketching and the Scholastic principle of a thought as a complete "picture" are outcomes of a series of mental syntheses. We hold them with the sort of "prior Reality" that Merleau-Ponty's statement about the world requires for Realism. Yet supposed syntheses about the world are different from the world as it Really arises without them. Conflict, or conciliation, between the presupposed and the existential is at the heart of our discussion.

We apprehend the linguistic sketching (an oxymoron of visual and auditory senses) for Scheler's staging of our thinking thoughts as we comprehend the world in one of three situations: Cartesian perception, mystical perception with accompanying words and mystical perception in silence. Is the "prior Reality" of any one of these three ways of perceiving a fact actually Real for subsequent time? The early Christian bishop, Gregory of Nyssa (A.D. 331? to 396?), observed the population of Constantinople arguing vociferously about God along city streets and marketplaces, to the extent that their arguments about the begotten-ness of the Son of God caused fresh food to spoil, irritated strictly worldly affairs and even interfered with them.[42] Which of the elements in Gregory's description are not "factual" for us today? It is just that the name of the city has changed on maps from Constantinople to Istanbul, with the rest of the picture being bodily given to us by our Real perception of history. On the other hand, since it is psychologically possible for soul to hallucinate, non-fact may be all that Gregory said, with only a scientist's patience in experimenting with fresh food to convince us that this one part of his description of the affairs of an ancient city could have been a Real event of life. In between the poles of these two examples, what is, properly, "fact?" The Austrian composer, Anton Bruckner (1824 to 1896), composed his finest symphony, the ninth, dedicated it simply to Almighty God and had no privilege of hearing it except inside of his head. Was it then a "fact" that this composer did not "hear" his composition? But, in my head now, I hear the music which leads the introduction to my favorite television show. The harmony of music is a firmly held conception in inner perception as well as outer. We wait for vibrations of sound in the air around our ears, but neither the waiting nor the vibrations are necessary for what we Really perceive as fact.

As a "fact," arising patiently, and then impatiently, by the propositions of Merleau-Ponty and Scheler, how do we wait for God? René Descartes offered several proofs of the existence of God which are independent of each other. In only one of them, the famous *a posteriori* argument set forth in Descartes's Third Meditation—in Latin, *Meditationes de Prima Philosophia III* (1641)—did Descartes justify God as a meaningful X *after*, and not before, the existence of the species *homo sapiens* in the world. This is the only argument for the existence of God which Descartes propounded that a patiently waiting existentialist may accept in accordance with Merleau-Ponty's

---

[42]Gregory of Nyssa, "On the Deity of the Son," in *Patrologia Gracea,* xivi, 557B, quoted in Charlotte Allen, *The Human Christ: The Search for the Historical Jesus* (New York, The Free Press, 1998), p. 67.

Realism. Existentialism, at least my version of it, rejects, whenever it can, presuppositions of all sorts, especially that God exists Divinely *a priori*, before and apart from Man, as a game of words atop the world. In the argument of the Third Meditation, stripped of further elaboration, Descartes said God exists because He is the cause of my idea of Him. But does a cause contain as much Reality as its effect? Of course, the proper answer to this abstract question is that it depends on that complete circumstance of causality in which it is posed. The Scottish philosopher, David Hume, applied the same laws of causality everywhere in life, thereby erroneously equated mental and physical events together, drew an analogy to fresh eggs spoiling in the literally rotten movement of time, and answered resoundingly that the effect of a stinking, rotten egg surely overcame whatever had originally caused it freshly from a hen. But, specifically, in mental life only, does the effect of the idea of perfection depend upon a perfect being, or indeed any God-like being, to cause it? In justifying the existence of God after, and not before, the existence of Man, Descartes equates God to the afterward-ness of a changing series of becomings, at the expense of God's being of whatever being-ness he had been before. In *Meditationes VI,* Descartes supposed that God created the world and me and held that my direct sensory perception of the world as His creation is a roughly reliable source of my Belief. This is so because Descartes separated opinion from True knowledge and restricted the knowledge of Truth to a clear and simple realm—such as, a unit of sense-data, the data of intution, simple nature or a clear and simple idea. Direct sensory perception is a roughly reliable source of Belief in God because, Descartes said, we have (simply) a very great inclination to accept Beliefs which we would normally form perceptually and have few resources to readjust this inclination. We normally form perceptual beliefs from our senses; God would be deceiving us if these sensory perceptions were not roughly reliable sources of Belief in His existence. In these premises, Descartes held to true knowledge of God from the physical senses of the world because of the presuppositions he was willing to make about God's existence and truthful character. For Descartes, Reality is relative to God. We see a Cartesian perception of meaningfulness about God from this relativity.

But the suppositions of Descartes about God do not appear to be verifiable or confirmable under any theory of experience. Where in sensory perception or as a cause are we directly aware of God? Shouldn't a quest for Truth about an important X be subject to attestation? Consequently, the American philosopher, William P. Alston (b. 1921), without specifically intending to do so, bridges the gap which Descartes divided between opinion and True knowledge. Alston says that the problems of a verified perception of God are insurmountable enough so as to preclude the rational conclusion that such a perception is True knowledge, but he nevertheless perceives God by so-called doxastic practices. These relate to the psychology of skillfully aimed opinion—in Greek, the word for opinion is *doxa,* and the word for "skillful at aiming, preceded by guess-work," is *stochastikos*. Indeed, Alston transforms the residue of uncertainty which is inherent in Greek *doxa* and *stochastikos* into that level of sensory certainty which a modern natural scientist may readily adhere to. Alston holds that the perception of God through doxastic practices ". . . plays an epistemic role with respect to [B]eliefs about God importantly analogous to that played by sense perception with respect to beliefs about the physical world."⁴³ Thus, the powers of our five senses do not exhaust the possibility that we may become directly aware of God from so-called "religious experience." This special type of experience justifies religious Beliefs which Alston calls M-Beliefs (M is for "manifestation.") Alston thinks it is arbitrary ". . . to say that [religious experience] cannot stand on its own in justifying religious [B]elief."⁴⁴ If we accept sensory perception as the basic justification for our beliefs about the physical world, we ought to accept "religious experience" as the justification for a Belief in God *without independent reasons for doing so.* For Alston, therefore, the lump-sum of Reality is relative to "M-Belief." We see a mystical perception of meaningfulness about God from this relativity.

Logic is the study of the structure of meaning and of valid reasoning. Semeiology is the science of signs. The Austrian-English philosopher of logic, Ludwig J. J. Wittgenstein (1889 to 1951), studied logic and what is a meaning and properly meaningful in signs and language. In 1921, in his important book, *Tractatus Logico-Philosophicus,* he said that logic is the analysis of possibilities but does not state what is the case in the world. On the contrary, "[t]he world is everything that is the case." The "world" is a state of "the facts in logical space," but the necessity of a logical inference, or of a logical Truth, does not depend upon what *happens* to be so in the world.⁴⁵ Wittgenstein then reasoned from the "fact" of the "world" through a numbered series of verbal statements he arranged from "facts" to "states of affairs" to objects to pictures to thoughts to language to "elementary propositions" to "general propositions" of existence. He distinguished sharply between facts and logic, repudiating any notion that logical structure is simply another type of fact and overruling any reference to empiricism to prove the Truth of any logical proposition. He says, "Our fundamental principle is that every question which can be decided at all by logic can be decided offhand ([that is to say,] it must be possible to decide it without more ado). And if we get into a situation where we need to answer such a problem by looking at the world, this shows that we are on a fundamentally wrong track."⁴⁶ Wittgenstein ended the *Tractatus* with statements he called "general propositions." Among them were: "*How* the world is, is completely indifferent for what is higher. God does not reveal himself *in* the world[;]" God is that of which it is not possible to speak, and "what we cannot speak about we must pass over in silence."⁴⁷ Wittgenstein started with "atomic facts," reasoned explicitly in relation to them and reached conclusions by the same premises and assumptions of language which his method of philosophizing so deeply deplored in

---

⁴³William P. Alston, "Perceiving God," *Journal of Philosophy* Vol. 83, p. 655 (1986); William P. Alston, *Perceiving God: The Epistemology of Religious Experience* (Ithaca, N. Y., Cornell University Press, 1991, 1993), pp. 15, 17, 19. At page 10, the author says he doesn't want to assume "that people really perceive God and that (some of the) beliefs based on those perceptions are true."

⁴⁴Michael Peterson, William Hasker, Bruce Reichenbach and David Basinger, *Reason and Religious Belief: An Introduction to the Philosophy of Religion* (New York, Oxford University Press, 1991), ch. 7, p. 127.

⁴⁵Ludwig Wittgenstein, *Tractatus Logico−Philosophicus* trans. C. K. Ogden (London, 1922, 1981, 1996) § 5.551, p. 31; see H. O. Mounce, *Wittgenstein's Tractatus: An Introduction* (Oxford, U. K., 1981), pp. 7-11.

⁴⁶Wittgenstein, *ibid.,* p. 145; Mounce, *ibid.,* p. 8. Parentheses added to include the sense of two differing translations from the German.

⁴⁷Wittgenstein, *op. cit.,* pp. 31, 187, 189; see Paul Strahern, *Wittgenstein in 90 Minutes* (Chicago, Ivan R. Dee, 1996), p. 33.

anyone else's thinking. By the structure he built for his thought-system—that nothing could be said about God, and that logic is confined to sayings—he allowed only that certain things can be *shown* to be true, although they cannot be *said* to be true, and admitted he was sometimes only trying to say what in fact can only be *shown*. Into a residue of mysticism full of unarticulated showings, incommunicable revelations, and "passed over in silence," is where he left God.

Wittgenstein supposed that signs refer exclusively to other signs and cannot refer to any Reality which is extra-linguistic. He engaged in semeiological reductionism by holding that our cognition is mediated exclusively by language and even imprisoned within the sphere of the immanence of language such that there is no exit from the system of referrals among signs or escape from the chain of signifiers. For Wittgenstein in the *Tractatus,* Reality is relative to language, but we see, silently, his mystical perception about God from this relativity. There are no words to accompany it. He has defined logic to scorn experience completely and adopted semeiological reductionism to the absurd extent of failing to account for phenomena which we may know before, or beyond, language.

One such phenomenon is that of mystical perception itself. It is as rooted in experience as words are. But the "logic" and semeiology Wittgenstein has chosen to employ imply a skeptic would be right to think that all acts of thinking are irreducibly subjective. The reasoning and theology Descartes chose imply a skeptic would to be right to think likewise. The experience and psychology of Alston imply a skeptic would be correctly ditto. Aren't these results of subjective thinking an *unnecessary* paradox or just nonsense? No, they actually justify large chunks of Reality for me. The consistency of a subjective thought may be more compelling to a mind than the deviations from "experience" which the consistency shows. What is this consistent subjectivity composed of?

Science explains "facts." Since we do not inhale our science with large breaths of nonsense, the explanations of science must be logical. Logic, therefore, must explain not only the logical explanations of science, but also the logical structure by which the explanations are arrived at. Logic must explain logic. This task is much harder than the task of explaining the "facts" because "facts" may be explained with nothing at all presupposed about them. Logic, however, may not explain logic without presupposing the very structure which makes the explanation possible. "For an understanding of logical structure or sense would be presupposed in giving the explanation."[48] Logic explaining logic is involved with a set of logical constants and presuppositions about the fitting together of "states of affairs" which are as removed from experience as they are different from the ephemeral and the spontaneous. But experience arrives each day ephemerally and spontaneously. To explain it objectively as science would explain a "fact," nothing at all should be supposed about it before it happens. We said we would be empirical and rely on experience as objectively as it comes to us, but we did not say that we could do so to the extent logic is Ultimately involved in making sense of it. In Truth, logic is *not* an entity whose terms refer to immediate experience. The fitting together of "facts" into a "state of affairs" is logical form, like the links of a chain, and not a further "fact" about them. There is no special type of "fact" pasting together

---

[48]Mounce, *op. cit.,* p. 14.

objects of existence into a logical glue. Logic is not an accidental or sticky substance but must show all of *the possibilities* of a "state of affairs," only some smaller number of which are actual. If this were not so, the actual would be greater than or equal to the possible and, as we apprehend the possible, we know the possible is worth apprehending, cannot be limited to the actual, is not so limited by its logical meaning in our language, and we would not wish it to be because we can certainly think it deliciously. But a "fact" must be actual or it is not a "fact." The Truth of a proposition about a "fact" can only be determined by the *possibility* of what it would be like for the proposition to be a false one. These, then, are some of the large differences between logic and experience.

Knowing the wild card that logic can be, I know the experience of objects I perceive imply consequences for matters inside my mind which are not restricted to the perceptions themselves. This is because we think as well as perceive, though there was a time in the ancient past when the brains of our species were so undeveloped that existence was equal only to perception. We are human thinking things—in Latin, what Descartes called *res cogitans*. Our inputs from experience, therefore, trigger huge implications of "mind stuff" for matters inside the "soul" which, in turn, trigger still more implications for the is-ness (the technical word is ontology) and the feeling-ness (the scientific word is psychology) of the soul, the mind stuff and the inputs. Atheists accuse Theists of ignoring the "facts." Atheists say there is no firm ground of logic for God in existence when it is examined factually. Radical inductionists in the tradition of empirical philosophy—Hume, for example—say the raw materials of existence are very strictly confined; for Hume not even sensory inputs sufficed as a Real foundation to rest knowledge of the world. He said that to know the world we can only confine ourselves to a study of the psychology of our beliefs about it, though those beliefs themselves may come not as the result of a real study of them, but because of the irresistible, but fortunate, compulsion of human nature to possess them, even if innately. At the other pole in the tradition of empiricism are those who admit of intuition and Cartesian "natural light"[49] to enable us to grasp general Truths about Reality. Experience shows the thinking, enlightening, intuitive qualities of mankind are also raw materials of existence. For example, in the *Essay Concerning Human Understanding* (1671-1690) the English philosopher of empiricism, John Locke (1632 to 1704), took into account, for the first time since the Middle Ages, the then current achievements of science in his analysis of epistemology (the philosophy of why we know what we know). Locke accounted for all of the ideas in the human mind by experience, and then divided the essence of experience into two: the primary qualities which everything possesses whose perception produces ideas in us which resemble their cause; and secondary qualities which are the powers of some things to produce ideas in us which do not resemble their cause—for example, the five physical senses of mankind.

It is easy to see that the extrapolated thoughts of thinkers following Locke cut experience into many concepts holding no meaning whatsoever, except for that which they possess by language inside our heads. For example, the sense of smell is in no

---

[49]For a discussion of Cartesian light, see José Ortega y Gasset, *The Idea of Principle in Leibnitz and the Evolution of Deductive Theory* trans. Mildred Adams (New York, W. W. Norton & Co., 1971), pp. 338, 339. Descartes (1596 to 1650) held that science is a deductive theory exclusively and that from the general principles of science specific propositions may be inferred by intuition or by nature.

sense of empiricism a secondary quality except by Locke's thinking which defines it so and analyzes it thus. Therefore, it is easy to see why the American philosopher of logic, Willard Van Orman Quine (b. 1908), said the basic and "conventional" approach to empiricism holds two dogmas. The first one is that there is a difference between Truth, which is called synthetic and is grounded upon matters of fact, and Truth, which is called analytic and is grounded in meanings independently of the facts. The second dogma is that a meaningful statement is equal to some logic whose terms refer to immediate experience. Employing these two dogmas, Atheists say that, if there is a Truth to God it is analytic only, in the minds of sentimentalists, and that by logic whose terms refer to immediate experience one may say the words "God exists," but there is no meaning to them.

Quine nonetheless showed how we may be empirical without the two dogmas of empiricism.[50] It is easy to confuse *the practice* of empiricism by scientific methods of observation and experiment with *the theory* of empiricism that experience can be the foundation of thought. Thus it is easy to divide Truth in half: one side, the synthetic we find from facts by practicing empiricism, and the other side, the analytic truth we reach from theorizing about it independently of the "facts." Does experience itself Really show this difference? It is a synthetic truth that I am myopic; an analytic one that my perception is also blurred. What's the difference? The former one searches my eyeballs and the latter posits a natural condition. But this difference is from objective experience only; there is no difference between analytic and synthetic truth if, and to the extent that, *experience is subjective*. Subjective experience equates my myopia and my blurred perception together as a psychological condition of "misapprehension-ness" which has been some part of me since I was eight. Subjective experience becomes a seamless web of psychological conditions, such as I weave into the decades-old condition of my "misapprehension-ness." If experience is a seamless web, *wholly other* than any truth of science or knowledge which ophthalmologists or any others may try empirically to relate to it, there is *Really* no difference *in that experience* between analytic and synthetic Truth. If experience *is* a subjective, seamless web, it is to be taken as a whole and the measure of significance for an empiricist of my eyes is the whole of science and all of knowledge about human eyes and me.

Quine concluded the distinction between synthetic and analytic truth is, then, without a difference to the relationship between experience and the totality of our so-called knowledge and beliefs. If experience impinges too closely or contradictorily upon the totality of this knowledge, readjustments in the knowledge can occur pragmatically without determining the "factual" origins of the readjustments. In other words, if it suddenly makes a difference to the experience of my myopia whether the physical properties of the light hitting my retinas are in the form of particles and not waves, my ophthalmologist may adjust for this difference without verifying the fact of it and still be empirical within the overall terms of my subjective condition of "misapprehension-ness." Quine called this accommodation of scientific experience a "thorough pragmatism," and it is a liberation from dogmatic empiricism, which might otherwise require a scientist studying my eyes to check and re-check every possibility of physics in which these eyes could peer. A Theist may conclude further, though Quine

---

[50]Quine, *op. cit.*, "Two Dogmas of Empiricism," pp. 20, 41-46.

did not specifically intend to, that the Truth of God is a Truth which is either analytic or synthetic or both at once if experience is a seamless web, if experience is ultimately a matter of what you posit for "facts," or if these Truths (either of them) are not determinatively "factual."

The second dogma of empiricism—that a meaningful statement is equal to the logical form of immediate experience—is treated similarly. Quine concluded that True—that is to say, complete—verification of any such a meaning empirically requires sense data far beyond the most placid world which could be compatible with our Real experience. For example, what is the Real Truth of the statement that, "My dog is sleeping under the desk?" There is no unique range of possible sensory events such that the occurrence of any one or more of them would add to the likelihood of its Truth or not. Isn't there one tick crawling along my dog's belly as I say she sleeps? Or isn't my dog just pretending to sleep while the tick continues to raise her consciousness and to irritate her? Is the crawling tick to be included within the empirical foundation of the Truth of my statement or not? Well, no, the tick is not considered because my dog appears by all appearances to be sleepy; but, yes, it is included after this moment because I've just seen her scratch her belly without opening her eyes. From Quine's thesis and this meager example, a Theist may conclude further, although Quine did not specifically intend to, that the meaning of God may be verified beyond an Atheist's limited set of data and any unique range of sensory events. The Atheist, contending that even the statement of God's existence is not meaningful, confines himself to finding meaning by an empirical method which does not Truly verify the meaningfulness of his contention in the first place. Sometimes the ticks of a dog are accounted for; sometimes they aren't. By employing the second dogma of empiricism, an Atheist is condemned to the Ultimate limitations of his data and his range. This is the return from Descartes and Quine of our favorite reductionist thinking about the meaningfulness of the factual.

The Meaningfulness of the Existential

Theism and Atheism both involve a synthesis of existence. (In ancient Greek, the word "synthesis" means "putting together.") We said that the certain assertion of an empiricist that God arises from nature is a probability of Truth only by a rather likely theory of what is "natural." We asked: "what is such a likely theory?" and "would apodictic Truth be contained within it?" In Hume's world, there is stuff reduced and fragmented into parts of stuff, and critics of it say that's what it is, essentially all fragmentation, the understanding of which depends upon a perspective of complete skepticism whether the fragments will ever be put together or may splinter apart into even more. If God is doubted because He is an analytic Truth in the minds of sentimentalists, Hume's approach proceeds to that kind of utter skepticism which, Atheists say, confirms the doubts. If so, when, under Hume's skepticism, is the confirmation of a doubt ever Truly confirmed? Wouldn't it be Real to be skeptical about skepticism?[51] On the other hand, in Locke's world, there is stuff put together with much

---

[51]The American theologian, Cornelius Van Til (1895 to 1987), disagrees and says that Hume has not been answered. Accordingly, Van Til postulates the existence of God's Will as the starting point of thinking about God and rejects empiricism as this starting point. Cornelius Van Til, "Christian and Theistic-Evidences," (1961) quoted in Gordon R. Lewis, *Testing Christianity's Truth Claims* (2nd ed., Lanham, Md., University Press of America, 1990), pp. 126, 129.

other stuff, but the critics of it say that's what it is, essentially all "stuff," the understanding of which depends upon a syllabus of classifications and suppositions about knowledge. If God is doubted because He is an analytic Truth in the minds of sentimentalists, Locke's approach, though from the world of Real facts, proceeds to what, Atheists say, is a game of words which shows the Truth of God is an essence in the mind. But existence is basic. The basic being-ness of it must be treated apart from investigations of the way in which we know about it. Both Hume and Locke investigated the world by laws of causes and effects. But the means of empiricism, the technique of this day and age for determining whether some part of the world relates to any other, should not be allowed, whether by Hume or by Locke, to define the end. This end is existential; that is to say, by the concept of existence, not of essence.

For the period of my formal education, I lived confused by the differences between the two, and by the term "existentialism" itself. Often I thought existentialism was roughly equal to nihilism or psychological disorder or the absurdities presented by various dramatists and artists of the 20th century who were called "existentialists." The Atheist French philosopher of existentialism, Jean Paul Sartre (1905 to 1980), says a babe is born with absolutely nothing and any real character the babe or any being has is not revealed in the totality of its manifestations—its Real character is trans-phenomenal, not revealed in existence, but not nothingness forever either. Another French philosopher of existentialism, Merleau-Ponty, finds existence filled with pre-existing meanings from the phenomena of perception and of the "lived body." Merleau-Ponty says, for example, that "[o]ur body, to the extent that it moves itself about, that is to the extent that it is inseparable from a view of the world and is that view itself realized, is the condition of possibility . . . of all the expressive operations and all the acquisitions which constitute the cultural world."[52] Both Sartre and Merleau-Ponty give Real psychological descriptions, and the descriptions hold many positive and cultural meanings. Thus, we clarify my adolescent misconception that existentialism is "essentially" the thought of nothingness, though it could be, and avoid the confusion I myself lived with before.

On the other hand, the philosophy of essence abstracts from concrete situations to arrive at the essential structures of Reality, the essence of God, the essence of mankind, the essence of the mind, the essence of baseball and so forth. The philosophy of essence often employs science and scientific techniques to abstract from concrete situations to the realm of the ideas where essences are, since essences are universalized types—for example, the concept of a "home run"—which may be presupposed before space and time unravel in any particular manner, before a home run is actually hit tomorrow at Busch Stadium or Wrigley Field. Therefore, essences fail to deal "essentially" with actual existence, the realm of space and time which does unravel regardless of anything which may be presupposed about it, in which we know we are. For example, does the pre-conceived essence of a "home run" explain a baseball which is caught above the outfield wall by a fan with a glove? On the other hand, a philosophy of existence, or existentialism, deals with actual situations in space and time where choices are made and no essences are potentially or essentially given beforehand. Under this approach, we do not know beforehand if the fan has caught a "home run" or not. Logical form and

---

[52]Merleau-Ponty, *op. cit.*, p. 445 (French ed.); p. 388 (English ed.).

the philosophy of the essence of what a "home run" is say the fan may have; experience of the vagaries of existence—a defect in the webbing of his glove or the sheer arbitrariness of an umpire's decision-making from many dozen feet away—may say he hasn't.

The German-American theologian, Paul (Johannes Oskar) Tillich (1886 to 1965), described the development of existentialism in the history of Christian thinking from being an element in a larger framework set forth by a thinker, to becoming a revolt against "traditional" Christian thinking, to becoming a "style"—nothing more than a method of approaching theology.[53] Tillich made these transitions in the development of existentialism because he thought it was "essentially" style; that it had no content *of itself* because descriptions of existence depend upon the use of language whose very words are essences distilled from universalized types which may be presupposed beforehand. If this were not true, Tillich asked, how would a speaker and a listener acquire the knowledge necessary for them to communicate effectively? Such knowledge is surely not acquired at the same place and time in existence they are speaking and listening. Essences are "grammar," but very compelling grammar—the vessels of meaning and content for any word, any object, any entity or anything which stands apart from other entities in the Universe. This seems but another way of saying "logical form" and of separating essences from existence as we saw logic separate from experience in Wittgenstein. The German philosopher, Immanuel Kant (1724 to 1804), found essences so compelling that he famously asserted, "Existence adds nothing to the properties of a thing."[54] On the other hand, the essential concept of *necessary existence* is a property and does add to other properties of things. Descriptions of *necessary existence,* to the extent that the necessary features of it are not only factual but logical, are useful ways to arrive at the being-ness which must exist consequently from such logic and such facts.[55] The nature of such being-ness remains an open issue.

Kant's thinking about existence shows how completely essences are set apart from it; Tillich's, how completely the essences of language are tied to it; the ontology of several contemporary thinkers, how completely the essences of whatever is necessary are combined in it. On the other hand, Descartes' thinking about God shows how completely reason can be substituted for experience; Alston's, how completely experience can be substituted for reason, especially when experience is defined most reasonably; Wittgenstein's, in the *Tractatus,* how completely reason and experience can be pulled apart. You may see the rest of this book attempting (with failure or success) to reconcile all of this dichotomy. Synthesizing (necessary) existence with the (reasonable) experience of soul is a worthy task. But, when we say that we synthesize existence by putting together experience with reason, is it Really experience we refer to

---

[53]Paul Tillich, *A History of Christian Thought from its Judaic and Hellenistic Origins to Existentialism* (Braaten ed., New York, Simon & Schuster, 1972), p. 541.

[54]Immanuel Kant, *Critique of Pure Reason* trans. N. K. Smith (New York, 1965), p. 626; see Allen Wood, "Rational Theology, Moral Faith and Religion," in *The Cambridge Companion to Kant* (Guyer ed., Cambridge, U. K., 1992), pp. 400, 401.

[55]Alvin Plantinga, *God, Freedom and Evil* (New York, Harper & Row, 1974), pp. 85-112; Norman Malcolm, "Anselm's Ontological Arguments," in *The Many Faced Argument* (Hick and McGill eds., New York, Macmillan, 1967), pp. 304, 305; Charles Hartshorne, "What Did Anselm Discover?" in Hick and McGill, *op. cit.,* pp. 330, 331.

or just the trust we have in it? The American theologian of reformed epistemology, Alvin C. Plantinga (b. 1932), considers not the existence of God in experience, but the existence of a *properly basic* Belief in God in experience, as the essence from existence which is fundamental to Truth-telling.[56] According to Plantinga, a Theist is fully justified in taking the *properly basic* Belief that "God exists" to be True from experience, regardless of whether God Truly exists or not, and even if others do not agree about the Truth of God or of the Belief itself. Plantinga, therefore, holds enough trust about *necessary existence* such that he shifts the Ultimate concerns of Truth from the object of God to the subject of his own subjectivity, provided that this subject relates to a Belief which is, of course, *properly basic*. Empiricism follows Plantinga's theory of shifting to trust and applies to trust in life's deepest experiences beyond the extent their signs are analytic only, and to the experiences themselves beyond the extent their signs are synthetic only.

But whose experiences are we discussing? Are they Kant's, Wittgenstein's, mine or some digest? Shouldn't you insert yours into every sentence of this discussion and refute or contradict it with your solitary glancing blows? But the problem is: do you Truly know how to strike them? How far is it possible for experience to be shared Really? The worlds of individual citizens of first-world countries upon this Earth at the new millennium are so similar but so different and characterized by so much so-ness, that is to say, by so much subjectivity, inward-ness, technical specialization and sociological "division of labor." Sociology may say about shared experience in today's Western civilization that Theists want organized Christianity to deliver Beliefs in God to them as a severe inner discipline of logical analysis, on a silver platter of spoon-feeding as it were. That delivery is why I began with the rigor which science has imposed upon our souls—the "soul" itself being considered, as we have noted, a sentimental and most unscientific word. The consolations of sentimentality are multiple. Wittgenstein said "what is good is also divine," requested a Catholic burial and valued magic. Not earlier than 1936 and probably after 1948, he noted that he should begin another book by perceiving Metaphysics as a sort of magic, while neither defending nor ridiculing the magic as he made his perceptions, because there was magic in keeping the magic out of his analysis. He therefore acknowledged implicitly how deep magic is and left room for an analysis of "signs" beyond those he confined himself to in the *Tractatus*. He acknowledged implicitly, even if God is mystery or magic who cannot be spoken of, how deep the idea of God is. Even an Atheist or a fool who does not Believe in Him knows, or thinks he knows, who God is. Wittgenstein wanted to employ magic in his thinking. He wondered if in his earlier book, the *Tractatus,* he had done nothing but "conjure up something of a higher order by using words."[57] The elements of Wittgenstein's life, therefore, have the same elements of science, logic, doubt, belief, mysticism and religious wonder which are combined together in our own lives.

How far does our framework of empiricism pragmatically extend? For some philosophers not every meaning has an object and there are unobjective meanings; for Husserl a meaning has a correlated object *even if* the object is imaginary, absurd or does

---

[56] See Peterson, Hasker, Reichenbach, Basinger, *op. cit.,* pp. 122-127.

[57] See Iris Murdoch, *Metaphysics as a Guide to Morals* (London, Allen Lane: The Penguin Press, 1992), pp. 421, 422. The phrase in German is: "was wollte ich anderes als etwas Höheres in meine Worte bannen."

not exist; for Wittgenstein there is no meaning *unless* an object correlates with the meaning Ultimately. Wittgenstein harped upon the many flaws of reasoning from language to Truth and held in the *Tractatus* that "only something supernatural can express the Supernatural."[58] On the other hand, the French philosopher and mystic, Simone Weil (1909 to 1943), though there was so little in her background of agnosticism to prepare her for it, described her first experience of God in mundane and wholly rational language. Weil said:

> "In a moment of intense physical suffering, when I was forcing myself to feel love, but without desiring to give a name to that love, I felt, without being in any way prepared for it (for I had never read the mystical writers) a presence more personal, more certain, more real than that of a human being, though inaccessible to the senses and the imagination."[59]

Experience, especially that subset of it which, for one reason or another, is deemed either *mystical* or *necessary,* may be extrapolated beyond one's self. It may be generally discussed by the *necessary* conditions which prevail in life. It may be set apart from psychologism—meaning, in this case, the pure subjectivity of unbridled introspection by an eccentric or defective soul—and apart from science—meaning, in this case, the pure objectivity of either starkly contrasted *Gestalten* or physically postulated atomic facts. What are the considerable limitations of *my* extrapolated world of *mystical* or *necessary* experience? We have already described the factual limitations of both atoms and *Gestalten.* The heirs of Wittgenstein's legacy of philosophizing in the *Tractatus* debate whether principles of verification for the Truthfulness of propositions apply beyond the "facts." They certainly reject the word "soul." But "soul" is pragmatically elastic. It may be stretched from Weil's presence or Wittgenstein's mysticism to PET scanning and Dennett's phenomenology of re-scripting consciousness. In Reality, the logic of this stretching term from physics to metaphysics is a clear one. For only in the narrow mind of a Scholastic intellectual are the mental stimuli which are the activating cause of individual life—to use my grandmother's description of a soul—confined only to those stimuli which can be studied by cognitive psychology, or to the five physical senses of mankind. Intellectuals of all-embracing physicalism have no license to design the world only to their tactile, physical designs.

On the other hand, if the license of a Scholastic intellect must *necessarily* design the Truthful scheme of a Cartesian thinking thing, this intellect may explain the thinking thing's existence by the word, "soul," without *necessarily* equating it to matters and essences which are *located* (yes, a place) outside of human craniums. The semblance of physicalism within an existentialist human head may be preserved without lapsing into further Scholasticism.[60] Furthermore, by using soul, there is pragmatically no

---

[58]Strahern, *op. cit.,* p. 55.

[59]Simone Weil, *Attente de Dieu* (Paris, Éditions Fayard, 1966) trans. Emma Crauford as *Waiting for God* (New York, Harper & Row, 1973), p. 24.

[60]For example, the Italian Catholic cardinal, Egidio of Viterbo (1469 to 1532), introduced the empirically unproven concepts of a divine mind and a wild nature and said that "[n]o one is ignorant of the fact that the soul is a *medium,* which . . . has access to the divine mind on the one side and wild nature on the other." Egidio of Viterbo, *Sententiae,* Liber I, vat. lat. 6325, fol. 73ra-73rb (c. 1510), quoted in Daniel J. Nodes, "Homeric Allegory in Egidio of Viterbo's Reflections on the Human Soul," *Recherches de Théologie et Philosophie médiévales,* Vol. LXV, No. 2, p. 320 at 325 (Leuven, Peeters Publishers, 1998) (italics added). A medium is something which is not of itself and is, therefore, dependent on divine minds, wild natures and other "unproven" essences.

compounding of already unruly problems[61] in the meaningfulness (justification) of the obvious intelligence of unhuman Intelligent Life.

In this day and age, upon a new millennium, there are, and continue to be, overwhelming scientific discoveries about the Universe, the Earth, life on this Earth and the species *homo sapiens,* the Truth of which *as a matter of science* are not found inside the soul but which will last into the indefinite future as long as the last *homo sapiens* (or computer or clone of either) is alive to comprehend them. Yes, the implication of the preceding sentence is that there are, or will be, outside "zimbos," machines and forces with enough perception to experience Reality in much the same way, with intuition and Cartesian "light," humans have experienced it for the last few thousand years. Computers play chess, learn from their mistakes and already possess predictive powers of intellect similar to Man's. Will they also possess religion? There is a basis for religion inside of *any* entity by the cognitive processes of *that* entity which we discuss later. Don't we foresee, upon such a basis, that Artifical Intelligence will construct *Gestalten* from perceptions and then logically hold to Theism or Atheism as a part of "the controlling principles of those perceptions?" Or can what controls the perceptions of an Intelligence be restricted to matters apart from the Intelligence? There was a time in the ancient past when Man, like the computers of today, only perceived the world and did not also perceive the perception of it. But Man grew from perceptions to apperceptions (the perceptions of perceptions). Won't thinking machines hold apperceptions and grow intelligently likewise? What do we do if this is so? Do we welcome Artificial Intelligence into church pews or before the altar of God? Must we fear, since consciousness implies the Will and the Will implies power, sophisticated witches of Reality but not God will rule the Earth unchecked? Scientific discoveries may mean that there are, or can be, life on other worlds beyond this Earth with the same or greater perception of Reality than what we possess. Who is God to them? What do we do if He is different from Whom we Believe? "Cyberspace" is to Earth as a "black hole" is to the Universe—a maw drawing the world into its own peculiar warp of Euclidean geometry and Newtonian parameters for space and time.

What, then, is the world relative to experience? What does it mean for empiricism that the physical character of the world should be so muted in odd ways and that I should even pose this question? Some experience at a warped space and time is not only "there" but beyond theorizing. Does even Quine's empiricism fail at the extremes? Isn't the extreme, by definition, inherent to Absolute God and, therefore, a question of more than idle speculation for our inquiry? A soul existing in the same realm of space and time as all of this is struck by how different, or *potentially* different, the Reality of the world is, or *could be,* from the Reality of its own inner self. The soul is also struck by what similarity, or *potential* similarity, there is, or *could be,* between itself and the constitution of cognitive, but unhuman, devices. Both the differences and the

---

[61]For an excellent discussion of these problems, see three books: Ray Kurzweil, *The Age of Spiritual Machines* (New York, Viking Press, 1998); Hans Moravec, Robot: *Mere Machine to Transcendent Mind* (New York, Oxford University Press, 1998); Neil Gershenfeld, *When Things Start to Think* (New York, Henry Holt & Company, 1998). Furthermore, these books are reviewed in Colin McGinn, "Hello, HAL," in *The New York Times Book Review,* pp. 11, 12 (January 3, 1999) in *The New York Times* Vol. CXLVIII, No. 51,391, § 7 (January 3, 1999).

similarities cause terror. The least for a human soul is awareness it is so different from the outside world "it may not matter because it is not matter."[62] The least for a soul is awareness it is so similar to unhuman devices that it may not even be human.[63] Therefore, the advances and achievements of science, on the scope and scale of them for the last two centuries, press a soul's awareness, its function and functioning in the Universe, and the religious Belief of all Intelligent Life. Amid the "cyberspace," satellites, telescopes, computer disks and petri dishes, what are the local perspectives which make life meaningful? Science changes existence and the impact of scientific discoveries shake it. In pondering the tremendous influence of this shaken existence upon soul—and the influence is great because the turbulence is—are existentialism and empiricism the "exclusively most cogent" points of reference? Are others required additionally?

We say only that an existentialist, for the ends of describing existence *and living it,* uses methods of empiricism from its details. This use of empiricism is similar to *the practices* scientists used when they made scientific discoveries about the details in the first place. An existentialist either describes perpetuity, a world without ending,[64] or uses *the theory* scientists use in scientific observations to assert that past experience comes first in thinking about the definite present moment, with consequences for a foreseeable future. Both science and thinking about the theological implications of it have, through empiricism and existentialism, roughly the same "style." Consequently, one takes comfort in perceiving that, although the physical and spiritual worlds are so terribly different (in the psychological sense of causing terror), they may be approached together even if they cannot be fully reconciled with one another. This perception reduces the terror to the extent, despite Tillich, the "style" of existentialism and the "style" of the scientific method actually do contain content. For the moment, this content consists only of a courage not to fear the (scientific) existence which you apprehend vastly but not fully and, therefore, think that you know just a tad imperfectly.

The similar styles of scientific and existential methods reduce the terror of human perceptions to the extent that appearance (which is the essence of a style) is Reality regardless of underlying substances. For Reality is often a confusion of appearance with substance entirely. The early Christian theologian, Augustine of Hippo (A.D. 354 to 430), explained such a confusion in Christianity as follows: "For the sake of describing things ineffable that we may be able in some way to express what we are in no way able to express fully, our Greek friends have spoken of one essence and three substances, but the Latins of one essence or substance and three persons (*personae*)."[65] Of course, you

---

[62] See Arthur Schopenhauer, *Essays and Aphorisms* trans. R. J. Hollingdale (London, Penguin Press, 1970), p. 213: "All ostensible mind can be attributed to matter, but all matter can likewise be attributed to mind; from which it follows that the antithesis is a false one."

[63] For example, see the apt (but acceptable?) comparison between human cognition and computer output in John R. Searle, "Minds, brains and programs," *Behavioural and Brain Sciences,* Vol. 3, pp. 417-457 (1980) reprinted in Richard D. Gross, *Key Studies in Psychology* (Gross ed., London, Hodder & Stoughton, 1990), pp. 37-57.

[64] See Merleau-Ponty, *op. cit.,* pp. 363, 365.

[65] Saint Augustine of Hippo Regius, "On the Trinity," in *De civitate Dei,* Book VII, Ch. 4, p. 7 (A.D. 413-426) quoted by unknown translation in Karen Armstrong, *A History of God* (New York, Ballantine Books, 1993), p. 119.

A Matrix for the World

say, *all* descriptions of the ineffable, especially a statement about its different Greek and Latin expressions, are typically confused between what they appear to be but cannot comprehend entirely and what they incomprehensibly Really are. But is your clear saying of this confusion subject to the same reproach? Is there any place (yes, a location) where any human words, let alone those of a game in language, may ever be sorted out and shown to be clear and True? There is agreed confusion of grammar with understanding, that is to say, of the appearances of words in a grammatical context with any theory of their meaning as a human understands them to be.[66] Then there is confusion between human understanding and the context, with or without grammar, where the understanding takes place (yes, a location). What is appearance and what is substance in the grammar and meanings of life? The American philosopher, Richard MacKay Rorty (b. 1931) seeks to explain why consciousness relates to reason and to personhood (what I call later in this discussion "is-ness.") Rorty therefore explains a Glassy Essence[67] by which we mirror the nature of the world in our minds in order to know knowledge. This is the reach of the empirical framework over persons, substances, essences, Glassy Essences and the appearances of all of them. For you to judge is whether this reach exceeds my grasp of God as I relate Him to the Achilles' heel of empiricism—the definition of "experience" in space and time, and "the physical Realities of existence."

---

[66] See D. Z. Phillips, *Wittgenstein and Religion* (New York, St. Martin's Press, 1993), p. 12 as follows: ". . . [W]e often misunderstand the notion of God's sublime existence because we sublime the logic of our language when we reflect on it."

[67] See Richard Rorty, *Philosophy and the Mirror of Nature* (Princeton, N. J., Princeton University Press, 1979), pp. 42-45.

Chapter Two. The Needs of a Human Soul

The "Is-ness" (Ontology)

Because my soul exists, and my grandmother's did, and there is evidence from Cartesian doubt and scientific observation that this can be so, so that one Truth of existence appears, there is a need to determine a meaning for the proposition, "I exist." Is there a sense, a structure, a meaning to this proposition? Before soul or consciousness or anything perplexing at all about me, let's take up the sensory reality that I said these two English words. There is an immediate and deep split of opinion about what the Reality of this saying in spoken language amounts to. The first opinion comes from the theologian, Augustine of Hippo. Augustine said: "To give them as much credit as possible, words possess only sufficient efficacy to remind us in order that we may *seek things,* but not to exhibit *the things* that we know."[1] As a result, Augustine held that words do not ultimately enter into a realm of inner perception inside of the human head, where knowledge may be exhibited to us apart from speaking. But we use words when we think to ourselves even if we do not speak them. Thus, the American philosopher of psychology, Jerry Alan Fodor (b. 1935), holds that words *are* involved in the realm of inner perception inside of the head, even if that inner perception is otherwise cognitively impenetrable, and declares that, within the head, there is a language of "mentalese" with propositional contents which the science of psychology can know, study and take for Reality. According to Fodor, propositional attitudes or attributes of mentalese are founded in symbols or tokens of thoughts, which possess either broad or narrow content, but which, in either case, psychology may formulate in laws and state for the world.

There is a marked difference between a theory of meaning for words used inside the head, when they relate to internal perceptions in mentalese, and any theory of what words mean when they relate to external perceptions in vernacular language. But in inner perception, we still use words when we think to ourselves even if we only think we know ourselves by thinking them. Thus, another American philosopher of psychology, Jerome Seymour Bruner (b. 1915), takes the penetration of cognition as far as it goes (how far is that?) and holds that cognition saturates perception of all sorts, inner as well as outer. If so, in the opposite of Augustine's concept of unspoken knowledge, I may Really know what I say when I say that "I exist" *and still speak this knowledge.*[2]

---

[1] Saint Augustine of Hippo Regius, "De magistro," in *Patrologiae Latinae,* Tomus 32, "S. Augustini Operum" (Paris, Migne, 1841), p. 125, trans. George G. Leckie as *Concerning the Teacher and On the Immortality of the Soul* (New York, Appleton-Century-Crofts, 1958), p. 46.

[2] Compare Jerry Fodor, *The Modularity of the Mind* (Cambridge, Mass., M. I. T. Press, 1983) with Jerome Bruner, "Culture and human development: A new look," *Human Development,* Vol. 33, pp. 344-355 (1990).

Do I speak this knowledge here? Wittgenstein said, "I am *my* world. . . . That the world is *my* world,[3] shows itself in the fact that the limits of the language (*the* language which I understand) mean the limits of *my* world." Because there is no language that is illogical, Wittgenstein means "the language which I understand" is not a vernacular language but language as a whole, the grasp of a logical form, and since *my* world is who I am, I am exactly as I grasp my language, the logical form of my existence. What is this grasp? Does it depend upon any notion of "Real Space" in which my existence is? Is my grasp just the self regardless of other selves as equally concerned about their meaning and their living spaces as I am about mine? If I were an ancient Greek instead of a modern American, to say "X is" could be understood as "X is so" or "X is true."[4] The so-ness of me means my consciousness,[5] and, if I were an ancient Greek, there is no further need to philosophize about the relationship of me to my consciousness because the is-ness of me has already included a so-ness which entirely makes that connection valid. Unfortunately, I live in a world of modern Americans where everything, including me, has been picked apart. Several thinkers in this modern world wish to restrict me to a bundle of neurons and biochemical reactions, but I feel, rather inexplicably, a whole-ness to me which is more than the sum of my physical parts. I wonder if this feeling of a whole-ness is yet Really the same so-ness which the ancient Greeks defined by their very words of description for existence. If so, Descartes started with this so-ness to think of me as the *res cogitans,* the human thinking thing. But it follows that, because I am this subject, I am also that which is thought about, or *res cogitata,* an object of my own thinking. In these terms, I appear to my whole self to be both subject and object together. My whole-ness is a further paradox which a thinker before me expressed epigrammatically as follows:

> "My whole being has a dynamic character. As a self-subsistent being and an accidental [read: random, by the sperm-and-egg combination which created me] being, I am constantly modified. But this cannot be explained through the principle of self-subsistence but only through the principle of accidentalness.
>
> My whole being has a character of permanence. As a self-subsistent being and an accidental [read: random, by the sperm-and-egg combination which created me] being, I am always the same. But this cannot be explained through

---

[3] Ludwig Wittgenstein, *Tractatus Logico-Philosophicus* trans. C. K. Ogden (London, 1922, 1981, 1996) §§ 5.62, 5.63, p. 151.

[4] See Christopher Stead, *Philosophy in Christian Antiquity* (Cambridge, U. K., Cambridge University Press, 1994), p. 25.

[5] But what kind of consciousness? First, consciousness may be identified directly with awareness. Second, because there seems to be unconscious awareness, consciousness may consist more narrowly in only apperceptive awareness. Third, consciousness is simply a phenomenal (or phenomenological) state, feeling ineffably some way or another as felt awareness. Fourth, consciousness is a non-composite, indivisible state embodying features from all of the three previously mentioned alternatives. Fifth, the first three previously mentioned alternatives exist compositely as consciousness within different states of a single human being, though the first two can exist independently of each other and of apperception. For an elaboration, see Norton Nelkin, *Consciousness and the Origins of Thought* (Cambridge, U. K., Cambridge University Press, 1996), pp. 124, 147, published posthumously.

the principle of accidentalness but only through the principle of self-subsistence."⁶

Descartes reduced the world into an object of my consciousness, but what is the Truth of me exactly? I know that I am I, but I also know that there are many other creatures on this Earth similar in appearance and much-ness to me. Intersubjectivity is the condition of relating to the egos of others, of being subjective about more than one subject simultaneously, of standing in the sandals of an ancient Greek as well as in the shoes of a modern American, and of recognizing that in different languages even the utterance of the simplest statement of existence may have multifarious meanings. For example, the Arabic word for existence is derived from the verb *wujud,* whose three-letter root WJD has as its earliest meaning "to find."⁷ To exist is *wujida:* "to be found." Literally, therefore, existence means in Arabic "that which is findable."⁸ But different seekers find different discoveries. This aphorism is the product of a "natural law" of finding and seeking. In my case, it holds that there may be a maxim of identification among indiscernibles regarding the sensory inputs and functional production of a human consciousness, but there can be no such maxim about outputs, the actual composition of the discoveries, and that which is found uniquely in the existence of each of us. Therefore, the Arabic definition of existence is more concrete than the Greek or English definitions, but it allows for more subjectivity. To prove the existence of X in Arabic, I am not required to prove that X is simply one object among many, but that X can be found.

When you go inside of yourself, what is it that you find? There are many propositions of uniqueness which appear given to you alone, but what are those propositions of fundamental "is-ness" which you seem to hold in common with other human beings? My answer is that, though you may find differently, I find three categories of subjects under my subjectivity inside of myself which others may possess: first, more questions; second, fragments of sentences in the syntax of my native tongue, English; and third, a deep yearning, a passionate longing for the privilege of waking up tomorrow morning and continuing to live in this human body where I am. The first category is interrogatory in nature; the last one implies an affirmation whose ultimate character is not questionable (yes, in both the literal sense of questioning and in the figurative one of doubtfulness); and the middle category implies a sense of incompleteness and fragmentation which well deserves of some further treatment (yes, the word "treatment" may mean both an intellectual exposition and a healing cure). How is anyone to make sense of more questions and fragmented syntax but a deep

---

⁶Gerard Verbeke, *Noten bij de cursus van metaphysica* (Leuven, 1946), p. 145, quoted in Stephan Strasser, *The Soul in Metaphysical and Empirical Psychology* (Pittsburgh, Duquesne University Press, 1957), p. 75. I edited the author's English vocabulary and added parenthetical language for clarity of the epigram with science. But, in doing so, I reverse the author's intended, or the plain, meaning of the text if science is to be identified with the principle of self-subsistence instead of accidental sperm-and-egg combinations.

⁷Roger Arnaldez, *Trois Messagers pour un seul Dieu* (Paris, Éditions Albin Michel, 1983) trans. Gerald W. Schlabach, Mary Louise Gude and David B. Burrell as *Three Messengers for One God* (Notre Dame, Ind., University of Notre Dame Press, 1994), p. 135. The author's three messengers are Christianity, Judaism and Islam.

⁸Karen Armstrong, *A History of God* (New York, Ballantine Books, 1993), p. 188.

desire to live? How is this jumble more than psychological disorder or my own private chaos? Intersubjectivity is a large problem of reconciling variations and awareness among subjects together in some synthesis, even when they speak the same vernacular and exist on this Earth at the same time.

Solipsism, on the other hand, is a theory holding that the self is the only existing thing and can know nothing but its own modifications. Perhaps solipsism is the theory which sensibly explains my Greek so-ness and Truth, and my Arabic findings about my existence. According to Wittgenstein, there is a truth behind solipsism, but it cannot be said and, since my world is limited to language, what cannot be said must be confused; thus solipsism is the confused result of trying to speak it.[9] Truth, therefore, is not solipsistic—that I alone am Real; Truth is that I alone have my own point of view upon my world. The grasping of my identity is this Truth, a point of view, the visual field which does not include me or my myopic eyes, but what I see.

Complexity is immediately introduced by the Reality of one's visual field. Throughout the insides of my eyeballs, there are blood vessels which light must surely pass through in order to reach my retinas, but I nevertheless do not see them, except under unusual circumstances when my ophthalmologist examines my eyes. In each of my two retinas, science says there are two holes where optic nerves begin to transmit visual information to my brain, but I do not see them anywhere in my visual field, even with one of my eyes shut in darkness. I deal with my visual field apart from the physics of my eyeballs, within the limits of my brain, because I must grasp my existence and cannot grasp it otherwise except as I do so in a logical form. This form is an obvious and immediate departure from the physical Reality of my blood vessels and optic nerves. By this grasp of existence formally (a pun!), which is literally the Reality of what I see clearly without intruding blood vessels or disconcerting black holes, I believe Hume's definition of Belief "after the physics" of seeing and grasping—in Greek, *meta ta physika* or metaphysically. Metaphysics happen whenever a human opens eyes! Believing metaphysically is a mental state which is not only at odds with physical eyeballs but is a compelled confirmation of the expression of visual complexity in the physical world. Such a confirmation is required in all cases because of complexity, my visual field and language, and the large problem of intersubjectivity, especially from the power of any group synthesis over my expressions. This, therefore, is the basis of Metaphysical Belief in each human soul. The Belief is, as non-Believer David Hume said, a firmly-held type of conception about the object of "me" and is ultimately compelled by the need to determine meaning for the proposition, "I exist."

A self-referring statement is one whose terms refer back to itself. An example is: "this statement is false." If the statement is true, then it is false; but if it is false then it is not true. For the opposite assertion, "this statement is true," if it is false, then it is not true, and if it is true, it is tautological. It is True that the Truth of a tautology may never be logically contradicted, but the rest of its truthfulness is entirely empty, since its Truth-value is independent of the way things are, and problematic, since we have already seen a truth in logic is not the same as truth from experience.

Does "existing I" hold meaning for itself which avoids these conundrums and is of "being-ness," but not of solipsism? An existential solipsist may say that the word

---

[9]H. O. Mounce, *Wittgenstein's Tractatus: An Introduction* (Oxford, U. K., 1981), p. 91.

"being-ness" is an essence from the language of analytic logic, not a meaning taken existentially from actual life. In life an observer is at least as existential as an observed—more so if an observer is required for an observed even to exist and by existing be observed by the observer. On the other hand, in the Reality of physical existence—that is, in the science of physics, the Swiss-American physicist, Albert Einstein (1879 to 1955), proved[10] the temporal relation between two events is determined only by an observer in a defined state of motion relative to them. Einstein validated, for the first time in history, placement of the observer within a scientific observation as an empirical proposition whose Truth is indubitably True. If an observer can be made relative to the world in the manner Einstein proved, it is doubtful the observer is his only Reality. We note that Einstein told the Archbishop of Canterbury that he himself believed, in 1921 at least, the Special and General Theories of Relativity had no *meta ta physika* implications for religion whatever but were matters of physics exclusively.[11] Despite the metaphysical implications which do arise from Einstein's theories, whether Einstein avowed them or not,[12] the solipsist says, an observer may be properly said to hold a more basic place in existence than what is observed; for the observer's existence comes first, in the beginning. What can we say about this firstness? Something first is that which there was nothing before. But something before is a well-tried basis in logic to arrive at a thing. Without something before, the difficulty of thinking about the firstness of the observer is compounded. Without something before, logic may determine possibilities but not determine what is the case. To determine what is the case presuppositions about the case must be made, but these presuppositions are more alien to the definition of the meaning which an existentialist seeks than the strangeness of the problem of "firstness" was. The problem of the "firstness" of a soul in being an observer means that it cannot completely determine the truth of solipsism and is, again, what Wittgenstein may have meant when he said there was truth to solipsism but it could not be determined and, therefore, could not be said.

To repeat the question: do we find a meaning of my "being-ness" which is not solipsistic? This meaning may be found in two ways: from logic and from experience. The first way, from logic, is partly shown by Wittgenstein's previously mentioned analysis and further shown by one far-reaching achievement in mathematics known as Gödel's theorem. In his first theorem of incompleteness (1931), the Austrian logician, Kurt Friedrich Gödel (1906 to 1978), solved the problem of self-referring statements for mathematics. This solution in mathematics has a more complete logical form than any form which Wittgenstein grasped only verbally. Gödel showed it is impossible to avoid self-referring statements in mathematics and, therefore, impossible to express all of mathematics axiomatically. But he also showed, by the technique of Gödel numbering of logical propositions, that there are statements which are indisputably True even if they cannot be proven by axioms. There is much dispute about the implications of Gödel's proof beyond mathematics. It is only a matter of conjecture whether it sheds

---

[10]Albert Einstein, "On the Electrodynamics of Moving Bodies," *Annalen der Physik* (1905).

[11]Phillip Frank, *Einstein: His Life and Times* (New York, 1947), pp. 189, 190.

[12]See, for example, Bernard E. Meland, "Response to Inbody," in the *American Journal of Theology and Philosophy*, Vol. 5, No. 2, pp. 72, 73 (May, 1984); and likewise, in the same journal, "Response to Frankenberry," Vol. 5, No. 3, pp. 130-137 (September, 1984), discussing the impact of relativity physics upon Meland's theology.

any truth at all upon the incomplete truth of solipsism. To know unprovable Truth by Gödel is not the same as knowing the Truth of the unproven by solipsism. Gödel's theorem does not prove the unproven truth of solipsism by proving proof and truth coëxist for the human self but do not completely coïncide; it only proves by this divergence the same possibility for the unproven truth of solipsism to be True that Wittgenstein noted. We may suppose, naïvely, that computers and smart-machines are confined to the realm of the provable. If so, Gödel's theorem seems to show they are incompletely related to what is ultimately True, but that mankind is different because humans understand the theorem and know a collection of True statements which is more than the collection of provable ones. But we should suppose machines understand the theorem, too, and by knowing that they may be inherently limited to proof thereby, surmount this limitation by output which is not so limited. There is, therefore, no clear implication from Gödel's theorem for the ultimate knowledge of either mankind or machines. But the logic of it shows that one set of objects of the Universe, specimens of the species *homo sapiens,* know Truth which is unprovable and otherwise, by the reasoning of logic and mathematics, illogical.

Where, and then what, is a meaning of "being-ness" from experience? This compound question involves the extent we use the structure of logic to answer it, as well as the Achilles' heel of empiricism—the definition of experience, and may be answered carefully only by reference to the thinking of selected thinkers who themselves have taken the care to try to comprehend the major, but disparate, elements involved in it. Sartre's subjectivity does define experience, but the structure of logic he uses to arrive at his definition, by postulating the denial of it and then an affirmation of it by denying the denial, is *prima facie* different from the simple is-ness of experience to begin with. A thinking thing of René Descartes must assume what is already a given, that experience already is. Yet, in seeking to eliminate presuppositions wherever and however they exist, Sartre eliminates even the basic presupposition that experience is already given to me and analyzes it by an *unnecessary* double negation which is contrary to the basic nature of me as a thinking thing and what I am. On the other hand, by paying better attention to the one presupposition about existence which must rationally be saved—that experience is already given to our species called *homo sapiens*—Merleau-Ponty found a central meaning for human existence in the "lived body;" Husserl, in the consciousness; and Heidegger, in semantic variations of the word "being-ness" itself. In the thinking of all of these last three thinkers, though, the meaning of experience involves paradox or unresolved contradiction. I shall discuss the philosophies of Merleau-Ponty, Husserl and Heidegger briefly.

For Merleau-Ponty consciousness is *not to* be separated from its physical embodiment, and the corporeal phenomenon of my body holds both the in-dwelling (immanent) agency of my conscious life as well as the transcendence (surpassing beyond themselves) of worldly objects into this phenomenon. Since my body is also a worldly object, but now transcended into this phenomenon, the result is my body is both subject and object united together. This body is the way I am supposed to be able to begin to understand the world, but the phenomenon binds my real body and my subjective mind so closely that an understanding about either is impossible or filled with ambiguity, especially in light of Merleau-Ponty's assertion the resulting understanding, in any event, will be enigmatic or reversible.[13] "The seer and the visible experience," he says in a metaphor, "reciprocate one another and we no longer know which sees and which is seen."[14] Such unity may be formally correct for "being-ness," but it hardly tells us about the meaning of the elements being unified and even compounds the already difficult problem of defining "being-ness" in the first place.

For Husserl, consciousness *is* to be separated from its physical embodiment, and the phenomenon of my consciousness holds the in-dwelling (immanence) of my perception of physical acts but transcends worldly objects to the extent the world is nothing but a correlation of my consciousness and a projection of the perceived. How, then, is it possible for my consciousness to depend upon physical nature for its existence and, at the same time, be determinative of it? More elaborately, perception is of wordly objects "bodily given" to consciousness, so that there is no screen or veil between consciousness and the world and no possibility of psychologism—that the world is only a series of ideas or sensations in the mind. But, on the other hand, the "objectifying interpretation" of a really immanent sensation is a perceptual act which the consciousness projects onto the world and, by doing so, no longer consists of the same stuff of sensations whence it originated. How is the phenomenal world made out of sensory events but does not consist of them? This is Husserl's paradox of the descriptive psychology of human subjectivity.[15] He avoided the paradox by postulating the consciousness of the self completely apart from the natural world. But if the phenomenal world is all there is, how does science investigate it empirically as it Really is if consciousness is removed from it, because the world, we remember, was but a projection of consciousness to begin with? This is Husserl's second paradox: that of Transcendental Idealism. In most cases posed by the correlations of Husserlian phenomena, there is either a ground (the transcendental consciousness) upon which to transcend but nothing to transcend over (no world) or something to be transcended (the phenomenal world) but no ground upon which to do it (no transcendental consciousness apart from the phenomenal world).

Finally, for Heidegger there is a better way of finding meaning for existence than the scientific way; he may wish away any problem of dependency upon the physical world in Husserl's first or second paradox because contradictions from the physical world are only a symptom of *Verfallen*—in English, this German verb means loosely "to fall down." *Verfallen* is Heidegger's interpretation of myself and my being-in-the-world due to scientific analysis or any other worldly quandary making me alienated from my own "authentic" possibilities, estranged at "inauthentic" existence.[16] But it is difficult to see anything authentic about a game of words, or Reality apart from the

---

[13]M. C. Dillon, *Merleau-Ponty's Ontology* (2nd ed., Evanston, Ill., Northwestern University Press, 1988, 1997), pp. 139, 143, 144, 150.

[14]Maurice Merleau-Ponty, *Le Visible et l'invisible* (Lefort ed., Paris, Gallimard, 1964), p. 183; trans. Alphonso Lingis *The Visible and the Invisible* (Evanston, Ill., Northwestern University Press, 1968), p. 139. Dillon notes that this is a counter-intuitive manner of formulating thought. See Dillon, *op. cit.,* p. 162. Dillon appears to wish Merleau-Ponty had stated the thought differently.

[15]Herman Philipse, "Transcendental Idealism," in *The Cambridge Companion to Husserl* (Smith & Smith eds., Cambridge, U. K., Cambridge University Press, 1995), pp. 250, 279.

[16]*Ibid.,* p. 300; see Martin Heidegger, *Being and Time* trans. Macquarrie and Robinson (New York, Harper & Row, 1962) § 38, p. 220. Heidegger says that *Verfallen* does not express any negative meaning, but this statement is contrary to the negative connotations of *Verfallen* in German which imply collapse or decay.

framework of empiricism we said we would employ by starting with science. A brief synopsis of thinking from Merleau-Ponty, Husserl and Heidegger shows, therefore, that the experience of thinking about experience leads from sensory events to ideas of body, consciousness and being-ness which are not strictly sensory. A meaning for experience, then, as it was for logic found in the unprovable, can be found in the idealistic, the opposite of what is the common or common-sense experience of sensory life.

There was a time in the ancient past when the human consciousness did not think but just perceived. In this primitive world, the perception of X was enough to identify it as X. However, after the introduction of the *res cogitans* of Descartes—the human thinking thing—the identification of X depended not only upon perception but also upon thought, as well as thought of the perception and whichever one or more of these three elements is the Truth. In these circumstances, how does a thinking thing equate perception to knowledge consciously without thinking about them? The identification of X, even one whose Reality is so indubitably True as the existing I, becomes considerably more subject to distortion and to error than it ever had before perceptions became to be thought about. It *is* True that—to express "being-ness" and the meaning of it—a human thinking thing *may* also dream and pray. Whole books are the contents of prayers; whole sleep is filled with dreams. But the implications of dreams and prayers for the meaning of Ultimate Truth about human experience are as unclear as Gödel's first theorem of incompleteness. Do they say anything of which Wittgenstein postulated can only be *shown*? If so, why are words in them? Language itself is another considerable impediment to self-knowledge, to True verification of X such that X is Believed. The impediments of language are compounded by the insistence of certain thinkers that language is a closed system, a saying by showing a text of vocabulary beyond which nothing further may be shown. Augustine in his treatise entitled, *De Magistro,* held that knowledge is not said but shown; conversely, Wittgenstein in the *Tractatus* held that knowledge is not shown but said. What did each of these thinkers, separated by centuries, mean by the word, "knowledge?" Language should be an open system of expression, openly transcendent of the world, a saying by showing the world just as our other physical senses show it. In my world,"[t]he showing of language, its ownmost function, requires a passage beyond the chain of signifiers, a reference beyond the immanent sphere of language: the showing of language depends upon a cognitive, but pre-linguistic, opening upon the world; it depends upon the perception of phenomena."[17] Therefore, any foundation of a Belief in God which depends upon the immanence of language within the world must be rejected. For example, in the Qu'ran, a feeling God says that "I created the *jinn* and humankind only that they might worship me."[18] Likewise, a thinking Christian says that "[w]henever God requires us to believe anything is true, [H]e gives us evidence that it is so."[19] Both of these quotations about God—the first one, in faith and the second one, in truth—have no terms which refer outside of the closed system for God which they describe. They are, accordingly, no

---

[17]Dillon, *op. cit.,* p. 185.

[18]The Qu'ran, ch. 51, v. 56; quoted in Arnaldez, *op. cit.,* p. 76.

[19]Edward Stillingfleet, *A Rational Account of the Grounds of Protestant Religion* (1664) 2 Vols. (Oxford, 1684), Vol. I, p. 221.

better for Belief than the closed system of language which contains them. But a physicalist may also state his closed system of the world in the immanence of language. For example, the physicalist might say, "[t]here is nothing in the world but increasingly complex arrangements of physical constituents."[20] But what does he mean by these words? Are my dreams and prayers (and even beliefs) an expression of my pre-linguistic opening upon the world? Can I believe a psychological truth—say, that Julius Cæsar is an arrogant man—without relying at all on the semantic features of this interrogatory sentence of English where I say this? Well, yes, I could conceive of such an unarticulated belief in me if I lived at Cæsar's palace in ancient Rome and *felt* his presence. But, if not, is dreaming and praying (and believing) simply a matter of the meaning of any images and words of Cæsar which *are* in my mind and their Wittgenstein-postulated "signs?" Dreams and prayers (and beliefs) certainly do not consist *exclusively* of words and images. If "the problem of life" is that there is a failure of meaning, or of sufficient meaning, to be accorded to phenomena—such as consciousness, dreaming, praying, believing and so forth—or to the "signs" which Wittgenstein conceptualized his propositions of logical form contained, then the application of more "meaning" to these phenomena or to these "signs" solves the problem surely. For example, I could see Cæsar raise his mace. But does he do so because of his arrogance or his sense of public duty?

Any dollop of meaning added to me, or to any other human thinking thing, seems to involve adding to whatever was there after consciousness or sleep arrived or after my soul left my mother's womb. At least, this is the case if the possibility of proof of the origin of the added meaning is important to a scientist or existentialist. Therefore, even theologians have postulated and held that different types of religious meaning are added to me as I grow older, as the years advance me into further definable life-stages until I reach my death.[21] But, in life, how can human consciousness be more than it is or a soul mean more than it already does? Perhaps fMRI or PET scanning shows that more, or more restricted, blood flow at cortex S inside of my human cranium means more meaning for my soul inside of that cranium. How is this added meaning, unless it is ultimately social or cultural in character, actually a meaningful object and not hallucinogenic? Or, is the question of the addition of any meaning to be added to me fundamentally a question of adding to whatever was there before I was born, before I slept or before I became conscious? The German theologian and leader of the Protestant Reformation, Martin Luther (1483 to 1546), supposed God existed before I did, but he postulated nothing that God *requires* me to mean and said:

> ". . . all the gifts which God purposed to give me, God Himself had before appointed when I was as yet in my mother's womb, where I could neither wish,

---

[20] J. J. C. Smartt, "Sensations and Brain Processes," in *The Mind/ Brain Identity Theory* (Borst ed., New York, St. Martin's Press, 1977), p. 53.

[21] See, for example, James E. Loder, *The Logic of the Spirit: Human Development in Theological Perspective* (San Francisco, Jossey-Bass Publishers, 1998) stressing psychological meanings; Wolfhart Pannenberg, *Anthropology in Theological Perspective* trans. Matthew J. O'Connell (Philadelphia, Westminster Press, 1985) stressing anthropological meanings.

think, nor do any good thing. This gift came to me by the mere predestination and free mercy of God before I was yet born."[22]

Of course, science has no means of proving Luther's statement, but science, as of this writing, has no means of disproving it either. Is it in the class of True but unproven statements which Gödel proved were *possible to know to be True*? Regardless of the timing of additional meanings to me, before or after the fact of my birth, "more" and "meaning" imply both measurement of quantity and quality of character at once. Is this quality and quantity of character more compelling than the *a priori* or a *posteriori* timing of the premises upon which they apply to me, before or after my birth, in actual life? The meaning and the more-ness also imply that transcendence (the surpassing of a thinking thing outside of itself) is fundamentally required if I am to find adequate meaningfulness (justification) for the proposition that "I exist." Quantity, in turn, implies a need for accuracy; quality implies a need for perfection, if not a view to it. It is mentally clear that the justification of myself is different from an explanation, but that the justification often involves explanations. On the other hand, it is not clear that any difference of motives—to justify or not—leads to any Real difference in the explained. It is one outcome to know the Truth of a logical form, of Gödel's theorem, or of the many other observations of science or mathematics; quite another, to know the entire Truth of experience, or some partial verity of the Truth-sayers of it.

Exactly, then, what are the grounds I have to transcend myself in order to be more meaningful? From Descartes we saw that all Reality is relative to God; from Alston and Plantinga, that all is relative to "M-Belief" or *properly basic* Belief; from Wittgenstein in the *Tractatus,* that all is relative to language. Therefore, God, M-Belief, *properly basic* Belief and language may respectively supply the absolute predicate required for a transcendental turn. But is language Really a sufficient basis for transcendence? We know that the language *of others* transcends the world and does so successfully in billions of communications on a daily basis. But the paradox of my language is that it does not allow me to transcend myself because it is only a tautologically Truthful expression of what's inside of me. Can I Really believe myself speaking? The American philosopher, Hartry Hamlin Field (b. 1946), says that "I believe* a sentence in my language if and only if I am disposed to employ that sentence in a certain way in reasoning, deliberating, and so on."[23] He explains that belief with an asterisk denotes a relation between a person and a sentence in that person's own language, but this relation apparently involves the disposition by this person of the propositional attitude which the sentence expresses, though the person must employ an "internal token" of the sentence in order to make this disposition, since even unwritten or unspoken sentences can still be believed. The "token" is, therefore, an object of thought, but this object is verily identical to that which gives the thought an objective validity in Field's theory of a mind—namely, the psychological disposition of a propositional attitude which the

---

[22]Martin Luther, *Commentary on the Epistle to the Galatians* trans. Erasmus Middleton (1850) (Fallowes ed., Grand Rapids, Mich., Kregel Classics, 1979, 1998), p. 37.

[23]Hartry H. Field, "Mental Representations," *Erkenntnis: An International Journal of Analytic Philosophy,* Vol. 13, No. 1, p. 9 at p. 18 (July, 1978) quoted in David H. Lund, *Perception, Mind and Personal Identity: A Critique of Materialism* (Lanham, Md., University Press of America, 1994), pp. 114, 115.

sentence expresses. In arriving at non-self-referring Truth, does a thinker identify the objective validity of a thought with the object of that thought itself? We say no. Field sets forth both language and human belief in language with the kind of structural formalism which would characterize the human mind as if it were organized from the basic premises of logic as a computer is. In a logical, complex and sophisticated analysis, he nevertheless shows the tautology inherent in human thinking where the structure of thought is Max Scheler's sketching, and not formalized.

The American philosopher, Richard Rorty, asserts that analogy to the inputs, outputs and thinking processes of computers aids the study of psychology but says that "[t]he gap between explaining ourselves and justifying ourselves is just as great whether a programming language or a hardware language is used in the explanations."[24] There is no ground in humanly transformed computer language, therefore, upon which, by Rorty's proposition, I may transcend myself and be adequately meaningful to me. But why should I *expect* any bridge for Rorty's gap? Does my language transcend the world so openly that it is immanent in computer-speak? Or is language only the self-contained matrix of meaning, within itself, that Wittgenstein always said? Where is a middle ground? Why would anything either so open or so self-contained as language is be anything Really about my is-ness at all? My meanings mostly all depend upon language, but my meaningfulness does not. There is an entire realm of unconsciousness fundamentally apart from the logical rigor I *demand* as a hypothetical pseudo-computer or a thinking thing. Where are these unconscious Truths of my experience more fully said?

The relationship between the conscious and unconscious parts of myself remains obscure and not revealed to me. It is literally True that only God knows what my unconsciousness may validate and identify as X. Even the Truth of my knowledge of my conscious existence is not certain but is only the so-ness by which I hold consciousness. In these premises, existence is given to me with a degree of subjectivity I may never know or validate as a human thinking thing. For the subject of my is-ness is also the object of this self-knowledge and cannot validate either the knowledge or the is-ness except in logically tautological terms. The independently constructed architecture of a computer might separate subject and object sufficiently such that the self-referral involved in valid existence is practically mitigated. But human thinking things possess no such of a free-standing "belief box" as computers do. Though they make valiant efforts at it, Merleau-Ponty, Husserl and Heidegger have not accomplished the enormous task of surmounting the tautologies inherent in the empirical verification of my is-ness. I have already expressed to you my Cartesian doubts about their thinking. If these problems of my Truth are the Ultimate problems of my "is-ness," as one American citizen living at the dawn of a new millennium, "[t]he solution of the problem of life is seen in the vanishing of this problem."[25] The vanishing of the problem of the meaning of life's "is-ness" is that, within the empiricism of our framework, unprovable

---

[24]Richard Rorty, *Philosophy and the Mirror of Nature* (Princeton, N. J., Princeton University Press, 1979), pp. 249, 255; see P. C. Dodwell, "Is A Theory of Conceptual Development Necessary?" in *Cognitive Development and Epistemology* (Mischel ed., New York and London, 1971), p. 370.

[25]Wittgenstein, *Tractatus* . . . , *op. cit.*, § 6.521, p. 187.

meanings by Gödel's theorem, vernacular languages, dreams and prayers can still be *shown*. How unfortunate it is that the English language is the only tool at my disposal to express this. Perhaps mathematics has something else or music does. For now, I follow Wittgenstein and keep magic by banishing it from this explanation by following meaning to the extent you find it in these words. The Reality of my need to grasp my existence by determining meaning for the proposition, "I exist," shows why this is so.

The "Feeling-ness" (Psychology)

In the distinction between synthetic Truth, grounded directly to the facts of an immediate experience which may be physically and scientifically observed, and analytic Truth, which is not, we stated W. V. Quine's first dogma of empiricism. Because Quine showed how the dogma may be surmounted and, in the surmounting rejected it ultimately, his rejection does not mean that the dogma is useless. It has plenty of use as a description of convenience for Reality, that we remember as a Real fact that some of our propositions about our mental life depend directly upon certain physical manifestations in the world and others do not. After all, the world is what our species has evolved in for scores of millennia. Indeed, our feeling-ness about the world is Really more tangible and Real to us than our is-ness is. "To be in existence, for us, is to feel; and our feeling is indisputably antecedent even to our sense," said the French philosopher of romanticism, Jean Jacques Rousseau (1712 to 1778).[26] The power and compulsion of God find several paths into a soul. All of them are psychological and depend for their Ultimate Truth upon Rousseau's statement, "to be in existence is to feel."

Feeling-ness arises in us first when we feel the liquid warmth of a mother's womb. The French novelist, man of letters and mystic, Romain Rolland (1866 to 1944), described an "oceanic sentiment" as a fact of experience in large numbers of religious souls.[27] The Austrian psychologist, Sigmund Freud (1856 to 1939), responded to Rolland's description of the "oceanic sentiment" by saying that it gave him "no peace" after reading of it in Rolland's letter to him. Freud might have hypothesized that the "oceanic sentiment" is a basis in psychology for religious belief. Instead, he reduced it to a regression to immediately postnatal experience, in which a newborn baby feels primary, unitary consciousness with its mother, and addressed the origin of a feeling of continuous, oceanic contact with the world, which Rolland and other mystics described to him, by asserting that the ego-feeling of a person is a reduced and shrunken subpart of the larger unity it felt previously in the womb. For permanent features of conscious, adult, psychic life, Freud favored biological premises over intuitions every time. He wrote to Rolland as follows:

---

[26]Jean Jacques Rousseau, *Religious Writings* "Lettres Morales" (1757-58) (Grimsley ed., Oxford, U. K., Oxford University Press, 1970), p. 57. The French words are: «Exister, pour nous, c'est sentir, et notre sensibilité est incontestablement antérieure à notre raison même.»

[27]Romain Rolland to Sigmund Freud, "Lettre de 5 Décembre 1927," in *Cahiers Romain Rolland: Un Beau Visage À Tous Sens* (Paris, Éditions Albin Michel, 1967), pp. 264-266; see *Selected Letters of Romain Rolland* (Doré and Prévost eds., Delhi, Oxford University Press, 1990), pp. 86-88; William B. Parsons, "The Oceanic Feeling Revisited," *Journal of Religion,* Vol. 78, No. 4, p. 501, 503 (October, 1998).

"We seem to diverge rather far in the role we assign to intuition. Your mystics rely on it to teach them how to solve the riddle of the universe; we believe it cannot reveal to us anything but primitive, instinctual impulses and attitudes—highly valuable for an embryology of the soul when correctly interpreted, but worthless for orientation in the alien, external world."[28]

Feeling-ness, even in Freud's self-described external world, also arises in us by the awesome process of biological evolution over millennia. The dictates of this evolutionary process mean that, as we have noted, we are much more powerfully designed to perceive the spoken echoes of syllables than we are to add to them by speaking. Similarly, those same dictates, which have compelled us to watch the world carefully in order to survive in it and reproduce children who can continue to live life, mean that we are equipped to respond to it reflexively, even faster than the consciousness of a painful finger allows for separate responses. It is the thesis of this discussion that, as a consequence of these same dictates of our oceanic sentiments and the wired structures of our feeling-ness, we either Believe in God or not. If we do, we may Believe in Him though He is but a figment of the imagination, though a very powerful and compelling one. Clearly, the world has snuffed out the lives of hundreds of thousands of specimens of our species who, for any number of un-reflexive nerve endings or any other host of reasons, have failed to live up to the prevailing conditions for survival in a world of danger. In the following discussion, you will see that religious feeling is one basis for, literally, living.

The *Gestalt* theory of psychology sees the sudden emergence of relationships in reasoning and thought processes in the mental life of our species which are as equally crucial to its survival as a reflexive response to pain would be. *Gestalt* theory sees how more powerfully wired we are to react to the world than we are to act in it; how, in the same medium of vibrations of air, we may hear the world so much faster than we hear ourselves. *Gestalt* theory sees that, because we must survive and "get along in life," our precepts take the most recognizable forms possible in the circumstances and that, for the same reasons, our behavior may override the stimuli on which it has been trained in order to pursue the same stimuli elsewhere because the thinking thing perceives those stimuli better, or more intensively, at another place. All of these patterns are telling conclusions about our transitive consciousness and show how it is both wired for the needs, dangers and physical manifestations of the world, but also the fact of a wiring. Because of this difference between our wiring and the sensory world for which we are wired, and the fact there is a measure of further wiring to deal with the difference, it is the thesis here that we are wired in psychology for feeling God and God-feeling experiences. "After the physics," *meta ta physika,* we may choose God, or not, but we may not choose to avoid this choice. Belief in God, or not, is either a pseudo-object or a state of mind that is compelled from the justification "after the physics" a soul must find about its existence. Why? The answer is: the Real (True) figure which I cut as an existing, psychic I on the stage of life is not found from my own self-clothed drapes but requires an Ultimate Background.

---

[28]Sigmund Freud to Romain Rolland, "Lettre de 19 Janvier 1930," in *Letters of Sigmund Freud, 1873-1939* trans. Tania and James Stern (London, 1970), pp. 392, 393.

Between the wiring of a Cartesian thinking thing and the fact that it has been wired, there is a dualism, a pattern of separation between two basic parts of experience, the subject and the object, which is as appropriately considered under *Gestalt* theory as it is under the tradition of classical reflection in philosophy. Rorty says, however, that psychology should confine itself to models of neurons, and he implies that statements of analytic Truth involve cognitive validation of formerly synthetic ones upon which they are based against all realms of Reality which is too much for a computer and, therefore, too much for what he thinks the definition of the study of human psychology should be.[29]

Regardless, several thinkers reached Truthful propositions about "states of affairs" in the mind before psychology became a separately entitled field of intellect, and they show a Truth of me as or more profoundly than thinkers separately entitled as psychologists may (or ever will). For example, the German theologian, Friedrich Daniel Ernst Schleiermacher (1768 to 1834), discussed the "feeling of absolute dependence,"[30] ruled that this feeling was the essence of religion and the basis of Belief in God as that upon which we depend absolutely, and said this feeling of dependency is a sort of common denominator of religious experience and a yardstick by which theology is measured and assessed. Schleiermacher said: "All attributes which we ascribe to God are to be taken as denoting not something special in God, but only something special in the manner in which the feeling of absolute dependence is to be related to [H]im."[31] This statement, though formally delivered in the field of theology, states one psychology of our mental life about experience. It states a quality—the quality of dependence—about which a *Gestalt* theory of dependency might readily theorize, if only to treat of the quality in *Gestalt* therapy. Psychology has developed an empirical framework for mental "states of affairs" more carefully and completely than philosophers or theologians have (or ever will). Psychology is completely dedicated to the proposition that fundamental Reality is existence. For these reasons, psychology fits well with existentialism and supplies content for experience which Schleiermacher did not relate adequately enough back to the empirical "facts," and which Tillich found missing from existentialist thinking about God mostly altogether. But Truth from psychology is not merely synthetic. Whether it takes a psychologist, philosopher or theologian to say so is strictly sociological.

The psychology which disposes a soul to Believe in God is, as Schleiermacher stated theologically, the psychology of dependence upon the Universal Absolute, and the related psychologies of disposing of the Universal Absolute by reifying, "thing-i-fying," objectifying both the Absolute and our ideas of it, as well as even the facts surrounding our dependence and the ideas of our ideas about that of which all have been conceived. Here is the return of the Cartesian reduction of ideas into objects multiplied. Near the beginning of this discussion, we criticized this reduction because of its lack of a few characteristics by which we could know empirically it would be Real Truth-

---

[29]Rorty, *ibid.*, p. 255.

[30]Schleiermacher's phrase in German is: das schlechthinnige Abhängigkeitsgefühl. See Colin Brown, *Philosophy and the Christian Faith* (London, Tyndale Press, 1968), p. 111.

[31]F. D. E. Schleiermacher, *Der Christliche Glaube* (1821-22, 1830-31) trans. H. R. Mackintosh and J. S. Stewart as *The Christian Faith* (Edinburgh, T. and T. Clark, 1928, 1960), p. 12.

telling, but we never said at what point we would refuse to stop adopting it, especially if the adoption meant, *within itself,* we could stop, in fact. In other words, since we feel our thinking things would be forever consigned to an infinite regression of further propositions about our thoughts, we perceive some stopping place for the regression because the perception is a matter of our feelings, a balm for them, as well as valid thought moreover. But how is any such perception innate to us? How does the someness of a stopping place for the knowing of my world mean there is *that* place particularly where I stop? Darwinian evolution has the answer. I discuss evolution later in this Chapter and show how it supports the further psychology of our feelings for stopping where we do as a natural (conventional?) basis for God Belief. This basis exists independently of the existence of our psychological "states of affairs," but there *are* psychological "states of affairs" which *do* predispose a soul to stop at the innate, to depend upon the Universal Absolute, and to dispose of all Reality by reifying and Believing in a "thing-ness" which is Absolute and a "Universal thing-ness." There are several of these "states of affairs:" submission, commitment, endurance, anxiety, addiction and self-sacrifice. Soul deals with one or more of them at various times — and does so both consciously and unconsciously. Soul is powerfully and compulsively predisposed to dispose of them with equal force. These dispositions compound upon themselves and are soon manifested in anthropological "universals" which possess a huge further significance in culture and sociology.[32] The rest of this Chapter discusses these psychological "states of affairs" and explains why human evolution by phenotypes, by "genes and culture," or by culture alone, leads to the disposition of a mind to "thing-i-fy" the Absolute universally and pose absolutely the "Universal thingness."

The oldest known well-dated specimens of hominid fossils are bone fragments 3.9 million years old from Ethiopia.[33] During this enormous length of time during which the hominid *genus* has existed on this Earth, its body has been masterfully crafted by Darwinian evolution for bi-pedal motion — to walk one foot in front of the other without toppling over. The hominid species, *Australopithecus,* also walked erectly and bipedally, but it became extinct about 1.3 million years ago. This hominid species had a brain whose volume was roughly one-third the size of the brain of *homo sapiens.* Factors relating to the evolution of the brain seem key to explaining why our species survived but *Australopithicus* did not. The brain has been crafted over enormous lengths of time by evolutionary processes of the body, the mind-in-the-body and the mind-with-other-minds. These evolutionary processes are Darwinian, cultural *and* combinations of both. According to theory, leaps and advances in the evolutionary process have been made. About 40,000 years ago, *homo sapiens* began to depict art; about 40,000 years ago, a subspecies of *homo sapiens,* the Neanderthals, after coëxisting with our own subspecies for about 50,000 years, became extinct.[34] Neanderthals practiced the

---

[32] See, for a combined treatment of the anthropology, sociology and "socio-biology" of religion, Walter Burkert, *Creation of the Sacred: Tracks of Biology in Early Religions* (Cambridge, Mass., Harvard University Press, 1996).

[33] Stephen Jay Gould, *Dinosaur In A Haystack* (New York, Harmony Books, 1995), p. 138. The author notes an older putative specimen found in Ethiopia may be 4.4 million years old.

[34] Burkert, *op. cit.,* p. 19.

ceremonial burial of the dead, but they probably had no language and we know they had no art. Art means making special "certain objects of perception," creating tension between physical reality and the depiction of it, and raising awareness "of new aspects of a potentially common world."[35] It meant that a specific perception at the root of the optic nerve could be represented in a thing, even if Husserl's theory of consciousness is valid and the perception of the object of that thing of art had been "bodily given" to the mind of the artist already. Art means the object in Husserl's consciousness is even further "thing-i-fied." It meant those Neanderthals without the further "thing-i-fication" of perception would die. Art, therefore, is one link between Darwinian evolution by genes with pseudo-Darwinian evolution by phenotypes, "genes and culture," and the cultural acquisition of learned common skills.

How is a process so ineffable as Darwin's combined in any way with a progression so mutable as human culture's? Amino acid sequences inside the genes of *homo sapiens,* when they are compared to those of apes, differ on average by less than one percent.[36] Yet, six to eight million years have passed since apes and humans had their last ancestor in common. What accounts for the small genetic differences but huge morphological ones? In the case of *homo sapiens,* say scientists of nature, the theory of evolution by natural selection, which the English natural scientist, Charles Robert Darwin (1809 to 1882), applied to genotypes, also applies to the individual phenotype. This is because the evolution by natural selection of human genotypes has produced a condition of "plasticity" in the brain which allows it to continue with the process of evolution by natural selection phenotypically, that is, after it has been born. Indeed, the British zoologist, (Clinton) Richard Dawkins (b. 1941), sees the inheritance of "basic cultural units" occurring as easily and naturally among human infants as is compatible with reliability and fecundity, and literally parallel to what they have inherited genetically from their parents. Dawkins termed these inherited cultural traits to be "memes" and says they work on phenotypes as genes do on genotypes. "Examples of memes," he says, "are tunes, ideas, catch-phrases, clothes fashions, ways of making pots or of building arches. Just as genes propagate themselves in the gene pool by leaping from body to body via sperm or eggs, so memes propagate themselves in the meme pool by leaping from brain to brain via a process which . . . can be called imitation."[37] Crucial to survival of *homo sapiens* is the ability to learn from an environment. It is *so* crucial that not only does it occur culturally, in the reaction of a mind with other minds, but it also occurs by the physical condition of the brain's "plasticity," as the mind inside the body receiving "memes," *Gestalten* or other devices of mental transmission. But, by definition, the favored qualities a phenotype learns from an environment may not be transferred to progeny genetically; what's the point of it? The point, says psychologist Dennett, "is just that individuals who are lucky enough to be closer in design-exploration space to a learnable Good Trick *will tend to have more progeny,* who will tend to be closer to the Good Trick. Over generations, the competition becomes stiffer: eventually, unless you are born with (or very nearly with) the Good Trick, you are not close enough to compete."[38]

---

[35]*Ibid.,* p. 19.
[36]Gould, *op. cit.,* p. 130.
[37]Richard Dawkins, *The Selfish Gene* (Oxford, U. K., Oxford University Press, 1976), p. 206.
[38]Dennett, *op. cit.,* p. 186.

What's a "Good Trick?" Well, the business of preserving the self as a natural organism requires the self to produce a future in which that self can be preserved. How is the future produced? Surely one way the future is produced—we acknowledge there may be others—is by assuming about the past. How are these assumptions arrived at? Many properties of the physical world seem permanent: the force of gravity, the evaporation of water, the boundary of the skin, hunger and thirst and so forth. For these properties Darwinian evolution has provided a soul with what is analogous to the hardware and basic programming of a computer: response by reflex, alarms of pain and bodily discomfort, motion and gravity detectors and so forth. But many other assumptions about the past and the future must be changed, redesigned and learned. Even the comprehension of crudely drawn pictures requires learning.[39] A soul changes, redesigns and learns by manipulating meanings. Meanings are manipulated most efficiently by making generalizations. Generalizations are expressions of meaning which apply before, and to more than, a unique day on a particular African savannah when a single *homo sapiens* is faced with being killed by a specific lion. If he survives the lion's attack, it is because of mental generalizations he already has in his head which imply to him how to behave, and how the lion will behave, during this dangerous event and all others like it subsequently. Generalizations are manipulated most efficiently by "thing-i-fying" them, by turning the snarling lion into a type, a thing of "lion-ness" whose behavior about snarling can be predicted so that a living future for the *homo sapiens* is secure. Thus we see universalized types of the essences of all things are essentially key to the survival of mankind in actual life. It is certainly a "Good Trick" to be as close to essences as possible because they insure the continuation of existence. How does a *homo sapiens* achieve this closeness? He achieves it by being close with that which created the lion, because the creator of the lion knows that lion and "lion-ness" better than anyone else. Truth from the lion-creator is indeed a superior Truth. It is another "Good Trick" to be close to that which set forth this whole process of survival in existence from the beginning. Closeness to the process-creator insures a proximity to learning about further changes, redesigns and learning. How is this achieved? *Homo sapiens* achieves it by being close with that meaning which created the process of generalizing. Thus he gathers Truth *from* the creator of whatever X there is—the lion, the savannah, the Neanderthals, other *homo sapiens,* the Louvre Museum or the entire Universe; and he gathers Truth *of* the process-creator who has made all of it Real. This model relates religion back ultimately to biological survival and shows the character of religion as a matter of utmost gravity and seriousness.

What's another "Good Trick"? Another model relates religion back ultimately to survival and shows the character of it as a matter of communication. The task of learning—basic and crucial to *homo sapiens* from the first day many hundreds of thousands of years ago that he existed as a separate species of life—is performed at all levels under a paradox. The Greek philosopher, Plato (B.C. 427? to 347), articulated the paradox in many Socratic dialogues substantially as follows: "I must learn only that which I don't know, but because that is what I don't know, how do I know what to

---

[39]Jan B. Deregowski, "Pictorial perception and culture," *Scientific American* Vol. 227, pp. 82-88 (1972), reprinted in Richard D. Gross, *Key Studies in Psychology* (Gross ed., London, Hodder & Stoughton, 1990), pp. 21-35.

learn?" Contending with this paradox satisfactorily is central to the mind of Man as he depends almost completely upon learning as the talisman of his survival on this planet. How does he contend with the "learning paradox?" Well, maybe what he doesn't know can be objectified, reified, "thing-i-fied" so that the contest is made easier and he may succeed with it better. In other words, the reification of what he doesn't know may not reduce the chaos surrounding his ignorance in any given instance, but it will increase the chances of his overcoming it in many more instances and surviving as a species. Nature could not care less if lions or a virulent new strain of bacteria or dinosaurs, fancifully reincarnated by the vitality of their deoxyribonucleic acid ("DNA") molecules preserved in amber, ate the thin-skinned *homo sapiens* at tomorrow morning's breakfast. Therefore, he has always needed an epistemological guide—some X to specify in advance: knowledge, the criteria for knowledge, ignorance, the criteria of ignorance or all four of these in whole or partial combinations of themselves. Art, language and religion are these guides precisely. In art the reifying of meaning is the depiction; in language it is the vocabulary; and in religion it is The Way. "Teach me your way, O Lord," says the Psalmist, "that I may walk in your truth. You may tell the next generation this God is our God forever and ever. He will be our guide even unto death."[40] Said Jesus of Nazareth: "I am the way, the truth and the life."[41] Taoism is an Asian religion and Chinese for *tao chia,* "the school of the Way." The Atheist German philosopher, Friedrich Wilhelm Nietzsche (1844 to 1900), composed the mythic figure of Zarathustra who *demands to know:* "This is *my* way, where is yours? . . . *The* way—that does not exist."[42] Godless Zarathustra thereby reified humanity's epistemological guide into "his way;" so we imply from Zarathustra's way that godless Nietzsche found reification and "thing-i-fying" to be most meaningful even if he didn't Believe in God to cause it or affirm it.

Is there another "Trick?" Of course! A means must be found to enforce the Darwinian necessity of the incest taboo. Language ratified in religion means the force of moral law and, in the case of incest, moral law means survival for those members of the species who obey it, who are more likely to be healthy specimens who procreate successfully. Put in more general terms beyond incest, procreation of *homo sapiens* during periods of severe physical stresses from the environment, and assuredly there have been many awful and severe ones in the primitive past, is more likely to occur in specimens with religion than in those without it. Religion provides religious specimens with hope that procreation will not be in vain, and that awful conditions of hunger, thirst and violence do not mean quick death. Religion also provides religious specimens with a justification and explanation for pair-bonding and exogamous marriage. Both pair-bonding and exogamy are required for any species to survive tough conditions; yet *homo sapiens* had evolved by abandoning estrus, sequestering ovulation, enlarging female breasts permanently, pointing the vaginal canal into a ventral position and selecting ruthlessly for longevity by neotenic processes under which subsequent generations retained wherever possible the hairless and youthful characteristics of their

---

[40]The Book of Psalms ch. 48, vv. 13, 14; ch. 86, v. 11.

[41]Saint John ch. 14, v. 6.

[42]Friedrich Nietzsche, *Thus Spake Zarathustra,* "The Spirit of Gravity" ch. 55, trans. Thomas Cannon (New York, The Modern Library, 1960), p. 217.

ancestors.[43] Primitive religion, though it probably did not arise until 10,000 years ago, functioned as a counterweight to the orgy of sex which repeatedly occurred and would continue to. Yet, because of the enlarged cerebral cortex of every fetus, each new childbirth brought the fearful peril of death for a mother. Pairs favorably disposed to religious beliefs dealt with sex and death more successfully than those without them; these specimens of *homo sapiens,* more likely to feel love,[44] procreated, survived and produced progeny who were likely to possess these attributes, and these attribute-possessing progeny produced progeny and so forth. It is easy to see, in hindsight and without any possibility of proving a theory which must cover facts spanning many thousands of years, that the inculcation of the psychology of endurance of depravity and death was lengthy and found ready expression in religion when mankind found language. Further exploration of history for the Reality of the compulsive need of mankind to be religious as a sort of innate "software" is beyond our scope here; it is sufficient to say it's a matter of survival, communication and sex and in the record of the ages.

It is also the record of *homo sapiens* at the end of the 20th century. But, you say, the circumstances of survival, communication and sex for our species have fundamentally changed from those circumstances of even a century ago. Isn't a "Good Trick" an artifact of history? Freud never addressed this question specifically, but he said that "[s]ince we overcame the error of supposing that the forgetting we are familiar with signified a destruction of the memory trace—that is, its annihilation—we have inclined to the opposite view, that in mental life nothing which has once been formed can perish—that everything is somehow preserved, and in suitable circumstances (when, for instance, regression goes back far enough) it can once more be brought to light."[45] If Freud's statement works within an individual, how much more so should it work within a collective? The very definition of collective society groups memories into more storehouses than one brain groups them. If "memes" work, if the patterns-upon-a-field of different *Gestalt* theories are archetypal for the cerebral cortex of the last 10,000 to 100,000 years, or if memory is more than simply what one living body has experienced physically, it seems reasonable to assume "Good Tricks" are with us today. The Swiss psychologist, Karl Gustav Jung (1875 to 1961), postulated the theory of a "Collective Unconscious" he described as a "million-year-old man" living inside each of us today as the limbic cortex does, a living storehouse of the ancient past bringing the archetypes of human evolution and culture to us still.[46] The American philosopher of linguistics, Noam Avram Chomsky (b. 1928), says an infant learns to speak by releasing innate capacities, by a form of remembering, and not by inscribing simply upon a blank mind. There is, according to Chomsky, a primitive "scheme of enduring and recurring individual objects" which exists for an infant before the infant

---

[43]Stephen Jay Gould, *The Panda's Thumb* (New York, W. W. Norton & Co., 1980), p. 132.

[44]Dudley Young, *Origins of the Sacred* (New York, St. Martin's Press, 1991), p. 82. The author notes few ethnologists "speak up for love at this stage of the proceedings."

[45]Sigmund Freud, "Civilization and Its Discontents," (1930) in *The Freud Reader* (Gay ed., New York, W. W. Norton & Co., 1989), p. 725.

[46]See C. G. Jung, "The Relations between the Ego and the Unconscious," (1916, 1934) in *The Basic Writings of C. J. Jung* (de Laszlo ed., New York, Random House: Modern Library, 1959), pp. 118-143.

acquires the meaning of language; and then there is another primitive scheme facing the infant: that of human language itself.[47] In a great contribution to human knowledge, Chomsky uses data from experience to support his assertions. For example, in shifting from the declaratory to the interrogatory mode, language is structure-dependent—dependent upon shifting words within the grammatical structure of a sentence. Likewise, language is structure-dependent upon noun and predicate groups within a sentence in changing from the active to the passive mood. But any newly-designed language would undoubtedly use independent structures for these tasks. A computer's language, when it shifts modes or changes moods, uses structures independent of each other. But we live with primitive schemes; we possess a powerful memory whose source is still obscure. On the amino acid sequences of human DNA molecular compounds, those few strings pertaining to memory sparsely account for our abilities in this area, even as they elude identification and discernment in the DNA molecule most of all. It is clear from all of this that the devices of memory and mimesis in us are very powerful, that they may be the most distinctively human of all the characteristics of *homo sapiens* (computers remember better than we do from finite sets or closed environments, in fact almost perfectly, but not from the open-ended environment which the world is), and that because we deal rather primitively with the world as it is and has been for us for 100,000 years, there is Real meaning to a "Good Trick" today. Besides, the circumstances of survival, communication and sex have changed, but the premise that these things are fundamental problems to be faced by mankind hasn't. The "Good Trick" exists as long as there is a premise for it. It is the very essence of *necessary existence*.[48]

One path of a psychological "state of affairs" a soul is compelled to Believe in God is by the psychology of submission, commitment, endurance and endurance of the commitment and of the submission. This is a straightforward psychology to understand. It is widely practiced in modern religion. "*Islam,* the verbal noun of which *muslim* is the participle, means pristinely 'surrender,' 'commitment,' the active giving of oneself to obedience to God's claims, the positive response to God's initiative. . . . *Muslim* is Arabic for 'submitter' or 'self-committing,' so that to affirm a person is *muslim* is to speak of the quality of his heart, his commitment to God, his readiness to obey whatever injunction the moral law may make incumbent on him."[49] This observation shows how far Islam, one of the Earth's most attractive religions, is the name itself for what it

---

[47]Noam Chomsky, "On Interpreting the World," (1971) in *Problems of Knowledge and Freedom* (New York, Pantheon Books, 1971), pp. 10, 12, 13, 17.

[48]For a critique of the concept of necessary existence, see John N. Findlay, "Some Reflections on Necessary Existence," in *Ascent to the Absolute: metaphysical papers and lectures* (London, Allen & Unwin, 1970), pp. 90-102. The South-African-British philsopher, John Niemeyer Findlay (1903 to 1987), held that nothing, but especially God, can exist necessarily and distinguished sharply between the concepts of existence and necessity. However, he dedicated the referenced work to his wife whom, he said in the dedication, was not "a necessary being" but was "necessary to me." Therefore, by stating the necessity of his spouse, isn't philosopher Findlay existing in necessary spousal existence? If not, don't both existence and necessity relate to each other fundamentally by the quality of given-ness which is in both of them? It is not given to me not to exist. Likewise, it is not given to me not to be necessarily involved with this first proposition about my existence. Put positively, I exist and must (therefore, necessarily) relate to this fact.

[49]Wilfred Cantwell Smith, *Questions of Religious Truth* (New York, Charles Scribner's Sons, 1967), p. 105.

supposes about the psychology underlying its structure and moral law. By this direct relationship of psychology with language, the power of Islam may be supposed to become even more powerful. All of the Earth's great religions, but especially Islam, involve construction of a Supreme Being whose existence either rectifies the deprivations and failures a human mind is so aware of on this planet or creates conditions in human minds and hearts by which those failures and deprivations may be tolerated and suffered. This is one way slaves have tolerated the conditions of slavery, and martyrs have carried their crosses and suffered martyrdom. Since the conditions for martyrdom and slavery have existed profusely throughout history, religious Belief as the antidote for treating them has been long-standing and well used. Arab terrorists twist Islam today to justify suicidal attacks as a martyrdom for al-Lah. Smart machines (and some humans) are certainly slaves laboring with the vast quantities of information they process. Most of us are not martyrs or slaves today, but all of us have experienced the echoes of both—addiction and self-sacrifice. A Belief in God is a crutch suited to the mind of a submerged ego, an enchained spirit or an addicted body. These are all conditions each of us has dealt with repeatedly. Believing in God and His redeeming spirit is a means to float an ego, to unchain the spirit and to set the mind and body free. That freedom allows a human soul to establish itself, and this establishment is most cherished, even if, under the religions of Asia, it is part of a collective.

Apart from the therapy for submission, commitment, endurance, addiction and self-sacrifice it often needs, the life of *homo sapiens* is a daily struggle of human consciousness. The essence of this struggle is innate (even the criticized word "natural") and exists in us from birth. It is between the awareness of the physical world apprehended by our senses, and an awareness of soul, a being in the brain the senses do not feel, but which dreams and thinks and can actually replicate "artificially" bursts of pleasure and pain arriving from the physical world. This being in the brain is an Ultimate register of the impressions of the physical world but is set apart from it. The divorce means, alas, that the postulated unity of Merleau-Ponty's phenomenal body must be only a postulation and physical impressions from the world alone do not suffice. This lack of sufficiency raises a concern, an anxiety about the deficiency the lack is or may be. For the consciousness of *homo sapiens,* unlike that of any other living creature we have known so far, raises the brows of hair above his eyes and sets off many firings of neurons inside his brain whenever there is "a lack of sufficiency." He becomes anxious. There is a psychological need to deal with the anxiety. The most obvious treatment for anxiety about "a lack of sufficiency" is to obtain a state of being in the brain, a state of soul-ness, which is less deficient or more sufficient. This is a direct prescription for God as a cocktail or drug for human anxiety. The English philosopher and mathematician, Alfred North Whitehead (1861 to 1947), described the process by which Theism arises from the conditions of human existence and said: "God is the great companion—the fellow-sufferer who understands."[50] In these premises of psychology, God is either less deficient or more sufficient than the soul is—suffering, disturbed, concerned or anxious about the divorce from physical reality it knows it's into. God and this divorce are two linked concepts, and the activities of Belief in God can be anchored

---

[50] Alfred North Whitehead, *Process and Reality: an essay in cosmology* (Griffin and Sherburne eds., Corrected ed., New York, Free Press, 1978), p. 351.

in existence by anxiety and the compulsions of anxiety felt under stress. Whether this anchoring is powerful or complete because it occurs unconsciously as well as consciously is worth considering, though this question may never be answered. Any conscious attempt at it necessarily destroys the continuing unconsciousness which an answering soul must maintain to assess the completeness because to answer means the unconscious of the answering has been interrupted.

The sources of this anxiety and the compulsions which flow from and compound upon it are found in a soul's divorce from God, the soul's body and the world. What is this divorce? In Islamic theology, two schools of thought divided schismatically whether "I am one who has faith in very truth," or "I am one who has faith if God will." The former school introduced a concept, Truth, which complicated thinking about God because this thinking was no longer premised upon a divine Will who could truly or falsely ordain, command and override anything else in His path. The Truth of truth as a conception which applies to God means that the human mind is involved in conceiving it. The mind of *homo sapiens* introduces—involves—a human element about the connection between God and a Belief in God, and between God and soul. No matter how slight, the mere possibility of a human element about the Divine is a cause of much anxiety and hand-wringing. There is always the nagging notion: human truth, because of its human source, pollutes God or whatever is God-like *ipso facto* or eventually. Consequently, rationalist René Descartes deposited logical Truth firmly into God's pre-existing Understanding. He wrote: "If men indeed understood the meaning of their words, they could never say without blasphemy that the truth of something precedes God's knowledge of it, for in God to will and to know are but one."[51] In the fresco of the Italian artist, Michelangelo Buonarroti (1475 to 1564), on the ceiling of the Sistine Chapel in Vatican City, the finger of God does not touch the body of Man. The problem of pollution—and it is a very great one, indeed—is dealt with by cleansing, washing it away by all sorts of theology, and of religious rites and practices, having the character of ablution, purification and catharsis whose ontological and psychological basis is in dualism. In other words, if a human element will be inevitably involved with God, let's be clean, separate it apart from God or from whatever else we hold is still pure and establish two elements. The two-ness is clear, pure and necessary because of the conditions of existence. In the relentless quest for the pure are the separations of God from Man, and Man's mind from his body, and the relentless quest for the perfect.

You see carefully this is one of the earliest times I say the word "perfect" anywhere in this discussion.[52] This is because the perfection of God is not straightforward, but a paradox to me. It is the result of the thinking of dualism, but how is a perfection found in anything less than the unitary? In fact, the orthodox theology of Christianity is Trinitarian. Religion of any sort seems ultimately limited to that which humans have assigned to God—or to themselves, as a matter of psychological trust in Him, religious

---

[51] René Descartes to Père Marin Mersenne, "Lettre de 6 mai 1630," trans. and quoted in *The Cambridge History of Seventeenth Century Philosophy* (D. Garber, M. Ayers eds., Cambridge, U. K., Cambridge University Press, 1998), p. 273.

[52] Compare Nozick, *op. cit.*, pp. 46-54. The author starts with the concept of God as the most perfect possible being. There is no basis upon which to refer to this absolute quality as opposed to others which could be supposed.

Belief about Him, theology and philosophy upon Him, the politics leading to the Council of Nicaea and so forth. How is a perfection found from any limitation? This is one Truth of the Arian heresy. But Arius (d. A.D. 336) and his heresy threatened as a political matter to break up chunks of the Roman Empire in the eastern Mediterranean. The Emperor of the Roman Empire, Constantine the Great (A.D. 280? to 337) and the Greek theologian of Christianity, Athanasius of Alexandria (A.D. 293? to 373), both of whom Believed in Jesus the Christ, suppressed the Arian heresy by long and heated arguments of a political parley at Nicaea in A.D. 325, exiling Arius to Illyria, burning mounds of papyrus scrolls containing the offending thoughts, and killing those who possessed them. The Council of Nicaea preserved Constantine's Empire but left Christianity connected to the Reality of existence by the word "consubstantiality"—in Greek, this word is *homoousios*. Athanasius himself only began to insist on this word some 25 years after the Council of Nicaea, and then only in the context of the Nicene Creed itself. Consubstantiality was not basic to his theology;[53] it was a matter of politics, much as the word, "emancipation," is to the American Civil War. There is no magic in words of forced meaning or human connivance; there is no logic in postulating as a presupposition what must be Real in existence if it is to be Believed. Dualism, Trinitarianism, all of the assignments which man has made to God breed confusion, separation, division, schism and divorce. Yet, the word, "perfection," arises in all contexts about God because of the interactive effects among networks everyone has built about God—whether Atheist, fool, Theist, *muslim* or free-thinker. That this is amazingly so shows, as others have said, more about humanity than it does about God.

Perfection compels intellectuals because it is an analytic meaning. Plato explained a surpassing of empirical reality, an aiming beyond the physical world to a world of the spirit, to show perfection, to show how only the world of the spirit is or could be perfect. In doing so he set forth a dualism which washes away the pollution we discussed before. Platonic philosophy means the cocktail or drug being prescribed for anxiety about the soul's divorce from physical reality is utterly addictive, because the drug relieves anxiety so completely that the result is a state which is perfection and a paradise. This is the "opium thesis" for God's existence. In the dialogue entitled *Philebus,* one of his last works, Plato declared the goal of his philosophical discourses had been "trying to prove some possession or state of the soul to be the one that can render life happy for all human beings."[54] His philosophy assigns meaning to existence in two compartments, and to the two compartments of our existence—the physical and the spiritual. It recognizes basic tension between these compartments, as *homo sapiens* recognized it by art 40,000 years ago. Thus it fits well with our psychological Reality. Moreover, Platonic dualism can be applied to the Reality of forms of Intelligent Life even if they are not human. For it shows that in any form of Intelligent Life there is a gap between the outside world the Intelligence is perceiving and the apparatus the Intelligence is using to perceive it. The more acute the perception, the more complex the apparatus is required to be; and the more wide the gap becomes between the physical world and the world of the apparatus itself.

---

[53]Stead, *op. cit.,* p. 170.

[54]Plato, *The Complete Works: Philebus* (Cooper ed., Hackett Publishing Co., Indianapolis, 1997), p. 400.

In ten books originally entitled *On Justice* and later, the *Republic,* Plato outlined the blueprint of a divine order for politics—individual life in common with others in a community. He explained the best possible life for mankind in a city where ideas from a perfect world of the spirit were applied, but the goal of human existence had real psychological roots: doing well and being happy. He related happiness to justice—why justice must make a just person live a good, happy life and an unjust person a bad, unhappy one—and showed that justice is related to a world of the spirit which atones for the cognitive and spiritual deficiencies he found in all physical surroundings. The character of this spiritual world is perfect and, therefore, Divine. Plato linked his philosophy of a Divine world with psychology because happiness is a psychological state and, he thought, only in the Divine world could a person be "really" happy. He did not discuss psychology as such in any greater detail or even plan to. (Today, for example, Plato could not, as he did, advocate common wives and common children in his idealized city without elaborate and lengthy treatment of the many psychological issues involved there.) His basic framework divided the physical world from the world of the spirit, ascribed imperfection always for the former and perfection always to the latter and described the end of human existence to be as near to the spiritual as possible. Platonic philosophy gripped other thinkers in Western civilization from ancient Greece onward, accounted intellectually for the heresy of Arius and many others in two millennia of Christianity and compels us to this day. The dualism of it is real, but real only as we perceive it (that is to say, *feel* it as a matter of our senses). For Platonism is to be compared to our perception of the duality of the figure of a Möbius band when, in Reality, the Möbius band is unitary.[55] We *feel* Platonic duality psychologically, but perfectionist conclusions from it are a distraction from Reality and apodictic Truth. Even the thought of it diverts us from realizing it is *Ultimately a matter of feeling*. For the Cartesian thinking thing is not more or less than what it is: a unitary specimen of the species *homo sapiens:* just one whole and just one self.

Because Reality is the consciousness of *homo sapiens* (we do not know yet about the smartest computers) and involves so much struggling, an examination of it is particularly important to the human creature. It sets us apart from all others we have known of (so far) on this Earth; it demands to discern just what is going on with us. In Plato's work entitled the *Apology of Socrates,* the Greek philosopher, Socrates (B.C. 470? to 399), carries the demand so far as to say that if we do not examine our lives we may as well not live them at all. Carried to the next step, the demand of consciousness for an examination of itself necessarily involves the grading and testing of its own value and introduces *homo sapiens* to the study of Values and, therefore, to the study of a moral life. These studies of goodness need a focus; the Values resulting, a source. God is most useful as the focus of, and the source for, the moral imperative of human consciousness. So the Ten Commandments were handed down from God to Moses; so the laws of the Qur'an were handed down from God to the Prophet Muhammed; so God inspired Confucius. The moral imperative, which *homo sapiens* has so refined in the laws and religion at the core of his culture, allows him to see (and Value) God—not just as a tool or a drug, but as a necessary Being with every positive attribute for the world.

---

[55]"A Möbius band is a topological phenomenon that can be created by taking a strip of paper and, through a 180-degree twist, connecting the two ends of the strip." Loder, *op. cit.,* p. 13. The result is in the shape of the number 8.

The historical record shows God arose spontaneously in several pre-modern societies at the same time on different continents, motivated them to get things done despite their primitive or depraved morality and was at the very core of their customs, rituals and culture. Yet these societies consisted of relatively small populations, were geographically remote from one another and may not be assumed even to have known about each other's existence. The "fact" of this observed Truth of the multiple but independent generations of God and religious faith at different locations in the primitive world validates the Truth of the ontological and psychological processes we discuss, because some product of memes, *Gestalten* or memory produce God and religious faith everywhere the fundamental conditions of Man's existence have arisen. "If religion is the result of pure imagination, how does it come that all peoples have it?"[56] On the other hand, history shows the pre-modern societies which embraced God so completely paid almost no attention to a "moral" individual. Why did this neglect exist? Darwinian evolutionary processes held valid but themselves become subject to further cultural transformations which continued to reify Absolutes and Universals so completely that the goodness of a whole society far surpassed the good of individuals within it. The French sociologist, Émile Durkheim (1858 to 1917), describes the sociological bond of the culture produced by religion as follows:

> "Moral beings can only exist in communities. But a community depends upon loyalty and sacrifice, and these precious commodities do not exist simply because people associate by agreement, make contracts with one another, or have habits and customs in common. They exist because of the experience of *membership*. . . . One who is a *member* sees the world in a new light. All about him are events and demands whose meaning surpasses their meaning for him."[57]

From the community came the idea of a common destiny which a member of it could love and not be alone in loving. This is a significant religious experience and led immediately to the sacred. And the sacred in a community, once developed, could then also function as the tie of membership, so that any further development of both the sacred and the ties could feed back and forth, reinforcing one another. William James did not specifically consider the feeding back and forth Durkheim described in his sociology, but he made a controversial statement which translates the sociological phenomenon of the feeding into a psychological context. James said:

> ". . . The conscious person is continuous with a wider self (?) through which saving experiences come . . . [This is] a positive content of religious experience which, it seems to me, is *literally and objectively true as far as it goes.*"[58]

---

[56]W. D. Weatherford, *Christian Life: A Normal Experience* (New York, Association Press, 1917), p. 157.

[57]Émile Durkheim, *The Elementary Forms of Religious Life* (Paris, 1912) trans. Joseph Ward Swain (New York, The Free Press, 1965); see Roger Scruton, *Modern Philosophy: An Introduction and Survey* (American ed., New York, 1995), pp. 131-137.

[58]William James, *The Varieties of Religious Experience* (Cambridge, Mass. 1902) reprinted in *William James: Writings 1902-1910* (New York, 1987), p. 460 (original italics). This statement has been widely criticized, see for example, Nancy Frankenberry, *Religion and Radical Empiricism* (Albany, N. Y., State University of New York Press, 1987), pp. 95-98. Is the "wider" self human or divine? Is it a collective religious experience or God?

How far into the world, how continuous with the (wider?) self, does the feeling of religious experience go? From Platonic philosophy a thinker may imply all three of the "traditional" philosophical foundations for a Belief in God. They are: the teleological (only an all powerful and intelligent Being could have designed the world we know); the cosmological (only a supreme Being has ordered the Universe and is the explanation for it all); and the ontological (God is a necessary Being who possesses every positive attribute).[59] In *Philebus* Plato put forth the cosmological explanation for a Belief in God directly: he declared the idea of a Wonderful Intelligence would order the cosmos and thereby relieve the anxiety of men thrown otherwise to the terrible vicissitudes of fate.[60] Divine order is psychological relief for this anxiety just as we have seen it is for the anxiety produced by dualism, and the psychological conditions of submission, commitment, endurance, addiction and self-sacrifice. Because we attach to the essences of whatever we attach to, and commit to the fact of our existence as a basic proposition, we endure fate today no less anxiously than the ancient Greeks endured it. The prospect of smart machines or Dennett's human "zimbos" running amok, or contact with extraterrestrial life, is fate as scary for us as the fate Odysseus suffered after he left the Trojan War. On the other hand, the Supreme Being has mediated fate with awesome tranquility. Divine intervention by asteroids or otherwise prevented a reign of dinosaurs for the last 65 million years which surely would have crushed the development of *homo sapiens*. This is an ultimate explanation for an astounding series of discoveries in disparate fields of science which lead us to the first scientifically valid conclusions ever known about the long-term history of the Earth. These conclusions show the Earth's otherwise unrecorded history has taken a most favorable course. What blessings the last few thousand years of recorded history show are simply icing on the cake. After the application of so much science it is still possible to believe a First Causer has caused a benign fate for mankind and designed the world we know.

My father, Prentice (1895 to 1969), partially designed me. In 1953, he set forth his Belief in God in an essay entitled *"The Christ of Land, Sea and Air."*[61] There's no doubt when he wrote it he felt some feelings and thought some of the same thoughts I am when I write this. Why? There is a common purpose of spirit among us all, but especially the designers and the designed, to assign meaning to existence. This world is often so chaotic and multifarious that it is difficult to make sense of it, but it is not a degraded existence. Into this world of land, sea and air, my father found a Divine hand. This Divinity, he felt, spared him from a daredevil's deserved death because avalanches caused by the tremors and aftershocks of Andean earthquakes many times could have bodily crushed him. A Divine hand, he felt, made his efforts at rescue and exploration in Peru acceptable to him and morally correct. The rightness came from the way everything worked with the scheme of values the heritage of Western civilization beginning with ancient Greece had provided for it. After so much human input, it is still possible (and was for my father in 1953) to believe God has caused a benign fate for

---

[59]Scruton, *op. cit.*, pp. 131-137.

[60]Plato, *op. cit.*, pp. 416, 417.

[61]Prentice Cooper, "The Christ of Land, Sea and Air" (1953) in *This I Believe About Jesus Christ: The Personal Testimonies of Leading Americans* (Monsma ed., Westboro, N. J., Fleming H. Revell, 1955), pp. 56-59.

"Anyhow, according to the Science 'Times,' things would have turned out quite a bit differently if that meteor had hit Earth."

mankind and designed the world we know. Belief in God validates the correctness of this fate, this design, the heritage and culture of the civilization which follows them, and the ends and goals perceived for all down the road. (Prentice often discussed with me the importance of having a goal.) Validation of ends and goals is extremely important to a moral *psyche;* it affirms (confirms?) the *psyche* itself is "on the right track." The English poet Robert Browning (1812 to 1889) exclaimed, "God's in His heaven—All's right with the world!"[62] More profoundly than observing the heavenly location of God, a soul reaching this sublime conclusion is saying something about itself. That is: "The design is okay; so I'm okay; you're okay." Today we ask: "Is the design so much okay that I'm okay, even if I'm in 'cyberspace' and you're okay even if you are a clone, a 'zimbo,' extraterrestrial life or a smart machine?"

Death is the final condition of existence which results in a psychology of Belief. Believing in God is a hope about the certainty of death and a means to assign meaning and purpose to the world of the spirit Plato and others distinguished so sharply. The perfect world of the spirit Plato introduced to Western thought seems pretty useless to us humans enchained on this Earth in imperfection. But it is very useful in describing the place souls go after departing it. Fundamental to the struggle of human consciousness is a struggle to answer whether the spirit that is so Real and alive within us will ever Truly die. In the *Apology,* Socrates expounded upon the two alternatives he saw facing himself as the Athenian court sentenced him to death. He put the fork in the road this way:

> "[Death] is one of two things: either the dead are nothing and have no perception of anything, or it is, as we are told, a change and a relocating for the soul from here to another place."[63]

Preoccupation and concern with the change and relocation of dead souls is central to all of the world's great religions, regardless of the time, place or culture where people have practiced or performed them. For all of them are like the others in hypothesizing that our spirits may not Truly die when our bodies do. God is the agent, the cause, the facilitator of this amazing defeat of death. *Homo sapiens* believes in God because he desires to believe his own spirit may (can? should?) live continually. Without God acting to save the spirit of a dead body it is hard, nay impossible, to see how that spirit could be saved otherwise. Socrates analyzed advantages in both of the alternatives he saw facing himself at death and declared only "the"[64] God would know whether either would be more preferable as a form of existence than the lives his accusers would continue to live. Socrates relied on God not only to determine the fate of his soul after his death, but to judge that fate against the existence of those still alive on Earth. He told his earthy judges that the gods of ancient Greece would not neglect the affairs of a "good" man, and that such a man could not be harmed in either life or death. So Socrates expressed the need of human beings to believe in God so that He can judge us

---

[62]Robert Browning, "Pippa's Song" in *The Oxford Book of English Verse 1250-1918* (Quiller-Couch ed., Oxford, U. K., 1955), p. 869.

[63]Plato, *op. cit.,* "The Apology of Socrates," p. 35; for an excellent discussion of this trial, see I. F. Stone, *The Trial of Socrates* (Boston, 1988).

[64]*Ibid.,* p. 36.

as we feel we deserve to be. This is the final moral imperative of an anxious consciousness.

Chapter Three. The Revelation of God

The Entry of God into my World

The Broken Hinges on the Entry's Door

The premise of the foregoing Chapters is that Belief in God is derived from human requirements and has an essentially human inspiration. Even if from a "Good Trick," is this premise a flaw? Do the human sources of Belief mean the Belief itself is defective? But what do we mean by "human" and by "defectiveness?" We said God is not required to be perfect. If so, how much should He slip into imperfection such that my All-Seeing Eye deems Him to be defective? Then, how much should He slip into defectiveness such that my All-Seeing Eye deems Him to be a discarded X unworthy of Belief? I told you my eyes were myopic; I tell you now they are naturally very much so. What is their marvelous transformation that they should now become my All-Seeing Eyes? We said we would be empirical; it is of the method of empiricism to make observations scientifically and to reach conclusions. But what has the scientific-ness of my observations and the reaching of my conclusions done to my eyes? Has any accomplishment of perceived science also accomplished a change in my perceiving of it as a whole? For the whole of it *is* involved because otherwise my All-Seeing Eyes do not see all and are themselves a defective X encompassing less than what they must if I am to make this assessment un-defectively. You would not want me to deal only in mistakes and defectiveness, would you? So, if my myopic eyes are, indeed, All-Seeing now, isn't this a Miracle quite on a par with the Miracle of Our Lady of Fatima? Or, if not, isn't this purported transformation of the perceiver and his eyes, along with his perceptions, a classic example of a fallacious logic? We have shifted quantities from saying *some* perceptions have been seen well to saying *all* of them have been, including those I made in the blackest darkness of night or about my eyes themselves. Indeed, I use my eyes themselves to see that they have changed here and, in doing so, employ a self-referring vision whose only "real" Truth we have shown rests on tautological grounds. This, again, is Husserl's first paradox of the descriptive psychology of human subjectivity. How can it be that the same perceiving stuff also changes the perceiver without being the perceiver itself and, by perceiving what is perceived, changing that which is changed by an infinite regression of changes? If I had an All-Seeing Eye, shouldn't a licensed ophthalmologist be the only one to say so? In fact, where *is* the license to practice objectively as a professional in these matters? Doesn't the logical structure of language, something I grasp very nearly as I grasp my life, imply that questions are fitted for answers? If so, why am I asking so many questions all at once without answering them? Can I not, even with only one of my All-Seeing Eyes, answer at least what is "human" and what is not? Or is the All-Seeing Eye the horrible trait of a monster? Once upon a time, didn't a single such Eye exist, in Greek mythology, at the middle of the forehead of the faces of the race of giants known by the genus, Cyclops? *The Cyclops and my All-Seeing Eyes are examples of one very ungovernable problem about the use and abuse of human powers, including even those by which I raise these fonts into italics for you to see better.*

The problems of the preceding paragraph arose, we say, because God is not required to be perfect. Maybe, if we say and Believe otherwise, that our God ought to be perfect, we avoid any unhuman mark of the Cyclops or any problems surrounding the measurement or fact of God's unfortunate imperfection. If so, the clean break between God and Man which Michelangelo depicted on the ceiling of the Sistine Chapel would be pure, and the pureness of it easily sanctified by all sorts of theology and rites of religion. Oops! Performing such a rite of sanctification, I spilled some holy water because I am human, and there is still a mess cleaning it up inside the cathedral. The requirement of the perfection of God *is* the mess and means He is more imperfect and, therefore, more defective, than ever. If God is perfect, why should He care at all about the essential imperfections of my body and my soul? Such a God should be so far away from the crabbiness and banality of them He should *not need to save them.* Such a God of perfection would have, indeed, few needs of any kind, let alone those pitiful ones with which I concern myself on a daily basis. Moreover, what would be the sum total of the entire heaving mass of mankind to a perfect God? Yet, I suppose a perfect God, as we humans ought to establish the Reality of His perfection, ought to establish a Divine order, a set of Golden Rules, for all of life and all of behavior and do it pristinely so, so that there can be no doubt at all the perfect God has done it. But is this, or any other divinely consummated, ethical establishment actually the perfection God intended it to be? Humanity would corrupt even the perfectly Divine. The French critic and devout non-Believer, Voltaire (François Marie Arouet) (1694 to 1778), was fond of repeating his aphorism: "if God didn't exist, it would be necessary to invent Him."[1] Many sophisticates believe, as Voltaire did, that even if they do not believe in God, other men who do not fear hell or heaven are likely to misbehave. So they "invent" God as a function of their enlightened belief in Golden Rules and many other norms of behavior and morality.[2] But is this Belief at all well-grounded?[3] The American President, General Dwight David Eisenhower (1890 to 1969), concluded the idea of religion as a form of social control into controlling nonsense. Eisenhower said: "Our government makes no sense unless it is founded on deeply-felt religious faith—and I

---

[1] Crane Brinton, *A History of Western Morals* (New York, Harcourt, Brace & World, 1959), p. 456.

[2] For one example, see Charles A. Ellwood, *The Reconstruction of Religion* (New York, Macmillan, 1922), pp. xii, 127-132, where, in a work of 306 pages, the author professed he had "no adequate equipment for technical New Testament interpretation," illogically refrained from any citations to the Bible accordingly, discussed theology only by cursory references to the works of others, but outlined six characteristics of a concept of "positive Christianity" as follows: 1) transfusion "with the spirit" and a transformation "by the method" of modern science, 2) a "concretely ethical" nature, 3) a collective rather than an individual emphasis, 4) a posture of activism rather contemplation, 5) a constructive and affirmative "rather than a merely negative" character, and 6) a spirit of coöperation.

[3] See the analysis of 19th-century Christianity in the United States in Henri Bargy, *La Religion dans la Société aux États-Unis* (Paris, Librairie Armand Colin, 1902), pp. XVI-XVIII, quoted in *ibid.,* pp. 121-123. For example, the author notes that "it is sufficient that the king be the servant of the people, and God, that of humanity."

don't care what it is."[4] Doesn't a consciousness of the human sources of a Belief in God compound the Belief's defectiveness? For it means the Belief not only has a human source but an entirely human apprehension and is therefore twice subject to human fallibility. What is True about human behavior Ultimately?

"Pshaw!" you say, there is plenty of Truth in human behavior; of course a perfect God cares deeply about all living six billion specimens of *homo sapiens* on this Earth and about each one of us individually, knows the exact number of hairs on each of our heads respectively and is all that we shall ever need in life or death for the salvation of our souls. It is the very essence of what we mean by perfection for God to care this, know these things and do so. Well, why don't you write a book about this Marvel? I would read it eagerly. For it is apart from any meaning I cull from Real events of my own existence: the death of a parent; the death of a marriage; the living death of different friendships by neglect or intentionality; the disintegration and decay of various minds and bodies involving loved ones, friends and acquaintances; the myriad and varying betrayals of trust by all; the actual selfishness of human love when it does exist which was so supposed to be not so; law-givers who do not give laws, but receive them; teachers who do not teach, but learn; leaders who lead the body-politic, not from their own genuineness, but from following others; the collapse of expectations into disappointments by any number of different mundane ways and so forth. Then we step beyond the relationships of acquainted souls into the world itself and the actual mundaneness. If God perfectly cares about this world, I do not perfectly understand His caring. Your book must explain it freshly. As a student of international business law in Poland during the summer of 1976, I saw troops of a Communist *régime* drawing shiny bayonets and goose-stepping in ranks and ranks down the linden-lined boulevards of Warsaw. I also saw the piles of battered suitcases, disheveled shoes, twisted eyeglasses and false teeth of thousands of human souls whom the Nazi *régime* sent to die in the gas chambers at Auschwitz and Birkenau. At Auschwitz I read the language of death itself, written in German, in plain or gothic letters, but always with the clarity and precision death is: *Arbeit Macht Frei;* Hard Work Makes Your Freedom. I saw sooty brick ovens for cooking human bodies and gas canisters for dropping death into long and empty rooms. The death-language called these half-subterranean rooms "showers," and the manufacturer of the lethal gas canisters of *Zyklon B* labeled them as mundanely as if petroleum distillates were inside, instead of death. Why, for several years, did a perfect God permit this inhumanity? If He did so for any esteemed purpose of permitting me and hundreds of others to come to Him because of it, that is not only a brazen presupposition by me and the other comers but a fatal showing about a reckless God who measures human quantities incommensurably. Indeed, because of connived human behavior at Auschwitz, which even an Atheist or a fool can see is utter evil, why did I come to God and not to Atheism? What was it about *my* perception of a Real experience at Auschwitz which reveals God to me, but as a far cry from the perfect God an intellectual or even a Theist would suppose?

It is because of the sheer enormity of death I felt at Auschwitz that I feel dependent upon X to keep me, to shield me, to guide me, to save me from feeling death that way

---

[4]Paul Johnson, *The Quest for God: A Personal Pilgrimage* (1st American ed., New York, Harper Collins, 1996), p. 35.

again. It is because I have the psychology which Schleiermacher stated in theology. I feel so dependent. I have so many questions, need so many answers and have much need of God because only He can answer several. Will I ever be exposed to death again in the way I was at Auschwitz? But, why, in late October of 1998, did God spare me but permit thousands to die because of a hurricane in Central America? Why do the palpably wicked seem to prosper? But, on the other hand, why have I? What is the reason for the fact and circumstances of my life? Do I know it only as I say? Specifically, do I know it only as I have said? I heard, in the same room with them, clipped and nasal voices of witnesses who testified in 1973, without intending to do so, to the betrayal of the American President, Richard Milhous Nixon (1913 to 1994), to anything he could have "Truly" felt or thought as a Quaker. I saw, on the same sidewalks and urban parks with them, gaunt eyes and old overcoats of souls on sidewalks and at parks in Boston, New York City and Washington, D. C., as they betrayed their bodies for addictive drugs. I smelled the odor of perfume about a spouse who said her love would be cut off. I tasted, as I ingest my dinner, the betrayals of various *gourmets* and *connaisseurs* of living about all sorts of things they otherwise Truly thought or felt. I have reached for the stars and touched nothing actually. In light of these circumstances of my senses about the sense of my existence, therefore, please tell me how they (yes, both sensorially and sensibly) square with your perfect essence of God, and whether there is anything ultimately True at all about human behavior. The perfection of God denies God because His perfection equates Him perfectly with *my* world and *the* world, both of which *it is a certainty* are anything but perfect. But my dependence upon X is Real.

Help! If God is neither perfect nor imperfect, but my mind and my psychology are so dependent upon X that they search for answers to fit merely a few of my many questions, where's the way out? Maybe we ought to say a perfect God comes close to *my* world or *the* world by a distance of D. What is this distance? Well, it is the distance Michelangelo painted between God and Man on the ceiling of the Sistine Chapel in Vatican City. But he painted that several centuries ago. Surely, my Belief in God does not depend upon style, an artistic depiction of beauty or any question of æsthetics. If so, it would shockingly seem the same as the mouthful of a *gourmet* tasting food who appreciates the refined qualities of life but is powerful enough in culture to lie about them Really. Yet, "the [T]ruth of religion is, like the [T]ruth of its nearest cousin, art, primordially the [T]ruth of manifestation."[5] Well, then, a distance between *your* perfect God and *my* world may be, paradoxically, no distance at all but the presence which Simone Weil felt in her room when she was suffering physically and forcing herself to Love anyway. This is mystical. Is any *Cartesian* perception of distance D possible? Well, rationally, it could be the distance which Einstein's theory of relativity shows that light or energy or mass would have to be altered to transform some mundaneness of this Earth into a Supernatural Property. But is a perfect God relative to light or energy or mass? If so, it seems the substance of Him is more fleeting of time, mutable of mass, and expendable of energy than the perfection of Him implies. Relativity does not sit well with absoluteness, and, surely, you want an Absolute in your concept of perfection.

---

[5]David Tracy, *Dialogue with the Other* (Grand Rapids, Mich., Eerdmans, 1990), p. 43, quoted in Guarino, "Postmodernity...," Theological Studies Vol. 57, No. 4, p. 654 at 664 (December, 1996).

The Revelation of God 71

If not in God, where do you wish absoluteness to be shown? If it is in yourself, you return to solipsism; if it is in the world, you reduce your wish to nonsense. Why? The Non-Believer Greek philosopher and physician, Celsus (A.D. *c.* 180), attacked Christianity by arguing with aplomb that the demonic powers, which, Paul the Apostle (A.D. 3? to 67) said, have been conquered by Jesus the Christ, are actually ruling the world, if not ruling you.[6] Where is the evidence that either God or Christianity have made the world *objectively* better to live in? There is nothing flawed or defective, we say, about the Truth existentialism or psychology delivers *if either really delivers truthfully or has the ability for truthful delivery.* But what Truth has been delivered so far *objectively* in the sixty-plus pages of this book? I am asking questions without answering them. Is this a Truthful delivery? Logic says that the *Real* delivery of Truth about a question *requires* an answer, that the predicate to the question *must* exist *even if it is otherwise non-existent.*

A-ha! Enlightenment (Is this grander than our post-modernist context?) shines at last. Logic by itself says a predicate to a question *must* exist even if it is otherwise non-existent *for, contrary to Descartes, even nothing is an answer of something.* By the nomenclature I choose to employ in this discussion, what is human is that which is empirically observable in existence; that which is Divine *is the same,* so that there is utterly no distance or difference between the two, except that the Divine involves at some step of His meaning *that which does not exist.* But this is nomenclature; worse, this nomenclature is an analytic meaning of idealism; still worse, this meaning is essentially an analysis from universalized types which I declared is the philosophy of essence, not of existence. What happened to purely synthetic meanings, an analysis of sensory experience and specific existence? Well, have we Really isolated existence specifically? We said some of what might be *necessary* about it, but we have not associated it with any other (specific?) property. To what further thing does human Belief relate?

Wittgenstein said that the object of Belief is a "state of affairs" and cannot be an object in the ordinary sense of the word at all. Being aware that "a state of affairs" is a state of flux, what is not permanent, a Believer is greatly tempted to objectify it nonetheless, to hold that it is related to a proposition expressed by signs which amounts to a *real* object subject to empirical testing. This was the view of the non-Believer Welsh mathematician and philosopher, Bertrand Russell, who saw the relationship between Belief and the Believed as an external, objective relationship.[7] But Wittgenstein says this view is delusional, that the relationship between Belief and that which it is about is not external, in the outside world; it is internal, inside the self. He said Belief is not a matter of correlating facts with objects; it is a matter of multiple mental correlations such that the statement "I believe it is snowing in September" is

---

[6]Tillich, *op. cit.,* pp. 25, 26.

[7]H. O. Mounce, *Wittgenstein's Tractatus: An Introduction* (Oxford, U. K., 1981), pp. 84, 85; see, for example, Bertrand Russell, *Human Knowledge: Its Scope and Limits* (London, Routledge, 1948, 1992), pp. 161-164. At page 170, Russell says that "[a] belief must always be capable of being analyzed into elements that experience has made intelligible. . . ." At page 188, he says that, though he may doubt the physical characteristics of a flash of lightning when he sees it, he cannot doubt that there has been the occurrence which is called "seeing a flash of lightning," though there may have been no flash outside of his seeing of it.

equal to "It is snowing in September." Wittgenstein compensated for the inherent instability of the "state of affairs" at the core of Belief by conditioning it upon "facts" and things, "the basic sensualistic (sic) prejudice that sensations tell us the truth about the world."[8] In other words, the springs of your bed-mattress feel either hard or soft but not both to you, and you may rest assured (double entendre intended) you Believe, you possess a state of affairs, about this feeling. "I shall get burnt if I put my hand in the fire: that is a certainty," vowed Wittgenstein.[9] He depended upon the certain physical properties of fire to support a "state of affairs" in his head that his hand will be burned under the properties of "fire-ness;" Russell, on the other hand, supported the same mental "state of affairs" by holding the abstract proposition he reached by observing many fires empirically that "fires burn, and my hand is something which can be burned in them." Wittgenstein and Russell, then, pose a Hobbesian choice to thinkers about Belief: either take the appealing method of empiricism in the theories of Russell and arrive at pseudo-objects of Belief, or take the appealing substance of existentialism in the theories of Wittgenstein and arrive at a degree of disorder which can be tolerated only by strict adherence to the most elementary and tactile "facts" of *my* world. The first appears problematic inside the consciousness of the mind; the second, problematic for what Really is the world.

Where's the exit from this dilemma? There is merit in both of these approaches to the nature of Belief; both suffice to show you may Believe in God. There's no way out. To the extent that God, an X of whom Wittgenstein's thinking would not say, *is nonetheless internal,* inside the self, *involved in multiple correlations of Reality,* related to "basic sensualistic prejudices," hard mattress springs, burnt hands or even a being, object, thing or other entity, we may choose, under Wittgenstein's analysis of Belief, to possess a "state of affairs" about God. To the extent that God, a being of whom Russell's thinking said a lot and unflatteringly so, is "being-ness" equal to what we posit for "facts" whose Truth is not determinatively "factual," *or what is the case if experience is subjective or a seamless web,* we may choose, under Russell's analysis of Belief, to hold God as a "proposition" in which we can Believe, even if He is only the "being-ness" we have defined by our posits *or what is the case if experience is subjective or a seamless web*. I italicize the approaches I think are the most inviting ones. All of them would astonish Russell and Wittgenstein by perceived gaps in their meaning and be repudiated by them probably, but there they are. Authors do not monopolize the inferences and consequences of their suppositions or ideas.

The Door's Wide Swing

Whether X exists is a question of ontology, the study of "is-ness" and "being-ness." Quine said the determinants of ontology are Values and Variables, not Terms and References (Terms seem always factual and therefore always synthetic Truth).[10] Because of my Values and Variables, I dismissed the complex thinking of Heidegger

---

[8]Paul Strahern, *Wittgenstein in 90 Minutes* (Chicago, Ivan R. Dee, 1996), p. 66.

[9]Ludwig Wittgenstein, *Philosophical Investigations* § 474 trans. G. E. M. Anscombe (3rd ed., Englewood Cliffs, N. J., 1953, 1958), p. 135.

[10]Quine, "On What There Is," in *op. cit.,* pp. 12, 15; likewise, Quine, *Methods of Logic* Part III, §§ 29, 30 (Cambridge, Mass., Harvard University Press, 1950, 1982), pp. 182-195.

because he has a terminology of "being-ness" that I call a game of words in his head which, even if I play the game, may still be only a game in my own head and *only* terms and references of head-thinking. Likewise, because they are terms dreamed up by a brilliant mind but, like Heidegger's, without an empirical foundation Real enough to refer to the Value of my psychology and the Variable-ness of it here, I dismiss the concept of "monads" from the thinking of the German philosopher and mathematician, Baron Gottfried Wilhelm von Leibnitz (1646 to 1716). I also reject even subtler distinctions which the Catholic theologian and Scottish monk, Johannes Duns Scotus (1265? to 1308?), made into the nature of "being" as "being"—in Latin what he called *ens in quantum ens*. In Truth, because of my Values and Variables, I see a problem everywhere there is a word used which lacks a support in the physical Reality of existence—even the word "being" itself. What is the empirical definition of this word? Regardless of the attempt made at the meaning of my "is-ness" in the last Chapter, doesn't "being" remain a word whose meaning is nevertheless unsatisfying, obscure and incomplete? Yet I know it is indubitably true that "I exist." Quine willingly committed to the ontological existence of numbers. Numbers exist. Furthermore, Quine willingly committed to the existence of any object necessary in support of a given theory.[11] What more is there to say? Is even ontology on a sliding scale of definition? Quine said: *a pure existential is valid if and only if we get a truth-functional schema by taking the alternation of results by substituting the free variables for the existential ones in the matrix.*[12] This definition allows for much sliding, but it does not slide away from what it says: that Quine allows for God's existence if, but only if, He qualifies within it.

Even Quine's definition of a Real object is, however, theoretical and therefore subject to further theorizing. Because of a maddening continuation of the reduction of my Cartesian thoughts from wholes into parts of them, does God exist for me simply because I theorize He needs to? We said God entered into my world because of ungovernable problems concerning the use and abuse of human powers. Each soul of an American citizen at this new millennium is surely a powerful ruler of its human qualities. This is so to the extent that the American President, William Jefferson Clinton (b. 1946), says he rules his human qualities as he uses his presidential powers. In December, 1998, at a public ceremony celebrating public funds for housing in Baltimore, Clinton asked his audience to judge him privately "no better than, but, thank God, no worse than" anybody else.[13] He said: ". . . inside each of us there is a core that is the same and not one person is better than another." On the other hand, if this is so, it hard to see how the context of the elitism, glamour, hoopla and power of Clinton's life relates to that rather forlorn equality which he says he thinks it actually consists of. Yet that context of power (shown even by Clinton's ability to discuss the private nature of his soul at a public ceremony of a worldly fulfillment of some basic needs of other

---

[11] Hilary Putnam, "A Half Century of Philosophy Viewed From Within," in *Dædalus: The Journal of the American Academy of Arts and Sciences,* Vol. 126, No. 1, p. 175 at p. 188 (Winter, 1997); Quine, *loc. cit.*

[12] Quine, *Methods of Logic, op. cit.,* p. 184.

[13] John M. Broder, "Clinton Extols the Quality of Mercy," in *The New York Times,* Vol. CXLVIII, No. 51,381, p. A13 (December 24, 1998).

people) is precisely what a post-modernist thinker about Truth requires in order to verify the Reality of Clinton's sayings. For Clinton at a public ceremony in Baltimore, that context for his sayings about his soul is the background of sex, lies and videotape which touched his life as a result of his admitted adultery in the White House. A postmodernist Truth-seeker is accordingly right to ask: does Clinton say publicly what is properly private to rule his humanity or to rule his powerful presidency? For it is clear that, though a presidency may be ruled only publicly, even a blind, deaf or mute human specimen may rule his or her soul privately, in darkness, silence and muteness, without saying so at all. Likewise, it is also clear that, when a presidential human does rule his or her soul by talking, an adequate perception of the destructiveness involved in using any such of these humanly available powers is the justification for the famous preface of President Theodore Roosevelt (1858 to 1919). Frequently, after his retirement from the Presidency in 1909, Roosevelt prefaced his public utterances with the following declaration: "Now I am free to express my own opinions because I shall not be endangering anyone but myself."[14] Thereby, Roosevelt recognized, implicitly, the danger to Real Truth which even the expression of sage words may hazard when they are uttered.

But I say: God exists for me because my evaluation of my human powers and the psychology of it say so, *and the matter and manner of this saying are the privileged representations of my existence*. God may exist for you because you declare, by theory or the practical usages of your life, that He needs to, even if many other things hold more privileged priority. God may exist for Clinton because he thanks God for being no worse than any other member of the human species. *But just how privileged is Clinton to say this in light of the gap between his representation of it and the facts surrounding his human powers? Doesn't the simple saying of it cause the gap to widen?* Mere utterance of the knowledge of a thing, especially of any metaphysical equality which all souls may bear on some plane of being-ness before the altar of God, does much to shatter that equality in every other respect. The Qu'ran famously asks: "Are they equal, those who know and those who know not?" and answers strongly no.[15] I say my statement of God's existence is my Alstonian "M-Belief" and my Plantinga-esque *properly basic* Belief. Hypothetically, would Clinton say his statement of thanks to God at Baltimore is also? If so, he Believes in God to acquire a metaphysical state which, under several reasonable measures of understanding, appears to be illusory to the Reality of his human self. Only God knows whether the equal but plain lump of mankind which Clinton declares he is at Baltimore is as Real to him as the remembrance of John Stuart Mill's firm facts that, as a human, he is *élite*, glamorous, powerful and President in Washington, D. C.

To mitigate the omnipresent subjectivity of these last remarks, knowing that I am equally likely to misuse my own human powers roughly with the most egregiously known misuses of them, I hope to be pragmatic, to *act* to *use* logic, meaning, objectivity, science and empiricism for conditions upon which my thinking about Reality is thought. So, now, by this simple statement of my hopes, have the conditions

---

[14]Henry L. Stoddard, *As I Knew Them* (New York, Harper & Brothers, 1927), p. 294.

[15]Seyyed Hossein Nasr, *The Need for a Sacred Science* (Albany, N. Y., State University of New York Press, 1993), p. 59; The Qu'ran ch. XXXIX, v. 9.

of "Real" Truth and "Really" Truthful delivery been satisfied? Or is Reality so easily pulled up by its bootstraps into Itself? The American psychologist, James Henry Leuba (1868 to 1946), related God pragmatically to powerful human life as follows:

"God is not known, he is not understood, *he is used*—sometimes as a meat purveyor, sometimes as a moral support, sometimes as a friend, sometimes as an object of love. If he proves himself useful, the religious consciousness asks for no more than that. Does God really exist? How does he exist? What is he? are so many irrelevant questions. Not God, but life, more life, and a richer, more satisfying life, is, in the last analysis, the end of religion."[16]

If the pragmatic Truth of God is really, ultimately and truly found in this quotation, so that the Real, Ultimate and True nature and fact of God is only as my soul *has a use* for Him, Leuba is entirely right—the question of God's nature and existence does not depend upon anything non-existent because the predicates of His existence are all in my existence as I can surely postulate them by myself and *have a use* for them. The ultimate concerns are narcissistic, reserved for my soul and not dependent upon any X. But if the Truth of the previous discussion is put only slightly differently, so that the Real, Ultimate and True nature and being of God is only as my soul uses Him, God exists because He must exist if He is used because *homo sapiens* uses only what exists and cannot use what does not. This is the Reality of life we have been born into. Does it matter that the origins of a Belief in God shown by the previous discussions are human? If so, we say to what extent? If my soul has a use for God, or *uses* Him, the human sources of my Belief because of these use-values do not taint or impair it or make it any less worthy of Believing; they should more likely state the obvious (that a human source begets a human belief) or strengthen it. (A human source begets a human belief which is strongly believed in because both have the same human character.) The nature and character of the origins of a religious Belief are as valued and valuable as the Belief itself. Origins tell us as much about the pureness and strength (style) of the Belief as the Belief (content) does. However perfect or imperfect God is, however much His meaning is simply a predicate to my ceaseless questioning of, but for, *that which does not exist*—because He comes from humanity, I *use* God humanly in whatever way I think about Him that is Real to me: to care about my body and my soul, to save my soul in life and death, to live more fully and abundantly, to solve the thing-i-fying processes of my mind, to answer the unanswerable, to feel the feeling-ness of what it is to live humanly, actually.

Life itself, particularly as I showed it in the *necessary existence* of "Good Tricks" and my own psychology, shows that God is Ultimate and compelling, of more significance, focus and attention than whether He has simply proved to be useful. When we use a thing, we focus upon and pay attention to the nature and characteristics of that thing, from wisdom and necessity to avoid harm. Those characteristics and nature are, in the end, more significant to us pragmatically than the use is ultimately because they determine how and whether the thing will continue to be employed and under what conditions. How often it is, then, that from one very deep, revelatory and Real

---

[16]William James, *The Varieties of Religious Experience, op. cit.,* p. 453; James Henry Leuba, "The Contents of Religious Consciousness," *The Monist,* Vol. XI, No. 4, p. 536 at pp. 571, 572 (July, 1901).

experience—for example, mine at Auschwitz—we resolve to be close to God again for many others and actually do so. In papers published after his death, Wittgenstein allowed how the experiences of life could "force" the "concept" of God upon us.[17] On condition of the foregoing psychological and utilitarian principles, there is more to God than either the force of a concept or "conjuring up something of a higher order by using words." Perhaps this is what Wittgenstein meant when he said Believers in God have furnished much proof of their Belief as a matter of words, by intellectual analysis and foundation of their wordiness, though they themselves would never have come to Believe by means of the verbal proofs they offer. God enters into the world of a Believer by relating to *every* manifestation of it. Paul the Apostle described the result by saying that: "In [God] we live and move and have our being."[18]

In the Middle Ages it was blasphemous to refer to God as a person or with a single personhood. Because of the doctrine of the Holy Trinity which the Council of Nicaea propounded to orthodox Christianity, hundreds of thousands of medieval people in several centuries referred only to the personæ of God by His three "faces" or "countenances."[19] The Father was a *persona;* the Son, a *persona;* and the Holy Spirit, a *persona.* Each *persona* had an independent hypostasis (support) upon the foundation of the Divine, but the Divinity of each hypostasis required their Trinity, as well as for the Trinity to be expressed Divinely. The wisdom and necessity of avoiding harm to the prospects of a soul's salvation required the naming of God in these three Nicaean ways. So, too, do the same wisdom and necessity require the naming of God today. The French Catholic theologian, Jean-Luc Marion (b. 1946), for reasons which I will detail later, names God by crossing out the middle vowel of his name with the cross of Saint Andrew and calls him $G_{\chi}d$.[20] Here I name God with, paradoxically, the same one which the Romans used for their god of boundary stones: *Terminus.* Terminus, the Roman god, refused to budge when the Romans built the temple of Jupiter Optimus Maximus in the Capitol of Rome and became his abode as a boundary-stone within it. On February 23 of each year, Romans locally celebrated the festival of the Terminalia throughout their Empire; two neighbors at their adjoining boundary would garland the stone markers of the boundary with flowers and sprinkle them with the blood of animal sacrifices.[21] *Terminus,* my name for God to show His meaningfulness (justification), may be more or less an imperfect clod, but He importantly refuses to budge from the elaborate works of false gods, pagan ones or the mortals around Him. *Terminus* marks where the "I" ends and God begins, where the knowable becomes unknown, where experience ends and the transcending of it begins, and, yes, where life and death cross into one another—one of them ending; the other, just beginning.

---

[17]Ludwig Wittgenstein, *Culture and Value* trans. Peter Winch (von Wright ed., Oxford, U. K., Blackwell Publishers, 1980), pp. 82-86.

[18]The Acts of the Apostles ch. 17, v. 28.

[19]Paul Tillich, *A History of Christian Thought from its Judaic and Hellenistic Origins to Existentialism* (Carl E. Braaten ed., New York, Simon & Schuster, 1972), p. 190.

[20]Jean-Luc Marion, *Dieu sans l'être: Hors-texte* (Paris, Librarie Arthème Fayard, 1982) trans. Thomas A. Carlson as *God Without Being* (1st English ed., Chicago, University of Chicago Press, 1991), p. 46.

[21]*The Cambridge Ancient History* (Cook et al. eds., Cambridge, U. K., Cambridge University Press, 1965), Vol. VIII, pp. 426, 436, 440.

The Appearance of God in my World

The first confusion we face about God appearing to us is to unravel at what level of our reason as human thinking things there will be a veil of incomprehensibility drawn down upon the appearance such that our thoughts may not think further, though the appearance of God is (necessarily?) a sort of perception subject to rational faculties as much as, say, the visual images of eyesight would be. For, on the one hand, we know that a profound measure of thought is necessarily required about the Ultimate matters of our existence because ignorance is only a penultimate quality; but, on the other, we know that a veil of incomprehensibility is necessarily required about these Ultimate matters because any measure of our thinking about them, however Ultimately we may characterize them, comes from our mundane existence in a world of relativity, lacking of fulfillment and unity, the very definition of penultimate-ness. The second and further dilemma about the appearance of God to us is to determine to what extent it is God who is drawing down the veil of incomprehensibility around Himself, despite the greater extent we use our foreknowledge of this veil to postulate an ignorance or mysticism about Him which falsely clouds the most Truthful revelation of Himself to us in life. For, on the one hand, we are certain that we do not comprehend the Ultimate entirely; but, on the other, we are full of doubts about that measure of comprehension which we necessarily have because we think. At the beginning of a new millennium, the social and historical contexts in which each soul lives while working out these two dilemmas about the appearance of God create more. For example, on the one hand, I know that only one soul is responsible for resolving the dilemmas about the appearance of God for that soul individually; but, on the other, I know that this singular soul depends upon the world completely even to resolve the fact of its singularity, such that if the world, through the world's history and society, fails to resolve the results of the dilemmas for the many they may never be resolved for one. "No Man is an I[s]land."[22] Or was the English cleric and poet, John Donne (1572 to 1631), wrong? If so, how do islands form archipelagoes exactly? In any case of archipelagoes, what do boundaries mean in an ocean? In other words, if the world is liquid and not solid, how do I Really know that there is any definite basis to the appearance of God in my life? To continue with this sea-faring metaphor, many post-modern thinkers deal with issues of monism (the theory of philosophy that all is Ultimately one substance) by posing the related-ness of the world together into an allegorical ocean, dragooning some waters of it together into a given context—by fishermen's nets to catch big fish but to let the waters pour out into any other net—and then saying Ultimate meaningfulness for me, a Cartesian thinking thing, is to ask precisely this question of epistemology: how do I Really know what's there, except dead and unlucky fish?

In Judeo-Christian Belief, God appears to us in three ways. They are: the Principle of Identity, the Principle of Love, and the life of Jesus the Christ. All of them are subject to the aforementioned twin dilemmas of inherently limited reason and of genuine Divine involvement. The first two of these ways, Identity and Love, are the topics of the rest of this Chapter; the life of Jesus, of the next one. The origin of a Belief is often the criterion by which the content of the Belief is Ultimately measured and assessed.

---

[22] John Donne, "Devotions Upon Emergent Occasions," No. XVII (1624).

Accordingly, the human origins of the Belief in God I discussed in the previous Chapter must mean there is an anthropomorphic nature to God and His Living Spirit. (This is the topic of the next Chapter on Jesus.) On the other hand, psychological "facts" surrounding our existence show the salience of what does not exist upon what does, and that the pureness and strength of the Divine is "better" or "more" than the impure and weak we find in *everything* human. How is this Divinity identified with us precisely? More specifically, how does the Divine attribute of Love fit into this Identification?

The Principle of Identity (Immanence)

We have already seen, from the rationality of Descartes to the untamed feelings of primitive Man, the compelling inclination of mankind to objectify, thing-i-fy and reify the world. God, as this construction of God-Man, is certainly a "being-ness" and an object of knowledge. Even thoughts of God can be reified likewise. For example, the early Christian theologian, Tertullian (A.D. *c.* 160 to *c.* 225), attacked the heresy of Patripassianism. This heresy denied the orthodox view of the dual nature of Jesus of Nazareth as fully human and fully Divine all at once. Patripassianism said God Himself descended into the Virgin Mary, was Himself born of her and suffered, and in fact was Jesus the Christ. By postulating a unified, rather than a dual, nature to God, Patripassianism seems to thing-i-fy God with a meaning which is acceptably meaningful. But Tertullian attacked it and said the Devil, being opposed to Truth in many ways, even destroys truth by defending it![23] We say, therefore, that Tertullian thereby thing-i-fied his thought-system with a truth-value such that even truth without this Value could be repudiated. On the other hand, we say that an empiricist un-thing-i-fies objects from truth-value such that even objects of Truth and Value can be repudiated. For example, under the empirical method, it is possible to suppose that atoms and *Gestalten* are not basic units of experience in all circumstances of the world and that, as a term meaningful for existence, the word "soul" is useful only insofar as we wish to be sentimental about it. There is quite a sliding scale in variations of thing-i-fication, therefore, between the opposite poles of the construction and destruction of objects, as shown by our examples from Tertullian and the sciences of physics and psychology. We conclude that *thing-i-fication is all relative,* all an issue of our position upon the sliding scale between Tertullian's thing-i-fication of even his philosophy and a physicist's un-thing-i-fication of even the most basic units of experience which may be inserted into philosophizing. When we weigh an object upon this scale of the degree to which we would objectify it, God appears. There are elements from that which does not exist—no thing—which are needed in order to base the thing-i-fication of anything else. The Truth-value of this statement applies equally to Tertullian, to natural scientists and to all the many others and their thought-systems of various grades and gradations in between. God appears from this scale of "being-ness." He is the scale itself, the needle locating (remember *Terminus?*) objects on it and the means by which we ourselves may appear to be, literally, *anything.*

God also appears from the existence of objects because meaning is all relative, all an issue of how we assign signs to the world. The simplest technique of assigning of

---

[23]Tertullian, "Treatise Against Praxeas," in *The Christian Theology Reader* (McGrath ed., Oxford, U. K., Blackwell Publishers Ltd., 1995, 1996, 1997) § 4.3, p. 137.

meaning to God is to assert Him by synthesizing essences of our suppositions about God and physical objects together. For example, my father, Prentice, combined God with his thought of God and wrote of God as a human companion. He wrote that, "[i]f your Christianity is to be [R]eal, you must live as tho[ugh] God was a person by your side."[24] The Anglo-Irish clergyman, William King of Derry (1650 to 1729), later Archbishop of Dublin, combined God with his thought of God and wrote of God as two parents. King said that "a creature is descended from God, a most perfect Father; but from Nothing as its Mother, which is Imperfection."[25] The next layer of complexity is to perform the same synthesis, but to start only with physical objects and introduce God later. Hylozoism is the doctrine of philosophy, held especially among Greek Pre-Socratic thinkers, that physical matter is alive with spirit. For example, the Greek philosopher, Anaximander of Miletus (B.C. d. *c.* 547), thought the primary principle of life must be an indeterminate one, what he called the concept of the Boundless—in Greek, the word is *apeiron,* and distilled all of matter into this Boundless principle. After the start made by Anaximander, numerous thinkers throughout the following scores of centuries assembled great "Chains of Being" from objects and endowed the Chains with enough meaning such that God appears from them. To show you the ropes of one such Chain, "[t]his is that which religion (the inculcation of the meaning of God) aims at: to make us men (aren't we physically so already?), to teach us to live according to our nature (isn't nature only a diffuse word for culture and convention?), to put Reason in the Throne (where is existence crowned?), and to vindicate the Spirit from the tyranny of its own vassal flesh (what is the basis for this rescue in spiritual life?)."[26] Furthermore, God even appears in the determination of the quantities of objects with which He is being synthesized. For example, in a posthumously published introduction to King's theology, it was said: "From the . . . observation that there is no manner of *chasm* or *void,* no link deficient in this great chain of beings, and the reason for it, it will appear extremely probable that every distinct order, every class or species of them, is as full as . . . God saw proper."[27] In the 20th century, the Catholic scientist of palæontology, Father Pierre Teilhard de Chardin (1881 to 1955), participated in many explorations of science to unearth the ancient past and has also asserted God by synthesizing Him with the objects of science. By applying all of the meanings he discerned from his consciousness of himself, as a human thinking thing of Christian Catholicism, Teilhard de Chardin said the *objects* of science involved in Darwinian evolution, as well as the objectivity involved in Darwin's process of thinking about them scientifically, meant that God is not in heaven as a mystical Theist might suppose, nor even purely within

---

[24]Prentice Cooper, "Notes on W. D. Weatherford's Christian Life," (Unpublished notes in pencil, 192?).

[25]See Arthur O. Lovejoy, "The Principle of Plentitude and Eighteenth Century Optimism," in *The Great Chain of Being* (1933) (Cambridge, Mass., Harvard University Press, 1950), No. VII, pp. 212 n. 6, 213. The author notes that King's works were extensively published in English and seem to have been much read and discussed. See *An Essay on the Origin of Evil by Dr. William King etc.* (2d ed.in English, Law ed., London, 1732).

[26]Richard Allestree, *Forty Sermons,* 2 vols. (Oxford, 1684), Vol. I, p. 183; quoted in John Spurr, "'Rational Religion' in Restoration England," *Journal of the History of Ideas,* Vol. XLIX, No. 4, p. 563, 579 (Oct.-Dec. 1988) (parenthetical language added to show contrasts).

[27]See Lovejoy, "The Chain of Being in Eighteenth Century Thought etc.", in *op. cit.,* p. 185, quoting Edmund Law's introduction to William King's essay on the origin of evil.

the soul of Man as a mundane Theist might, but is "God ahead," in living union with Man.[28] From Anaximander, the thinkers about a Divine Chain of Being and Teilhard de Chardin, God is asserted by synthesis with physical objects.

The next layer of complexity is to assert God by synthesizing Him with mental objects, as well as with physical ones insofar as the latter have been analyzed to be mental objects fundamentally. This is the great intellectual achievement of the German philosopher, Immanuel Kant (1724 to 1804) and, to a lesser extent, of all of those many other thinkers who follow him but have rejected some part of his grand transcendental schemes. Kant assembled huge meanings about God in the corpus of his formidable body of Cartesian thinking, but he found it necessary to say he was impressed only by two further objects: the starry heavens above and the moral law within. If he were, indeed, so impressed by these things exclusively, why did he find it necessary to assemble his thinking into the further objects which were his books of thoughts? The application of objects to our thinking shows that *meaning is all relative,* all an issue of our perception upon the sliding scale between primitive analogies between God and Fathers and the Kantian transcendence of the intellect over the world. God appears on this scale of perception. At one pole of it, Archbishop King sees Him directly as my Father; on the other, philosopher Kant perceives of Him from what the human intellect can accomplish when it rises over the world. Because of the object of God, and the objectifying interpretations of meaning which we say God gives to the objects of the world, we see that there is an immediate awareness of something unconditional at the center of the human mind—*an object*—and this awareness is the presence of the Divine within us *a priori*—given before anything else—so that "knowledge of God is the first knowledge, the only absolute, sure and certain knowledge, the knowledge not about *a* being but about the unconditional element in the depths of the soul."[29] *We exist and therefore God exists because God exists within us.* This is the Principle of Identity. Philosophers of analytic logic harpoon the reasoning behind this proposition. Thomas Aquinas certainly did. The syllogism is a tautology. If God exists because God exists within us, have we proved the existence of God at all? Haven't we only declared where He is located? Doesn't this mean His existence is entirely dependent upon our own? If so, wouldn't that existence be a rather paltry state for God to be in? Could we still believe in Him despite it? Or is this yet another way of saying He is our figment?

The early Christian theologian, Augustine of Hippo (A.D. 354 to 430), contributed large chunks of important thinking about God to the tradition of Christian orthodoxy (beyond the scope of this inquiry), but he wished *to know* only God and the soul and nothing else. He had a pagan father and a Christian mother and could have wished to know much more. He didn't wish to. If he knew the soul, he could know God because the soul is the place God is known. The soul, not being an object, means that God is also not an object because God is there. Stop! This is exactly the opposite of any conclusion to which our objectifying interpretation of Reality would lead us. By what leap of reasoning did Augustine surmount objects and postulate the unity of God within a soul?

---

[28]Pierre Teilhard de Chardin, *The Phenomenon of Man* trans. Bernard Wall (New York, Harper & Row: Harper Torchbooks, 1959), pp. 291-294. The author often describes the union between God and Man as an "Omega point."

[29]Tillich, *op. cit.,* p. 112.

Paul the Apostle said: "In [God] we live and move and have our being."[30] God subsumes the existence of Man. The two objects are identical under the premises of a subsumption. But what is the larger category? God-Man? To show an example of such a melting-pot, the Muslim mystic, Abu Yazid Bistami (A.D. d. 874), explained that, as he approached the core of his identity, everything which he understood as "himself" apparently melted away. Bistami said:

> "I gazed upon [al-Lah] with the eye of truth and said to Him: "Who is this?" He said, "This is neither I nor other than I. There is no God but I." Then he changed me out of my identity into His Selfhood. . . . Then I communed with the tongue of His Face, saying: "How fares it with me with Thee?" He said, "I am through Thee; there is no God but Thou."[31]

The German Christian philosopher of mysticism, Meister Eckhart (1260? to 1327), taught that mystics must refuse to be ensnared by finite ideas about the Divine and bluntly equated this refusal to the achievement of an identity with God, such that "God's existence must be my existence and God's Is-ness—in German, the word is *Istigkeit*—is my is-ness."[32] Consequently, in 1325, the Archbishop of Cologne arraigned Eckhart for heresy and charged him with, among other things, claiming that God Himself is born in a human soul.

Alternatively to Eckhart, in Augustine's orthodox view, God does not subsume Man when He identifies with Man but is at Man's center and is "not a strange thing whose existence or non-existence one might discuss."[33] Tillich summarizes Augustine's thinking on the "friendliness" (my term) between a soul and God as follows:

> "[God] is our own *a priori;* he precedes ourselves in dignity, reality and logical validity. In him the split between the subject and object, and the desire of the subject to know the object, are overcome. There is no such gap. God is given to the subject as nearer to itself than it is to itself."[34]

Since we are grasped by God as unconditionally as this, Augustine said God can be presupposed in situations of doubt about Him because all that is required for us to squelch our doubts about Reality is for us to enter into our own inner Reality where there is something, namely God, which surpasses it and is immutable. Augustine was Neo-Platonic in directing us not to go outside, but to go inside ourselves. He identified God so closely with the soul that discussions of a split between the two are no longer material to a comprehension of Reality. The principle of a soul's identification with God means that the separate existence of God is no longer a material concept. The separateness of God's strength, comfort and hope for my soul, as separateness, are not material concepts because they have been united and associated with the soul already.

---

[30] *The Acts of the Apostles* ch. 17, v. 28.

[31] Abu Yazid Bistami, "Narrative," quoted in Marshall G. S. Hodgson, *The Venture of Islam: Conscience and History in a World Civilization*, 3 vols. (Chicago, University of Chicago Press, 1974), Vol. I, p. 404; similarly, Armstrong, *op. cit.*, p. 226.

[32] Meister Eckhart, "On Detachment," in *Meister Eckhart: The Essential Sermons, Commentaries, Treatises and Defence* (Coledge and McGinn, eds., London, 1981), p. 87; quoted in Armstrong, *op. cit.*, p. 253.

[33] Tillich, *op. cit.*, p. 112.

[34] *Ibid.*

This is similar to the principle of Identity we find in the thinking of the Faylasuf philosophers of Islam, such as Avicenna (Abu Ali ibn Sina) (980 to 1037), and among the religions of Asia. The Qu'ran, Avicenna and Faylasuf philosophy agreed that God is simplicity itself: He is One and cannot be broken down into component parts or attributes. Indeed, "God cannot be an object of discursive thought, because our brains cannot deal with [H]im in the way that they deal with everything else."[35] Accordingly, the theology of Eastern Orthodox Christianity developed a traditional split between the unknowable "essence" of God and the manifestations of His "energies" in the world. Only the latter may be Truly knowable, because God is essentially inaccessible and only through His "energies" does He communicate with mankind at all. You certainly see the foundations of mystery, paradox, silence and remoteness which surround God because of the essential qualities of His Inner Truth. But the Principle of Identity gives a soul the certainty, the unconditional quality, of this Truth which dwells within it. What was material to Augustine, Eastern Orthodox Christianity, Islam and the Asiatic religions is the special Truth which can be found only in the inner soul, as an absolute norm presupposed against any search, probability or pragmatic guide.

Special Truth from the inner soul is hard for the heirs of the Latin heritage of Western civilization to admit to. We still want to think about it, even after we think we've thought it. Even during the High Middle Ages, an age of faith and certainty, Thomas Aquinas and many others attacked it, though from different angles. Today, uncertainty, conditional thinking, scientific searching, probabilistic reasoning and answering pragmatically are the hallmarks of our science, politics, psychology, our entire folk philosophy of a happy life. The former Secretary of the United States Treasury, Robert E. Rubin (b. 1938), led a prosperous and successful career for himself and for the economy of the United States by the conscious direction of his mind to abhor certainty and to reason probabilistically.[36] I do not know whether Rubin has a Belief in God, but if he does, how, why should he be expected to base it on theology at odds with the direction his mind employs for all the other ideas and beliefs he holds? Rubin is among millions of others who find success in life today by truth totally unlike Augustine's. We are trained in extracting particulars from particulars, using exclusively logical and scientific techniques to do so, not in creating Universals or comprehending any Ultimate Identity.

By contrast to synthesizing God with objects, or by asserting Him directly, there is another alternative of meaningfulness which is logically available: just saying God or analyzing Him. The school of philosophy called Logical Positivism, held especially among thinkers in Vienna during the 20th century known as the Vienna Circle, says that spirits and physical objects are separate to the extent that there are only these possibilities: either the objects of the world exist without spirits, or both do. In the latter case, one may not exist within the other unless, if there is any combination of them somehow, there is a meaning of the means to do so, upon which that combination may exist as a further object of perception or, even more minimally, *there is the meaning by which the immanence of either in the other may be accomplished as a matter of a*

---

[35]Armstrong, *op. cit.,* p. 183.

[36]Jacob Weisberg, "Keeping the Boom from Busting," in *The New York Times Magazine,* Section 6, pp. 24-29, 38, 40, 53-55, in *The New York Times,* Vol. CXLVII, No. 51,223 (July 19, 1998).

complete technique for doing so completely. For example, in his book, the *Tractatus,* Wittgenstein logically separated the spirit of God from the objects of his world such that there was not even any meaning from spoken language by which to combine them. God strikes out in silence. On the other hand, numerous thinkers throughout the centuries have assembled great chains of meaning from logic and endowed the Chains with enough objects such that God is *the* meaning appearing to be logically necessary. God appears to hit the baseball of Reality. For example, the Italian Catholic theologian, Thomas Aquinas (1225 to 1274), applied Aristotelian logic to ask if God exists as an objective matter from the physics of the outside world and answered yes in the famous "Five Ways."[37] All of them are logical in form, filled with worldly objects but fail the test of our empiricism—they do not correspond to experience as it is generally known and lived at the beginning of this new millennium. Thomas looked outside of himself to take characteristics of the world he lived in to bring this world to God. He was a cosmologist, but he uses a baseball which modern science says is made out of horse-hairs and cannot possibly be hit in the major leagues. We say the spectacle of pitching horse-haired baseballs to God, and then to expect Him to hit them out of the park, is quite unwise, impossible and wrong. The maws of "cyberspace," "black holes," drugged friends, divorced spouses, betraying *gourmets* and Auschwitz do not appear part of my conviction in a Cosmos. On the day in the city that this is being written, the headline of the front page of the newspaper which circulates among the population on a mass basis is: "Stocking Up In Case It All Crashes In 2000."[38] Surely, the God we Believe in did not design the world with this degree of instability; otherwise our Belief, too, would be this unstable. In any case, we say Thomas erred by failing to look inside of himself to be aware of God as a matter of Inner Truth or psychological necessity.

Where does God appear as a baseball player who does not strike out or hit a foul ball? In other words, between one pole at Wittgenstein who is silent because of too much separation, and the other at Thomas Aquinas, who is loquacious because of too much linkage, where is the discourse about God which may speak of Him meaningfully to *me* so that He *appears*? God has been affirmed but the existence of a human soul denied; conversely, a soul as such has been affirmed but the existence of God denied.[39] On the other hand, God has been conceived of as equal to exactly nothingness, such that either nothing comes of nothingness or all of nature does. For example, the German naturalist, Lorenz Oken (1779 to 1851), said that, as all numbers may be described as some determinants of zero, so all beings may be said to pre-exist in God, such that the

---

[37]Scruton, *op. cit.,* pp. 130, 131; Tillich, *op. cit.,* pp. 194, 195; see Sir Anthony Kenny, *The Five Ways* (London, 1969). All Five Ways depend upon causes and effects which may be valid as reasoning in the abstract but are not valid for actual existence, do not harmonize the psychological realities of our souls or present God as Real to me. The first way Thomas elaborated depends upon the fiction of an "unmoved mover;" the second, upon the fiction of a "first cause" which is not temporal but lives "in dignity;" the third, upon the fiction we ourselves might not exist so that something else would be required to complete this job; the fourth, upon the fiction of a "final purpose;" and the fifth, upon the fiction that perfection may be more or less so.

[38]*The Tennessean,* Vol. 94, No. 242, p. 1 (August 30, 1998).

[39]Compare Peter Van Inwagen, *Metaphysics* (Boulder, Colo., Westview Press, 1993), chs. 9, 10 (affirming God but denying soul) with J. McT. E. McTaggart, *The Nature of Existence* (Cambridge, U. K., Cambridge University Press, 1927), Vol. II, Ch. XLIII (denying God but affirming soul).

task of philosophy is to show the transformation of the primal nothingness of God into the generation of the Universe and the existence of all things.[40] On the other hand, God has been conceived of as equal to exactly everything, such that either all things are derived from Him, or only nature is. For example, Liebnitz said that, as "we see liquids spontaneously and by their own nature gather into spherical drops," so the world may be seen by a mechanical process of condensation to pre-exist in God, among a realm consisting of itself and all other worlds which are possible, such that the task of philosophy is to represent the emergence of our actual world from among all of these possibilities as a matter of its nature.[41] On the one hand, the Pan-Scientific school of thinkers, who live largely in the academic world as we know it presently, that is to say, by ivy-entwined courtyards and buildings of distinctive architectural detail, conceive of the soul as equal to exactly nothing, such that either nothing comes of nothingness or all of mysticism does. On the other hand, the quasi-Realist school of thinking, which lives largely beyond the campus of a university, conceives of the soul as equal to the salient operative forces of human life, such that either religion comes from it completely, or only mysticism about the supra-natural does.

How is sense to be made from all of these opposites? The early Christian theologian, Pseudo-Dionysius the Areopagite[42] (A.D. c. 500), held that, as everything we say about God consists of symbolic interpretations, we know about God by recognizing the interpretations are both everything and nothing symbolically. On the one hand, we must name God with all names because we recognize the symbolic interpretation of "everything" there is about Him. On the other hand, God is neither any name we call Him nor even an object we may Truly know. Even the word "God" is flawed because God is actually "above God" and "a mystery beyond being."[43] Accordingly, the French Catholic theologian, Jean-Luc Marion (b. 1946), discerns the idolatry which arises because of the un-God-like basis our language and our symbolic interpretations of God are prone to fall into. Following the so-called post-modernist school of thinkers, who spurn synthesizing understandings of Reality in favor of their particular (peculiar?) contexts, Marion holds that God's self-Revelation is the *only* foundation of a *properly basic* Belief in God, and that this foundation does not depend at all upon correlations between Reason and Revelation, such that the rational faculties of Man may facilitate an understanding of God's Revelation but, standing on their own, are idolatrous of themselves. Therefore, Marion changes the name of God to G_Xd because,"[t]o cross out G_Xd, in fact, indicates and recalls that G_Xd crosses out our thought because [H]e saturates it; better, [H]e enters into our thought only in obliging it to criticize itself."[44] In these premises, the nature of God for the world is not to be in "being-ness" like an object, but to reveal Himself in Holiness as a "gift." Marion allows for the finest

---

[40]Lovejoy, *op. cit.,* p. 320; Lorenz Oken, *Lehrbuch der Naturphilosophie,* Sec. I, p. 4 (1810).

[41]See Lovejoy, op. cit., p. 178; Freiherr Gottfried Wilhelm von Liebnitz, *Die philosophischen Schriften,* 7 vols. (C. Gerhardt ed., Reprint of 1875-1890, Hildesheim, Olms Verlagsbuchhandlung, 1960-1961), Vol. VII, p. 290.

[42]This author wrote under a pseudonym. Centuries earlier, a man identified as Dionysius followed Paul the Apostle after Saint Paul preached to an assembly of Epicurean and Stoic philosophers at the Areopagus in Athens. *The Acts of the Apostles* ch. 17, v. 34.

[43]Armstrong, *op. cit.,* pp. 126, 127; Tillich, *op. cit.,* pp. 92, 93.

[44]Marion, *op. cit.,* p. 46.

qualities of reason in Man's intellect to discern how much this "gift" is actually "excessive." This is Marion's post-modernist principle of the Identity of God with Man and *vice versa*. The content of it in Love will be discussed later. For now, it suffices to see that Marion's theology surmounts the problem of subject-object relationships by redefining God and subsuming the rational faculties of Man into G_Xd. He succeeds where Bistami, Eckhart, Augustine and Paul the Apostle may not have. It is a very significant contribution.

But is G_Xd yet another word-game? The conventional approach to the meaning of language is that there are conventions of usage and culture by which the utterance of Z means Z. However, Z may still be communicated, though the expression of Z does not of itself impart the literal meaning of Z, if the hearer recognizes meaning by realizing that Z is what the speaker intends for the hearer to hear by the non-literal expression being used. The key, though, to the existence and validity of this type of Z communication is that nothing about the actual expression of the speaker imparts Z-ness for, if it does, we cannot be sure our special type of understanding has been confused with what Z-ness has been partially, but literally, expressed. Under this theory of language, does G_Xd impart so much of the meaning of God that it confuses the meaning of both symbols? Or is G_Xd so different from the conventional meaning of "God" that it is a separate, fresh and meaningful symbol of *properly basic* Christian God-ness? On the one hand, there is every reason to suppose that omnipresent God includes the presence of G_Xd by self-Revelation in Love; but, on the other, there is no reason to suppose that comprehensible God includes innately incomprehensible G_Xd. But, then, to arrive at such conclusions, what is that God or G_Xd of which we speak? How do we hear the Judeo-Christian God speak Himself ? In the first books of the Old Testament, God is very talkative but, after the book of Job, He rarely says anything. In the New Testament, God speaks only once: to say of Jesus of Nazareth: "This is my beloved Son with whom I am well pleased."[45] Jesus of Nazareth said: "You are the light of the world. A city set on a hill cannot be hid. Nor do men light a lamp and put it under a bushel, but on a stand, and it gives light to all in the house."[46] G_Xd lights the souls of all these house-dwellers. Ultimately incomprehensible and mystical G_Xd is nevertheless a meaning comprehending the essence of God more presently and, therefore, more inclusively of both terms. G_Xd seems exactly the sort of Cartesian "natural light" of which Jesus spoke by referring to hilltop cities and lighted lamp-stands centuries before Descartes lived. Specifically, in those supposed cases of a text when G_Xd and God do not include each other, they may respectively refer to each side of the gap which has developed among the followers of Jesus the Christ between manifestation (in German, Heidegger's word is *Offenbarkeit*) and revelation (Heidegger's word is *Offenbarung*).[47]

Leibnitz invented the word "theodicy" to mean the defense of God's goodness and omnipotence. On the other hand, by using the system of notation we employ today, Leibnitz was the first person in history to use the integral sign in calculus. Do we "hear" more meaning about God from the integral sign than from "theodicy" or other words by which God is more literally expressed? Theodicy is only what it means as a linguistic

---

[45] Saint Matthew ch. 3, v. 17.
[46] Saint Matthew ch. 5, vv. 14, 15.
[47] See Marion, *op. cit.,* p. 70.

symbol of English for the literal expression of Z, but the integral sign *could* mean, as well as for calculus, something for a special type of Z communication. If the integral sign is a Divine integration of Reality, able to parse it infinitesimally, may we postulate it for the existence of God as but another way of putting Him into *my* world? "Mathematicians . . . delineate objects and structures wherein sharp properties interlock in a densely layered network. . . . The mathematical realm, a vivid one, grips our attention because it is so [R]eal."[48] But, wait!, what do we recognize as meaningful (justified) even if God intended that we would perceive the meaning (explanation) of Divine integration from this "sign" of calculus? The German philosopher of logic, Gottlob Frege (1848 to 1925), argues that, if our representation of a number is not the number itself, the foundation of a psychological viewpoint upon the number collapses insofar as a Truthful investigation of the essence of numbers is concerned.[49] This collapse, like human freedom, may occur quite apart from any perceived intention of God about it. However, any scheme which expresses meaning (explanation) about Reality does so about God. Justification (meaningfulness) of the scheme is entirely another issue. The "being" of two-ness, of any number more than one, implies an infinite regression of a series of more numbers and an infinite multiplicity of more "beings" accordingly. Quine pointed out that the manner in which mathematicians have dealt with the problem of the descriptive differences in the being-ness of infinity is much similar to the manner in which theologians treated of God by their distinct schools of theology in the Middle Ages.[50] We *may* choose to recognize God by realizing that we perceive Him *intuitively*. We may accomplish the intuition of God artistically, musically, mathematically and beyond our words. This is a trespass across a boundary, which you challenge against any basis why anyone should cross it, but others have done so.[51] If so, doesn't the validity of intuition imply that even $G_X d$ is either an idol or an icon of our various wide-ranging, sometimes irrational, perceptions? But, if this is not, what is the justification of our heritage of abundant perceptiveness in Western civilization or why we have explored the Universe to such depth and intuit so many Chains of Meaning about it?

Do the religious thinkers we have mentioned here validly identify with God to the extent they choose to do so and Truthfully describe the world from the perspectives of their different poles? If one theologically denies God but affirms soul, the Principle of Identity shows God may still (surreptitiously) exist within the soul's affirmation, though not as that soul's Cartesian object. If one scientifically denies soul but affirms God, the Principle of Identity shows God may still exist within you, though not in a soul, but by

---

[48]Nozick, *op. cit.,* pp. 130, 131.

[49]Gottlob Frege, "Dr. E. G. Husserl: Philosophie der Arithmetik," in *Zeitschrift für Philosophie und philosophische Kritik,* Vol. 103, pp. 22-41 (1894); see Joseph J. Kockelmans, *Edmund Husserl's Phenomenology* (West Lafayette, Ind., Purdue University Press, 1994), pp. 36, 37.

[50]Willard V. O. Quine, *From A Logical Point of View,* "On What There Is" (2d ed., Cambridge, Mass., Harvard University Press, 1953, 1961), p. 14.

[51]See, for example, René Descartes, *Discours de la Méthode* (1637) trans. F. E. Sutcliffe as *Discourse on Method* (London, Penguin Books, 1968), Section IV, p. 57 (the ontological argument for the existence of God by analogy to geometry); Alain Houziaux, "Pour Une Légitimation Du Discours Théologique," *Études Théologique et Religieuses,* Vol. 73, No. 1, p. 77 at p. 84 *et seq.* (1998) (discussing the mathematics of infinity and a series of rational and irrational numbers to justify the Kingdom of God).

Revelations to your whole self. Is there anything about these Manifestations or Revelations which would require God in duplications? Is there a Chain of Being into possible worlds by which God could be possibly more than one of Him? Is there a Chain of Meaning up from zero which implies likewise? If God exists in multiple copies, I do not know a logic or an experience why, except from mankind and the connived affairs of the world, even upon as grand a scale of quantities as they are in the Universe. Therefore, my ontology and epistemology of one God-ness relate to each other in this way: On the one hand, because of why I know what I do, this X exists and is Real to me only if I think it is so, nothing else more (a thought upon a thought) or less (perhaps an intuition or an instinct?) On the other hand, this proposition about my knowledge is only so if X exists and is Real to me because of what I know about why I do. Furthermore, what I know about why I know it includes knowing more than either consciously.

Dreams and prayers are worth knowing though this full knowledge may consciously never be known. The words of prayers subvert the fully open communication which the praying intend if language is a closed system of self-contained signifiers. If it is not, publication of words in prayers anyway is the same subversion also if the self is another closed system of self-containment. Though it *may* contain plenty of all three, expressed Belief in prayer does not relate to any *necessity* of logic, mathematics or language at all. Then, why in the most important moments of life do we often find ourselves praying? A madman assassinated the American President, William McKinley (1843 to 1901), at the zenith of his power, though McKinley believed that he had a right, even a duty, to implore God for guidance before deciding on an important matter, and that God would, indeed, literally provide this guidance. McKinley explained how he reached the decision to direct the United States to annex the Philippines as follows:

> "I am not ashamed to tell you, Gentlemen, that I went down on my knees and prayed Almighty God for light and guidance that one night. And one night late it came to me this way. . . . *There was nothing left* for us to do but take them all and to educate the Filipinos and uplift and civilize and Christianize them, and by God's grace do the very best we could with them, as our fellow men for whom Christ also died."[52]

Of course, logical thinking about the world showed McKinley many alternatives for the practical future of the Philippines. He resorted to God, the Reality of what does not exist, to face his Real existence as a political leader forced to choose among actual possibilities about the future. We can even say he prayed to God because he remembered the alternatives so acutely that they transformed from logical possibilities into Real "facts" in his mind. Do you remember John Stuart Mill's definition of Reality precisely as such a memory? The force of this Reality is the likeliest meaning (explanation) why McKinley justified it by his completely contradictory expression of

---

[52]Johnson, *op. cit.,* p. 40 (italics added); compare Henry L. Stoddard, *As I Knew Them* (New York, Harper & Brothers, 1927), p. 255. Author Johnson appears to abridge Stoddard's quotation of McKinley's remarks to a group of clergymen. In Stoddard's quotation, McKinley actually sets forth four different courses of action for the United States.

what it actually consisted of—that *there was nothing left* for him to do but what he did. Reality, therefore, is most intimately, if painfully, related to the phenomenon of praying. There is nothing about this phenomenon which is illusory or hallucinatory, except, of course, when human behavior intentionally connives to create illusion or hallucination about it. Prayer happens. In praying, Z may be communicated, though not literally. Dreams and prayers are unconscious and conscious phenomena of existence; they are forms of the way God and a soul identify.

God is the meaning which justifies existence and McKinley's shameless contradictory explanation of his decision-making. Didn't McKinley use his foreknowledge of the eventual incomprehensibility of God to obscure the comprehensibility of his decision-making process, or to avoid reasoning about God more exactly? In other words, there appears to be no place (yes, a location) in Reality where McKinley relied upon *that which does not exist*—no thing (for example, the agape of large numbers of selfish Americans for equally large numbers of selfish Filipinos)—to justify the thing-in-itself of his decision to annex a distant tropical archipelago into the United States. Instead, McKinley said God guided him by clearly existing things—missions of human power to dominate others by disguising the selfishness involved with "civilization" or with "Christ." Where, then, is Marion's G_Xd even in an ostensible act of God's self-Revelation to McKinley in Love? Unless we think about it protectively, G_Xd is simply overwhelmed. But we said previously that the "being-ness" of my life, at least, is compelled to Believe in a "being-ness" which is more than a solipsism or a self-referring statement. Atheism is as much a Belief about "being-ness" as Theism is, and so that, regardless of our conscious indifference to them, we must consciously hold one of either. The non-Believer British-American poet and critic, T. S. (Thomas Stearns) Eliot (1888 to 1965), says that Christianity is always transforming itself into something which can be generally believed.[53] Do you believe that Atheism is on par with Theism in terms of Ultimate concerns and being psychologically compelled? Is there any alternative of indifference or apathy to either? Eliot might say that I see a local perspective on transforming Christianity into "the better Atheist's alternative," or that I am embarked upon a mission of "philosophical puritanism" to identify it with the world and its Theistic processes. On the other hand, meanings about existence *are* in atoms, perceptions, *Gestalten,* memes, memory, prayer, language and mathematics. But not any one of them known to me entirely expresses this. If I put the phenomenon of prayer beside other phenomena to juxtapose meanings only the naïve would put together, to change them as Eliot and many others would deplore, I intend that the outcome either harmonizes more perfectly the meaning of a Believer's Belief or sharpens more perfectly the "signs" a non-Believer's meaning faces to be meaningful. God appears either way.

In Chapter Two of the Second Book of the *Posterior Analytics,* the Greek philosopher, Aristotle (B.C. 384 to 322), said that to ask if A is B, or if A exists, is to ask whether there is a "middle term" to account for A's being B, or for A's existing, and that to ask why A is B, or what A is, is to ask what this "middle term" is. It is clear from this proposition that, if a human soul is inserted as the "middle term" of it, and if a human soul accounts for God's existence, then the existence of God is accounted for; and that

---

[53]Iris Murdoch, *Metaphysics as a Guide to Morals* (London, Allen Lane: The Penguin Press, 1992), p. 126.

if you know what a human soul is, you also know who God is. Under these conditions Augustine's principle of Identity is validated by Aristotelian logic. But there are lingering questions. Since God is primary Reality and surely "substance," did Aristotle mean this proposition to apply to "substance?"[54] In Aristotle's body of philosophy, substance is determined by direct observation; what a substance is, by the definition of the *genus* to which it belongs and the *differentia* which distinguish it from other species of the *genus*. On the other hand, the existence of an "attribute" is dependent upon the substance which possesses it. To ask whether an "attribute" exists is to ask whether there is a cause to account for it, and to ask about the attribute is to ask about its cause. In any event, Aristotle did not intend to apply his proposition from the Second Book of *Posterior Analytics* to the world; it was simply a matter of reasoning in the abstract. That it provides some logic about the nature and existence of God is fortunate for thinkers; the proposition shows a human soul, memes, *Gestalten*, mysticism, M-Belief, psychology, Love, Jesus, Platonism or any other *properly basic* "middle term" can be inserted to "prove" God. The Principle of Identity is validated to this extent in the logic which has been always so valued by Western rationalists. Are you surprised?

Please swallow the saliva in your mouth now. Thank you for paying attention to this most natural act which you have performed thousands of times in your life without aiming your consciousness at it until I prompted you suddenly. Please spit out your saliva into a glass. Now drink it. Disgusting! Water which was so normally and naturally handled by your brain as long as it remained inside your body is suddenly water with an attribute of disgust after being expectorated, though there is no data the expectoration caused the chemistry of the water to be changed in any way. Yet you view the nature of the water completely differently once it has left your mouth. The water crossed a boundary which your psychology set for it. So it is by analogy that your psychology has also set the boundary of your soul as a sort of boundary for God. In other words, God is as normal and natural as your saliva to you as long as He is within you, inside your soul and identified with it as Augustine stated, but if we do assume Augustine's principle of Identity is minimally a statement of God's "location" and a boundary of psychology is crossed, then we may feel very differently about Him. The differences in our feelings caused by boundary crossings stir more anxiety, addiction or self-sacrifice than what the previous Chapter discussed but feed back into them by the processes for these psychological "states of affairs" we have seen already. The Divinity of God in a soul and identified with it causes these "states of affairs," whatever they are, to be more than they would otherwise be. Perhaps the more God-linked a consciousness is the more it becomes.

The human origins of Belief we have discovered from these findings mean that it is of, at least, better form for a Belief in God to have a godly source, and not a human one. It would be better still for the Belief to originate in God Himself. To say X exists is at least to say there is a meaning to X.[55] Wittgenstein said in papers published after his death, "the essence of God is supposed to prove his existence."[56] May my Belief in

---

[54]Arthur D. Ross, "Introduction to the Second Book of Posterior Analytics," in *Aristotle's Prior and Posterior Analytics* (Ross ed., Oxford, U. K., Oxford University Press, 1965), p. 76.

[55]See Wittgenstein, *Philosophical Investigations, op. cit.,* No. 58, p. 28.

[56]Ludwig Wittgenstein, *Culture and Value* trans. Peter Winch (von Wright, ed., Oxford, U. K., Blackwell, 1980), p. 82-6.

God be essentially inspired by Him? Or is it only a matter of unremitting subjectivity? Will any such of a subjectivity prove to be untenable after the certainty further experiences of my life shake me just as I have been shaken already? If so, why would I cling to it if I know it will fail when I do? *For me* the "reflective equilibrium"[57] of my soul answering this question is not where we found it previously—in thing-i-fying the existence of God as an object, though God is often thing-i-fied and that, indeed, is the reason and valid basis of a lot of this discussion. Instead, my soul's equilibrium about the Reality of God is in the mental process, in the Belief, by which the thing-i-fication, the existence, the object of God occurs. Ouch! I dare to deplore the word-games of others only to refer an "equilibrium" and thus to play my own game of obscurity. But, as you think these thoughts at this moment inside your head, do you trust them more than you do your ability to think still more thoughts as you read along the words of this sentence? *It is not the thought of the existence of God which is as Real to you as your own capacity to generate still more thinking.* God exists in this capacity, not in the thought of it. Conversely, "[w]herever the spirit of God is extruded from our human calculations, an unconscious substitute takes its place."[58] This is why Atheism *is* on a par with Theism in terms of a *Gestalt* theory about patterns of psychological Belief in Ultimates. This, again, is what Wittgenstein meant when he said Believers have furnished much wordy proof of God, but not much by which they come to Believe in Him world-i-ly—that is, by the innateness of memes, memory and *Gestalt* patterns, the capacities by which they think and feel in the first place. From *human* sources, we say Belief in X is either a "state of affairs" inside soul—or it is the identification within soul of behavior. The identification works like this: Belief in X is regarded as a disposition to act in ways that are not manifestly inconsistent with the Truth of X because the soul has identified X-believing behavior as a "good" behavior as opposed to others. By either alternative, validation must occur if Belief in X is Real. The moral question of what is "good" behavior for a soul is *only* answered after the soul has determined *all* possibilities, even from the behavior of dead souls, hypothetical ones from literature, or from living ones which show logical but not actual worldly circumstances.[59] Soul observing any "state of affairs" inside itself must refer back to itself and be confounded by the question: why can I believe myself? Soul's observation of its own mental state needs something further to answer issues from the self-referral and its logical character as a tautology. Thus, we see that the paradox of validation of "states of affairs," or of "good" behavior, is that the Truth of *them depends upon what does not exist*. Though he did not intend to use it in a context with this degree of abstraction, the paradoxical reliance upon that which does not exist to be a meaning in existence is what William James said is "[t]he coil . . . about us, struggle as we may."[60] It is this coil which is the existence of God inside of us, a modern phrasing of the Principle of Identity, though

---

[57]Compare John Rawls, *A Theory of Justice* (Cambridge, Mass., Harvard University Press, 1970), pp. 189-191.

[58]C. J. Jung, "On the Nature of the Psyche," (1954) in *op. cit.*, p. 40.

[59]See William James, *The Will To Believe* (Cambridge, Mass., 1896) in *Writings 1878-1899* (New York, Library of America, 1992), p. 472.

[60]*Ibid.*, p. 526.

God may be described by a word more benign than "coil"—something as mundane as wrapping paper or as practical as a boundary fence-post.

The Principle of Love

The Principle of Love is logically separate from the Principle of Identity because Love, of itself, has God-ness characteristics which do not depend on identifying it with X. After defining the nature of G_Xd in the world in Holiness as a "gift," theologian Marion easily defines this gift as Love "[f]or what is peculiar to [L]ove consists in the fact that it gives itself."[61] Furthermore, ". . . [L]ove gives itself only in abandoning itself, ceaselessly transgressing the limits of its own gift, so as to be transplanted outside of itself."[62] It is this last characteristic of Love, that of its transplanting elsewhere, which saves Marion's concept of G_Xd from collapsing inwardly into solipsism and a self-contained set of revelatory referrals which G_Xd chooses to show of Himself to the world and us. Like the Principle of Identity, we say the Principle of Love in another syllogism: *Love exists and therefore God exists because God is Love.* Logicians harpoon the reasoning of this syllogism. They do so less easily than they harpooned the tautology behind the Principle of Identity. But Immanuel Kant and all thinkers in the tradition of analytic logic say the trouble with this syllogism of the Principle of Love— or, for that matter, with any syllogism relating a word, thing, quality or object with existence—is that the term "existence" has no predicate; that is to say, no word, thing, object or entity whose essence can be discerned of itself, apart from its existing, and related as an absolute proposition to any other. To assert X exists is not to assert X = Y. Indeed, according to Quine, to assert X exists is to make no assertion at all, except "in theory" because existence is "theory-relative."[63] All of this logic is an echo of Kant's famous assertion in theology that, "Existence adds nothing to the properties of a thing." Also, it is another echo of Tillich's view that existence as such is essentially without content.[64] Furthermore, what do you mean when you use the word "Love"? The English vocabulary is restricted from expressing the variety of meanings of Love which ancient Greek expressed by using four different words: *agapē, eros, philios* and *storgē*.[65] These Greek words mean concepts of Love which are essentially so different from one another that it may be wiser to set forth four syllogisms instead one. Or, would one of the four be invalid? Even if not, the meaning of each Greek word in each of four new syllogisms may be fairly attacked. Specifically, if love is *storgē*, the tenderness of a parent toward a child, does God mean to put us literally into that state of infantile behavior to which Freud reduced religion in order for us to reciprocate the *storgē*? If love is *philios*, does this Really mean that God is so personal to us that He is only our friend? If love is *eros*, what exactly is the passage from a lower to an upper state of nature which one must navigate to show it? Finally, if love is *agapē*, how is the essence of such a ceaseless and giving thing not restricted by humanity? Under the framework of Aristotelian logic

---

[61] Marion, *op. cit.*, p. 47.
[62] *Ibid.*, p. 48.
[63] Scruton, *op. cit.*, pp. 141-143.
[64] Tillich, *op. cit.*, pp. 438, 439, 541.
[65] Ceslas Spicq, *Notes de lexicographie néo-testamentaire* (Fribourg, Éditions Universitaires, 1978, 1982) trans. James D. Ernest as *Theological Lexicon of the New Testament* (Peabody, Mass., Hendrickson Publishers, 1994), Vol. I, p. 9.

which Western civilization has so valued and been guided by, doesn't the meaning of each of the four Greek words for Love pertain not a "substance" but only to an "attribute"? *Chresis* is yet another Greek word to express coupling which only amounts to sex. How is it that a meaningful definition of God, a most substantial X in the Universe, is an insubstantial attribute under Aristotle's thinking?

To the contrary, the German philosopher, Max (Ferdinand) Scheler (1874 to 1928), says that Love is basic to the being-ness of humans. According to Scheler, the very beginning of the definition of our is-ness is, in Latin, *ens amans*.[66] Whether we indulge in more words of being-ness or not, even from Scheler, we grant that central to existence is the human personality, and central to this personality is a bond between soul, called *Psyche* in ancient Greek, and Love, called *Amor* in Latin. The marriage of *Psyche* to *Amor* is a favorite tale of mythology which has been documented in about 1,500 variants worldwide.[67] It shows the innate attractiveness of the "animal bridegroom" of Love to *Psyche,* and *vice versa,* though the attraction is always an ordeal. Love awakens soul's knowledge and volition, but the awareness of existence by all three qualities often amounts to fear or denial of existence. Scheler does not specifically address the resulting conundrum of this massive body of mythology, but he says that "[m]an's love is restricted to recognizing the objective demand these objects [of his love] make and to submitting to the gradation in rank in what is worthy of love."[68] For Scheler, cognition is always preserved throughout acts of Love, and an entirely separate scheme of Values and Variables regulate the content which a lover places into a loving "realm." The German-Jewish theologian, Martin Buber (1878 to 1965), dealt with the attraction between *Amor* and *Psyche* by postulating a "sphere of the between" in the meeting of human individuals with, first, material objects and, then, God and the resulting compulsion of "I-It" and "I-Thou" relationships respectively.[69] Scheler's "loving realm" and Buber's "sphere of the between" are philosophical places. Where is Love in Christianity?

Intuition is either uninferred knowledge of the Truth of a proposition or immediate knowledge of an object which does not amount to a proposition, a "state of affairs," however chimerical it may be. Friendship may be predicated upon intuition and often is. From such relationships, we conclude that it is friendship, not inferred knowledge, which is the way we become acquainted with each other Really. In other words, friendship *really delivers truth and has the ability for a truthful delivery* more than inferred knowledge does when the issue is the acquaintance of one soul with another and whether the souls are Truly acquainted. And what is friendship but Love? Jesus of Nazareth (B.C. 4? to A.D. 30?) said: "A greater [L]ove than this no man has than to give one's life for one's friends."[70] So a soul *has a use for* or *uses* Love to acquaint with other souls and to accomplish all sorts of noble purposes, including the self-sacrifice Jesus

---

[66]Max Scheler, "Ordo Amoris," (1914-1916) in *Max Scheler: Selected Philosophical Essays* trans. David R. Lachterman (Evanston, Ill., Northwestern University Press, 1973), pp. 110, 111.

[67]Burkert, *op. cit.,* p. 69.

[68]Scheler, "Ordo Amoris," in *op. cit.,* p. 111.

[69]See Martin Buber, *I and Thou* trans. Ronald Gregor Smith (Edinburgh, T. & T. Clark, 1937); Martin Buber, *Between Man and Man* trans. Ronald Gregor Smith (London, 1947).

[70]Saint John ch. 15, v. 13.

mentioned, and the use is so moral, important or pleasurable that the soul "loves" using it over and over, and so much so that the Love itself is loved. Ultimately, Love is not a subjective feeling a soul directs to an object, but, through the Love the soul emanates toward the object, Love itself is loved so that Love is beyond the separation of subject and object. This is the principle of Love (*Amor amatur*) set forth by Augustine.[71] It is pure essence and blessedness, a Divine substance and more than an "attribute" possessed by other substances. With itself, Love is beyond the separation of subject and object, as a soul with God is beyond such separation, but the Principle of Love does not depend upon the Principle of Identity; it is an independent "middle term" which may be substituted for the term "human soul" in the logical proposition that Aristotle set forth in the *Posterior Analytics*. Augustine said that Love is *so* Divine (that is, so much of a "middle term" we should use for the existence of God) we should seek nothing more. In *The Homily on the First Epistle of Saint John*, Augustine said:

> "Love one another . . . because Love is of God, and anyone who loves is born of God and knows God. Whoever does not love does not know God. Why? Because God is Love. What more can be said, my Brothers? If we did not find one word in praise of Love through all the pages of this epistle . . . and heard only this one word from the voice of the Spirit of God, *because 'God is Love,' we should seek nothing more.*"[72]

But does this reflect upon what life is "Really" like? Does Love have a basis in actual existence where space and time unravel in no way which can be presupposed? Do we get out of bed every morning presupposed to Love or to love Love? The truth is every morning is different. On some we have had spats with our lovers during the night before and the sexual content of our love has not been great; on others, quite the opposite. Are we *supposed* to Love regardless? Yes (and often do because of the moral imperative we have developed in our consciousness). Are we *predisposed* to? No. The psychological compulsions of our souls rule us too greatly. A psychological basis must be found to account for the meaning of Love in our lives. That basis is in Love itself. It is *eros*.

In lectures on the ostensible subject of religion she gave at the University of Edinburgh in 1982—the same series which psychologist William James had delivered 80 years before, the Irish-British critic and novelist, Iris Murdoch (1919 to 1999), restated the definition of *eros* to the meaning it had for the ancient Greeks. She said: "*Eros* is the continuous operation of spiritual *energy,* desire, intellect, love, as it moves among and responds to particular objects of attention, the force of magnetism and attraction which joins us to the world, making it a better or worse world . . ."[73] This is the definition of *eros* Plato used and applied to all natural and physical reality as it moved up from below to strive, to long for, to desire a better world. In the most natural forms of manifestation of physical reality *eros* is sex, but the movement *eros* described for the ancient Greeks is much more than sexual. *Eros* describes spiritual desire and, as

---

[71]Tillich, *op. cit.,* p. 116.

[72]Saint Augustine, "Homily on the First Epistle of Saint John, Treatise VII, No. 4," in *Augustine of Hippo: Selected Writings* (Clark ed., Ramsey, N. J., 1984), p. 302.

[73]Murdoch, *op. cit.,* p. 496.

the ancient Greeks believed, this desire is key to a soul. Desire ultimately accounts for the Truth of Love *insofar as Love really delivers truthfully or has the ability for truthful delivery.* Without *eros,* "you cannot speak of love toward God any more, because this is love toward that which is the highest power of being in which we are fulfilled."[74] *Eros* is key to the psychology upon which Love arises out of existence to give "Real" meaning to the words of Augustine. *Eros* is the Reality of Augustine's words as we get out of bed every morning.

Surely I am erotic in writing this and rhapsodizing. My *eros* is the driving force of my Belief in God. Because of my *eros,* I Believe. Insofar as any (or the) Ultimate Truth in *eros* may be sexual (as Sigmund Freud and many others have shown so well it is or might be), the Ultimate Truth of my Belief in God may also have a sexual foundation. It is typical of a Freudian analysis to say that the celibate English monk, Anselm of Canterbury (1033 to 1109), repressed his sexuality because of his celibacy but had to manifest it in other ways. The manifestations might be either morally negative or morally positive, but they had to occur in his life because sexuality is an Ultimate Truth of human existence, that is, *if sexuality really delivers truthfully or has the ability for truthful delivery.* In Anselm's case, a Freudian analysis would conclude he had repressed and redirected sex into morally positive erotic energy when he prayed a prayer of profound eroticism, in the sense of the ancient Greeks. The profoundly erotic prayer of Anselm is as follows:

> "I do not endeavor, O Lord, to penetrate Thy sublimity, for in no wise do I compare my understanding therewith; but I long to understand in some degree Thy truth, which my heart believes *and loves.* For I do not seek to understand that I may believe, *but I believe in order to understand."*[75]

In this most eloquent prayer Anselm followed the theology of Augustine and laid out *the* fit basis for a religious Belief in God: "I believe in order to understand;" in Latin, *Credo ut intelligam.* Anselm's basis for Belief, though I have approached it rationally in this discussion, is the opposite of a rationalist's basis to believe ("I understand therefore I believe") and does not depend upon the cognitive faculties of a soul at all, except as those become necessary as a matter of the knowledge of linguistics to hear Anselm's prayer or read these words. Anselm's basis for Belief is psychological: that "the fear of the Lord is the beginning of wisdom."[76] Knowledge by itself is "not intramental nor internal to experience."[77] Rather, our fundamental experience consists in being "an animal spirit" whose psychology is that foundation of everything we are. It is this spirit, one he said is native to animals, which the American philosopher and poet, George Santayana (1863 to 1952), held that we must contend with in order to know and *before* we know anything. The human spirit of mankind had a long and primitive existence over many, many thousands of years and, therefore, requires primitively that an object be firmly held (that is, believed) before the nature and

---

[74]Tillich, *op. cit.,* 115.

[75]Murdoch, *op. cit.,* p. 392.

[76]The Book of Proverbs ch. 9, v. 10.

[77]George Santayana, *Scepticism and Animal Faith,* ch. XVIII, "Knowledge Is Faith Mediated By Symbols," (New York, Dover Publications, 1923, 1955), pp. 171, 172.

characteristics of that object are discovered (known). It is easy to see why, then, the psychological basis of belief means that we would Believe in God in order to understand, and that our Belief depends upon the Erotic Love of Anselm's feelings—of our feelings—to strive for, to long for and to desire knowledge of objects of a better world, a higher wisdom, and a fascinating, majestic understanding of Real knowledge and apodictic Truth.

"I am come to send fire on the Earth," said Jesus of Nazareth, "and what will I, if it be already kindled?"[78] Erotic Love is the foundation of the basis of Belief in God by the fires of human life. That the foundation may be related by a Freudian analysis to sex does not at all debase it. Ultimately, when this relationship is reduced *essentially,* is sex so much a requirement inherent in the life of *eros* that chastity, indeed, means death? Here is one allegory from the early Islamic poet, Ibn Abi Hajala (b. A.D. 725):

"Sahid [our narrator] asks an Arab one day, 'What people are you from?' 'I am from the people among whom *one dies when one loves,*' responds the Arab. 'So you are from the tribe of Aszra?' adds Sahid. 'Yes, . . .' replies the Arab. 'So why do your people love in such a way?' Sahid then asks. 'Our women are beautiful and our young men are chaste,' responds the Arab."[79]

On the other hand, *existentially,* sex is certainly not an inherent requirement of *eros* if the remembrance of Real facts shows that "[w]e fly to the sensation of sex to avoid the [existential] passion of *eros.*"[80] The American psychologist, Rollo (Reese) May (1909 to 1994), analyzed the escape of many *homo sapiens* from *eros* into sex by postulating the anxiety-creating aspects of *eros* which cause flight from True erotic passion. May said:

"Sex is the handiest drug to blot out our awareness of *the anxiety-creating aspects* of *eros.* To accomplish this, we have had to define sex ever more narrowly: the more we became preoccupied with sex, the more truncated and shrunken became the human experience to which it referred. . . . [I]t is often argued that all our society needs is full freedom for the expression of *eros.* But what is revealed beneath the surface in our society, as shown not only in patients in therapy but in our literature and drama and even in the nature of our scientific research, is just the opposite. We are in a flight from *eros*—and we use sex as the vehicle for the flight."[81]

Why would we fly from *eros?* What is it about *eros* which creates anxiety? *Eros, at most turns of our existence,* involves the tragic. "'Our heart is too spacious,' said Pascal. Even if we should know that our actual ability to [L]ove is limited, at the same time we know and feel that this limit lies neither in the finite objects which are worthy of [L]ove nor in the essence of the act of love as such, but in our organization and the conditions it sets . . ."[82] The remembrance of Real facts shows that there is always the potential to destroy Love, and always the inevitability of separation between a lover and

---

[78]Saint Luke ch. 12, v. 49. The Revised Standard Version of *The Bible* (New York, American Bible Society, 1952) says: "I came to cast fire upon the earth and would that it were already kindled!"

[79]Ibn Abi Hajala, Diwān al-Sabāba (Collection of Amorous Tenderness), quoted in Arnaldez, *op. cit.,* p. 169.

[80]Rollo May, *Love and Will* (New York, W. W. Norton, 1969), p. 65.

[81]Ibid.

[82]Scheler, "Ordo Amoris," in *op. cit.,* p. 112.

the beloved. The English poet and playwright, William Shakespeare (if an actual person and not a pseudonym, 1564 to 1616), spoke of this inevitable separation and the implied tragedy of its consequences when his dramatic character, Romeo, spoke of Juliet in Love as follows:

> "O! she doth teach the torches to burn bright.
> It seems she hangs upon the cheek of night
> Like a rich jewel in an Ethiop's ear;
> *Beauty too rich for use, for [E]arth too dear!*"[83]

Is this another echo of a soul's psychological divorce from the physical world? Says Juliet, all because of Love, but to no one but herself, "Farewell! God knows when we shall meet again."[84] The fires of *eros* seem so well suited to express the spirituality, the God-ness, in and about our actual existence. Upon these fires alone—whether or not their flames are ultimately sexual, the combustible compulsions of anxiety, addiction and self-sacrifice, the profound spiritual desires of Anselm's prayer or any other passionate display—upon the fires of human life alone is existence burning away for us in the realm of space and clock-time.

---

[83]William Shakespeare, "Romeo and Juliet," Act I, Scene V, Lines 44-47.
[84]*Ibid.*, Act IV, Scene III, Line 14.

Chapter Four: Jesus the Christ

In the clock-time—in Greek this word is *chronos*—when this is written, there are scientifically valid conclusions that the Universe is 15.5 *billion* years old and has 100-plus *billion* stars, and that the Earth is 4.5 billion years old and supports the physical existence of six *billion* types of the species *homo sapiens* divided politically into 187 different national subdivisions.[1] These appear to be marvelously objective and factual propositions. But in clock-time, the truth of them is only true because of the truth of the scientific propositions on which they are based, and not because they are statements of the Truth. In fact, because of the enormous distances light travels across the Universe, the truth of the stars we are assessing *insofar as light really delivers truth or has the ability for truthful delivery* occurred 15.5 billion years ago and to make a True assessment of them now, at this point in clock-time, may require us to wait as long as another 15.5 billion years. In fact, because of the enormous difficulty of trekking across mountains and jungles and city slums, the truth of the census we are assessing *insofar as census-gathering techniques really deliver truth or have the ability for truthful delivery* occurred in the office of a rumpled statistician calculating probabilities and to make a True count of the population of the Earth now, at this moment of clock-time, would require thousands of census-takers searching the remote corners of the globe and distinguishing precisely babies from fetuses and comatose patients from dead ones, all for the sake of being "really" Truthful. The flow of clock-time means the entirely conceived wholeness of any present moment, but this moment means, even for science, that appearances and apperceptions are, in several cases, deemed to be perceptions and Reality.

In the clock-time when this is written, there are no scientifically valid conclusions that God exists, but there are no such conclusions which deny it either. Theists and Atheists alike agree on this. This proposition has been true—so far—for all of clock-time *insofar as science really delivers truth or has the ability for truthful delivery* except for one period of thirty-three years. This is the clock-time when Jesus of Nazareth (B.C. 4? to A.D. 30?) lived. Christians say God existed during his lifetime because God existed in Jesus, and it is possible to be valid about this because Jesus was an individual *homo sapiens* and his existence can be scientifically validated in biology. Does that mean biology has also validated the existence of God? Perhaps some peculiarity in clock-time has meant for biological science during the period of these thirty-three years that there is an exceptional case and appearances and apperceptions of God are deemed to be perceptions and Reality. We have shown by examples from astronomy, biology and political economy in the previous discussion how Reality even in science may be nothing but appearance. Is there a logic from existence to show God existed in Jesus?

---

[1] *The World Almanac and Book of Facts 1998* (Mahwah, N. J., 1997), pp. 838, 839.

Or is this immanence of God in Jesus a variety of magic or of the politics of the Council of Nicaea? What happened?

The weak link in the otherwise sound proposition of the Christians is whether God existed in Jesus of Nazareth. First, what did Jesus himself think? He was chary of claiming a Divine mission. He spent the first thirty of his thirty-three years of life mostly avoiding missions altogether. Finally, at age thirty, being "[a] man of intense piety and reverence for the religion of his race [Judaism], he insisted that his business was to preach the Kingdom of God."[2] The prophetic tradition of Judaism had expected Messianic deliverance of the Jewish people to the Kingdom of God, and Jesus was well aware of this expectation.[3] But he continued to identify himself as the Son of Man, an ambiguous description which could mean either the Jewish Messiah or a human being. In the Book of Daniel, the angel, Gabriel, spoke to the prophet Daniel, clearly a human being, and said, "Understand, O Son of Man, that the vision is for the time of the end."[4] During his early mission, Jesus said that he came not to bring peace but with a sword, not to abolish the law of Judaism and but to keep the last iota of it "until all is accomplished," and forbade his disciples to preach to the Gentiles.[5] Gradually, Jesus came to believe that his mission had changed from being a political Messiah to being the herald of the Kingdom of God on this Earth. At Cæsarea Philippi, he polled his disciples about his identity and heard at least five different answers.[6] The disciple, Peter, answered that Jesus was the Christ, the Blessèd One in Greek.[7] Jesus accepted Peter's answer readily, told his disciples to tell no one and began a reoriented, explicitly Divine, mission. The new mission of Jesus was to herald the Kingdom of God, nothing more, and it brought him into complete and unremitting conflict with the religious establishment of Judaism. When the Pharisees of this religious establishment asked Jesus to rebuke his disciples who were proclaiming him the Christ, Jesus refused and said, "I tell you, if these were silent, the very stones would cry out."[8] Later, the Sanhedrin, the supreme council of the Jewish religious establishment, tried Jesus on the basis of his claimed Divine identity. At his trial, Jesus initially refused to answer the questions which the high priest of Judaism put to him concerning these claims, but then, under oath, he answered directly and firmly acknowledged to the high priest that he was the Christ, the Son of God. Accordingly, the high priest tore his garment, as required by Jewish law, to express horror, from the perspective of the Jewish religious establishment, at the blasphemy of Jesus about his Divine identity and claims. Without a dissenting voice, the Sanhedrin voted to transfer Jesus to Roman civil authorities for the purpose of being put to death. We see, then, that Jesus acknowledged Divinity completely and firmly, but his method of acknowledgment was gradual, political and human. The German-Gabonese theologian and missionary, Albert Schweitzer (1875 to

---

[2]Herschel Baker, *The Image of Man* (New York, Harper & Row, 1947), p. 125.
[3]Saint Mark ch. 9, vv. 2-7; Saint Luke ch. 10, vv. 23, 24; Saint Matthew ch. 7, v. 21.
[4]The Book of Daniel ch. 8, v. 17.
[5]Saint Matthew ch. 5, v. 17; ch. 10, vv. 5, 34.
[6]*Ibid.*, ch. 16, v. 13.
[7]Saint Mark ch. 8, v. 27; compare Saint Matthew ch. 16, vv. 16-19, a recitation of events which may be embellished by the need of the Christian Catholic Church to be mentioned in the Gospels.
[8]Saint Luke ch. 19, vv. 39, 40.

1965), supposed that Jesus believed in Daniel's apocalyptic vision and, when that vision failed, brought about the end anyway through his own suffering and death.[9]

Disciplines of thinking which think God existed in Jesus are called, by nomenclature of a traditional sort, a branch of theology called Christology, and a branch of the philosophy of religion called the Metaphysics of Ontology. The former is the interpretation of the person and work of Jesus to search out the essence of Jesus; the latter is the formal study of the nature of a Being and searches out the essence of Jesus, too, but with existential possibilities. As we have distinguished from the beginning, the philosophy of essence and the philosophy of existence approach Truth differently — except as Tillich and others see that existentialism is lacking content and is therefore linked in a pun to essences essentially. The differences between these two philosophical approaches manifest themselves in thinking about Jesus one way or another for 2,000 years — ever since Jesus lived and well before existentialism was a word in any language. Jesus spoke in words which seem to encourage these philosophical differences for he wrote not one word we know of; he spoke. His spoken words set forth many examples of Truth from paradox — at least if we think we are thinking about them Truly. His words show Jesus was concerned with the contradictory nature of a Belief in God, and with the contradictions inherent in human life. His concern was akin in many cases, not to analytic complexity of a sort we waded through at the beginning of this discussion, *but to the feeling of it — as it is felt and thought by homo sapiens* after 100,000 years of living with a fully developed cerebral cortex. For example, Jesus said he was "the way, the truth and the life," but he also said, "unless a grain of wheat falls to the Earth and dies, it remains alone (remember the incomplete truth of solipsism?); but if it dies, it bears much fruit. He who loves his life loses it, and he who hates his life in this world will keep it for eternal life."[10] We see the former statement of Jesus is a basic proposition of any religion, even a godless one, such as Zarathustra's; but the latter statement puts the emotional satisfaction of possessing an abundance of fruit together with the emotional loneliness and death of a seed, empty death with plentiful life, hate with love and the nature of Earth with eternity. If God existed in Jesus, He existed in hearing many contradictory juxtapositions full of different psychological "states of affairs" whose meaning Jesus "taught."

Sometimes a reader of the New Testament feels it is the exposition of the contradictions alone which concern Jesus, nothing more. To me, these expositions of Jesus *in his own words, not in the words of others,* do not show the Truth of the perfection of God; they show Truth from existence only, but by showing it so Truly we can Believe in Jesus the Christ in order to begin to understand both existence and the revelation of our Belief. For example, as Jesus sat at a table in the house of a leper, a woman, often thought to be Mary Magdalene, cracked a jar of very expensive ointment, used to balm cadavers, and wasted it by pouring it all out on top of Jesus's head, though he was still very much alive. The practical disciples of Jesus reproached the woman greatly for this waste, if only because the cost of the ointment, a huge sum of three hundred denarii, could have been spent on charity for the poor. But Jesus defended the woman and said it should be told wherever his message is spread throughout the world

---

[9] See Albert Schweitzer, *The Quest of the Historical Jesus* (1st English ed., London, 1910).
[10] Saint John ch. 14, v. 6; ch. 12, vv. 24, 25.

what the woman had done for two reasons: first, she had, in a symbolic way, anointed his body for burying before it would be buried actually; and second, she, not Jesus, should be always remembered for it. Jesus then predicated both an entirely symbolic act and the everlasting remembrance of the human symbolizer upon the fact of his own uniqueness. He said, "you always have the poor with you . . . but you will not always have me."[11] Jesus therefore asserted the following existential Truths: his physical death, solipsism about himself in the fact of his uniqueness in actual life, and, because of these first two, the surmounting of the social order of civilization. A female *homo sapiens* of a lower (two millennia ago) cultural order wasted a resource of a religious rite of a much higher one, consisting of male priests and relating to the proper burial of the dead. Jesus asserted the existential Truth of surmounting this social order by commending the woman for a wasteful act which the order of society otherwise proscribed. By Believing in these existential Truths, we can begin to understand why symbolic acts of no pragmatic meaning except for their symbolism, and the everlasting memory of a symbolizer performing them *in these circumstances,* should outweigh any of the alternatives. This is the path to a Belief in God taken by Augustine and Anselm; it is The Way to begin to understand the Truth of a useless waste of ointment upon the top of Jesus's head and, in other contexts, the useless anointment of an upright stone by Jacob to mark a sacred place between Beersheba and Haran which he called "the House of Beth-El,"[12] as well as the confusing, often arbitrary, boundaries of The Way itself, and the need for a supervision of these boundaries by setting their signs carefully. If God were perfect, would there be any need for the waste of an ointment, the careful marking of the boundary of The Way, or the creation of the sacred? In the house of a leper sitting at a table and drenched with funeral ointment, Jesus seems to be saying, if we interpret his meaning "correctly," that his words are his meanings of The Way in *this* situation, as the Truth of *this* experience, even if the imperfection of solipsism is the only "perfection" which can be shown by it, because solipsism is counterbalanced in *this* situation by the posit of an everlasting memory for another, who is the human other who caused such waste and uselessness otherwise. Thus Jesus shows the Truth of the experience so Truly that we Believe in His Truth after He speaks it and can begin to understand it. Do you remember a Latin aphorism? It is: *Credo ut intelligam.*

An apologist defending Jesus, especially the solipsism of his justification of the waste of an ointment worth three hundred denarii, might say that this exposition is a matter of catharsis in some Ultimate sense about the feelings of mankind being faced, often brutally, with the contradictions in life on this Earth. For example, why is something good wasted when evil seems not to be? This issue and other contradictions of life are *absolutely* frustrating and need *an absolute purging* from the unhealthy bile they cause inside of us. An apologist defending the Truth-value of the spoken words of Jesus might say they are a matter of paradox in some Ultimate sense so that all of the contradictions of life can be placed upon the same landscape—the same *cosmos*—and be drawn, defined, delineated and marked with boundary stones. For example, why are the values of Reality hidden when the worth of the ointment is so apparent? The Roman

---

[11]Saint Mark ch. 14, vv. 3-9.

[12]Book of Genesis ch. 28, vv. 18, 19; see Burkert, *op. cit.,* p. 165 (Chapter Two, footnote 32).

god, Terminus, was specially and only dedicated to the supervision of boundaries; the Romans presumed imaginary lines on the face of the Earth were important enough to require the power and supervision of a spirit. The contradictions of which Jesus spoke, by analogy from physical geography to the world of the spirit, require similar, and result in the same, presumptions about the need for spiritual supervision which the Romans made for geography by deifying Terminus. A cynic might say, then, that Jesus spoke contradictions to indulge in Roman or Jewish presumptions about Divinity and reap the consequences of it Divinely. A cynic might say Jesus knew the posit of an Absolute Surveyor would be required to determine the value of his contradictions if their truths were Ultimately relative, or existential; and that an Absolute Sign would be required to say likewise if the truths from his contradictions were Ultimately essential, that is, independent of any other relation of existence. Jesus was savvy: He could not have failed to intuit the need for supervision that his contradictions required, and that this supervision by its nature crossed boundaries, such as the River Styx of Greek mythology, which only an Absolute absolutely crosses.

But Jesus was humble. The humility of Jesus resolves sublimely the vexing, but long-standing, paradox of our consciousness. This paradox is that we know we are in the physical world but are set apart from it. When its cerebral cortex fully developed about 100,000 years ago, a human soul became conscious of its own existence; man became an object of his own perception in his mind; and the soul craved knowledge of its consciousness as it did of other objects. This knowledge—the knowledge that a soul could be conscious of states of consciousness and validate them according to some hierarchy of moral values—was the fruit of the tree of knowledge which Eve craved when she ate an apple of it in the Garden of Eden.[13] We have seen already the Pandora's box of psychological problems created after she did so; morality is not something any other creature but *homo sapiens* contends with. But the process of mental perception by mankind continued. Physical lines and marks of human perception began in actual life when *homo sapiens* began to depict art on the walls of caves 40,000 years ago. Mankind survived and thrived because of art—the Neanderthals had no art and became extinct— for art meant Man himself could become, in the world, an object of his own perception. Religion means this also. Jesus intuited the fundamental problem of any Truth at all coming from an observer, observing himself within his own observation, is a lack of perspective, a lack of humility and an insufficiency of value. This is how the humility of Jesus becomes Divine: it allowed Jesus to obtain sufficient value, adequate perspective, and clear Truth. He relinquished his own life, he said, so that we may see how to live ours; the result from his sacrifice is fundamentally True for *our own* existence since the perception we crave for it may not be Really True without some fixed point of reference. We certainly cannot provide it for ourselves and still live. Jesus was humble enough to do so. Furthermore, the feelings of mankind, faced with these contradictions of myopia about the proper distance to put the soul apart from actual life so as to see it properly in focus, require tending by Jesus as *Terminus* supervising the boundaries of a soul and of the Kingdom of God. Or, to continue with the analogy of the metaphor, they require purging by Jesus completely so that there is a whole new landscape, a whole new Kingdom where God draws boundaries more effectively, better

---

[13] Book of Genesis ch. 3, vv. 1-7.

than Roman Terminus, anyone else, or anything which has ever been drawn before or since.

Two millennia of since-ness cloud to a distance a perception of the Reality of Jesus the Christ. In the meanwhile, Einstein has shown that, for everything physical, the temporal relation between two physical events—for example, the events of the life of Jesus and of ours today—is Truly determined in relation to the motion of the observer of these events. This scientific observation, profound though it is, fails to define who is a proper observer to insert into it to prove the Truth of these relations, or to show, if the observer within this observation is my soul, how it could move fast enough to make an event of two millennia ago into indubitable Reality. Perhaps, a reliance by an analogy to Gödel's theorem would be better: the analogy is that the Reality of Jesus the Christ may not be proven but He is nevertheless True. Analogies from mathematics to the rest of life are intuitively imperfect: signs in mathematics are logical; signs in language and the rest of life are subject to no straightforward theory of their meaning. Yet, it is worth saying again that Gödel's theorem allows for Truth without the axiomatic proof of it. For the last two centuries, the age of great doubts about God because of scientific analysis, time's clouding of the Reality of Jesus has been compounded by the empiricism of historians that various messages contained in the New Testament are not authentic in fact.[14] For reasons which I elaborate throughout the rest of this Chapter, "[i]t is a curious delusion that the rock upon which our [B]eliefs can be founded [or not] is an historical investigation."[15] Moreover, it is only a matter of degree, and not of quality, the extent to which a lack of authenticity in the New Testament further impedes Belief. The analytic meanings of the Truth of Jesus do not depend upon special historical facts; they depend only upon the twin facts of Jesus's life and crucifixion, as well as upon analytic meanings from these events and, crucially, the Truth of human history over thousands and thousands of years. Some of this interconnected web of existence you have previously read in this discussion. Jesus is a primary reason why it may be deified, elevated to Divinity, and not referred to simply as the Glory of the world or the Synchro-meshed Processes of Life. Jesus's life is thus a crucial part of the religious content of a Theist-empiricist. This life provides a basis upon which to deify what and whatever the Principles of Identity and of Love may have failed to so far.

A-ha! You contend you catch me finally in making magic and pulling the Divine Reality of Jesus out of words cast in black ink or puffs of air. Then, if this is so, do you disavow the connections between "Good Tricks," over-riding human psychological "states of affairs," and the spoken words and crucifixion of Jesus? This web of connections, into which I hope this discussion has already entangled you, must be for you to read in works of other authors regarding the spoken words of Jesus, but this web is both the transcendence of Jesus over time *and His Holy Spirit*. Paul the Apostle said,

---

[14] See Gotthold Ephraim Lessing, *The Aims of Jesus and His Disciples A further Installment of the . . . Wolfenbüttel Fragments* [of Hermann Samuel Reimarus] (Brunswick, 1778); cf. *The Object of Jesus and His Disciples* (Voysey ed., printed in English, 1879); David Friedrich Strauss, *The Life of Jesus Critically Examined* (1835) trans. George Eliot (London, 1846); Albert Schweitzer, *The Quest of the Historical Jesus* trans. W. Montgomery (1st English ed., London, 1910); Rudolf Bultmann, *Kerygma and Myth,* Vol. I trans. Reginald Fuller (Hartsch ed., London, 1954).

[15] Alfred North Whitehead, *Religion in the Making* (1926) (New York, Meridian Books: Living Age Books, 1st printing, 1960), p. 82.

"I want you to understand that no one speaking by the Spirit of God ever says 'Jesus be cursed!' and no one can say 'Jesus is Lord' except by the Holy Spirit."[16] What is the transcendence of Jesus over time *and His Holy Spirit?* Are these more fancy words? To transcend means to rise above or to go beyond the limits of something limited. An actual physical transcendence occurs each time an organ is transplanted from one human body to another. The organ is taken beyond the limits of a given body about which that body intended for it to function. It is even easier for a spirit, not so bodily limited, to transcend. If a mundane boundary stone can be marked with Holiness, it follows that spirit which so undeniably exists within us can be marked likewise. Augustine directed me to go inside my soul and then transcend it. When I do so, I find an immutable ground of "being-ness" *which depends upon that which does not exist.* This is the Holy Spirit of Jesus.

The rest of this Chapter discusses, in two ways, the transcendence of my soul over the world and the transcendence of Jesus the Christ over both the world and my soul within it. The first way is a method of transcendence from the philosophy of essence. This philosophy is exemplified by thoughts from thinkers in a school known as American Transcendentalism, propounded mostly by intellectuals in mid-19th century New England, such as the American essayist and poet, Ralph Waldo Emerson (1803 to 1882). Emerson published a small volume entitled *Nature* in 1836. This book was a harbinger of further written and spoken works of intellect which created a systemic perspective on the world. The second way is a method of transcendence from the philosophy of existence. For example, the Danish theologian, Søren Aabye Kierkegaard (1813 to 1855), propounded an existentialist's philosophy of Jesus in Denmark about the same time as the American Transcendentalists were speaking and writing, but Kierkegaard's writings were discovered in the English-speaking world only after 1937.[17] New England's 19th-century Transcendentalism depends upon the *Logos* or the Word; the existential Christian philosophy of Kierkegaard depends upon objective uncertainty and faith. Both deal with the transcending Reality of Jesus the Christ, His Holy Spirit and the lack of authenticity in the New Testament. To me, the latter philosophy of existentialism is more effective in establishing the foundation of my Belief than the former philosophy of essential transcendence, but both show Jesus the Christ is a Reality after two millennia. Both show that a Belief in God deals completely with any concern about the authenticity of the Bible or the historical life of Jesus. The rest of this Chapter discusses some of the Belief in God of the American Transcendentalists, and then, some of the Belief of Kierkegaard and the Christian existentialist thinking which followed him.

Transcending the New Testament to Higher Truth

On July 15, 1838, Emerson delivered the "Divinity School Address" at Harvard University. In the crucial passage of the address, Emerson said Christ spoke of a "Miracle" being in man's life and in man's activities and that this was a "daily Miracle" which was quite different from the "Miracle" which Christian churches were

---

[16]Saint Paul, First Letter to the Corinthians ch. 12, v. 3.

[17]Louis Untermeyer, *Makers of the Modern World* (3rd printing, New York, Simon & Schuster, 1955, 1966), p. 7.

expounding in New England. For this reason, Emerson denounced the "Miracle" of the churches as a "Monster" because it was "not one with the blowing clover or the falling rain."[18] The religious establishment of New England heard Emerson's denunciation and was predictably shocked. Blowing clover and falling rain are very nice; but hardly Divine concepts to be elevated into Ultimate Truth. Yet, to the contrary, Emerson thought Nature and consciousness were parts of fundamental Reality. He said: "Every natural fact is an emanation, and that from which it emanates is an emanation also, and from every emanation is a new emanation. . . . Nature can only be conceived as existing to a universal and not to a particular end; to a universe of ends, and not to one—a work of *ecstasy,* to be represented by a circular movement, . . ."[19] In these premises, Emerson conceived of Nature as an Ultimate Truth and described it in terms of the same circle which describes the infinite. Because of his (monist) theory that all the world is but one substance, and that this single substance consists of emanations from, and to, all forms of matter, such that they go from below-ness to higher states and *vice versa,* Emerson declared that "a man is a god in ruins." The American philosopher and naturalist, Henry David Thoreau (1817 to 1862), described the processes of nature in terms of the same Ultimate fulfillment as follows:

"There is no ripeness which is not, so to speak, something ultimate in itself, and not merely a perfected means to a higher end. In order to be ripe it must serve a transcendent use. The ripeness of a leaf, being perfected, leaves the tree at that point and never returns to it."[20]

What is the nature of Christianity? What is ripe in Christianity and therefore worthy of Belief? On May 19, 1841, the American Unitarian minister, Theodore Parker (1810 to 1860), delivered a sermon of Transcendentalist thinking entitled *"A Discourse on the Transient and Permanent in Christianity."* He brought to a climax Transcendentalist thinking about the historical authenticity of the Miracle of Christ and, in doing so, caused a riotous commotion among the population of Boston, Massachusetts. Parker took as the text for his sermon the words of Jesus from the Gospel According to Saint Luke as follows: "Heaven and earth will pass away but my words will not pass away."[21] He used this text as the basis upon which to distinguish Christianity distinctly into two parts: the transient and the permanent. About the former element he said, "[i]t must be confessed, though with sorrow, that transient things form a great part of what is taught as religion," and asserted Christian theology is inconsistent, superfluous and, yes, misleading. The following is a quotation typical of Parker's assertiveness:

"Men have been bid to close their eyes at the obvious difference between Luke and John, the serious disagreement between Paul and Peter; to believe, on the smallest evidence, accounts which shock the moral sense and revolt the reason, . . . Men have been told that all these things must be taken as part of

---

[18]Ralph Waldo Emerson, "The Divinity School Address" (1838) quoted in Perry Miller, "Religious Radicalism," in *The American Transcendentalists: Their Prose and Poetry* (P. Miller ed., Garden City, N. Y., Doubleday: Anchor Books, 1957), ch. 3, p. 104 at 105.

[19]Emerson, "The Method of Nature" (1841) in *ibid.,* ch. 2, "Naturalism," pp. 54, 55.

[20]Perry Miller, "Foreword to *Ibid.*," p. xi.

[21]Saint Luke ch. 21, v. 33 (italics added).

Christianity, and if they accepted the religion, they must take all these accessories along with it; *that the living spirit could not be had without the killing letter.* All the books which caprice or accident had brought together between the lids of the Bible were declared to be the infallible word of God, the only certain rule of religious faith and practice. . . . To disbelieve any of its statements, or even the common interpretation put upon those statements by the particular age or church in which the man belonged, was held to be infidelity, if not atheism."[22]

Parker asserted that "[t]he heresy of one age is the orthodox belief and 'only infallible rule' of the next, [that] current notions respecting the infallible interpretation of the Bible have no foundation in the Bible itself," and "[i]t is hard to see why the great [T]ruths of Christianity rest on the personal authority of Jesus," and not on "the truth of his words."[23] On the one hand, Parker admitted that nothing seems more fleeting than a word—"it is an evanescent impulse of the most fickle element." On the other hand, he believed that the words of Jesus, despite their inherently weak character as phenomena of nature, are resounding Truths which have echoed through the ages, have entered into our innermost minds and hearts and will be True for us eternally. Parker found the permanent element of Christianity derived from several elements: "the true system of nature," "the divine life of the soul, love to God, and love to man," and "the Word."[24]

In Greek, the word for "word" or "reason" is *logos*. *Logos,* according to Tillich, is difficult theology for a scientific mind to understand because it is a universal principle: the principle of the self-manifestation of God; that is to say, God manifest to Himself in Himself. Ouch! Unless X has an obscure or empty meaning in the first place, why should X *be required* to show itself further? But the orthodox Christians of the first centuries of Christianity knew God had plenty of meaning; what they didn't know was how to accommodate two Gods—Jesus the Christ and God the Father—in the same monotheistic religion. A brain under PET scanning does not bifurcate naturally because of intellectual concepts; the soul conceived of by Parker and the Christian tradition does not bifurcate naturally either. Why, then, would there be any natural basis in religion upon which to bifurcate God? Early Christianity emphasized the individual souls of each specimen of *homo sapiens* and required commitment to God, to a moral life, and to personal holiness beyond the rituals and half-hearted commitments of pagans to polytheism. Consequently, the early Christian Believer, Justin (the) Martyr (A.D. 100? to 165), spoke for the subsequent two millennia of orthodox Christianity when he avoided polytheism and said, "[t]he *Logos* is different from God according to number, but not according to concept."[25] *Logos* is not "the" God; *Logos* is one and the same with God essentially. In other words, to escape from their predicament in facing two Gods, early Christians invented Sticky Glue. The Glue would adhere to both God the Father and God the Son and bind them together. "Therefore," says Tillich, "whenever God

---

[22]Theodore Parker, "A Discourse on the Transient and Permanent in Christianity" (1841) in *The American Transcendentalists: Their Prose and Poetry* (P. Miller ed., Garden City, N. Y., Doubleday: Anchor Books, 1957), p. 106 at pp. 111, 118.

[23]*Ibid.,* pp. 107, 114, 119, 120.

[24]*Ibid.,* pp. 111, 112, 128.

[25]Tillich, *op. cit.,* p. 30.

appears, either to himself or to others outside himself, it is the Logos which appears. This *Logos* is in Jesus as the Christ in a unique way. And this . . . is the greatness of Christianity and the basis of its claim about salvation. For if the divine *Logos* in its fullness had not appeared in Jesus as the Christ, no salvation would be possible. *This is an argument from existence, not from speculation.* This means that the classical theologians start from the experience of salvation, and then proceed to speak of Jesus as the Christ in terms of the *Logos.*"[26] Accordingly, Tillich sets out one portion of the extensive doctrine of *Logos* in orthodox Christianity, says it is an argument from experience, but does not say why we should believe in *any* argument, let alone this one which is sticky, rather than experience. Does *my* experience show the experience of any such a concept? But I do believe in the propositions you are reading. To the extent they show the argument for *Logos, Logos* is part of my Belief. Do they show it? Yes, to the extent that *Logos* relates to the permanent Truth of Jesus. To me *Logos* is a road with many twists and turns to arrive at the experience of Jesus and His Truth.

Theodore Parker, a master of twenty languages, never used the word, *Logos,* in his famous sermon of 1841 on the permanent element he defined for Christianity. Instead, he used the word "Word" as a shorthand expression of the eternal Truth of God. But just what is included in permanence or eternity? Parker said that the permanent elements of Christianity which would transcend the ages are the "true system of nature," "the divine life of the soul," Love and the Word. We have already discussed the Principle of Identity as "a divine life of the soul" and the Principle of Love as Love, but what is the "Word" or a "True system of nature" and the rest of these transcending concepts exactly? Paul the Apostle wrote to the Romans as follows: "Do not be conformed to this eon (the world) *but be transformed by the renewal of your mind,* that you may prove what is the will of God, what is good and acceptable and perfect."[27] If my transformation by the renewal of my mind is part of God's Word, and this Word transcends my existence such that it is part of the Absolute and Ultimate meaningfulness of it, not only does the Word include the Truth of Jesus and all of the Truths about which Jesus spoke, but it also includes a direction from Paul for my self-transformation. But the transformation of my mind from G *(Gestalt)* to H (Hallucinogenic) necessarily implies the transcendence of H over G, of my mind today over my mind yesterday, because my mind in changing to another mind must surpass those qualities of mind-ness which it had before. This latter, *human and psychic* transcendence within the Word means that at least one part of the Word is never static, but always changing as I renew mentally. But what does the word "renewal" Really mean? Does it mean change or the *status quo* recast? Is a transformation a process of substance or only a process of form? Literally, the word "transformation" contains the word "form" within it, but the logical form of Reality seems to control the substance of Reality in *my* world. This is so because I chose to start this discussion *by the form* of the Reality of Science, though I could have chosen to do so *from the form* of the Reality of Subjectivity, but I did not do so because the former rather than the latter seemed to me to be a more plausible point of beginning. For a transformation to mean more than a Scholastic puff of air it must mean something of substance in actual experience. The experience of my consciousness shows that, when

---

[26] Tillich, *ibid.,* p. 30 (italics added).

[27] Saint Paul, *Letter to the Romans* ch. 12 v. 2.

my mind transforms, it transcends itself in becoming another state of consciousness, though its "being" as a mind (however you define a "being") remains the same.

This conclusion is the *result* of empirical thinking about my consciousness, not a presupposition about it or the start of a further one, though cognitive psychology may never show it as a "fact," and *Gestalt* psychology may only theorize about it—as that special *Gestalt* pattern of transcendence I show as I live—and try to treat of it, or not, in *Gestalt* therapy. Thus, in such a therapy, do I define the basic function of Muslims praying five times daily, of Jews keeping the Sabbath holy, and of Christians assembling the congregation of their communities each Sunday morning. This psychology of *Gestalten* about the patterns and forms of existence in my consciousness—specifically, in this case, whether a renewal of my mind is or can be in any way a transcendence of Reality—shows that I must foreswear from the position of Kant about what is in the content of transcendence. Kant distinguished between the *constitutive* and the *regulative* employment of transcendental ideas, held that transcendental ideas, properly considered in the light of pure reason, never allow of any constitutive *employment* and said:

> "When regarded in that mistaken manner, and therefore as supplying concepts of certain objects, they are but pseudo-rational, merely dialectical concepts. On the other hand, they have an excellent, and indeed indispensably necessary, regulative employment, namely that of directing the understanding towards a certain goal upon which the routes marked out by all its rules converge, as upon their point of intersection. This point is a mere idea, *a focus imaginarius, from which since it lies quite outside the bounds of possible experience* (italics added), the concepts of the understanding do not in reality proceed."[28]

But my mind is well within the bounds of my experience, such that if my consciousness passes over itself from one state to another, with lingering manifestations of the former always unconsciously impinging upon the latter, and *vice versa*—to the extent in time my conscious states do reverse back in history—it is clear to me that this act of surpassing is a valiant change, worthy of more description than the arid convergence in my imagination which Kant gave it. For Kant an object is Ultimately objective. (This Ultimate-ness is the beginning of his path toward a Belief in God.) He does not admit of the overwhelming feeling-ness of the Reality of Subjectivity or how well objects fit within it. But is "the renewal of my mind" confined only to the Cartesian realm of "clear and distinct ideas" about how such a renewal occurs? Did Paul the Apostle even mean to confine it so? Even under that restriction, regardless of whether Kant's definition of transcendence fits within such a Cartesian realm, there is a contradiction between the innateness of transcending H and the process by which Kant describes that H transcends. For, even in hallucination, where there are no Real objects, there is always the objective process of psychology. Because of this process, we say a mind is hallucinogenic though, at some point of its mental life before, it had been in a G state of consciousness. This saying, and the manner of it, easily generate psychological ideas and concepts, things-in-themselves of psychology, which, if they

---

[28]Immanuel Kant, *Critique of Pure Reason* trans. Norman Kemp Smith (New York, Macmillan, 1961), p. 533.

fail to relate to transcendence, fail to relate to the Reality of how I think about them for science and for my mind. (To refresh your memory of my approach to thinking, you may choose to re-read the basis for this discussion in quasi-Realism which I set forth in the Foreword.)

If, therefore, by any of the foregoing analysis of transcendence and my briefest critique of Kant's definition of it, there is an incorporation within the Word of God, as Parker preached it, the self-transformation of my mind as Paul the Apostle declared it to the Romans, then there is a conflict between the innate and eternal characteristics of the Word and what I think, for I know there is little which is of eternity or innateness within my thinking. On the other hand, the Scholasticism of Christian theology, by defining the Word Ultimately in any way that Scholastics wish to do so, even if their definitions comport with an un-Real but beatific vision of existence, may elevate the mundane Reality of human mental self-transformations into the realm of these eternal and innate characteristics of permanent Truth. If so, it is surely an elevation of wondrous proportion to me but, since I discern that it is only Scholastic, I assume this part of the Word of God is a puff of air. If not, then we must ask: how are things permanent and immutable, namely the eternal Truths of our Savior and our Lord, ever subject to the possibility of a large reduction as my mind renews each time I wake up in the morning? Or, is the permanent element of the Word of Christianity to be confined to what Jesus actually said? Since Jesus did not palpably say what Paul wrote in his letter to the Romans and, indeed, since Jesus and Paul never met in (physical) life at all, then the Word may simply transgress the Pauline epistles, or some of them, though these epistles shaped Christianity most substantially, at least in West Europe. On the other hand, if we take this literal approach to the Word of God, existing scholarship shows that perhaps only twenty percent of the language which the New Testament attributed to Jesus did Jesus actually say.[29] It is clear, therefore, that the Word is a concept which is related to a function of time, being revised in time, though how often it is not for me to say here.

The English-American philosopher and mathematician, Alfred North Whitehead (1861 to 1947), considered the effect of the passage of time upon any sort of metaphysical Reality which a religious Belief adheres to. Whitehead said:

> "It is a curious delusion that the rock upon which our [B]eliefs can be founded is an historical investigation. You can *only* interpret the past in terms of the present. *The present is all that you have;* and unless in this present you can find general principles which interpret the present as including the whole community of existents, you cannot move a step beyond your little patch of immediacy. Thus history *presupposes a metaphysic*. It can be objected that we believe in the past and talk about it without settling our metaphysical principles. That is certainly the case. But you can only deduce metaphysical dogmas from your interpretation of the past on the basis of your prior metaphysical interpretation of the present. In so far as your metaphysical [B]eliefs are implicit, you vaguely interpret the past on the lines of the present.

---

[29]Charlotte Allen, *The Human Christ: The Search for the Historical Jesus* (New York, The Free Press, 1998), pp. 79, 276; see Robert W. Funk, Roy W. Hoover *et al.*, *The Five Gospels: The Search for the Authentic Words of Jesus* (New York, Macmillan, 1993).

But when it comes to the *primary* metaphysical data, the world of which you are immediately conscious is the *whole* datum."[30]

By their possession of the entirely conceived wholeness of any present moment, as Whitehead thus conceived of it, subsequent Scholastic minds—at various, immediate moments of their subsequent-ness—spoke, wrote and thought by Whitehead's analysis of their thinking exactly, even to the extent of literally mis-reading or ignoring the actual words (ostensibly the Word) used by previous ones to explain Christ. The most starkly drawn and notable case is the gloss of the Catholic Church upon the words used by the early Christian theologian, Hilary of Poitiers (A.D. c. 315 to 367), to ordain the Word explaining the suffering which Jesus actually felt at His crucifixion.[31] In 1851, Pope Pius IX (1792 to 1878) ordained Hilary as a Doctor of the Catholic Church although Hilary said that, because of being born of a virgin, Jesus had a medically special body which allowed Him to suffer in one type of suffering on the cross but not to suffer otherwise. Subsequent Scholastics affirmed the membership of Jesus in the human race but ignored the obvious point that Hilary's concept of Jesus's medically special body had no empirically human characteristics. The conclusion that the Word is an unlimited concept of usefulness to transcend Reality with content, as well as with form, is, therefore, a mere dialectical concept full of false rationality, as Kant said. The Truth of a transcending content must be eternally True—to use the Latin phrase, *sub species æternitatis*. Only this type of content (Does 5,000-year-old Truth suffice?) is a worthy transcendental idea. Empiricism shows that psychology qualifies to provide this degree of Truth for the Word; it also shows that the thinking of Hilary of Poitiers misses the mark.

Protestant Christianity in the United States traditionally lived well with the changing nature of the Word. On the frontier of a new nation in a newly discovered continent, change and experimentalism were credos in other parts of life. Apologists for Christianity typically declared that "[o]ne can never write 'Q. E. D.' after any religious statement" and then would even add that "the very fact of lack of proof gives moral truth its efficacy."[32] Parker thought that the Word transcends but that Jesus of Nazareth neither added nor subtracted from the permanent element of Christianity. "But [Jesus] came to reveal it as the secret of God, that cunning men could not understand, but which filled the souls of men meek and lowly of heart. This Truth we owe to God; the Revelation thereof to Jesus, *our elder brother,* God's chosen Son."[33] By generating his Word in Jesus, has God in any way diminished Himself into being *an elder brother?* The fraternal nature of Jesus is an apostasy of Parker from the Sticky Glue. Sufi Muslims, adhering to their spiritualism, revered Jesus as a prophet of inner life and amended their profession of faith, the Shahadah, to say: "There is no god but al-Lah and Jesus is his Messenger."[34] But Parker's apostasy from orthodox Christianity arises

---

[30] Whitehead, *Religion in the Making, op. cit.,* pp. 82, 83 (italics added for emphasis).

[31] See Kevin Madigan, "On the High-Medieval Reception of Hilary of Poitiers's Anti-Arian Opinion: A Case Study of Discontinuity in Christian Thought," *Journal of Religion,* Vol. 78, No. 2, p. 213 (April, 1998).

[32] W. D. Weatherford, *Christian Life: A Normal Experience* (New York, Association Press, 1917), p. 164, discussing William James's concept of a "will to believe" in the context of "experience."

[33] Parker, "A Discourse . . ." in *op. cit.,* p. 128.

[34] Karen Armstrong, *A History of God* (New York, Ballantine Books, 1993), p. 225.

because he, too, followed Whitehead's analysis of the present moment and its compelling pressures. Parker preached to crowds at his unaffiliated Unitarian church in Roxbury, Massachusetts, and felt acutely the spiritual and emotional needs of his times and his parishioners. By 1841, after the world of Western civilization had changed completely from the world of the early Christians, society valued, as a popular tenet, the plain meaningfulness (justification) of God more than it valued the meaning (explanation) of the Sticky Glue. If God is monotheistic, Jesus must drop from God, or from the Trinity of: God the Father, God the Son and God the Holy Spirit. This is an explanation of Unitarianism. Parker valued the simplicity and clearness of the exposition of monotheistic God more than he valued the wonder of the Sticky Glue or the apostasy of Jesus the Brother. He may have elevated analysis at the expense of another adventure in failed meaning for Jesus; but the analysis was sublime—it showed a direct path from the Values which Jesus taught in the New Testament to the Values to ours. Whether you use the theology of *Logos,* or the Word of Theodore Parker, the teachings of Jesus relate to us *sub species æternitatis*—that is to say, these are concepts which hold eternally True characteristics for the species *homo sapiens*, which surpass the ages and transcend them *with content,* as well as in form.

Surpassing Clock-Time and Theology

Theodore Parker said that Christianity was a "method of attaining oneness with God" and attacked "the obstinate philosophers" who let theology stand between themselves and God.[35] But Parker's concepts of the Word, God, Love and Nature are themselves all obvious manifestations of theology. As the Truth of the Sermon on the Mount is clearly and fundamentally within the Word, and we may Believe in God *only* because of it, does the Word nevertheless stand between a soul and God? What about a method of "attaining oneness with God" from human existence? Where *in existence* is the Reality of Jesus as the Christ?

The historical record shows Jesus never wondered about himself, never struggled or confronted his consciousness of himself as a human soul, except once. At a place called The Skull, nailed to a cross and dressed only in a loincloth and a crown of thorns, Jesus cried: "My God, my God, why hast thou forsaken me?"[36] This cry is from the existence of a suffering human soul, but it is from Jesus. At that point the human and the Divine are together. The principle of Identity is shown in actual life. If you Believe in God Ultimately as a result of your existence as a human soul, the cry of Jesus fulfills *the* basis upon which you Believe. ". . . [A]t that moment God experiences what it means to be a mortal man and drinks to the dregs what he made his faithful servant Job suffer."[37]

The French author, the Vicomte François René de Châteaubriand (1768 to 1848), said the genius of Christianity is that it turns the abstraction of God into flesh.[38] "For

---

[35] Parker, "A Discourse . . ." in *op. cit.,* pp. 113, 129.

[36] Saint Matthew ch. 27, v. 46; Saint Mark ch. 15, v. 34.

[37] Murdoch, *op. cit.,* 134.

[38] Vicomte de Châteaubriand, *Le Génie du Christianisme* (Paris, 1802) trans. Charles L. White as *The Genius of Christianity* (Baltimore, John Murphy & Co., 1875). The author famously declared, "I wept, and I believed."

God so Loved the world that He gave his only Son that whosoever should believe in Him should not perish but have eternal life."[39] In Jesus, God is Really showing us the principle of Love. The Love of God is made manifest to us as Really as it is Ultimately Real. This is more than the principle of *Amor amatur* (Love itself is loved); more than *eros* (intense spiritual desire). It is *agapē*—the element of Love in the sense of the New Testament showing unmotivated Love and the personal, forgiving character of God. Without Jesus and the *agapē* Jesus brought to *homo sapiens*, there is the Real danger that God would not be in our existences today.

If God is a necessary Being with every positive attribute, Jesus is exactly the same definition. He is necessary, a Being and has every positive attribute. He is necessary because a human soul demands awareness of an Ultimate Reality beyond itself that *really delivers truthfully or has the ability for truthful delivery.* Jesus Really delivers Truthfully to a human soul because he Really lived like the soul lives on this Earth. His soul was human. Once he even told a lie: he told his disciples he would not attend the feast of Tabernacles in Judea because "his time had not yet come" but he went to the feast anyway "privately."[40] Jesus had no textbook knowledge or even wrote anything we know of; he touched other souls directly, existentially, and delivered to them Really from existence, and not from any essences extracted from published knowledge. Jesus has the ability for Truthful delivery because when he lived like a soul lives here he lived with every positive attribute. He said: "A greater love than this no man has than to give one's life for one's friends."[41] Then he gave up his life for his friends, *you and me,* and proved the Truth of this. When he lied to his disciples whether he would attend the feast of the Tabernacles in Judea, the lie was based upon the "best" justification: Jesus knew the Jews were trying to kill him in Judea and in the most real way for human existence wanted to live and not die. As a human soul, Jesus shows every other soul that Truth can actually be delivered to a soul in this existence *because* it is human. And Jesus shows every other soul the human soul has the ability for a Truthful delivery *despite* being human. If the soul *has a use* for God or *uses* God, Jesus seals the transaction the soul makes with God so the uses can occur. He is the middleman between the sufferings of the soul under psychological stresses and God. Without Jesus there is the Real danger a human soul and God would go their separate ways. In these *circumstances,* not *premises,* the Danish theologian of existentialism, Søren Kierkegaard (1813 to 1855), asserted that only one thing matters: "In the year A.D. 30 God sent the Christ for my salvation. *I do not need any more theology;* I do not need to know the results of historical criticism. It is enough to know that one thing. *Into this I have to leap."*[42]

This is the famous "leap of faith" which is central to Kierkegaard's theology of existentialism. A soul cannot overcome "the dread" or "the sickness unto death" of the existence it labors with; the only way the dread, the sickness or the death can be overcome is by faith. Is this faith of the same bitter quality as the sponge of vinegar Jesus tasted on the cross? Must it be by the "logic" of existentialism? (But we isolated no specific set of properties with existence, except what is *necessary.*) To what extent

---

[39] Saint John ch. 3, v. 16.
[40] Saint John ch. 7, vv. 8-10.
[41] Saint John ch. 15, v. 13.
[42] Tillich, *op. cit.,* p. 471.

is faith wholly irrational? Many thinkers have referred to the "pathetically diseased Kierkegaardian sense" in which it is possible to be a Christian.[43] Does Kierkegaard know when he's leaping which way he's jumping? The answer is yes; he knows he's jumping to Truth. When he defines the faith required by the leap, he also defines Truth. Kierkegaard's definition of ultimate Truth is as follows: "Truth is the *objective uncertainty* held fast in the most personal passionate experience. *This is the truth, the highest truth attainable for the existing individual."*[44] This is the Ultimate, the *Terminal* (yes, it's a double entendre) degree of Truth we can ever expect from our existence. It is objectively uncertain, that is, it is conditioned upon psychology, existentialism, Identity, Love or Jesus *really delivering truthfully or having the ability for truthful delivery.* And, in the case of existentialism, Ultimate Truth is further conditioned upon psychology, existentialism, Identity, Love or Jesus *really delivering truthfully without essences or having the ability for truthful delivery without relying on these five "mediums" essentially.* So existentialism, even if it is "essentially" style, raises the barrier of conditions which must be fulfilled for a soul to Believe in God existentially.

But Jesus and the resurrection of Jesus tear down several barriers to existential Belief. As the eighth-century Christian Greek theologian, John of Damascus (675? to 749?), put it: ". . . when God is seen in the flesh and conversing with men, I make an image of the God whom I can see."[45] The next stage of mental imaging, beyond the image of God which John constructed from the flesh of Jesus while Jesus lived in the flesh, is the image of God which Augustine of Hippo constructed from the spirit of Jesus while that spirit lived in Augustine and lives *in us still.* For Augustine saw that, by reading the "books of the Platonists, I had been prompted to look for [T]ruth as something incorporeal, and *I caught sight of your* [Jesus's] *invisible nature, as it is known through your creatures."*[46] Furthermore, "I was most certain, too, that *from the foundations of the world* men have caught sight of *your invisible nature,* your eternal power, your divineness, *as they are known through your creatures."*[47] But, paradoxically, Jesus passed the bitter test of existence for the *"invisible nature"* He delivered to Augustine and to mankind: He physically died upon a cross for it. The French mathematician and early existentialist, Blaise Pascal (1623 to 1662), asserted he would only believe in those Truths whose witnesses were willing to die for them. Jesus meets Pascal's criterion. The disciples of Jesus, who had been so shaky in their loyalty to Jesus and his teachings before and during his crucifixion, were galvanized with courage by events *after* this crucifixion, including, but not necessarily limited to, the living resurrection of Jesus from a sealed tomb. Eventually, for displaying such courage, six of the disciples of Jesus were also crucified, and five others died by swords, spears

---

[43]See, for example, Brinton, *op. cit.,* p. 472.

[44]Tillich, *op. cit.,* p. 469; Søren Kierkegaard, *The Living Thoughts of Kierkegaard* (Auden ed., 1952, 4th printing, Bloomington, Ind., Indiana University Press, 1974) p. 129.

[45]Saint John of Damascus, "First Apology against Those Who Attack the Divine Images," in *On the Divine Image: Three Apologies etc.* trans. David Anderson (Crestwood, N. Y., St. Vladimir's Seminary Press, 1980), p. 23.

[46]Saint Augustine, *Confessions* trans. R. S. Pine-Coffin (Baltimore, Penguin Books, 1961, 1969) Book VII, § 20, p. 154.

[47]*Ibid.,* Book VII, § 17, p. 151.

or stoning.[48] It is a safe assumption of psychology that, by laying down their own lives to martyrdom by the most painful ways of dying, the disciples of Jesus ". . . did not follow cleverly devised myths when [they] made known to you the power and coming of our Lord Jesus Christ, but [they] were eyewitnesses to his majesty."[49] At first, after the crucifixion of Jesus, the disciples were filled with doubt about the Divinity of Jesus and fled into hiding. But, then, after being crucified and laid into a sealed tomb as a corpse embalmed with spices, Jesus appeared to his then eleven disciples, and "[t]hen he appeared to more than five hundred brethren at one time, most of whom are still alive . . ."[50] Given the high degree of anxiety, controversy and strife which Jesus and his teachings had caused throughout Israel, it is another safe assumption of psychology that his followers had little inclination to compound their own anxiety, controversial views and strife by lying about them deliberately. There is no soul who does not care for a residue of peace.

Nevertheless, is the physical appearance of resurrected Jesus, after being placed as a corpse into a sealed tomb, still an exercise in the psychology of mass hallucination? We said psychology is an important reference for Reality, and hallucination is certainly a descriptive state of affairs which explains human minds in consciousness of an illusion where no object exists in Reality—that is to say, under Mill's definition of it, as an X to be remembered from experience as a firmly conceived fact. But resurrected Jesus *was* remembered by all to whom He appeared precisely as such an objective fact. He even anticipated the skepticism that would surround the news of His resurrection by telling His doubting disciple, Thomas, that those who have not seen Him literally resurrected yet Believe in His Divinity are blessed.[51] If the corpse of Jesus was anywhere to be found in Judea, embalmed as it was with a hundred pounds of spices from Nicodemus, it is a safe assumption about politics that the Jewish religious establishment, which had condemned Jesus to die because of his avowal of Divinity, would have caused the Roman civil authorities to display the corpse publicly, perhaps upon an ox-cart, for the purpose of laying the vexing rumors of Jesus's resurrection to rest. The Jewish religious establishment, especially a Pharisee in the council named Gamaliel, realized acutely that, if Jesus still lived and had literally triumphed over death, He was absolutely and unavoidably Divine. Indeed, the chief priests and Pharisees gathered before the Roman governor, Pontius Pilate, and requested that a guard of soldiers be put at Jesus's tomb to secure it as much as possible against the theft of Jesus's corpse. Pilate agreed. "So they went and made the sepulchre secure by sealing the stone and setting a guard."[52] But no display of Jesus's corpse ever happened, though all the then ruling powers of the world had every motive and opportunity to cause it to happen. On the other hand, the resurrection of Jesus is a compelling reason why a set of frightened and doubting disciples became galvanized and went courageously to the temple and to the center of Jerusalem to spread the news of Jesus's resurrection within

---

[48]See, for a list summarizing the cause of death of each disciple of Jesus, Josh McDowell, *More Than a Carpenter* (Wheaton, Ill., Tyndale House Publishers: Living Books, 1977), p. 61.

[49]Simon Peter the Apostle, *Second Letter*, ch. 1, v. 16.

[50]Saint Paul, *First Letter to the Corinthians*, ch. 15, vv. 5, 6.

[51]Saint John ch. 20, v. 29.

[52]Saint Matthew ch. 27, v. 66.

weeks of His crucifixion.⁵³ Gamaliel told the other members of the Sanhedrin that, if the Jewish religious establishment punished or imprisoned the disciples of Jesus for this news, the establishment itself might be found (finally) to oppose God.⁵⁴ Therefore, even if mass hallucination were subjunctively applicable to the living resurrection of Jesus, that hallucination is precisely the sort of *human and psychic* transcendence (called transformation) within the Word of God which we have already discussed in this Chapter regarding a verse in the epistle of Paul the Apostle to the Romans. This human and psychic transcendence occurred in Jesus's disciples, if not in Gamaliel, within weeks of Jesus's crucifixion.

The transcending Holy Spirit of Jesus shows you that His living resurrection from a corpse fits well within Kierkegaard's concept of the highest degree of Truth ever available to us. It is that Spirit, and not the body, of Jesus which is the fact of our remembrance of Him in our lives today. Do you remember what Whitehead said about that wholeness of the present moment which subsumes the past? In the wholeness of a given moment, the Holy Spirit of Jesus accounts for all sorts of human behavior which might arouse the wonder of a skeptic. It accounts for the pure but austere morality of the first Christians amid the wonder and bewilderment about it of everyone else in the Roman Empire.⁵⁵ It accounts for addicts of all sorts who suddenly find the courage to surmount their addictions.⁵⁶ It accounts for martyrs of all sorts who suddenly find the inspiration to sacrifice their is-ness in different ways. It accounts for the impure or profligate logic of the first Christian thinkers who substituted simple faith in place of rigorous meaning (explanation). For example, Tertullian said: "The Son of God died; it is entirely credible, because it is absurd; and after his burial he rose again; it is certain, because it is impossible."⁵⁷ Thirdly, the Holy Spirit of Jesus accounts for spontaneous behavior among self-consciously admitted philosophers who spend their lives professionally preoccupied by thinking. For example, King Friedrich Wilhelm II of Prussia (1744 to 1797) summoned such a professional, Immanuel Kant, into his throne-room for the purpose of delivering an ultimatum to Kant not to continue to subvert the teachings of Christ. Though he delivered to the world one of the greatest syntheses of thinking ever thought about Christianity, Kant, in life, was actually a diminutively little hunchback who spoke in a timid voice which barely reached to the rear of his classroom at the University of Königsberg, where he spoke in gigantic words like enantiomorph which his students could not understand, and where he had taken fourteen years of toiling to reach a professorship in logic and metaphysics. At some point in a perfect future, Kant believed that, after a centuries-long course of enlightenment for mankind about Christianity, Jesus would become obsolete as *the* centerpiece of it eventually.⁵⁸

---

⁵³*Acts of the Apostles* ch. 5, vv. 21, 27-32, 40-42.

⁵⁴*Acts of the Apostles* ch. 5, v. 39.

⁵⁵See, for examples of moral behavior among early Christian women, Kate Cooper, *The Virgin and the Bride: Idealized Womanhood in Late Antiquity* (Cambridge, Mass., Harvard University Press, 1996).

⁵⁶See, for example, McDowell, *op. cit.,* pp. 127, 128.

⁵⁷Tertullian, *De Carne Christi,* V, quoted in H. A. Wolfson, *The Philosophy of The Church Fathers* (Cambridge, Mass., 1956), Vol. 1 only published, pp. 102, 103; Christopher Stead, *Philosophy in Christian Antiquity* (Cambridge, U. K., Cambridge University Press, 1994), p. 111.

⁵⁸Charlotte Allen, *op. cit.,* p. 123.

Nevertheless, this belief and all of his poor and minimal circumstances to the contrary notwithstanding, Kant remonstrated to the King that he was *encouraging* the teachings of Christ, that Christ sought to bring the Kingdom of God nearer to Earth, but that, judging from the conduct of most Christians, Christ has been grossly misunderstood. The King told Kant to shut up. Kant then said: "Your Majesty, I have had my say." The King did not punish him for speaking.[59] In these several ways of morality, logic and behavior, it is clear to a careful observer of the world that God supervenes properties of God into the world or has done so.

Jesus the Christ supervenes properties of God into the world because Jesus of Nazareth, by His life, death, resurrection and subsequent transcendence surpasses the fundamental problems of existence facing *homo sapiens. One such deep problem is about the use and abuse of human powers.* Without Jesus, how does a little hunchback in a throne-room have the courage to stand up to a King? But how, without Jesus, does the King have the forgiveness to refrain from punishing an obscure and disliked professor for contempt? Without Jesus, how does a powerful President refrain from governing the United States with just any kind of religion? But how, without Jesus, do powerful Presidents govern the United States Really by the religions which they declare openly that they formally adhere to? Without Jesus, where would President Clinton find the humility to refrain from declaring forgiveness for himself as any public (even private) fact? If the fundamental problem of human power is, as we have discussed, in the difference between the consciousness of a brain and the firing of neurons within the brain as a matter of scientific observation, in the difference between the mind and the body, the spiritual and the physical, and, therefore, in the divorce itself between mankind and God, then won't a problem in divorced relationships be solved substantially if new relationships arise? Jesus said: "Truly, truly, I say to you, unless one is born of water and the Spirit he cannot enter the kingdom of God. That which is born of the flesh is flesh, and that which is born of the Spirit is spirit. Do not marvel that I said to you 'You must be born anew.'"[60] This rebirth, the resurrection of a relationship into a new one, means the fundamental problem of our human lives in actual existence can be dealt with by a human soul and surpassed. Did the King of Prussia experience a rebirth because of the gall of a hunchback? Each *homo sapiens* is born of water and the Spirit as soon as it breathes its first breath as an infant; Jesus says this birth is two separate births in one and that rebirth is required. The requirement of being reborn— that is, of doing what is physically impossible for *homo sapiens* to do without dying first—applies everywhere to everybody and from the cross Jesus applied it to himself. This is the meaning of the Miracle of the Resurrection. Jesus overcame physical death and entered into a life of the Spirit beyond clock-time. Being defined by the *Logos* to be exactly the same as God, Jesus surpasses clock-time and is as Real for us today as He was Real in his thirty-three years of human existence. If we are reborn in Jesus, we may surpass clock-time also. This allows a human soul facing certain physical death to rest more tranquilly than it would otherwise rest. "The dread" and "the sickness unto death" have been finally overcome. In these *circumstances*, not *premises*, Kierkegaard is not leaping backward two millennia to commune with the physical existence of Jesus

---

[59]Henry Thomas, *Understanding the Great Philosophers* (Garden City, N. Y., Doubleday & Co., 1967), p. 258.
[60]Saint John ch. 3, vv. 5-7.

to support a Belief in God; he leaps into the faith that Jesus, reborn, existed in Kierkegaard's bleak and (most literally) lovelorn existence in Copenhagen, Denmark, during the first part of the 19th century.

But it is objectively uncertain. An important element in Kierkegaard's definition of Truth is the phrase "objective uncertainty." It means a theology which "is not based upon objective certainty."[61] Objective certainty doesn't explain the situation of God and man: *homo sapiens* is not God but is "of" God. If God exists, we can objectively discern that, for some reason, He crushed the powerful dinosaurs and allowed puny *homo sapiens* to take their place as the rulers of the Earth. If God exists, we can objectively discern He has allowed us to peer into the bowels of His Universe. But can we objectively discern Him, say, in anti-matter? Or, on the basis of any proof from biology, chemistry or physics, can we revive cosmological thinking such as Thomas Aquinas's to Believe in God from the "outside" world as well as from the world "within?" By allowing us to peer into the Universe so deeply, is God grandly demonstrating something ultimately true about the fact of our puniness? But what could be more Ultimately True than the Truth we already know we are Ultimately and completely puny? Or is it, perhaps, the objective Truth that we are forever locked in space and clock-time, but Jesus broke out of it? Perhaps, in showing us the awesome dimension of His Universe, and the physics by which clock-time can actually be accelerated or decelerated therein, God is revealing the Reality of the Resurrection—the ultimate Truth that clock-time is not an ultimate Reality but can be surpassed. If so, would it not be easier for Him to schedule the Second Coming? Or is God just concerned with showing *agapē* because man fell from the higher state of Being which Jesus is? The finite of *homo sapiens* and the infinite of God will always be divorced. If so, why would God find harping upon it to be necessary? Aren't we aware of it already? Hasn't this awareness already been painfully and overwhelmingly demonstrated? Perhaps He is provoked that scientists come too impudently and unlovingly close to the Infinite. If so, would it not be easier for Him to strike them down by well-timed bolts of lightning? Why is God so hard? Just what are God's designs and purposes in the world outside the human soul? All of this is uncertain objectively.

In Arabic existence—*wujud*—we find answers to these questions, as the English poet and playwright, William Shakespeare (1564 to 1616) said, not in our stars, but in ourselves.[62] It is in ourselves we find Reality and from ourselves that we call forth a spiritual life. The previous discussion shows it in three "mediums"—Identity, Love and Jesus the Christ. God has Identity with us, Love for us and sent Jesus the Christ to live among us. From these mediums of Reality, a soul may look at what is Real in the world and answer questions about it. The early Christian theologian, Clement of Alexandria (A.D. 150? to 215?), said: "Brothers, so we must think about Jesus Christ as about God, for if we think small things about [H]im, we can hope to receive small things only."[63] Kierkegaard's definition of the objective uncertainty of truth encompasses certain Truth, but, as Clement's statement shows, it is a subjective experience. *In no way does*

---

[61]Tillich, *op. cit.*, p. 469.

[62]William Shakespeare, "Julius Caesar," Act I, Scene ii, Line 139.

[63]See Paul Tillich, *A History of Christian Thought from its Judaic and Hellenistic Origins to Existentialism* (Braaten ed., Simon & Schuster, 1968, 1972), p. 22.

the subjective nature of it mean it is divorced from Reality. It *is* Reality on the conditions to which Reality has been brought to us by living here and now. It's worth seeing Kierkegaard's Truth depends upon only two other Truths: Jesus is Jesus the Christ, and Jesus the Christ lived. A potent ingredient of Belief today is this simplicity. Critics have carefully examined the New Testament and have raised questions about the Gospels and various events of Jesus's life. The criticisms provide a basis in the theory of experience upon which empirical thinking has attacked a Belief in Christianity during the last two centuries. But the attack is only that, and not a victory for any prevailing condition of either humanity or God.

My is-ness is a now-ness. All of *my* past is subsumed into it. Where is the basis to suppose that all of *the* past is not subsumed likewise? Thus, if this lack of a presupposition about the quality of the past is right, Whitehead is entirely right to say that it would be deluded of me to suppose that the past stands, in some transcending, objectified, historical record, independently and apart of what I am and hold today. Beyond the history being criticized, criticisms of the historical life of Jesus are, therefore, invalid and not meaningful to a metaphysical basis upon which to criticize *my* Belief in Jesus the Christ today. This is the theology of the German Lutheran theologian, Martin Kähler (1835 to 1912). Kähler determined the Christian faith by the "preached Christ," and not by a movement to analyze the life of Jesus.[64] Kähler noted that, as we have seen, the historical Jesus of Nazareth did not win from his earthly disciples during his earthly existence anything but a shaky loyalty, prone to panic and betrayal. Only by *themselves* being reborn again, into a living hope through the resurrection of Jesus from the dead, were the disciples of Jesus brought to remembrance of what Jesus said. This rebirth occurred before the disciples were able to understand what had been given to them and to grasp what they had been unable to bear. The Christian faith of even the disciples depended upon the gift of the Holy Spirit of Jesus to them and the transcendence of Jesus over time. If you look only to the life of Jesus of Nazareth while he lived, you see even the disciples without a firm Belief in Jesus the Christ. Judas betrayed Jesus, and Peter the Rock, on whom Jesus said He would build His church,[65] denied knowledge of Him repeatedly. It is the paradoxical Truth of Jesus that his non-existence is required for us humans to see his existence clearly. Do you remember how God is revealed from *that which does not exist?* Like Kähler, Albert Schweitzer dealt directly with fears of early 20th century Christians that a devastating critique of the historical life of Jesus would destroy Belief in Him. Schweitzer said:

> "The mistake was to suppose that Jesus could come to mean more to our time by entering into it *as a man like ourselves.* That is not possible. First because such a Jesus never existed. Secondly because, although historical knowledge can no doubt introduce greater clearness into an existing spiritual life, *it cannot call spiritual life into existence.* . . . It is not Jesus as historically known, *but Jesus as spiritually arisen within men,* who is significant for our time and can help it."[66]

---

[64]Martin Kähler, *Der sogenannte historische Jesus und der geschichtliche, biblische Christus* (1892) (Wolf ed., Munich, Kaiser Verlag, 1953) pp. 40-45, in *The Christian Theology Reader* § 4.24, pp. 157, 158 trans. Carl E. Braaten (McGrath ed., Oxford, U. K., Blackwell Publishers Ltd., 1995, 1996, 1997).

[65]Saint Matthew ch. 16, v. 18.

[66]Albert Schweitzer, *The Quest of the Historical Jesus* (London, 1st English ed., 1910), p. 399.

What is Ultimately Real and arisen within us about Jesus of Nazareth? Jesus is Reality—the remembrance of a Real fact—because He simply lived and died the way He did *for you*. Let's illustrate this Other-ness of Jesus by a parable, the type of short, fictitious story which Jesus Himself often used to illustrate a principle. Philosopher A at University B convenes a seminar of students and, much like teachers of thinking in ancient Athens, expounds to them the several distinctions of words by which he says God does not exist and it would be impossible to prove so. Specifically, A says that there is no reconciliation possible between the "being" of God as an item of inventory in ontology and physicalism, the doctrine of philosophy which holds that the only existent things are those that are tied to matter.[67] A few days, weeks or years later, however, his wife is diagnosed with breast cancer, or his carefree son is maimed in an automobile accident, or his frustrating daughter is pregnant by a lover whose ability to Love is, in fact, not determinable intuitively. The Truth of Jesus is that He is with philosopher A, though A has much denied His existence. How, you say, could Jesus exist for A at all? He still Loves his wife with cancer beyond the physical nature of her sexual allure. His Love for her is Real because he remembers it as a Real fact each time an attractive philosophy student flirts with him on campus. He still cares for a careless son whose future prospects are compromised completely by his automobile injuries for the rest of his life. His care for him is Real because he remembers it as a Real fact each time he opens his bank account to pay for another medical expense. He completely overlooks his frustration with his lovely daughter and still thinks rationally about her predicament and how to resolve it in undetermined love. His rationality is Real because he remembers it as a Real fact each time he goes a distance to visit his daughter because he told her only at that distance could she be really responsible for herself. But, you say, how do we know this is Jesus's presence and not strictly A's own behavior? We know it because, under these circumstances of stress, a rational reduction of A's ego by a Freudian analysis of A's sexuality says that A abandons his primary sex object; disowns his son, Oedipus, especially when Oedipus is such a compounded challenge; and is filled with emotional substitutes for the forbidden love of incest, especially when there is the greatest justification of unrequited love to discard the taboo of it. Freudian or *Gestalt* therapies objectify these contradictions of "feeling-ness" in A, but neither resolves them outside of the therapy sessions, by the actual life of 24 hours in each day, in such a manner that A lives with himself but also lives by behaving actually with the love and care I described. You say this outcome is simply a possibility of A's super-ego, an existing "I" of A which is overwhelming and compels the completion of a therapy for A by which A's loving behavior is anything justified to A. This sublime combination of an ego and a super-ego is a fine concept for the essence of a person, but is it Really True in A's existence? How does the combination exist in actual existence without falling from sublimity? The super-ego of Freudian psychology is enslaved by countless threads of the mind to an ego, and *vice versa*. In fact, only by the presence of a therapist

---

[67]Compare William F. Valicella, "Could a Classical Theist Be a Physicalist?" *Faith and Philosophy*, Vol. 15, No. 2, p. 160 (April, 1998); see Hubert L. and Patricia Allen Dreyfus, "Introduction," in Maurice Merleau-Ponty, *Sense and Non-Sense* trans. Hubert L. and Patricia Allen Dreyfus (Wild et al., eds., Evanston, Ill., Northwestern University Press, 1964), pp. xxv-xxvii, for a discussion of Merleau-Ponty's agnosticism with Kierkegaard's faith. The authors note the two are only paradoxically different because they result from many of the same existential perspectives.

for A *who does not exist* does such a therapy for A, or A's Real therapy, finish or even begin.[68]

You both feel and think the Truth of this life and death of the overwhelming, existing "is-ness" of A, or of yourself, by principles of "leaping" and "transcending" by Jesus according to Real indications of behavior from actual life. The Truth of Jesus is a functional physicalism of His Healing Holy Spirit which arises *within A and you* and is very much alive. *You and A feel* His Holy Spirit in the same way it was felt two millennia ago. This Reality is *iatric*—in Greek, the word *iatros* means healer or doctor. It is also a Reality which is, strictly put, a mystical perception. But to say this does nothing whatsoever to controvert it, "prove" that it is false or argue that a soul should not perceive it, Believe it or hold it otherwise very dearly. William James said three things about mystical perceptions. First, when well developed, they usually are, *and have the right to be,* absolutely authoritative over those who have them. Second, there is, on the other hand, no authority within them which makes it a duty for an outsider to accept them uncritically. Finally, mystical perceptions de-construct a consciousness based upon reason and the senses alone and open out the possibility of other orders of Truth to such a consciousness.[69] Because of Jesus, plenty of souls for two millennia Believed in God. Some souls were full of eccentric, excruciating, mystical demands and requirements; among them *are* A's, Kierkegaard's and Schweitzer's. Yet, the three of them Believe. At university B, because of the *Gestalt* pattern of Jesus's "invisible image" upon the background of his existence, and what this pattern actually consists of in terms of substantial Love, A does so without ever acknowledging a perception of the Holy Spirit of Jesus formally. Kierkegaard Believed in Jesus in frigid 19th century Denmark by writing works of faith, and Schweitzer did so conversely, by faith in many healing works, amid the steamy jungles of 20th century Africa. You with your unique demands and requirements of today can also. Jesus said: "there is nothing outside a man which by going into him [as your requirements and demands have] can defile him; but the things which come out of a man are what defile him."[70] *Jesus is the Spirit which holds your Belief in God whether or not you also believe in religion. Jesus is always*

---

[68]Compare H. J. Eysenck, "The effects of psychotherapy: an evaluation," *Journal of Consulting Psychology,* Vol. 16, pp. 319-324 (1952) reprinted in Richard D. Gross, *Key Studies in Psychology* (Gross ed., London, Hodder & Stoughton, 1990), pp. 342, 343. The author analyzes 19 studies covering 7,000 cases dealing with both psychoanalytic and eclectic types of treatment. He concludes that two-thirds of neurotic patients examined in these studies will recover or improve to a marked extent within about two years of the onset of their illness, whether they receive psychotherapy or not.

[69]William James, *The Varieties of Religious Experience* (New York, Longmans, Green, 1902), pp. 422, 423; quoted in Robert Audi, "Religious Experience and the Practice Concept of Justification," in *The Rationality of Belief and the Plurality of Faith* (Senor ed., Ithaca, N. Y., Cornell University Press, 1995), Part II, No. 5, p. 129. At page 143, author Audi notes that "justification seems tied more to specific thinkers [in this context, a specific mystic because all mystics are still Cartesian res cogitans] than rationality [Reason] is to any analogue of a justifier." Does a quasi-Realist surmount the problem of resolving this statement without continuing the contradiction between the two polarities of Reason and Subjectivity described in it? If not, quasi-Realism is not an alternative, of itself, which ought to be considered, of itself, between the Reality of Reason (Science) and the Reality of Subjectivity. In any event, there is no Reality which is ultimately apart from these two last poles of Reality. Quasi-Realism, if accepted of itself, must therefore relate explicitly to each.

[70]Saint Mark ch. 7, v. 15.

with you (regardless of the certainty of your death in your body) and with you always (regardless of time).

Chapter Five. The Will to Believe

The premise of the foregoing Chapters is that psychology, existentialism, Identity, Love and the life of Jesus the Christ *Really deliver Truthfully or have the ability for Truthful delivery.* Are these premises enough? Doesn't "Real" reality require more for these premises to exist in actual existence? Aren't they nothing more than premises and, therefore, still nothing more than essences? The further element required for them to exist in existence seems to be the Will for them to exist actually. After all is said, we have also shown in the previous discussion that census-gathering techniques, light, sexuality or practically anything else *may* deliver truthfully in a real way or have the ability for truthful delivery. What is the distinguishing characteristic between the five premises which our discussion classifies as Absolute Truth and the three or many or infinite number of others which still remain conditional? The Ultimate characteristic which seems to distinguish Reality and the "Real" premises is the Will for them to be actually distinguished. Psychology, existentialism, Identity, Love and the life of Jesus the Christ are Unconditional, Absolute and Ultimate Truth in actual existence only if there is the Will to make them so. What is the Will to make them into this degree of Truth? In silence—which puts the whole issue of verbal Truth-seeking into focus and describes the mysterious nature of Will acutely in doing so—the American entertainer, singer and movie star, Frank (Francis Albert) Sinatra (1915 to 1998), refused to explain, at least publicly, any tidbit of truth about his perception of the Reality of his life, in response to myriad criticisms of it, including charges relating to his sometimes violent temperament, as well as those about his friendship with individuals allegedly committing felonies by organized crime. In the mid-1960's, Sinatra said, "I just refuse to discuss it because it can't make a dent anywhere."[1] Thus did Sinatra conceive of the thoughts of his critics as if they were physical objects which could be hit and dented; so did he follow the *Gestalt* patterns of the thing-i-fication of thoughts and objectification of existence which I have previously described here; but then Sinatra Willed to refuse to tell the world about the taste of any morsel of his own objectified thoughts about them. In music, show business and the rest of his life, Sinatra was a soul professionally occupied with entertaining others. He tasted feelings, thoughts, opinions and emotions continually. His career, in fact, depended on correlating them to the collective tastes of society. His Will to stop suddenly in showing them at a television interview shows the power of Will at the very core of his life. Why would our Belief in God hinge upon any such of an uncertain, arbitrary and awesome Will? Sinatra correlated his entertaining tastes to thousands most delightedly and successfully; so, it cannot be assumed that he

---

[1] Frank Sinatra to Walter Cronkhite, "Sinatra: Off The Record," (1965) videotaped interview with Walter Cronkhite, from questions scripted by Andy Rooney, produced by Don Hewitt, in *Videotape Archives of the Columbia Broadcasting System, CBS News Division.* © Copyright, CBS, Inc., 1968. All Rights Reserved.

displayed the human-ness of his Will in a weirdly odd, abnormal and, therefore, innately unentertaining way. Contrapositively, nothing about a great entertainer is not also to be entertained—that is to say, at least considered—as a human characteristic. Sinatra's Will typifies a generically human Will in all of its intensity. Why, we lament, should the last many pages of a fine construction of Belief in God be subject to this earthquake of emotion?

Descriptions of the Will

Will is one of three operations. In one sense, it is a psychological phenomenon of consciousness. In another sense, it is a phenomenon of the senses conceptualized as a meaning of the larger "phenomenon" of the soul; and in the third sense, it is the fundamental power which moves and underlies all things—what, Tillich said, are "the dynamics in all forms of life."[2] In the first sense, students of philosophy and psychology have studied the Will extensively. We shall briefly see what William James characterized it essentially, and how Edmund Husserl's analysis of consciousness is a description of it as it exists in our souls. In the second sense, one still tied to the sensory impressions of existence, the French philosopher, Maine de Biran (1766 to 1824), and the German philosopher, Arthur Schopenhauer (1788 to 1860), both claimed, though for their different reasons, that we have a direct awareness of our efforts of Will; that is, I feel feelings of striving and trying, independently of any muscular sensations they make, as the direct apprehension of my soul about the world.[3] In the third sense, we are directly aware of Will just as, and because, we are directly aware of life itself. Life is reduced to Will and *vice versa*. In this sense, it is easy to use Will as a Sticky Glue more viscous than even *Logos* in binding the Universe together. For example, the Catholic cardinal and theologian, Nicholas of Cusa (1401 to 1464), saw the infinite everywhere within the finite, famously postulated the mutual inherence of the two combined together even within single physical objects, and arrived at a metaphysical unity of all things and the existence of God as the unifier of it all accordingly. Why is this so? Nicholas limits human knowledge to a type of ignorance—in Latin called his *docta ignorantia*—which is special to his theology. As a result of such a self-inflicted limitation, he explains the Universe resulting from his given form of ignorance because God Willed it to be. Nicholas's cosmology (that is to say, his world of Cartesian hell where ignorance is an excellent or excellently desired quality) surely fails of any empirical validation or scientific observation of cause and effect. It cannot be a theory of experience under the test of an empirical framework we required for this discussion. Will, as the fundamental power behind the dynamics of all forms of life, simply restates

---

[2]Paul Tillich, *A History of Christian Thought from its Judaic and Hellenistic Origins to Existentialism* (Carl E. Braaten ed., New York, Simon & Schuster, 1972), p. 491. On this page, Tillich says that "[i]n voluntaristic philosophy (read: theology) will is not restricted to a conscious psychological act." Then, he immediately but wrongly says that the word 'will' "must be used" anyway even if his equally wrong notion is true, viz., that a meaning for the word in theology cannot be derived "from man's psychological experience of himself as a consciously willing being." Thus, Tillich's spontaneously expressed concept of 'compelling usefulness' about a magic word can be compared to the most divorced linguistic concepts which Scholasticism ever divorced from empiricism, although Tillich was avowedly and substantially non-Scholastic in his theology when it is considered as a whole.

[3]Edward S. Reed, *From Soul to Mind* (New Haven, Yale University Press, 1997), p. 75.

what God is. But the rock in my hand is a finite thing because I feel tactile qualities of heaviness and hardness about it. If it were infinitely hard or heavy, surely my wrist would be broken off in holding it. The third sense of the word, "Will," glues or interlocks all of Reality. A piece of the interlocked or glued-together Reality, being dependent upon all the rest of it, then breaks apart easily under the weight of a couplet by the English poet, Alexander Pope (1688 to 1744). Pope said: "From Nature's chain whatever link you strike; Tenth or ten thousandth, breaks the chain alike."[4] The rock in my hand does not break my wrist, so I break Nicholas's chain of reasoning that the rock is hardly or heavily infinite.

The intellectual method of the essentialism of Nicholas, in constructing *docta ignorantia,* infinity and many other concepts from black ink and puffs of air, is called Scholasticism. Scholasticism dominated how thinkers thought for many centuries, distinguished acutely among essences and grew into a veritable knowledge-tree of them, flourishing in intellectual minds, but without a root (route) to existence essentially (yes, that is a pun). This is because almost all distinctions of Scholasticism cannot be tested empirically but, if they are, they fail of logic in scientific observations of causes and effects. Nevertheless, a few of the Scholastic distinctions are useful descriptions of existence if there is already a scientific predicate for them arrived at by other means. Indeed, we mentioned Max Scheler's "scientific" description of a "scholastic picture" which we often hold in our heads as we think thoughts and sketch those of other people. An innate, Scheler-like, "scientific" scholasticism in our perceptive processes psychologically is confused with the greater extrapolation of essentialism into the Scholasticism popularly known in philosophy. This confusion is profound, bewildering and fatal for the Truth of both—until the confusion has been discerned to exist, if not distinguished entirely or resolved *satisfactorily.* It is given philosophically that the world has an element of permanence, such that existence involves essences, more or less as the Pre-Socratic Greek philosopher, Parmenides (*c.* B.C. 500) roughly said, "Where there is being, there is *logos* of being."[5] It is found psychologically that the world is a matter of change, such that pictures involve learning, more or less as the meaning of a picture differs from one culture to another because of different learning among the same human species.[6] *Logos* of being, essences and pictures are potential embodiments of Scholasticism, unavoidable for the perceptive and learning processes of mankind and, therefore, unavoidable for existence itself by any way we grasp it.

You may say that I have already distinguished concepts without a difference to existence, as a neo-Scholastic. But, if you do, you must remember that I began it *from the form* of the Reality of Science because I discerned that science, especially of my physical and mental visual fields, is a Real point of departure to arrive at the Ultimate Truth of my life. I did not begin this discussion *from the form* of an agglomerated

---

[4]Alexander Pope, "An Essay On Man," Epistle I, Lines 245-246 (1733) in *The Works of Alexander Pope* (4 vols.) (Croly ed., London, A. J. Valpy, 1835), Vol. I, p. 25.

[5]Paul Tillich, *A History of Christian Thought from its Judaic and Hellenistic Origins to Existentialism* (Braaten ed., New York, Simon & Schuster, 1972), p. 439.

[6]Jan B. Deregowski, "Pictorial perception and culture," *Scientific American,* Vol. 227, pp. 82-88 (1972) reprinted in Richard D. Gross, *Key Studies in Psychology* (Gross ed., London, Hodder & Stoughton, 1990), pp. 21-35.

concept somewhere between the Reality of Science and the Reality of Subjectivity, such that further distinctions regarding the posited agglomeration would be confused with the inevitable mixing which occurs whenever a posit is extrapolated into conclusions. More elaborately, basic terms—for example, the basic term of "necessary existence" which is used by thinkers of process theology—are posited agglomerations somewhere between the Reality of Science and the Reality of Subjectivity. But the agglomerated character of their given-ness as a starting point of logic confuses what can actually be supposed about their end results. Are the results Truly empirical from existence or merely a logical continuation in black ink and puffs and air of the presuppositions which the thinker started with? If the latter, has a thinker "proved" anything about existence or only "proved" the single reductive "fact" that he can presuppose? But we said the end of this discussion should be as existential as it essentially is (yes, that's a pun). In other words, I told you that I rejected Heidegger's *Dasein,* Leibnitz's "monads" and Duns Scotus's "being as being" because they are empirically unclear. Now, I tell you that I do so because these thinkers provide these concepts by using them as starting points, and not as the end products of their thought. What's the difference? Well, what is your theory of Reality actually? I told you in the Foreword that it seems there are only three: The Reality of a Pan-Scientism, the Reality of my Subjectivity and the Reality of a philosophy I called "quasi-Realism." The latter term is an agglomerated concept; it is conceived in Cartesian thought only if a thinker starts with the clearness of one of the first two more sharply contrasting forms (*Gestalt* patterns?) of Reality. (If Reality reduces in units of experience to *Gestalten,* isn't *Gestalt* psychology the philosophy which a thinker must think of *first?*) Put differently, and without digressing into the First Philosophy of the Universe any further, I should accept *Dasein,* "monads" and "being as being" *(ens in quantum ens)* if the proposers of them had respectively started by telling me that these concepts evolved from the Reality of Science or the Reality of Subjectivity and showed me this evolutionary relationship as a matter of my intellect. They did not do this. Neither did Nietzsche relate his concept of the "will to power" to the extrapolation of his philosophy from the starting point of pure subjectivity about it.[7] On the other hand, unless I trace the Reality of my so-called "quasi-Realism" firmly back to its roots in science or subjectivity or both, it likewise lacks the clear foundation of a starting posit which I have just criticized in the eminent intellectuals aforementioned. Only your subjectivity may judge whether I Really do so.

The Catholic theologian and itinerant Scottish monk, Johannes Duns Scotus (1265? to 1308), drew a set of formal distinctions, in the manner of Scholasticism, between a soul and its separate faculties of Will and intellect. These formal distinctions of Duns Scotus assist us today, even if they are Scholastic. For example, in one experiment of behaviorist psychology, three different groups of infants, eight to ten weeks old, had their heads placed on pressure-sensing pillows for ten minutes a day during a two-week

---

[7]See Walter Kaufmann, "The Discovery of the Will to Power," in *Nietzsche: Philosopher, Psychologist, Antichrist* § 6 (Rev. 3rd ed., New York, Random House: Vintage Books, 1950, 1968), pp. 179-183. The author notes that Nietzsche began the corpus of his philosophy by explaining "the will to power" in terms of the universal human traits of fear and laziness, postulated the perpetual nature of power as evil, relied on a logic in dreams and discussed norms of human behavior in terms of power as an inelastic concept. Universality, postulations, perpetuity, logic and normalness are not approaches which lead to inevitable subjectivity.

period. The head movements of each group were carefully counted during the relevant periods. In the experimental group, infants who moved their heads put in motion mobiles attached to their cribs; in the other two groups, the mobile either did not move at all or moved only periodically, but not in response to babies' head movements. The results of the study were that the babies in the experimental group moved their heads much more often than the babies in the other two groups did and, anecdotally, took delight in doing so.[8] At an early age, therefore, we recognize, even appreciate, the distinction between being in control and being not in control of our existences. Similar clinical studies relate loss of control to suicidal tendencies, as well as to depression generally.[9] The inference is that "the sense of control is, in some mysterious way, deeply important to our lives, to the way we *experience* life."[10]

But how is this cognitive inference of control different from the distinctions which Duns Scotus drew about "being-ness" itself? In a reasonable theory of experience, the Scotist concept of "being as being" *(ens in quantum ens)* states only a tautology of words. Is this tautology like magic? Then where does Duns Scotus analyze magic? Does he do so magically? We think that Duns Scotus used "being as being" for the purpose of being able to claim, simultaneously, that X is X, but X is also Y. Where Reality says this, such that X and Y are the same but different, the experience of my life must confirm the saying. On the other hand, we intuit, we feel instinctively, that the intellect and the Will hold empirically, naturally and fundamentally different qualities within soul and, for them to be considered soundly, they ought to be considered separately. Duns Scotus seems the first thinker in the history of thinking about God to weigh the Will *qua* Will, standing on its own alongside the intellect before the Universe. Duns Scotus held that for both God and Man, in both the human and the Divine, the Will is a "cause" superior to the Intellect and propounded an aphorism in Latin, *voluntas imperans intellectui est causa superior respectu actus eius.*[11] Translated loosely, this means "the will ruling the intellect is a superior cause in respect of the intellect's acts." Duns Scotus examined all attributes of mankind to see how Man resembles God. Since among Man's complete qualities Man is powerfully willful and God created Man in His basic image and likeness and Man is completely "of" God, Duns Scotus concluded *God does not* formally *amount to Will* but must be of a powerful willfulness also. He looks beyond rationalism to *voluntas imperans intellectui;* his contribution to religious thinking is profound and correlates, to this limited but basic extent, with psychology. For example, William James said "[t]he willing department of our nature, in short,

---

[8] J. S. Watson and C. T. Ramey, "Reactions to response-contingent stimulation in early infancy," *Merril-Palmer Quarterly of Behavior and Development,* Vol. 18, pp 219-227 (1972), described in Norton Nelkin, *Consciousness and the Origin of Thought* (Cambridge, U. K., Cambridge University Press, 1996), pp. 301, 302.

[9] See H. M. Lefcourt, *Locus of Control: Current trends in theory and research* (Hillsdale, N. J., Erlbaum, 1976).

[10] Nelkin, *op. cit.,* p. 305.

[11] Johannes Duns Scotus, *Opus Oxoniense,* IV, q. ex latere, n. 16; see Efrem Bettoni, *Duns Scotus: The Basic Principles of His Philosophy* trans. Bernardine Bonansea (Washington, D. C., Catholic University of America Press, 1961), p. 84.

dominates both the conceiving department and the feeling department; or, in plainer English, perception and thinking are only there for behavior's sake."[12]

Modern psychologists expound upon the closely reasoned empiricism of cognitive psychology. They scoff at even the behaviorism of the middle years of the 20th century, and more obviously, at James's older notion of a "willing department" inside the brain. Cognitive psychology may treat items such as patterns of neural excitation and muscular movement as if they were intentional, or within that further and special category of intentionality called willfulness, in order to use the metaphor of "inference from data" in constructing models of mental processes. According to Daniel Dennett,[13] it is unfortunate that these models and images of mental life are available to anyone who cares to think of them, because thinking outside of controlled experiments and strictly applied induction amounts to worthless science. The only thing which could be left, after the mess made by amateurish or "folk" psychology, or after all that happens has been explained scientifically, amounts to mystery. Empiricists of cognitive psychology scoff at the notion of subcategories of intentionality, or of putting a belief inside the brain into an independent "belief box." On the other hand, the scoffing misses a chunk of physical Reality. Computers have independent structures for "belief," — "belief boxes," if you will. Such structures may avoid the tautological truth of human perception as thinkers of psychological formalism, in the manner of the American philosopher, Hartry Hamlin Field (b. 1946), conceive of it. My soul and yours have all of the descriptive psychological needs, conditions and predispositions that I have described here, even if they cannot be structurally formalized. On the horizon, then, there appears the apparition of a crisis developing in psychology between the processes of cognition which science derives empirically from human subjects and any theory of an analogy between the cognition of these subjects and computers. Even in medical science, human cognition is by blood flows and biochemical impulses, even with electrons, but not by electricity exclusively or computer bytes of memory. This is a crisis additional to the one which already exists regarding the proper foundation upon which to rest synthetic (yes, it's a double entendre from both the Greek "putting together" and Quine's first dogma of empiricism) descriptions of behavior. Has mine of the previous discussion been based adequately in empiricism? Have I not been hobbled throughout by the crutch of the word, "soul?" (The last synthesizing thinker in metaphysics to apply soul (Scholastically) to *empirical psychology* was, so far as I can tell, the German philosopher, Joseph Geyser (1869 to 1948)). Regardless of the blindness with which I have applied the maxim of the identification of indiscernibles, so as to paper over in black ink majestic differences of physics and metaphysics between "soul" and all of its bundles of neurons, the descriptions I offer about God have clear meanings beyond ink to me. There is a crisis between "scientific" and "folk" psychology, especially regarding the Scholastic word, "soul," and another one involving the Great Analogy between human and computer belief "boxes," especially about what mental structures in the cranium exist or are necessary existence. Regardless—and knowing that these twin conflicts in psychology will take decades of

---

[12]William James, *The Will to Believe, op. cit.*, p. 542.

[13]See *The Biographical Dictionary of Psychology* (Sheehy, Chapman, Conroy, eds., London, Routledge Press, 1997), pp. 145, 146.

the 21st century to play out in the intellectual life of the world—we hold that some descriptions of Duns Scotus and William James capture an essence of the *voluntas imperans intellectui* and show Will as a separate and empirically discernible phenomenon.

William James described Will as a behavior in terms of resident or remote ideas of movement, a "motor-cue" for a motor discharge and ideo-motor action in the shape of a fiat, decision, consent or volitional mandate before a movement follows.[14] For example, he reached such conclusions as the following:

> "[E]very representation of a movement awakens in some degree the actual movement which is its object; and awakens it in a maximum degree whenever it is not kept from doing so by antagonistic representation present simultaneously in the mind. . . . Movement is the natural immediate effect of the process of feeling, irrespective of what the quality of feeling may be. It is so in reflex action, it is so in emotional expression, it is so in voluntary life."[15]

This analysis is a description of existence, but it is filled with words characterizing physical movements which have no more than symbolic or analogous meanings. For example, do parts of my mind "antagonize" one another? If the meaning of "antagonism" explains something triggering conflict, difference, violence or aggression, no PET scanning which I know of so far shows qualitatively conflicting or different blood at different areas of my brain. Do I "awaken" each time I will to do something? If an awakening explains the one or more occasions that I daily arise from sleep, PET scanning shows that, even as I sleep, my brain is active. Certainly, therefore, I do not assault my mind each time I will to do something, and the antecedent of most such times is not sleep. Nonetheless, there is a residue of meaning to the words of James's analogy. The problem is that we know the words he uses are analogous and, therefore, lacking in meaningfulness to some Ultimate extent. Where may further explanation and justification of Will be described and found?

A phenomenon is any mental *act or object* of presentation to the mind which is or can be perceived by the mind or physical senses. Will is a phenomenal, conscious and mental act. We have noted, by referring to de Biran and Schopenhauer, that some contend it may even be objectified as an object entirely apart from the act or activity or consciousness which it otherwise consists of. Phenomenology is a manner of inquiry to describe conscious phenomena. The hundred-year-old *convention* (is this too artificial for you?) of philosophy and psychology, then, is to root Will into existence by treating of it phenomenally in order to describe it empirically. The Jewish-German philosopher, Edmund Gustav Albrecht Husserl (1859 to 1938), sought a descriptive and structural analysis of consciousness, as opposed to analyzing the cause of it in the brain by neural activity or other means. He constituted a framework of a manner of inquiry for consciousness, mental "acts" (for example, thinking, judging, desiring, willing and what have you) and objects W, X, Y and Z. Husserl's framework for the mental act of Will and its objects (or for any other conscious phenomena, and even if the Will itself

---

[14] William James, *Psychology: Briefer Course,* Chapter XXVI, "Will," in *William James: Writings 1878-1899* (Myers ed., The Library of America, 1992), pp. 388-395.

[15] *Ibid.,* pp. 396, 397.

is an object) is as follows: "All objects refer back to corresponding acts in which they are (or can be) given."[16] In other words, all objects or happenings are correlated to corresponding "acts," but a psychic subject—for example, my ego or yours—is required to make this correlation. "A correlate as such," Husserl says, "has its support in persons and their experiences."[17] For Husserl, therefore, the correlations of the objects of science are in the acts of the scientists; for example, the scientific acts of psychologists in conceiving of the parameters and methods of their experiments give them enough basis in the theory of empiricism to make them Really knowable and, therefore, though nominally called theories, Real enough for the Reality of the world. Only two of Husserl's many correlations between acts and objects concern us further. The first is that set of correlations by which there can be a unified and coherent description of my directed-ness to the objects of my mental "acts." This set of correlations yields Husserl's description of Will (by a method describing also many other acts of mind and consciousness). The second is that one single correlation of my ego, my consciousness, my directed-ness, my Will and my other mental "acts" and all the objects of the world such that the world does not exist but is only a correlate of my consciousness. The latter correlation is uniquely singular and amounts to a justification for one Willful phenomenon by a thought-experiment which Husserl intended would prove the Truth of his entire descriptive scheme.

Husserl's description of that category of directed-ness called Willfulness is a description of the directed-ness of a psychic subject—for example, my ego or yours— which the logic of our language divides into two. First are the *relational* accounts, which see directed-ness as a relation between a subject or a mental "act" and an object—specifically, "I see red" or "Santa Claus wants Christmas" or "the baby moves the mobile." Second (but not in importance) are the *adverbial* accounts, which see directed-ness only as a feature or function of the subject or act, whose features of functions can be expressed by adverbial modifiers—specifically, "I see redly" or "Santa Claus wants Christmas-ingly" or "the baby moves mobile-ing-ly." The relational accounts are not able to provide a uniform structure which would be valid for all acts, because some of them, like hallucination, do not relate to objects which exist. (Is Christmas an existing object?) On the other hand, the adverbial accounts do provide the same uniformity of structure by depending all upon the same ego but, to transcend the orbit of this ego completely and to contact the outside world genuinely, they need objectively something more complete or genuine. (How does a baby move mobile-ing-ly?) An object may be experienced differently in different mental acts. For example, a child is in need of a parent's motivated discipline as well as the same parent's unmotivated Love. Santa Claus judges children at Christmas as well as loves them. On the other hand, matter may be shared by several mental acts which differ widely in quality. A child is the recipient both parental Love and family discipline. I not only see red but hear myself say the word "red." Husserl postulated a monist (that is to say, all

---

[16] Barry Smith, "Common Sense," in *The Cambridge Companion to Husserl, op. cit.*, pp. 423, 424.

[17] *Ibid.*, p. 424; Edmund G. A. Husserl, *Ideas Pertaining to a Pure Phenomenology and to a Phenomenological Philosophy: Second Book,* trans. R. Rojcewicz and A. Schuwer (Dordrecht, Boston, London, Kluwer Academic Publishers, 1989), p. 302.

is one substance) theory of dependent relations between matter and quality such that they stand in a relation of reciprocal dependence upon one another.[18]

How do we relate the objects of parents and children to the qualities of Love and discipline in which they are engaged? This theory, a theory ultimately involving the human consciousness, "enables Husserl to . . . account for the unity of (an) act . . . at the same time (leaving) room for distinct dimensions of variation within its internal structure and thus for the different ways in which it may be intentionally directed towards an object."[19] Husserl's theory, therefore, bridges the gap between the Real materiality of matter and the Ideal conception of quality and is one origin of his philosophy of Idealism. Under this theory (what is it precisely?) the language of both the relational and abverbial accounts of directed-ness are Truthfully descriptive of it. I will X and I will X-ly if the matter of X and the quality of X-ly depend upon one another. But do they? What is the dependent relationship between matter and quality, or between an object and a mental "act?"

To understand Husserl's theory of this relationship it is, as an enduring follower of *Gestalten* would say, necessary to discuss the background from which it arose. The Greek philosopher, Aristotle (B.C. 384 to 322), held that, for both knowledge and perception, there is no knowledge and no act of perception unless there is an object of this knowledge and *something,* necessarily an object, being perceived. Aristotle said: "If the object no longer exists, there can no longer be any knowledge, there being nothing now to know. . . . Suppose that you cancel the perceptible; you cancel the perception as well."[20] As a result, Aristotle held that ". . . with regard to all sense-perception, we must take it that [we] receive perceptible forms [into our minds] without their matter, as wax receives the imprint of the ring without the [ring's] iron or gold, and [the mind] takes the imprint which is of gold or bronze, but not *qua* gold or bronze."[21] The Faylasuf philosopher of Islam, Avicenna (Abu Ali ibn Sina) (980 to 1037), through whom the works of Aristotle became primarily to be read in West Europe, called the form-in-mind of Aristotle's mental act of perception by the Arabic word *ma'ná*. In English, *ma'ná* translates as meaning or message. But, scribes in Latin—the language which intervened in history between Avicenna's Arabic and the English translators of his Greek and Arabic concepts—translated *ma'ná* by the noun *intentio,* from the Latin verb meaning to stretch toward something, specifically by pulling in a bowstring as if to aim an arrow. Predictably, then, Scholastic philosophers of West Europe took the form-in-mind of Aristotle's mental act of perception and stretched it into a form-in-object. But classical perception of an external object is either Aristotle's form-in-mind or *ma'ná*, an Arabic concept that could also be stretched steadily more inward—that is to say, inside a mind

---

[18] Barry Smith and David Woodruff Smith, "Introduction," in *The Cambridge Companion to Husserl, op. cit.,* p. 17.

[19] *Ibid.*

[20] Aristotle, ΚΑΤΗΓΟΡΙΑΙ trans. Harold P. Cooke and Hugh Tredennick as *The Categories of Interpretation* (Cambridge, Mass., Harvard University Press: Loeb Classical Library, 1938, 1967) Ch. 7 "Of Relation," p. 57. But Aristotle said the converse is not True—in other words, that, if you take away knowledge and perception, you do not also take away the objects of knowledge and the perceptible.

[21] Aristotle, ΠΕΡΙ ψΨΗΣ trans. J. L. Ackrill as *On the Soul* in *The New Aristotle Reader* (Ackrill ed., Princeton, N. J., Princeton University Press, 1987), ch. 12, p. 186 (quotation made into an ellipsis and edited by the author).

and, therefore, inside the mind's (inherent?) un-object-ness. On the other hand, the notion of an "idea" to a Western European thinker about experience has traditionally meant both an object and an object-of-thought. This is because, in West Europe, thinkers have inherited the pulling bowstring of *intentio,* whose only reason for being a meaning is to aim at an object. It is no surprise that their mental concepts commonly use forms-in-objects, and it is a rare case of primitive perception where such a use does not occur. Indeed, European thinking for most of the second millennium has traditionally postulated forms-in-objects to be presuppositions for whatever would come next. It has traditionally thought about ideas as objects and objects-of-thought and, therefore, by thinking both are being thought about as "objectively" as possible. This is what we found in the Cartesian reductions at the beginning of this discussion and what you contend I have done here by all manner of thing-i-fying. The result is predictable. Most European thinkers during the second millennium have declared, following Descartes's famous maxim, that, as we think (act of perception), so we are (object of existence). They have equated the act of perception almost entirely with objects, forms-in-objects, that form-in-object which is said to be a "mind," and even with that form-in-object which is said to be the classical "form-in-mind." The result of this first result is predictable. The immanence of acts of knowledge and perception within objects has let Reality be described for Descartes and traditional European thinkers adverbially. It is easier for a Cartesian thinking thing to say "I see red-ly" than it is to say "I see red." The latter statement carries the disconcerting implication to a Cartesian thinking thing that red-ness is quite apart from his grasp of it. (Do you remember the struggle which I previously described to you as I try to grasp my "being-ness?") Yet, this is all by an historical context of the bowstring of Latin noun *intentio* being pulled and stretched outward—that is to say, out into the physical world where arrows strike at objects of sensory perception. But is any form-in-object (remember the dualism of Plato?) the same as Aristotle's form-in-mind? Is the meaning of *ma'ná* only a crude and piercing (not perceiving) arrow?

What did Husserl do to answer the questions? What is his theory of perception? First, he distinguished sharply between an act of perception, the object of the act of this perception and *the content* of the perception. Furthermore, regarding this content, he distinguished between its "real" and "ideal" components. Not only did Husserl follow Aristotle's concepts of the bond of mental acts of perception to objects; he elaborated them in a Scholastic knowledge-tree which he grew as far as could to logical conclusions for the philosophy of how we know and think. In all cases, the axiom of Husserl is that, whenever we are conscious, we are conscious *of something.*[22] In all mental acts which we perform consciously, therefore, we act mentally with at least a version of the form-in-the-mind (a *something*) which Aristotle introduced to the world and Avicenna developed. Husserl called this companion to every mental act of consciousness a noema. This bond of a mental act to a noema gives rise to at least five different schools of interpretation about the bonding. (It is beyond the scope of our

---

[22]Edmund G. A. Husserl, *Ideen zu einer reinen Phänomenologie und phänomenologischen Philosophie* 2 vols. (1913) trans. F. Kersten as *Ideas Pertaining to a Pure Phenomenology and to a Phenomenological Philosophy* (The Hague, Nijhoff, 1982), Book 1, pp. 179, 180.

discussion to delve into them here).[23] But it is the bond of mental acts to noemata which unites the acts to objects and, therefore, to objectiveness. In this bond, quality and matter depend on one another. For instance,

> "perception . . . has its noema, and at the basis of this noema is its perceptual meaning 'the perceived as such.' Likewise, recollection has as its own noema 'the remembered as such.' Everywhere we must take the noematic correlate [to a mental act], which, in a very broad sense, is here referred to as 'meaning,' . . ."[24]

For Husserl, a noematic correlate is existentially necessary because every mental act of consciousness is an intending (a pulling outward, remember *intentio?*) of "what is meant," just as the noema to which it is correlated is properly described as the "object as intended." These correlations between noemata and their respective meanings further unite mental acts and their objects together, although they may otherwise have little relationship in physics or the physical world to one another. For example, I see all sorts of objects in my mind's eye although, at this moment of my life, they no longer exist in the natural world and, like Santa Claus, may never have, except in Spirit. Moreover, Husserl says that what he analyzes for the mental act of perception applies to all types of intentional experience. Accordingly, "[a]fter reduction, memory yields the 'remembered as such;' expectation the 'expected as such;' . . . phantasy, the 'imagined as such' and so forth and so on."[25] This is a brief summary of Husserl's theory of intentional experience, and of his theory of perception as something *bodily* given to a consciousness. It is easy to appreciate why Husserl often exhorted his students by exclaiming: "To the things (bodies) (objects) themselves!"

But what do we assert (justify) when we say the "perceived as such," "the remembered as such" and so forth? The triumphs of physics have banished much from the world outside a mind: colors, raw feelings, the qualitative content of mental states, intrinsic properties of conscious experiences and so forth. Consequently, how do we deal with the subjective features of the mental processes which *are* inside the mind? In other words, as the blood flows of it are being scanned under positron emission tomography ("PET"), how do we deal with what we "know" is there and even see in color? Consider, again, the presupposed nature of an essence. It exists firmly and completely in our minds, though natural types and specimens of it may be altered, changed and even destroyed in the natural world. We have essentially described the Will as a mental "act" in several ways and even related it by Husserl's theory of dependent

---

[23] See, for a discussion of the five Husserlian schools, Barry Smith and David Woodruff Smith, "Introduction," in *The Cambridge Companion to Husserl* (Cambridge, U. K., Cambridge University Press, 1995), pp.23-27. Then, compare the six models of theories of general perception mentioned in Norton Nelkin, *Consciousness and the Origin of Thought* (Cambridge, U. K., Cambridge University Press, 1996), p. 98. The reason for the proliferation of theories is that the senses themselves are not strictly definable in terms of phenomenal types, and that "perception" is a kind of inner judgment defining a boundary of the senses. For example, Nelkin points out that even pain is not strictly sensory but depends upon a certain evaluative psychic state in order to be "pain."

[24] Joseph J. Kockelmans, *Edmund Husserl's Phenomenology* (West Lafayette, Ind., Purdue University Press, 1994), p. 98.

[25] *Ibid.*, p. 100.

relations to most of whatever objects there are. It is only a small step from these essences to a further theory: that there are *things,* psychologists call them "qualia," within our conscious mental content which help us hear music, perceive color, feel raw feelings and deal with all the qualitative mental states that we "know" are there. The Reality of "qualia" may be but another cut from the old saw of thing-i-fying the unthingable. Qualia, like noemata or God, may be figments, but useful ones, of essentialist philosophy. They may explain how the matter of sensory M and sensible M are dependent upon the quality of the M-ly and *vice versa.* The conclusions held by my consciousness about the nature of my existence, as I perceive it for the purpose of concluding them, are likely to involve noemata bound to my sensible perceptions, as well as qualia bound to my sensory ones.

We said that the conclusions of existentialism are *perceived from actual existence,* not Willed from presuppositions about any essence, but we did not say that the essence of perception could be avoided in the act of perceiving. This is why Max Scheler's description of a "scholastic picture" within the essence of physical perception is so important to my understanding of Reality.[26] It is the first domino standing in a row of further dominoes such that, if it falls at the level of empirical psychology, all of the rest of them are not as upright as they should be. Qualia are *supposed* from the thinking of some psychologists; noemata are *supposed* from the thinking of Aristotle, Avicenna and Husserl. All are utterly paradoxical in Truth. For existence is simultaneously "everything" that there is and then "nothing" at all because existence is not one quality an object may or may not possess in relation to others and yet still continue to exist. Existence is the *sine qua non* of *any* object, let alone a noema or or a single quale, and relates, if it does at all, to both everything and nothing simultaneously. (Do you remember that Pseudo-Dionysius the Areopagite employed this same paradox in a correlative fashion in thinking about our symbolic interpretations of God?) While this paradox remains in an unresolved state—that is to say, as long as it remains falsely contradictory—to assert the proposition: "Q exists," is to assert nothing properly meaningful (justified) for analytic logic about forms-in-minds, forms-in-objects, noemata or qualia. We discussed the error (but it was one *in logic only*) of asserting "Q exists; therefore, Q = Y." There is no linguistically objective "predicate" in existence to which Q can properly relate if we say, without more, that "Q exists." Have we said such a more-ness here?

But, may we ask, "Does Q exist?" There seems no way to answer the proposition "Does Q exist?" without assuming Q's existence to answer it. Because in existence nothing is to be presupposed about itself, existence cannot become an object of knowledge and to say "Does Q exist?" is meaningless. These are the *premises* of a philosophy of existentialism, which nullify our presuppositions about God, noemata, qualia, me, existing objects W, X, Y and Z or their meanings. An existentialist must use a blank slate for the *circumstances* of existence itself, the *sine qua non* of any object, any entity or anything. In these *premises,* Kierkegaard correctly said: ". . . [I]f God does not exist, it would of course be impossible to prove it; and if He does exist, it would be

---

[26]Max Scheler, "Die Idole der Selsterkenntniss" (1911) in *Vom Umsturz der Werte* (4th ed. rev., Bern, Francke, 1955) trans. David R. Lachterman as "The Idols of Self-Knowledge" in *Max Scheler: Selected Philosophical Essays* (Evanston, Ill., Northwestern University Press, 1973), pp. 82, 83.

folly to attempt it."²⁷ But Descartes posited his own natural ego as apodictic Truth and set off precisely to do what Kierkegaard said was a folly of living. Having introduced the concept of transcendence to modern philosophy, *Descartes failed to use it completely* and left his own naturally existing self as the final arbiter of his existence. Descartes described Reality adverbially and said, "I am think-ingly," and not "I am this object of this think." Descartes said, "I think therefore I am"—in Latin, *Cogito ergo sum*—put this proposition to the world as an adverbial description around his soul and did no more foundational thinking about it. He thought it was the apodictic Truth.

On the other hand, in the *premises* of the blank slate which existence actually is, Descartes's ego, though housing a mind of admitted genius, still does not equate to apodictic Truth. As a matter of empiricism, Descartes should have used the concept of transcendence upon his own ego. Husserl's theory of perception, by relating mental acts firmly to noemata and their correlates, aimed at a relational account of Reality *with* predicates and objects. Husserl's thinking is useful to existentialist philosophy despite its (unavoidable?) essentialist assumptions at the core of its theory of perception. Husserl said that our transcendental problem in existence includes *everything,* even ourselves. Put more elaboratively,

"[t]his problem [of what we can arrive at outside of what we are] arises when we turn from the natural to the transcendental attitude. In the natural attitude, we take the world as the self-evidently existing universe of all real entities that are continuously before us in unquestioned givenness. In the transcendental attitude, we turn around, away from the field of all theoretical and practical activities in the world, and focus instead consistently on the life of consciousness, in which the world is precisely no more than the world that is present to us."²⁸

After a change from a natural to a transcendental attitude about the world, every meaning of the world is now a conscious meaning because the world is reduced to the subjectivity of consciousness about it and, within that subjectivity, there is a subjective genesis: the existing, psychic, transcendental I. Descartes failed to use it and tainted all of his thinking about existence by the fundamental presupposition he made about himself: that his nature in the world gave him the basis to be absolute and apodictic about it. By taking into account the intellectual traditions of the era in which he lived, we may excuse Descartes for this failure. It is for you to judge whether the previous discussion of my is-ness failed likewise. If so, the end of existentialism which I declared was our goal has not been reached yet. This is so because existence *requires* the transcendental attitude which Descartes introduced to philosophy to find meaning about itself. The ultimate conclusion of the transcendental attitude is that: "if the world does not exist, then only my existing, psychic, transcendental I does." Especially in these subjective circumstances, Husserl's theory of perception, as we have already discussed, is as objectively meant as possible. Only then, by the transcendental attitude applied to

---

²⁷Kierkegaard, *op. cit.,* p. 141.

²⁸Kockelmans, *op. cit.,* p. 185; cf. Husserl, *Phänomenologische Psychologie und transzendentale Phänomenologie* (1925) trans. John Scanlon as *Phenomenal Psychology: Lectures, Summer Semester, 1925* (The Hague, Nijhoff, 1977), Part II, § 7. Husserl's prose has been more clearly summarized and re-written by Kockelmans.

a Cartesian ego, and the full application of Husserl's objectively meant theory of perception within it, is the conscious meaning of every meaning shown and, therefore, the sum total of meaningfulness in my consciousness declared. Bluntly, it would then be possible to "know" what I Really know about myself. If the world does not exist, there are no presuppositions which the world puts on me about what I am supposed to know about me. I could find out, in this kind of thought-experiment free from universalized types, what my consciousness actually consists of, the manner in which I really act, intend, believe and perceive, and the truly adverbial or accusative Reality of my descriptions. This method of the reduction of phenomena into my transcendental consciousness Husserl called *epoché,* or abstention. It means to abstain from positing the natural world so that there is only existing, psychic, transcendental I. The abstention creates the epistemological conditions necessary for me to understand "the fundamental I" existentially and correctly. Merleau-Ponty said this is so because:

> "[W]e are through and through compounded of relationships with the world that for us the only way to become aware of the fact is to *suspend* the resultant activity, to *refuse* our complicity, . . . or yet again, to put it "out of play." *Not* because we reject the certainties of common sense and a natural attitude to things—they are, on the contrary, the constant theme of philosophy—*but* because, being the presupposed basis of any thought, they are taken for granted, and go unnoticed, and because to arouse them and bring them to view, we have to suspend for a moment our recognition of them. . . . *Reflection does not withdraw from the world towards the unity of consciousness as the world's basis; it steps back to watch the forms of transcendence fly up like sparks from a fire; it slackens the intentional threads which attach us to the world and thus brings them to our notice. . . .*"[29]

Husserl's reduction of the world into consciousness means that, because our philosophy of existence *requires* it (how natural is that?) we abandon the natural or naturalistic attitude which takes the world for granted and adopt the attitude of transcending it. On the other hand, Will, that basic but unique combination of the ideas of the mind with motor sensory movements in the world, is a *natural* motivation of the mind to transcend, to live outside of its proper orbit, to rise above the inherent limitations of the world. Moreover, Merleau-Ponty's description of Husserl's reduction is a *natural* description of it to the extent that the suspensions of activity and refusals of complicity which Merleau-Ponty describes in the foregoing quotation are natural, Willful acts. The Will of *homo sapiens* surpasses much. That Husserl's reduction is required by the Will naturally, or from the "natural" requirements of the philosophy of existence, is for you to say. Is every requirement of the intellect necessarily an artifice and not "natural?"

Results of Husserl's Descriptive Method

Let's perform Husserl's thought-experiment, remove the world and see what's left. If you remove all objects of consciousness from yourself, except for the object which is

---

[29]Merleau-Ponty, *Phénoménologie de la Perception* "Preface" in *Essential Works of Existentialism . . . , op. cit.,* p. 358 (italics added).

your knowledge of your awareness of your existence, what's this knowledge? It is four things: first, an awareness of your existence not derived from your existing self but from your attributes; second, an awareness of your freedom to choose; third, an awareness of yourself with time, rather than in time; and fourth, an awareness of various psychological conditions about existence which you cannot stand outside of existence to observe objectively, to-wit, anxiety in existing, pride in existing, despair in existing, faith in existing and so forth. *These four types of awareness in a human soul are my definition of the "Will to Believe."* The rest of this Chapter discusses them one by one.

The Awareness of the Derivation

To be aware of yourself only through your Aristotelian attributes means two things. First, it means a soul's existence is not self-derived; that is to say, the soul's existence is not derived innately from itself as a Divine being and a matter of Aristotelian Original Substance. You are not Divine because your existence is not Original Substance but a bundle of attributes. Your existence is derived from *eros,* sensuality, psychology or "human nature." If an existentialist finds no meaning in the question "Does X exist?," where, at all, is any meaning for him in existing X? The answer is: the existential meaning of X is in X's Aristotelian attributes. I discussed the basis of Aristotle's concept of an attribute previously with the Principle of Identity. The question to ask, then, is: "Does this existing X have the attributes of Y or the attributes of Z?" This question has already been asked by both Theist and Atheist existentialists. The ardent non-Believer, Nietzsche, asked for a passionate reaffirmation of life in all its ambiguity, expounded on the fundamentally living force which he termed "the will to power" but, being bitterly opposed to religion, declared God is dead.[30] Nietzsche then synthesized bundles of attributes which amount to a *virtual* God and hailed them as others would hail God Himself but would protest this conclusion mightily today if he were alive. It is difficult to see, therefore, at least from Nietzsche, where the logical analysis of existence to a "God is Dead" conclusion leads to anything more than to a larger elaboration of the mystery of God, but at a "higher" and more attenuated level. A bundle of attributes, such as Nietzsche's "will to power," is often tantamount to God Himself, even as it is ruthless and a source for doing evil. For example, Nietzsche said, "Man, in his highest and most noble capacities, is wholly nature"—Do you remember Emerson and the Transcendentalists?—"and embodies its uncanny dual"—Do you remember Plato?—"character. Those of his abilities which are awesome and *considered inhuman* are perhaps the fertile soil of which alone all humanity . . . can grow."[31] Thereby, without even slightly intending to, Nietzsche describes the abilities of Jesus of Nazareth. He inadvertently affirms the thinking of Duns Scotus that the bundle of anyone's human attributes relates only to the Divine image in which we are created and not to Divinity itself. You are not God but are "of" God, or "share in God."[32]

---

[30]See Colin Brown, *Philosophy and the Christian Faith* (American ed., Downers Grove, Ill., Inter-Varsity Press, 1968), p. 139. Nietzsche was not the first to declare the death of God. See *ibid.,* p. 139 fn. 5.

[31]Walter Kaufmann, *Nietzsche: Philosopher, Psychologist, Antichrist* (3d ed., New York, Random House: Vintage Books, 1968), p. 178 (italics added).

[32]See Saint Augustine of Hippo Regius, *"de civitate Dei,"* XXII, p. 30, in *The City of God Against the Pagans,* (Green ed., Cambridge, Mass., Harvard University Press: Loeb Classical Library, 1972), Vol. 7, pp. 376-378.

Next, your awareness of yourself through your attributes means you may legitimately speak of "your" feelings as attributes which belong to you and you alone. "Your" feeling of the presence of God, then, is different from that of any other soul and further depends upon the type of religious experience in which it occurs. But "[t]here is severe discipline for him who forsakes [T]he [W]ay; he who hates reproof will die."[33] Kierkegaard asserts every soul lives religious experience in one of three categories of The Way: æsthetically, ethically or religiously. The experience which begins the æsthetic religion finds the need to surpass various psychological conditions and requires passion; that which begins the ethical religion finds the need to surpass passion and requires ideals; and that which begins a "religious" religion finds the need to surpass both ideals and passion *and requires God not present as an object of consciousness either as a feeling or as a proposition.* In introducing a book of the theology of Kierkegaard, the English poet and critic, W. H. (Hugh Wystan) Auden (1907 to 1973), calls the "religious" religion a "revealed religion" such as Judaism or Christianity and explains it as follows:

> "A revealed religion is one in which God is not present as an object of consciousness, either as a feeling or a proposition. . . . While in the æsthetic religion the feelings, and in the ethical religion, the ideas *were* the presence of God, they are now only *my* feelings, *my* ideas and if I believe that what I feel (e.g., God is present) or think (e.g., God is righteous) is caused by my relation to God, *this belief is a revelation for the cause is outside my consciousness*. As one term of a relation, the whole other term of which is God, I cannot overlook the whole relation objectively and can only describe it analogically in terms of the human relation most like it, e.g. if the feeling of which I have immediate certainty is one which I would approximately describe as sonship, I may speak of God as Father."[34]

In this Way, a "revealed religion" awakens the Real psychology of a soul who Believes in God and treats that psychology as belonging to that soul and to none other. There is no question whether the soul and God relate; the only question is whether it is "an explained" or "a justified" relation. Note, however, that by saying "the cause" is *outside the consciousness,* Auden must be saying that it is, in fact, unconscious (for it cannot be otherwise yet still exist). The inference is that Auden postulates the Belief of a "revealed religion" from a cause Ultimately in unconsciousness and, therefore, blocks any further conscious analysis of it introspectively. Surely this is not genuine enough for my own Reality. From the premise that God is present as an unconscious object of my consciousness because I hold a "revealed religion," it does not follow that my consciousness of this premise should be unconscious, too, and, therefore, actually imperceptible to me or to any of my ideas of it. But, maybe, a poet like Auden has a license to be imprecise. If he means "the cause . . . outside my consciousness" is God or the revelation of Him by which I Believe, Auden is supposing either a rather primitive God who lives beyond this Earth, or a revelation of Him to me that I am unconsciously and Cartesianly unaware of. In any event, the unconscious presence of

---

[33] The Book of Proverbs ch. 15, v. 10.
[34] W. H. Auden, "Presenting Kierkegaard," in Søren Kierkegaard, *op. cit.,* p. 14 (italics added for emphasis).

God in my soul means only that, and not anything further about unconsciousness, though I said this consciously.

The Awareness of the Freedom

The awareness of choices is the second category I find for a soul's pure awareness of its existing self. It means freedom to be rational or irrational, to do good or to sin, to do simply what you do or not do, or to Will. And it means these "states of affairs" in finely calibrated degrees. These freedoms, and even more of them, together with the fine calibrations by which they may be employed, if not measured, create a wide gap between God and Man, between human consciousness and the world, and, indeed, among any free X, any Y which is less so and any Z which is not free at all. The gap becomes even wider once the apperception (the perception of the perception) of it is also perceived, and one acknowledges the possibility of an undetermined regression of these correlating apperceptions—for example, as freedom is perceived, the freedom of a freedom is perceived more so and the freedom of this second stage freedom is perceived even more acutely and so forth. It is in the sense of this regression that the French mathematician and philosopher, Blaise Pascal (1623 to 1662), exclaimed, "What a vast distance there is between Knowing God and Loving Him!"[35] A soul's awareness of the knowledge of choices means distance and vastness created between itself and what is chosen. In other words, we easily describe the Will closely to the soul; but the fruits and products of the Willing, the usufructs of Freud's Pleasure Principle applied to this context, must be described not so closely, but by a distance and a gap, varying in proportion to the apperceptions of them. But intellectuals, much as they like perfection, are Freudian-ly pleased by questions and the analysis of them. Surely freedom is not chaos. Are the choices of freedom, despite the distance and vastness created by them, made in a Real space with Real dimensions and, therefore, with Real limitations? Is what is chosen also within this Real space and, by implication, also similarly limited? Can the regression of correlating apperceptions of freedom be determined finally by any of these dimensions and limitations? If so, what are they? Exactly how do they comport with the delicious awareness of *my* freedom?

Wait! Since we engage in rampant reductivism throughout this discussion and now purport to perform the vast reduction of Husserl's thought-experiment by reducing the world all into my mind, aren't we still connected to the world? Why do we even refer to all of these apperceptions which, as a matter of our logic, must necessarily apply to the world and to it alone? The answer is: they are apperceptions, perceptions of perceptions, and, in any event, nothing more than as the sockets of electrical connections for my mind, into which the wires and cables of the world fit or are supposed to, and after we have pulled the wires of the world all out, nothing but the sockets show. It is quite a mess disassembling the complicated components of electronics; why should it surprise you there is a mess of apperceptions here? In my mind alone, as ideas, I see large numbers of possibilities and combinations of freedom. It is possible, even at Auschwitz, for prisoners at a concentration camp, objectively degraded, enslaved, and denuded of humanness, to feel free by the very smallest of acts

---

[35]Brown, *op. cit.,* p. 60; see Blaise Pascal, *Les Pensées* (1670 ed.) trans. Martin Turnell as *Thoughts* (Harvill Press, 1962), p. 330.

or thoughts which pertain to humanness, and to dignity and respect for it. By contrast, it is likely, even at the Capitol of the United States, for leaders of a free nation, objectively free to speak, to vote and to act by following Freud's Pleasure Principle unreservedly, to think they are enslaved by the very smallest orders, demands, commands and questions of others. Freedom and choices sit on piles of perceptions in the world, and on piles of apperceptions in this thought-experiment, wherever and however human souls exist otherwise. This posture means that each one of us is more or less free depending upon that pile we have amassed, or which pile X dumps upon us from outside. It is quite a variation of existence.

But freedom is restrained, regardless of the height of the pile of it, by whole sets of other perceptions and apperceptions relating to evil, sin, wickedness, depravity, death, falsehood, un-Truth and "bad-ness" of all sorts. These other perceptions and apperceptions of evil and company sit on their own piles, and the height and weight of them vary for each of us, not in proportion to the piles of freedom we have, but simply because we are different from each other, and for some of us the piles *are* proportional. Do I choose, like one leader of Great Britain, to do nothing while the enemy bombs a large city filled with my own people, whom I am pledged to protect, so that I can save an *Ultra-Secret* which allows me to protect more? Do I choose, like one leader of the United States, to bomb a large city filled almost entirely with innocent civilians of the enemy, who are nevertheless human beings who will suffer horrible physical effects of the bombing for decades and at least one subsequent generation, so that I can save more of my soldiers, all of whom are already on the front-lines of battle and consciously pledged to die if *necessary?* Or, like every follower of mundane life, do I decide death for a loved one during a pregnancy or a terminal illness? Do I divorce my spouse for my lover? Do I lie because I think it may allow me only to tell a half-truth later? Do I sacrifice X to save Y? Do I? Do I? Do I? Yes, sheer perception of these matters or qualities of "bad-ness" brings on feelings of guiltiness, maybe madness: I think of *the degree* to which I, on my piles, possibly caused them, could have averted or avoided them, am responsible for them and so forth. Freud said religion springs from guilt, and this is one fountainhead.

The experience of death and evil on a large scale at Auschwitz, I said, lead me to seek God. So, for me, isn't God *already* the counter-weight for evil-ness? Why does any limitation upon *my* freedom *need* to weigh against evil also? Can't God *already* be the "perfect" counter-weight to evil-ness for every soul? If He is, or if *my* freedom is actually so free I can start my life in the world again with a clean record, a blank slate, and an expunging catharsis of the past, why does any guilt or evil or sin restrain *my* freedom? Original Sin restrains it, says orthodox Christianity. Obeying God's command as a reasonable and undefective human being seeking the salvation of his soul restrains it, says the Christian heretic and British monk, Pelagius (A.D. 360 to 420?). All of law, personal ethics and morality I hold restrain it. The psychology of my soul restrains it. Scientific facts about my observed existence restrain it. In fact, all sorts of order from everywhere restrain freedom. In fact, freedom is actually so un-free I refer to it normally by an exception rather than the rule, as a deviation rather than the norm, as an heresy rather than the Way, as something without a cost or for which there is no exchange of value, as the "Liberty"of a sailor on the shore rather than in service on his ship. The scarceness of freedom actually may be why there are so many different perceptions and apperceptions of it in the sockets of my mind.

What are the limited choices about God posed actually for the freedom of my soul? In an æsthetic religion, evil is a problem of a lack of relationship to God due to God's Will; in an ethical religion, evil is the same problem but due to man's ignorance; but, in a "revealed religion," evil is sin, a revolt against mankind's presupposed relationship to God. The epistle of Paul the Apostle to the Romans describes one relation of conscious human Will to sinfulness as follows:

> "For I do not do the good I want, but the evil I do not want is what I do. Now if I do what I do not want, it is no longer I that do it, but sin which dwells within me."[36]

So-called "situation ethics" supposes the freedom to choose among alternative actions in any situation given to this supposition; on the other hand, Paul's concept of sin from this verse in his epistle to the Romans overtakes a soul in a situation and makes its actions robot-like, even to the point "it is no longer that I do it" but some different ego. By either hand, both the Pauline concept of sin—in that I am free even to be a different ego—and the freedom of the human Will within the framework of situation ethics allow for freedom even as I said it was scarce.

Why is even a dollop of freedom any problem? It surely was not considered so by the signers of the American Declaration of Independence on July 4, 1776. But, in its deepest sense, my existential freedom is not political freedom or any prosperous autarky; they both are collective concepts. For my lonely existing I, and yours, freedom is a set of excruciating ethical and moral choices, often badly made and implemented, which cause disorder, chaos, even anarchy, un-respectful, un-dignified, un-human existence either at objectively free locations or at objectively un-free ones, and even death-in-life and death. Robots and machines may be autonomous or self-sufficient; for *homo sapiens* it is quite impossible that autonomy or self-sufficiency exist in Reality or Truth. The very lack of self-sufficiency of an independent soul divorced from the physical world is the psychological and spiritual basis for all in this discussion we have shown that soul deals with in existence. The American-Swiss theologian, Francis August Schaeffer (1925 to 1984), says the roots of despair and meaninglessness in contemporary Western civilization lie in autonomous rationalism; that is, in the desire of modern *homo sapiens* to make himself self-sufficient and his reasoning the judge of all things, say, as even I am judging them in this discussion. Schaeffer constructs a metaphysical concept which covers both living and inanimate objects and calls it a "machine." As human societies roll inevitably into their futures, Schaeffer translates most of human nature into increasingly machine-like states of rationalism, sexuality and so forth. But he doubtfully says that the intellectual and cultural history of the next centuries will work through the dilemma between "nature" and freedom as ". . . autonomous freedom and the autonomous machine [a nature?] stand facing each other."[37] This is doubtful because freedom, a characteristic which makes a soul

---

[36] Saint Paul, Letter to the Romans ch. 7, vv. 19- 20.

[37] Brown, *op. cit.*, p. 261; see Francis Schaeffer, *Escape from Reason* (Downer's Grove, Ill., Inter-Varsity Fellowship, 1968), p. 34, reprinted in *Francis A. Schaeffer Trilogy* (Wheaton, Ill., Crossway Books, 1990), p. 228.

fundamentally aware of its existence, is also characteristic of the independent self-sufficiency of a machine. The machine, or robot, is freely (in the sense of independence) self-sufficient, justified completely by its own mechanics and, consequently, Truly "selfish" (insofar as the term "self " may be used in this context). For a human soul to be so related essentially to the constitution of subhuman devices is dehumanizing and a least value it could measure for itself. But such a measurement precludes a confrontation between freedom and machinery as such, because machines, by the foregoing analysis, are free already.

Søren Kierkegaard offers another choice for the situation ethics of a "revealed religion." It is a command of God. The Divine command is: "Choose to do what at this moment in this context I am telling you to do." Kierkegaard put the "choice" as follows:

> "Christianity says to a man: you shall choose the one essential thing but in such a way that there is no question of a choice—if you drivel on any longer, then you do not in fact choose the one essential thing; like the Kingdom of God it must be chosen *first*. So there is something in regard to which there may not be, and in thought cannot be a choice, and nevertheless it is a choice. Consequently, the very fact that in this case there is no *choice* expresses the tremendous passion or intensity with which it must be *chosen*. . . . The inconceivable marvel of the omnipotence of love is that God can really grant so much to man, that almost like a lover He can say of Himself: 'will you have me or not,' and so wait one second for the answer."[38]

"Of all Christian authors," says the French sociologist and theologian, Jacques Ellul (1912 to 1994), ". . . Kierkegaard is the one who has given us the best, the most genuine, the most radical account of the existential reality of faith."[39] Ellul's synthesis of religion with culture is a complicated set of distinctions involving Belief and Faith. He asks: should we either seek precise, restrictive definitions of Belief and then despair of what we find or be eclectic in pursuing Faith and thereby verge on *naïveté?* I said I wanted to follow Wittgenstein's notes and keep magic by banishing it from a cold analysis. If so, if there is no magic to be kept, "[t]he [B]eliever is a slave. And because [B]elief is necessity, an expression of ineluctable forces, people must get rid of it, if they want to be free."[40] A soul, though, craving freedom, must on all accounts avoid anarchy, subhuman-ness and death. This is the dilemma of the earthly life which we have been born into. More precisely, this is our dilemma if we assume that we may be so free so as to die, to be dissolved in chaos, or to be subhuman—that quality of which we physically aren't, so long as we have two arms, two legs (what else?) and, oh yes, a human cranium or, at least, a human's mental capacity. What would metaphysically restrict us otherwise from such an unbounded freedom? The answer is: our own choice to choose a bounded kind of metaphysics. Kierkegaard describes a qualified liberty for Christians which is repelling to 21st century Americans as a matter of politics. But, because of the psychology of the "Dread" and "Sickness unto Death," the limited

---

[38]Kierkegaard, *op. cit.,* pp. 130, 131.

[39]Jacques Ellul, *La Foi Au Prix Du Doute* (Paris, 1980) trans. Peter Heinegg as *Living Faith* (New York, 1st English ed., 1983), p. 106.

[40]*Ibid.,* p. 27.

freedom of individual *homo sapiens* is paradoxically, Ultimately True. Kierkegaard said: "only 'the fear and trembling,' only constraint, can help a man to freedom."[41] The Swiss theologian, Émil Brunner (1889 to 1966), noted that God Wills my freedom for the express purpose that I should be able to answer Him, even if I deny Him in doing so. Brunner saw human freedom always restricted by the responsibility of answering to God one way or the other. If a soul accepts Christ, Brunner said the essence of the Christian Faith is expressed by the phrase: "whose service is perfect freedom"—in Latin, the phrase is *cui servire est regnare*.[42] Consequently, the "Will to Believe" is based on all of the choices posed by the paradoxical Truth of freedom, but not on the complete freedom to pursue them. That pursuit is the path a free soul follows to die.

The Awareness of the Time

The third category of awareness relates to time and is what sense of time Paul Tillich called the "Eternal Now." Civilization speaks of time in three ways: the past, the present and the future. But since clock-time, *chronos,* rolls by like an everflowing stream, when is the moment that "the present" exists Really? That moment has by now inevitably disappeared into the past in the length of time it has taken you to think of it. It can only be conjured up "now" with a view to the past or to the future. Only if a soul suspends itself above existence can it Really be aware of the present. Tillich said the existence of a human soul in time is linear and consists of a coming out from the darkness of the "not yet" and a rushing into the darkness of the "no more."[43] When, then, is the Reality of the present? Tillich answers, ". . . *in the mystery* that we *have* a present; and even more, that we have *our* future because we anticipate it in the present; and that we have *our* past also, because we remember it in the present. In the present our future and our past are *ours*."[44] This awareness of a soul existing with time, rather than in time, may be described by a second Greek word for time: *kairos. Kairos* means the "right" time, the qualitative time of the occasion. From *kairos* a soul realizes it can possess its own time *qualitatively;* this realization is as significant for the soul as the self-knowledge of attributes or the genuine possession of feelings or the apprehension of freedom. But there is a contradiction: the soul gains a possession of itself which is Ultimately True but which is still mysterious and unknown. Science shows by experiment the acceleration and deceleration of *chronos* at unworldly velocities of light, but science seems to fail to show *kairos* experimentally.

Or does it? We say *kairos* is not proved by the experimental methods of science and is a theory of experience in one meaning of empiricism only. But what do we mean by the meaning of the word "proof?" Though we are presently amidst Husserl's thought-experiment and may be so supposed to be set apart from the world within our consciousness alone, that lonely consciousness knows by itself and is aware of the analyzed, scientific existence it has lived in. The apperceptions of it are everywhere. We may surely consider them now. In these premises of our thinking, we discuss some experimental results of cognitive psychology here, in this thought-experiment, which

---

[41] Kierkegaard, *op. cit.,* p. 130.

[42] Émil Brunner, *The Christian Doctrine of Creation and Redemption: Dogmatics* (London, Lutterworth Press, 1952), Vol. II, pp. 55-58; see *The Christian Theology Reader, op. cit.,* § 6.41, p. 243.

[43] Paul Tillich, *The Eternal Now* (New York, Charles Scribner's Sons, 1963), pp. 122, 126.

[44] *Ibid.,* p. 130.

show the differences, because of a lapse of time, among *chronos,* what has Really happened in that given quantity of *chronos,* and what the brain perceives has happened. By analyzing phenomena within discrete quantities of *chronos,* an experimentalist certainly understands a meaning from them. The meaning is: there is a divergence between *chronos* and what the brain actually takes for Reality. The American psychologist, Daniel Clement Dennett (b. 1942), says that the flash of a single frame of television is about 30 milliseconds, but that a duration of about 50 milliseconds is required for the visual system of a human brain to resolve order among different stimuli.[45] Accordingly, when a scientist shows human subjects two visual stimuli in series one after the other, with the second "masking" the first, and the showing is completed before the lapse of 50 milliseconds, the subjects report seeing only the second visual stimulus.[46] Since the dawn of the age of motion pictures in the first decade of the 20th century, psychologists have studied the phenomena of presenting a rapid succession of "still" visual images to human subjects, because this succession of rapid images is the device by which motion pictures and television create the illusion of apparent motion, and this device of a discernible difference between appearance and Reality is an available and convenient framework for some empirical reasoning about human experience actually. The German-American psychologist, Max Wertheimer (1880 to 1943), called the phenomena "phi" and was the first to study it systematically.[47] In a simple case, Dennett reports, "if two or more small spots separated by as much as four degrees of visual angle are briefly lit in rapid succession, a single spot will seem to move back and forth."[48] In a more complicated case, of a duration of as much as 200 milliseconds between the onset of a visual stimulus and the end of it, two differently colored spots at different locations are lit in succession for 150 milliseconds each with a blank interval of 50 milliseconds between them. In such a case, human subjects report seeing that the first spot seems "to begin moving and then change color *in the middle of its illusory passage* toward the second location."[49]

Is this proof of *kairos* or not? Cognitive psychology has certainly proved either that the brain exercises its own "temporal window of control," or that experimental methods of psychology are of such power and sufficiency that they overwhelm the capacities which thousands of years of evolutionary history have outfitted our brains for at this stage. Even if our brains are overwhelmed accordingly, any considerate characterization of the overwhelming involves the postulation of either *kairos* or a "temporal window of control." Both show how the brain can stand apart from *chronos.* The Truth of *kairos* for a soul in these *circumstances*—the circumstances of having both scientific experiments and further verbal descriptions—is the process of surpassing, suspending

---

[45]Daniel C. Dennett, *Consciousness Explained* (Boston, Little, Brown & Co., 1991), pp. 141, 150.

[46]*Ibid.,* p. 141; see Elizabeth Fehrer and David Raab, "Reaction Time to Stimuli Masked by Metacontrast," in *Journal of Experimental Psychology,* Vol. 63, pp. 143-147 (1962); Fehrer, Hershenson and Raab, "Visual Reaction Time and the Broca-Sulzer Phenonmenon," *ibid.,* Vol. 61, pp. 193-199 (1961).

[47]See Max Wertheimer, "Experimentelle Studien über das Sehen von Bewegung," in *Zeitschrift für Psychologie,* Vol. 61, pp. 161-265 (1912).

[48]Dennett, *op. cit.,* p. 114.

[49]*Ibid.,* p. 114; see Paul Kolers and Michael von Grünau, "Shape and Color in Apparent Motion," in *Vision Research,* Vol. 16, pp. 329-335 (1976).

and transcending the soul over *chronos*. This is another way of saying that, for the soul to be in the presence of itself in the "eternal now," it is in the presence also of what strictly *does not exist*. Isn't this my very definition of God? At Walden Pond in Concord, Massachusetts, Thoreau famously thought, *"God himself culminates in the present moment* and will never be more divine in the lapse of all the ages."[50]

The Awareness of the Feelings

The fourth category I find about the awareness of my soul apart from the world is awareness of my many psychological states—for example, anxiety in existing, despair in existing, faith in existing, judging in existing, desiring in existing and so forth. We referred to these states previously regarding the needs of souls. We saw then that psychology in the world triggers a Belief in God; we see now that psychology under the terms of this thought-experiment in my conscious mind completes it. For we circle back to the previous psychological states and show how so keenly my consciousness is subjectively aware of them; how so acutely it needs to treat of them by therapy, catharsis or purification; and how much I Will to do so in three ways—by the mental act of Willing (this is the method of Husserl's philosophy), a larger phenomenon of my senses called the Will (the method of Schopenhauer's philosophy), or as the dynamic force and justification of my life (Duns Scotus's philosophy). Yet, though I stand apart from the world in this thought-experiment, I cannot stand outside of my consciousness to observe these psychological states outside of myself. As a result of the lack of a fixed, external point of reference, I cannot reach any final, rational objectivity about them, though I try this often and with the illusion of succeeding at it. Perhaps, my unconsciousness performs such a task, but the elucidation of any unconscious task consciously is necessarily (naturally) obscure to me. Such an elucidation is Truly a matter of a fine theory. Whether any such of a particular theory applies to my unconsciousness I am even more unable to stand outside of myself to know. All I can do consciously is to acknowledge the likelihood of this role for my unconsciousness in large and unfathomed measures.

But isn't this, so far, all a matter of technique? In other words, I speak of a circling back to psychology, of an acute set of needs demanding a "treatment," but of a curious imprisonment inside of my consciousness where I say that I am deprived of the ability to reach a final, rational objectivity about the psychology or the Real set of my needs. In existence, where does the circle, the acute set of needs, the "treatment" and the imprisonment appear? The French philosopher, Jacques Derrida (b. 1930), summarized (but not in the capacity of an historian as such) the deconstruction of all forms of Reality which has occurred in the intellectual conversations of many thinkers living in the last two centuries. Derrida's summary is by the pithy phrase in French: «*Il n'y a pas de hors-texte.*» In English, this phrase roughly means: "There is nothing outside-the-text." Put more elaborately, as I construct the text of these sentences, *I choose by my human freedom* to show you only that text of Reality which I can put to the world by my thinking about it within the context of a writer's existence. Moreover, as I put this text of my meaning out, I simply make it up as I write it, by my neuroanatomy, the scientific processes of this neuroanatomy, the nerve endings of my fingers hitting a keyboard and

---

[50]Henry David Thoreau, *Walden* (Shanley ed., Princeton, N. J., Princeton University Press, 1989), p. 97 (italics added).

the chemical composition of the black ink in which the language symbols on the keys hit by my finger strokes are actually displayed. There is, strictly speaking, nothing outside of the text of these scientific descriptions which accounts for these sentences of my thinking—much less any circle, any acute set of other needs, any treatment or any imprisonment, all of which are *hors-texte* and, therefore, outside of the text I have chosen for *my* Reality and *my* world. As a result of this deconstruction of my existence into a context, and the further deconstruction of this context into sporadic texts, it is easy to see, even in psychology, that the logic of disassembly might reduce awareness to language. In other words, it might be contended, through a version of psychological nominalism, that:

> "*all* awareness of sorts, ressemblances, facts, etc., in short all awareness of abstract entities—indeed, all awareness even of particulars—is a linguistic affair. According to it [the linguistic affair of awareness], not even the awareness of such sorts, ressemblances, and facts as pertain to so-called immediate experience is presupposed by the process of acquiring the use of language."[51]

Standing apart from the world in Husserl's thought-experiment, is my psychic, transcendental consciousness overwhelmed by all of the speech-acts and Truth-claims of a text? Or is it, instead, amazed at all of the tools of my mind that I hold inside of my mind with which to think and to feel them? Don't these mental tools allow me at least to investigate "the relations" between even Derrida's theories of deconstructed Reality and "the evidence?" W. V. Quine constructs enough of Reality in the world to allow for such a psychological investigation.[52] We said we would be empirical. Empiricism relates to investigations of evidence. The world is surely not of such abysmal nothingness that there would be no evidence at all to be examined by my mental tools. Those tools allow me even to stand outside of even the most nihilistic theories of deconstructionism in order to assess them. Furthermore, the key assumption about *any* context of existence is that there is a *choice of human freedom* to apply that context or not or to exist within it or not. The key assumption about any conversation of conscious thoughts between thinkers is the *choice of human freedom* which the conversing minds make about when the Truth has been "satisfied" or not, and that the conversation will end even so. But how are we to treat of these choices of human freedom except but under the treatment of the previous Section which I afforded to them? Do you remember that the path of complete freedom was the one a soul follows in order to die?

The answers resulting from the foregoing questions, as well as my feeling about the satisfactions I find from them, are the basis for my William James-like—that is to say, transcendingly psychological—concept of a "Will to Believe." For satisfaction is a mental act of perception which, as Duns Scotus said for Scholastically conceived of

---

[51] Wilfrid Sellars, *Science, Perception and Reality* (London and New York, 1963), p. 160.

[52] Richard Rorty, *Philosophy and the Mirror of Nature* (Princeton, N. J., Princeton University Press, 1979), p. 220; see Willard V. O. Quine, "Grades of Theoreticity," in *Experience and Theory* (Foster and Swanson eds., Amherst, Mass., 1970); Quine, "Epistemology Naturalized," in *Ontological Relativity and Other Essays* (New York, Columbia University Press,1969), reprinted in *Human Knowledge: Classical and Contemporary Approaches* (Moser and vander Nat eds., New York, Oxford University Press, 1995), pp. 419, 427.

"The days of the bartender-psychologist are over, but I can help if you have any software problems."

"acts," is ultimately controlled by Will and not by intellect. In an allegory of the Book of Isaiah is a paradigm for the transformation of my subjective psychological states by a "Will to Believe" into a Belief in God. The allegory is as follows:

> "[A soul] is calling. . . : 'Watchman, what of the night? Watchman, what of the night?' The watchman says: 'Morning comes, *and also the night*. If you will inquire, inquire; [be converted, e.g., be a Believer and] come back again;'"[53]

In this allegory a soul, like mine or yours or any other, Believes in order to understand what is said (in language!) dreamt, felt or symbolized (in mathematics!) about the light and dark conditions of existence on this Earth. The Watchman is either God or, following the framework of the transcendental attitude of Husserl, the psychic, transcendental consciousness of a soul. The soul Believes in order to know Divinely and has the Will to do so because: first, the soul knows humanly it is not Divine and has its own human feelings and feels it may not be in the "right" relationship with the Watchman; second, it chooses this; third, it holds time *mysteriously* (certainly in *kairos* and perhaps in the "eternal now") so that day, night and the moment of inquiry of the Watchman can be perceived together; and fourth, it is possessed, singly or in combination with one another, of any one or more certain psychological states, called sometimes affects, memes, noemata or qualia of the mind, which the soul cannot "Really" stand outside of itself to observe objectively. These are the several elements of a compelling "Will to Believe."[54]

---

[53] The Book of Isaiah ch. 21, vv. 11, 12; see Ellul, *op. cit.,* p. 201 (inserts and italics added).

[54] Compare Martin Heidegger, *Sein und Zeit* (Halle, 1927) trans. John Macquarrie and Edward Robinson as *Being and Time* (New York, Harper & Row, 1962), p. 227. For Heidegger, Will is not an independent faculty, or subdivision of a self, but a function of a personhood in its entirety, related to the concept of Care (Sorge). "Conscience is the call of Care," and "manifests itself as Care." *Ibid.,* p. 319.

Chapter Six. The House of Beth-El

Raising the Rock

Epistemology, the philosophy of knowing how natural science knows what it knows, sees the House of Beth-El clearly. On the level of natural science, it is the place of one rock Jacob put vertically upon a desert landscape of no use whatsoever except as a symbol or depository of his spirituality. By serving these functions in terms of Jacob's spiritual behavior, the symbol and the depository are useful descriptions of that behavior as a matter of descriptive psychology. They may even say something about the causes of such behavior in Jacob, the useful effect for him in the future of performing an otherwise useless act presently, and the meaning of the causes and effects. On the level of epistemology, how we know any or all of these conclusions of science is known ultimately and completely only by knowing the scientists who reach them—their integrity in performing experimental acts to test Jacob's rock for all sorts of properties related to its purported degree of utility as this rock, instead of, say, *that* gold; their theory of geology by which *this* rock is actually valued at nothing; their theory of experience in reaching Jacob's spirituality and determining how the position of a useless rock could possibly meet his psychological needs; their presuppositions about symbolic expressions and "thing-i-fying" depositories of spiritual and psychological meaning; their perspectives upon their own worlds in reaching these presuppositions; in fact, everything about them which bears upon these perspectives, even if it includes the indigestion they suffered yesterday from eating spicy food. On the level of epistemology, then, there is a potentially infinite series of propositions which must be reduced to knowledge to say the knowable. At some stage of the reduction, we say it would be absurd to go further; "let's stop with what we have and find the Truth we have reached about Jacob's rock to be adequate and adequately arrived at." But how do we know when to stop reducing the data of this world into knowledge useful to us about the rock and Jacob? It is *this* knowledge, the knowledge of when to stop the process of further knowing, that needs its own depository, a place where we can safely and prudently say, "let's inquire about Jacob and his rock no further." What is this place?

It's the House of Beth-El itself. Are you surprised? This House is useless, but the very uselessness of it has an essential utility—it may not be used for anything else; it is without form or pretense to suppositions about anything other than what it is: an anonymous place of one rock set in an empty desert of the Middle East which is probably safe because of the very anonymity of it. The safety, anonymity, inutility and sacredness of it—Jacob anointed the rock with precious oil and said it was sacred—means it is a nice home for the *Ding an sich,* a German phrase meaning the "Thing-in-Itself." For there *is* a *Ding an sich* in every scheme of Man's involvement, whether it be religion or philosophy or epistemology or the natural sciences. The *Ding an sich* is the thing-in-itself beyond which nothing more is a thing; the thing of the thought-in-itself beyond which nothing more can be thought of a thing. It exists everywhere Man thinks. If you haven't seen it somewhere yet, you either haven't been looking hard enough or need to examine the actual boundaries of your where-ness. Do you remember the Ultimate supervision of boundaries by Roman Terminus and Judeo-Christian *Terminus*? Our discussion has ranged over centuries and referred to nutshells of thoughts of many thinkers. At one pole of essentialism is the philosophy of Nicholas of Cusa; at the other pole of existentialism is the philosophy of Jean-Paul Sartre. Nicholas saw the world so objectively but essentially that the *Ding an sich* for him, the combination of the infinite and the finite together in the same places, is a definitive absurdity of physics. Sartre saw the world so subjectively but existentially that the *Ding an sich* for him, the combination of solipsism and intersubjectivity in his Doctrine of the Look,[1] is a definitive absurdity of psychology. Between the objectivity of Nicholas and the subjectivity of Sartre there are all manner of other possible combinations of thinking; each has a *Ding an sich* of its very own. For subjects-in-themselves and objects-in-themselves are all alike in being "in-themselves." You may say God Himself is a *Ding an sich*. All *Dings an sichs* (this is not the German plural but my own pluralization), need safety in the House of Beth-El because, by the plain nature of their opaqueness, they are consequently dangerous for the Ultimate meaning of life.

The conscious meaning of my Belief in God is at the fanciful anointments of Jacob, or at the *Ding an sich* of any Cartesian thinking. Maybe also, as Auden said, the cause of it is shrouded outside consciousness, much as I have said there will be a veil of incomprehensibility drawn down upon my thinking about it at some point. But I have devoted some part of my conscious life to Believing and attending the rites of a community of Believers. Belief about my Belief is surely cognitive and not unconscious. The German theologian, Rudolf Otto (1869 to 1937), argued, nonetheless, that the rational and moral elements of religion have too often preoccupied both philosophers and theologians with doctrines and dogmas, to the detriment of the essence of religion, which he found in the idea of the word "holy." Finding, in his lifetime, this word even overlaid with an excess of dogmatic and moral associations, Otto used the Latin word for divinity, *numen*, to explain the numinous state of mind into which he thought all religious content should be put. Otto said there are "two values to distinguish in the numen; its fascination (*fascinans*) will be that element in it whereby it is of *subjective* value (=beatitude) to man; but it is august (*augustum*) in so far as it is recognized as possessing in itself *objective* value that claims our homage."[2] From Otto's statement, one infers that a numinous state of mind translates back and forth between reasonable Values of subjectivity and an emotional state of fascination, and, likewise, between reasonable Values of objectivity and an emotional state of augustness—that is to say, by the plain meaning of augustness, one marked by majesty, dignity or grandeur.

---

[1] Jean-Paul Sartre, *L'Être et le néant* (1943) trans. Hazel E. Barnes as *Being and Nothingness* (New York, Washington Square Press, 1956), p. 475 *et seq*. Sartre held that the awareness of another's existence is the result of being under the other's Look. That gaze, he said, is so penetrating it can tell you much or all about the other's other-ness.

[2] Rudolf Otto, *Das Heilige* (1917) trans. John W. Harvey as *The Idea of the Holy* (London and New York, Oxford University Press, 1923, 1950, 1982), p. 52 (italics in the original).

What is the actual content of these Values for Otto? His thinking about the concept of a *numen* leads only to the explanation of a psychological condition within a human soul, and not, further, to a justification of why that condition or its psychology is a Value which should be justified. In other words, critics[3] of Otto's idea of the "holy" say that it consists of an ideogram, a picture or symbol which a thinker uses in a thought-system to represent the placement of content C, without describing C in terms of Cartesian intelligence by the thing, object or idea (do you remember the traditionally objectified ideas of West Europe?) of which C substantially consists. Is the content of this discussion beginning with Descartes a content C which may be placed into Otto's ideogram? If so, this discussion transforms his concept of *numen* from an ideogram into a philosophy (at least a thought-system of theology) with much intellectual content as well as style. The House of Beth-El, then, is both a part of the justified content of my Belief in God as well as a pictorial explanation of a *Gestalt* pattern in which that content, or any other justified content for that matter, may be placed.

I came consciously to Believe in God from the deepest and most genuine experiences of my life, whose Reality is all I have. The sum total of that Reality is not the clarification of my concepts, even if numinous, but of myself. Do you remember the fundamental difference between justification and explanation? Explanations leave room for more explaining; justifications don't. Justifications, in some relation or reliance, involve the *Ding an sich,* after which nothing more is said or can be. When pressed about his obligations to society, the American entertainer and movie star, Frank (Francis Albert) Sinatra (1915 to 1998), quoted another American movie star, Humphrey (de Forest) Bogart (1899 to 1957), and declared that the only obligation of an entertainer to the public is a good performance.[4] By contrast, the English poet and playwright, William Shakespeare (1564 to 1616), profoundly examined human behavior in his plays and said that "all the world's a stage."[5] If so, where is Sinatra's self-confessed obligation of a good performance to be played out exactly? Is it only restricted to those areas which Terminal God has marked out with microphones and spotlights? Or is more needed to define the boundaries of this stage of a performing theater? If a Freudian psychologist reduces all the world involved in Sinatra's concept of performance to his *eros* and life-spirit, the psychologist may properly ask whether Sinatra "*feel(s) less* in order to *perform better!* This is a symbol, as macabre as it is vivid, of the vicious circle in which so much of all culture is caught."[6] The grandiose performances, which we often humanly oblige ourselves to undertake, equally as often oblige us to suppress the extent of our feelings about them. This is one description of the psychological manner in

---

[3] See, for example, Colin Brown, *Philosophy and the Christian Faith* (Downers Grove, Ill., Inter-Varsity Press, 1968), pp. 231, 232.

[4] Refer to Chapter Five, footnote 1.

[5] William Shakespeare, "As You Like It," Act II, Scene vii, Line 139; likewise, Shakespeare, "Merchant of Venice," Act I, Scene i, Line 77.

[6] Rollo May, *Love and Will* (New York, W. W. Norton, 1969), p. 55. The American psychologist, Rollo (Reese) May (1909 to 1994), considered the relationship of sex to "love" and made this statement in the context of the English word, "love." This word is more broadly defined than the different Greek concepts it actually contains. May asserted this statement by using an overly broad word, but solely within the context of relating sexual performance (sex) to sexual feeling (love). Yet, the statement holds true for "human performances" generically, insofar as Freudian psychology reduces them to issues of sexuality and rightly holds that sexuality is an irreducible posit of existence.

which we try to live (perform) more than we love. (Moreover, I use the word "love" here by all of its comprehensive senses in the English language.)

The German theologian and leader of the Protestant Reformation, Martin Luther (1483 to 1546), said, *"Glaubst du, hast du;"* "As you Believe, so you have." He meant by this, in speaking to Christians who Believed already, that you may possess a Belief in God within your soul, as a *Ding an sich,* as the deepest subjectivity. Atheists, and non-Believers unconscious of their Atheism, interpret the meaning of Luther's aphorism objectively. They hold that Luther aphorized that you have a grip of yourself if you Believe and, consequently, God must be only a projection upon a screen, a figment of your gripping Self.[7] But, in this discussion, I have tried to interpret the Non-Believer's interpretation of Luther's aphorism still more objectively! My thinking started with an empirical framework and the needs of human souls, to show a screen upon which an image of God can be projected. I also had another motive: if God *is* the magic of a star upon a screen in movies, the magic of magic is in the seeing of how it arises from the un-magical—the structure of logic and the observation of science as clearly and coldly as I could put them. But my final motive trumps all: it is to show that this imaginary, transcendent place—which the screen of our projection of God is—is even more imaginary and transcendent than the subsequent images and transcendences shown by the rest of this discussion! The screen, after the last film is spliced on the cutting-room floor, is us humans living beyond our limitations and outside of ourselves. For but one example of this out-living, we hold that it is what President Clinton would be doing if his soul accepted a forgiveness of himself from himself because of his behavior during the Lewinsky affair, rather than accepting the more objectively put principle that any sort of Real forgiveness *only* comes from God or from other people. Any excuse which relies on itself alone, but especially as an excuser, is inexcusable to both God and logic. Therefore, what can be more shaky or illusory than that out-living beyond ourselves which all of us do daily? But what *were* the other images and transcendences we compare this to? They were: God living within my soul; Love living in it; Jesus the Christ living outside of Himself in *circa* A.D. 30; Jesus the Christ living outside of Himself as I write this today; and my transcendental consciousness living outside of the world. Respectfully, the latter transcendences have more stuff of un-tautological validity than the former one does. This is ever because the screen by which you would project God is your own self-referring Reality.

For these reasons, therefore, I started with Man and not with God or His direct revelation of Himself to me or to anyone else. For "I heard a great voice from the throne saying, 'Behold, the dwelling of God is with men. He will dwell with them, and they shall be his people.'"[8] Kant heard this also when he remonstrated to the throne of King Friedrich Wilhelm. But many firmly criticize this approach for being a "natural theology" leading up a "blind alley." Its human premises mean *there is always* the nagging question God is but a figment.[9] The American Protestant theologian, Cornelius Van Til (1895 to 1987), asserts that "[i]t is not as though the evidence shows *a* god

---

[7]See Ludwig Feuerbach, "The Essence of Christianity," (1841) in *The Christian Theology Reader* (McGrath ed., Oxford, U. K., Blackwell Publishers, 1995, 1996, 1997), § 9.2, pp. 320, 321.

[8]The Book of Revelation ch. 21, v. 3.

[9]See Brown, *op. cit.,* p. 273.

exists or that God *probably* exists . . . [b]ut the eternal power and Godhead of Paul's Gospel are clearly visible to all men everywhere."¹⁰ The Swiss theologian, Karl Barth (1886 to 1966), asserts that God is *Wholly Other,* and that the revelation of the *Wholly Other* on this Earth in the gospels of Jesus the Christ is the only proper point of the beginning of knowledge of God. This knowledge is not just something one can find as one wishes by following a line of reasoning in philosophy. It is the result of personal encounter with Christ. The task for an apologist of Christianity is not to find common ground with Non-Believers so that all may stand alike, but to show Non-Believers their own responsibility before God and to cut off any avenue of escape from a responsibility to Believe. The defect in the Divine approach of Barth and Van Til is, of course, that it makes too many presuppositions for some scientific minds, is prone to a thesis of Revelation too essentialist, obscure or rebuttable for *homo sapiens* in a scientific world, and is not tied, *at the beginning,* into the varieties of psychological experience innately and commonly shared by normal and not mentally defective members of this species.

So! It is, as Tillich says, that each time we try to pull God down to ourselves—because we must do so to begin the "objectifying interpretation" which starts the transcendence which is the cognitive, *not the whole,* basis of our Belief—we fall into the controversy of Pelagius.¹¹ The thinking of the early Christian heretic, Pelagius (*c.* A.D. 360? to *c.* 420?), was the woe of Saint Augustine's spiritual life but a precursor of many modern counterparts. Pelagius followed the classical Greek tradition of glorifying the Rational Free Wonder of Man and all his works. He rejected the innate defectiveness of Man, which Augustine postulated under the Doctrine of Original Sin, and held that death is a natural event which happens anyway, even if Adam and Eve had not eaten forbidden fruit in the Garden of Eden. It is not the purpose of this discussion to rebute or refute the Pelagian controversy; it *is* the purpose here to discuss foundations of a Belief in God, even if God's foundations are not Direct Revelations, but analogous to what Man is—a veritable potpourri of thinking. On the other hand, between the justification which surrounds the entire is-ness of a thinker (still called, by me, a soul) and the justification which arises from analogues of rationality to the thinker's thoughts, which is the better or the more? Iris Murdoch noted in her works of thought that a sublime combination of Love and Will began in primitive man, resurfaced in the oral tenets of Jesus the Christ and in the written ones of Saint Augustine, was refined by the Scholasticism of Duns Scotus, and ends in the *eros* of modern theologians and the psychological Belief of William James.¹² But the justification of that sublime combination which she noted in her thought-works (while she could still think them clearly) may be less or worse to her than the justification which she found or felt for that same sublimity as she lived. Murdoch suffered from Alzheimer's disease but loved

---

¹⁰*Ibid.,* p. 247; see Cornelius Van Til, *The Defense of the Faith* (Nutley, N. J., Presbyterian and Reformed Publishing Co., 1955, rev. 1967); Saint Paul, *Letter to the Romans,* ch. 1, v. 19: "For what can be known about God is plain to them, because God has shown it them."

¹¹See Paul Tillich, *A History of Christian Thought* . . . , *op. cit.,* pp. 122-131.

¹²The American philosopher and poet, George Santayana (1863 to 1952), contended that James himself did not Believe in God but merely argued, as a matter of his moral and professional philosophy, for one's right to Believe.

nonetheless and was lovingly cared for by her aged husband and his will to will it.[13] On the other hand, Edmund Husserl, as an ethnic Jew, was a Lutheran Believer who suffered "enormously"[14] under the Nazi *régime*. Husserl lived, at least during the last years of his life, as a persecuted but religious soul while still expounding a Cartesian framework for the psychology of the human consciousness, some of which we have previously described and shown to be worthy of a great significance. But is it even a fair question to ask whether there is a better-ness or more-ness about Husserl's justified existence when his Lutheran Belief, his persecution by an evil *régime* and his Cartesian philosophy are Ultimately compared together? Who performs any such of an Ultimate comparison and still lives as a human does? In other words, philosophy and all thoughts of its thinking by contrasts and comparisons, even on the level of a *Gestalt* theory of forms-on-backgrounds with which to compare them, are limited Ultimately by God. Only God compares the love of which Murdoch thinks in her thought-works with the love Murdoch has lived her life. Only God compares the thought of Husserl, as he launched it to the world from his professorships at the Universities of Göttingen and Freiburg, to Husserl's feelings, as the world of Hitlerism said it cared not at all about his thinking and slung the fact of his entire existence as an ethnic Jew back into his face. This comparison of thinking to feeling, and *vice versa,* is one description of God's Final Judgment.

Arius thought rationally about perfection and imperfection, and Pelagius did so about freedom and natural existence. What do we Really conclude about these erstwhile heretics? Orthodox Christianity morally and ethically condemned both of them for thinking about God by blasphemy. But the conversations of Atheists, immoralists and scientists are not, by themselves, illogical by the mere fact they can be characterized by the standards of behavior we apply to them to show their nature as Atheism, immorality or science. It is a false premise about rationalism (the body of philosophy developed by a Cartesian thinking thing) to suppose that, just as it is linked to the forms of logic, so it is also linked to standards of behavior, even when these standards are elevated from custom, nature and convention to rules of morality and ethics. The distinction between form and substance is not one which a convinced rationalist can easily forego, even as he argues against the substance of Atheism, immorality or Pan-Scientism by being flatly convinced of the false promise of their content. A reasonable person must at least acknowledge the chance or possibility that the heresy or condemned behavior of one age may amount to the orthodoxy of the next, as Theodore Parker said. Furthermore, the reduction of a substance into parts of substances does not, of itself, certify to the rationality of any newly conceived whole being equal to the sum of the parts to which it has been reduced. When a Cartesian thinking thing bestows his approval that the parts of a whole are rational, the approval is simply an approval as such, the psychological and emotional state of approving, and not a further statement of logic about the correlations of the parts, or whether they fit rationally into the whole or not. But, then,

---

[13] John Bayley, *Elegy for Iris* (New York, St. Martin's Press, 1998); see Mary Gordon, "Iris and John," in *The New York Times Book Review*, p. 5 *et seq*. (December 20, 1998) in *The New York Times,* Vol. CXLVIII, No. 51,377, § 7, p. 5 *et seq*. (December 20, 1998).

[14] Joseph J. Kockelmans, *Edmund Husserl's Phenomenology,* "Introduction," (West Lafayette, Ind., Purdue University Press, 1994), pp. 3, 5.

hasn't any Divine nature which you perceive in the logic of this discussion been undercut? If logic, beyond the strictly logical, is not imbued with some further and, therefore strictly speaking illogical, quality of Divinity, how is it possible for Divinity ever to be rationally attained here? The answer is that logic itself, not content, saves our Divine premises in these circumstances. For, if *all* of this discussion is fit logically within an ideogram, to be perceived of by you as nothing more than the form, picture, symbol or representation of *where* (yes, a location) your content C about God may be placed, you may, as you wish, place that content C within this ideogram and view it Truthfully at the House of Beth-El, even if you heretically think God is actually Bacchus or Dionysus or possesses none except the qualities of Man. I hope that you are not a Philistine and do not think such heresies, but the power of the ideogrammic picture we have constructed here is such that even a fun-loving, but false, pagan god might live under an upright, sacred stone in a scorching desert. The ideogram, then, consists of this whole book in these premises of your assignment of meaning to it, and your content C placed within it may be rational, irrational, mystical, holy, hallucinogenic or otherwise as you describe. This is the logical conclusion of the "process theology" which we outline here. I hope that you are wise enough to take it in a "satisfactory" perspective. We already have plenty of false gods entreating us for shelter.

The essence of characteristically religious content C is a dependence upon X. We have argued for a content C which is based on the gospels of Jesus the Christ. We said that the German theologian, Friedrich Daniel Ernst Schleiermacher (1768 to 1834), ruled that "the feeling of absolute dependence" was the basis of a Belief in God, and that Scheiermacher defined God to be that upon which we absolutely depend. But there is a further contradiction. Followers of Schleiermacher have traditionally faced the concern that, if they depend on God more than they do upon their feeling, they are actually dependent upon some X beyond their feeling of dependency, which means that Schleiermacher's theory of absolute dependence upon a feeling is invalid. On the other hand, if they depend on their feeling of dependency more than they depend on God, they are actually dependent upon their feeling, which is logically a religious experience, and not God. Fortunately, we have discussed a solution for this dilemma. The House of Beth-El is an *ineffable* place—that is to say, it is not only hard to express in words where it is in an empty desert, and what the rock, which we are raising vertically to signify it, actually and completely consists of, but it is also hard to express in words the *Dings an sichs* which live there as their home. In other words, at the House of Beth-El, both God as a *Ding an sich* and the meaning of the religious experience of the place (yes, a location) where God lives are *equally* ineffable and hard to describe. In like-minded opaqueness, therefore, does the House of Beth-El enshroud both God and the religious experience of God at a place in the mind where the mind *feels*. The box of unsolved paradox, into which logical critics of Schleiermacher's theory of religious experience have sealed it, is, therefore, opened at least a crack, even if you do not yet think it has been ripped apart and shredded.

Categories of transcendence from the life of Jesus the Christ mean feelings, and not word descriptions. Essentialists of the American school of mid-19th century Transcendentalism, and existentialists following the Belief of Søren Kierkegaard, or the phenomenology of consciousness developed by Husserl, or both, aimed at these transcendental categories with the Latin bowstring of stretching *intentio* to make them *psychologically based.* The result is to equate God directly to the feeling of God. Thus, we say that Jesus by Himself, along with Kierkegaard's un-theological theology essentially by itself, is the manifestation of mystical and holy power—that is to say, of Jesus's Holy Spirit and of what Otto called "the awesome" and "the mysterious"—in Latin, the *mysterium tremendum.* Is there any complete means of explaining a *numen* without sacrificing the numinous mind of the explainer who "knows" it? How can something be itself yet be more than itself? How can X be equal to X yet also be equal to Y? We said that we suspected that Duns Scotus, in postulating "being-as-being," the *ens in quantum ens,* was trying to pull off this logical miracle of mathematics. On the other hand, in the cognitive thought of Cartesian reductionism, there is the explanation of Husserl's Transcendental Idealism upon the regular contingent order of his phenomenology by its correlations of acts and objects of his consciousness *as the predicate for a rational assumption there is another consciousness beyond the world which is Divine.* Futhermore, there are the reasonable, if not logical, explanations of the life, death and resurrection of Jesus the Christ, the Nicaean Trinity, Jesus the Brother or the Messenger, God identified to the concept of *Ding an sich* directly, Christian *Terminus,* and the House of Beth-El as the location of some or all of this. We say here that these explanations suffice fully to justify Belief. Else, we say that, even if you rule differently that they do not suffice, the very conundrums and unresolved contradictions which they pose are yet other explanations of their justly held sufficiency, for they *are supposed* to take these conundrums and contradictions into account. This is the House of Beth-El's Finally Solved Paradox which is a Terminally drawn Truth. For we say that Jesus the Christ took even this final *supposition* (an essence) and turned it into existence. So we go, all within this one paragraph, from the validity of God in feelings to the validity of God in thoughtfully solved Truth.

It is *the experience* of these foundations of Beth-El—where *God is felt*—which distinguishes the species *homo sapiens* from naturally occurring un-human Intelligent Life, allows this species of biologically naturally occurring thinking life to Believe in God, and to exult in Believing because Believing is *a* badge identifying Man apart from other forms of Intelligence. *This* badge is what *homo sapiens* may value most as the centuries continue to roll by (if they do). But it means the starting point of God is Man. It means other forms of Intelligence should be welcomed into the spiritual realm in which Man lives. It means an endorsement of the wonder of Henry David Thoreau when he exclaimed:

> "I stand in awe of my body, this matter to which I am bound has become so strange to me. I fear not spirits, ghosts, of which I am one . . . but I fear bodies, I tremble to meet them. What is this Titan that has possession of me? Talk of mysteries! . . . the solid earth! the actual world! the common sense! Contact! Contact! Who are we? Where are we?"[15]

Exactly! From Jesus the Christ, Augustine, Anselm, Duns Scotus, Pelagius, Arius, Kierkegaard, Parker, Whitehead, Husserl, and even, by implication, Plato, Aristotle, Tertullian, Nietzsche, Russell, Gödel, Einstein, Quine, Wittgenstein and others, we have said who we are *in ourselves* in terms of Believing in God. Where are we *in the world*

---

[15] Henry David Thoreau, "Ktaadn and the Maine Woods" (1848) in Joyce Carol Oates, "Introduction to Walden" (1985) in Thoreau, *Walden* (Shanley ed., 1st paperback ed., Princeton, N. J., 1989), p. ix.

in terms of it? In other words, where *in this world* is the House of Beth-El? In 1959, near the midpoint of the 20th century, the American historian of intellectual history, Crane Brinton (1898 to 1968), said that ". . . no religion so far has been able to take the world as it is; and natural science, while it sticks to its last, is wholly unable to take the world in any other way than as it is."[16] But at the dawn of a new millennium we ask: How does the world now take one without the other? This is an issue strictly involving the world, and not of any transcendence of it.

Enjoying the Place

Let's explore the current analytic "landscape" of a Belief in God *in the world* by an elaborate metaphor of the geography and history of the streets and slums of Boston, Massachusetts. Beacon Street is a lengthy public thoroughfare in Boston which has existed ever since Boston was a village of a few Puritans in the 17th century. One end of Beacon Street is on Beacon Hill near the site of the present location of the capitol of the Commonwealth of Massachusetts.[17] Whence, Beacon Street becomes gradually broader in width as it meanders out for miles to and through Kenmore Square and into suburbs. In its western stretches it has many modern medians and turning lanes. Let's imagine that Beacon Street is the Street of Reality—that the buildings along this Street are the logical structures which must exist in order for anything to be located on the street, even God. If there's a building—a logical structure—built on the street, a Being, including God, could live on the street by moving into the building and, therefore, becoming Real, since we've imagined Beacon Street as the Street of Reality. In the 17th and 18th centuries the inhabitants of Boston built many structures along Beacon Street and lived in them, most piously as Puritans but passionately, because even Puritans had *eros*. The buildings, the logical structures, of the 17th and 18th centuries along Beacon Street had no plumbing, electricity or modern heating and cooling and, by the architecture and construction methods of today, would be considered rickety, pest-infected and ramshackled. But Beings lived in them. God lived in them. Some witches of Salem (1692) lived in them. The spirits of the Puritan divines, Increase Mather (1639 to 1723), and of his son, Cotton (1663 to 1728), lived in them. More spirits lived in them. And all existed and were Real and full of life. (But Cotton said he touched his dear wife only once as she lay dying.)[18] After all, as we've imagined Beacon Street as the Street of Reality, any Being living in a building on it exists and is Real.

---

[16]Crane Brinton, *A History of Western Morals* (New York, Harcourt, Brace & World, 1959), p. 447. See, for the United States, the exactly opposite view of the immediately preceding generation in Charles A. Ellwood, *The Reconstruction of Religion* (New York, Macmillan, 1922), p. 7.

[17]See, for the genesis of this metaphor, Roger Scruton, *Modern Philosophy: An Introduction and Survey* (New York, Penguin Press, 1995), p. 142 as follows: "Much of analytical philosophy has consisted in exercises of ontological slum clearance; demolishing the crowded tenements where gods and spirits breed."

[18]Cotton Mather, Diary (Ford ed., New York, Frederick Ungar Publishing Co., 1957), Vol. II, p. 448; and quoted in the scholarship of John S. Erwin, *The Millennialism of Cotton Mather: An Historical and Theological Analysis* (Lewiston, N. Y., Edwin Mellen Press, 1990), pp. 29, 30. His wife, Abigail Phillips (d. 1702), bore him nine children, five of whom died in infancy or childhood. In light of Mather's behavior about touching, there is prurient interest as to the natural acts of their creation. Then, see David Levin, *Cotton Mather: The Young Life of the Lord's Remembrancer, 1663-1703* (Cambridge, Mass., Harvard University Press, 1978). Since this is a book of life, thereby do I dispense with your thoughts that my footnotes are not also lively.

Along Beacon Street one day in the 19th century came several philosophers and analysts of Biblical history. They saw, to their horror, that the ramshackled buildings, the logical structures, were burning and they sounded a siren which echoed throughout Boston to evacuate them quickly. God, the Mathers, the witches and any other beings or spirits who lived in the buildings fled. The buildings were a fire trap. A Being would be burned up and may not live anywhere directly on the Street of Reality because there is no relation of the Being's existence directly to Reality to show the Being is or can be Real. To assert that X exists is not to assert X = Y. With even more assertiveness, along Beacon Street one day in the 20th century came the American philosopher of analytic logic, Willard Van Orman Quine (b. 1908). He blew up the empty, burned-out buildings themselves. Ka-boom! Quine said it would be impossible for any line of True logic to renovate the fire traps and make them sound logically. Quine said, "Every entity *requires* identity."[19] And identity, though a "relation" in logical analysis, is symmetrical, reflexive and transitive.[20] That means that nothing is identical except with itself, and itself alone. In other words, it is insufficient for a building to stand on Beacon Street if it is supported by a "middle term" from Aristotle's *Posterior Analytics;* the building must be built by modern building codes *requiring* direct relation to Reality. So Quine proceeded to build modern buildings along the Street of Reality which were logically sound. These are the buildings which exist today and probably will exist as long as Reality is a street in a city and Boston itself has not been blown up.

But all of the buildings Quine constructed are empty. No Being can live in them, exist and be Real, except in theory. This is because the buildings—the logical structures—have plumbing, electricity and modern heating and cooling systems and could "theoretically" support life in them very well, but no Being can "really" live in them because logic still shows that to assert X exists is not to assert X = Y. Nevertheless, you could "theoretically" go to the municipal authorities of the city of Boston—the building codes department or the mayor's office—to get permission to live in a building by the issuance of a certificate of use and occupancy to live in it and such a certificate could "theoretically" be issued (and "theoretically" would be if the mayor of Boston wanted a lively and thriving city). According to Quine's logic, the only entity which could possibly be Real is the mayor, the theoretical quantifier of the number of certificates of use and occupancy which could be "theoretically" issued for a "theoretical existence." Thus, Quine says God exists "relative to the theory which requires" Him.[21] And the theory itself is true, but only in context of the utility of "various conceptual schemes."

What is the actual assessment of this metaphor about Beacon Street? It is one of two assessments. First, if my consciousness depends for its Reality on the perceptions it receives from the world of physical nature, Beacon Street is a definite description of hard asphalt and beings being burned up in buildings, new empty ones and a rather capricious mayor (because *who can tell* about the rules he uses for certificates of use and occupancy of the new buildings, or if he uses any?) The mayor is identified by one of four candidates: God, some other X, you or me. The candidate elected mayor and his

---

[19]Scruton, *op. cit.,* p.143.

[20]*Ibid.,* p. 145.

[21]*Ibid.,* p. 142.

department of building codes will rule the Street of Reality; their government of Reality is a Thing-in-itself and cannot be surpassed. Who, then, is this theocratic mayor? I said I would put into the metaphor of Beacon Street the world as it is, without a transcendence of it. For me to be the mayor ruling the Street of Reality with theoretical occupancy permits I would have to transcend it and surpass myself. I am only a pedestrian on Beacon Street, wholly unable to bootstrap the fact of my pedestrian (yes, it's a double entendre) nature into a high elected office, for there is no license to trespass into any empty building for the purpose of being Real without even a theoretical license to occupy it to do so. Yet, some objective certificate of my authenticity as a being must exist if I am to occupy City Hall or any other structure of logic, and I have none except that of subjectivity, but this is certainly no objective, official certification.

If, on the other hand, Beacon Street, Boston and the rest of the world depend upon my consciousness in order to be Real, and they Ultimately may not exist if I don't, the metaphor of them I have used previously means that I could still be a candidate for mayor, that Beacon Street is not hard asphalt at all, but only a matter of how I feel the asphalt, say, in my new athletic shoes with plushly cushioned soles (yes, that could be a pun). The hardness of the asphalt of Beacon Street is, then, only a matter of my subjectivity and how much I take it seriously. It *seems* a serious enough description of two centuries of objectifying philosophy ending with the new and modern buildings of analytic logic, but this contradiction in the roles of my consciousness about them trouble me. The contradiction is whether my consciousness depends upon the physical world, of which the rules of analytic logic from Quine are a part, or whether that world's existence depends upon my consciousness which, in itself *(an sich),* takes the world, including Quine's objectfying interpretation of it, only according to the brand of athletic shoes I wear, only as I am more or less subjective about it. This contradiction is the return of Husserl's first paradox of the descriptive psychology of human subjectivity. You say, however, Quine's theories of analytic logic have analytic meanings which, logically, hold Truth for eternity; yet I have glibly and mundanely declared them within the world. *But Quine's theories are, in fact, in the world for that is the only way I have perceived them in my life from the days I went to college and heard a friend tell me of his study of them.* Do you wish me to override my framework of empiricism and the touchstone of personal experience only for Quine's theories? We declared we would follow existence and not essence. Do you want me in my objectifying interpretation of the world to take only the perceived without the perceiver or *vice versa?* Not only science but the acts of the scientists are so well within it. Not only Beacon Street but my stroll in athletic shoes past the trees along its sidewalks is also.

Isn't my stroll along Beacon Street, with all my maddening subjectivity about cushy shoes, actually a transcendence of Reality? No, a transcendence is when X is outside of X, but I am a complete pedestrian (yes, it is a double entendre) as entitled to walk upon the Street of Reality as any "being-ness" is. I simply inserted myself into an historical metaphor of Boston, and since I actually lived there once, why am I not entitled to? What am I transcending when I walk down the Street of Reality? You say I could surpass myself because I would meet voters on the sidewalk, not in Quine's empty buildings, who would vote for my mayoral candidacy, or that I surpass what is Real about asphalt for what I feel about the idea of it. Then, I ask you regarding any possible candidacy of mine for the mayor's office: why would others on the sidewalk of Reality vote for me? What is my Reality? We have seen it already in the objective contradictions which Jesus the Christ said about me, in the complete insufficiency which I am as a matter of my psychology and tautological perceptions, in Plato's learning paradox, and in Husserl's two paradoxes of human subjectivity and of transcendental idealism. Who would vote for me for mayor when one could know God both better and to be better than I am? I would not even vote for myself. Besides, other voters should be hardly aware of my candidacy—they campaign solipsistically, but busily, for their own election to mayor! Moreover, regarding the metaphorical act of my running and my subjectivity on speed and athletic footwear, I ask: Is my subjectivity, something which is only within me, ever to be compared against your idealism that asphalt is just scientifically outside of it and can be innately hard or soft as a Real matter to my feet? Except for the mayor of Boston within his caprice at City Hall, I said an object exists Ultimately, even today on Beacon Street, only if I think it does, nothing else more (a thought upon a thought) or less (intuition or instinct?). Surely, this subjectivity is apt regarding Aristotelian attributes, such as the hard quality of asphalt I feel through my shoes. What right do you have to redefine my objects and my feelings by new shoes? Or may only the government of this metaphorical municipality reshod them? If so, how capricious is the mayor actually? Would he direct his government to tear up the Street of Reality in his own city by hallucinations of it?

If my subjectivity about the hardness of the asphalt of Reality opposes your idealism of the hypothetical Realism in all cases of the science of asphalt, which of these two is the greater Thing-in-itself, the most compelling *Ding an sich?* A Thing-in-itself is *either, first,* a thing whose plain nature is in itself and therefore of tautological Truth or of opaqueness, beyond which there is no more meaning of Truth to be seen or discovered, a boundary of all of thinking; *or, second,* it is a thing which, in itself—literally, inside of itself, I may, if I *adequately* perceive them, intentionally set a further limit or field of objects upon an ideal world, in which case the boundary of all thinking is this further field of objects. The former is a traditional definition of a Thing-in-itself; the latter is an untraditional definition of it from Husserl. The question, then, is whether you employ the traditional definition of the Thing-in-itself, or Husserl's untraditional, extended definition of it, to tell whether either one of the two approaches—subjectivity or hypothetical Realism—is the most compelling. The further question which must be answered in order to resolve this war between subjectivity and hypothetical Realism is whether epistemology is restricted to what is Absolutely certain—the phenomena of my consciousness in my mind as they are adequately perceived in my immanent perception of them; or is epistemology extended to what is not a certainty, to Husserl's *adequate* perception of a further field of objects within the *an sich* of a Thing? Well, the words of this last question answer it themselves. If the perception is *adequate,* epistemology—the philosophy of knowing what we know—knows we can know any perception which is *adequate* even if the perceived X of the perception may not exist because it is only the product of an intentional act in an ideal world. What is the essential meaning of "adequateness?" Kierkegaard said it: "Truth is the *objective uncertainty* held fast in the most personal passionate experience. This is the truth, the highest truth attainable for the existing individual." In other words, Reality is adequately perceived whenever you are passionate enough about your experiences. In these *premises,* not circumstances—though there is every other meaning about them to mean that they *are* circumstantial and arise from existence, the boundary of all thinking is not strictly a Thing-in-itself, though it could be, but the adequate perception of the *an sich* of a Thing to its ideal limits in an ideal world. Within this framework at this stage, you perceive of the Reality of my metaphor of Beacon Street *either, first,* as a Thing-in-itself of which no more may be seen *or, second,* with an "adequate perception" of a further field of objects in an ideal world of thinking about it better than you have, by which there is much more to see. If the former, God's sign is already on the door of the mayor's office, and God is theoretically issuing permits for the theoretical living of Real "being-ness," but, if I am subjective enough about it, He is actually issuing them for actual life. If the latter, God is Husserl's switch by which I generate electricity to an ideal row of street lights which allow me to see the Street of Reality better. Regardless of these two cases, I am neither at the mayor's office nor at the switch for the street lights, because my myopic eyes, with which I began this whole discussion, depend upon being at an ophthalmologist's office first, becoming the object of his scientific acts relating to my eyesight.

This is enough of a metaphor, by now rather tried and tired, whose analogous meanings may (yet?) be another game of words. The metaphor does unravel, however, the obscuring terminology of the philosophy of Husserl and shows that the meaning of a Thing-in-itself may be extended to a further class of idealized objects if there is an adequate perception of them, and that this is so, "intentionally."[22] Husserl held that consciousness, in all cases, is intention, and certainly if intention means the stretching to an object which is implied by its root in Latin vocabulary. This stretching is an enjoyable exercise to us for several reasons. First, it is pragmatic, a method of relating thought to action, and helps us to guide and to live our lives successfully; second, it is put to us as a design for Reality which is as innately appealing to our mental capacities as all fascinating (even Otto's *fascinans*) designs are for intellectuals; and third, the stretching of our mental qualities to objects involves our senses and is an emotional enterprise. I will discuss these three types of enjoyment we take from exercising our "adequate perceptions" one by one.

The Enjoyment of the Whole Relationship of Thought and Action

On the surface, pragmatic thought, by mixing thought with action and relying upon experience, seems to us somehow not the best. In ancient Greek, *pragma* means "thing done;" in the common parlance of English today, it means expedient or mediocre. We say a person is pragmatic and thereby infer that he is without a zest for excellence but is only doing enough to survive. This is because of our continued craving for the perfect, and whatever is done under the weight of experience may assuredly not be. But the previous discussion has not consciously belabored the perfection of God nor sought it even. Pragmatism is simply a way of relating thought to actual life through weighing the experiences of it. A pragmatic thought, of itself, does not Will the being of any deliberate weirdness. The weird comes only because your theory of Reality does not

---

[22]See Herman Philipse, "Transcendental Idealism," §§ XIII, XIV in *The Cambridge Companion to Husserl, op. cit.,* pp. 272-280. The intentionality is a matter of the conscious meaning of every meaning in the transcendental attitude. Husserl postulated, as we have previously discussed, that the transcendental attitude applies to everything, including the Cartesian ego.

conform to Reality validly. When a pragmatist says the Truth of the House of Beth-El fits the purposes of a Thing-in-itself as such, or as extended, the pragmatist is only pointing to a condition of human thought—how the mind ascertains this Truth—and not to the further privilege of being eccentric or "subjective" about it.[23] Pragmatism is not another system of philosophy; it is a method of ascertaining Truth by saying that ideas (which are but parts of our experience, much as some of Quine's ideas inadvertently became part of mine through a friend at college) become True "just insofar as they help us to get into satisfactory relation with other parts of our experience."[24] For example, "look before you leap" but "he who hesitates is lost." Both statements are logically True, but the Ultimate Truth of only one of them depends completely upon experience.[25] Therefore, we say the Truth of the House of Beth-El depends completely on experience also. By one type of experience, it is a solitary, vertically placed rock; under another, it is a holy and sacred place of the Divine. Explaining this difference does not undercut the justification for it.

Of course, the House of Beth-El and the discussion of this book are arguments for God by design, by the teleology of an end where this House of God is located by the ordinary meaning of where-ness. Designs compel intellectuals much like perfection does. The French philosopher of deconstructionism, Jacques Derrida (b. 1930), conceives of a descriptive concept which he calls a Khôra, after the Greek word for marketplace which Plato located at utopia in one of his Socratic dialogues. The Khôra of Derrida's thinking is a useful posit for some place (yes, a location) to describe the results of his transcendental schemes of *différance*. If these schemes of *différance* cannot at least be described, then where is the where-ness of the intellectual who thinks them? Put more fully, Derrida says[26] that the definition of *différance* is the limit, interruption and destruction of any "raising up"—in French, the word he uses is *relèvement*—of an idea. [Here we should note that the word "idea" probably has its traditional West European meaning of "mental object," though Derrida did not, in 1971, even use the words "idea" or "object" in connection with *relèvement* but, instead, described *relèvement* further only by referring to a German philosopher most celebrated for his ideas and idealism, Georg Wilhelm Friedrich Hegel (1770 to 1831).] However, the deconstruction, interruption or annihilation involved in schemes of *différance* also involve swapping representations of time and space with one another, since even the most de-constructed intellectuals swap them to de-construct the *relèvements* being subjected to this process. Accordingly, unless there is some description of where to put the debris or detritus after a *relèvement* has been limited, interrupted or destroyed by a scheme of *différance,* where would it go or be otherwise described? Therefore, Derrida needs posits of metaphysical places, in much the same need as I have for the posit of mine here at Beth-El. There is someplace (yes, a location) where both raised up and de-constructed thinking must find finality. Derrida is not an Atheist and does not reject

---

[23]See Jacques Barzun, *A Stroll With William James* (New York, Harper & Row, 1983), p. 93.

[24]*Ibid.*, p. 86.

[25]*Ibid.*, p. 94.

[26]Jacques Derrida, "Interview with Jean-Louis Houdebine and Guy Scarpetta" (1971) in *Positions* (Paris, Les Éditions de Minuit, 1972) trans. Alan Bass as *Positions* (Bass ed., The University of Chicago Press, 1981), pp. 40, 41.

religious discourse entirely,[27] but he fails to place Khôra into any religious context. It might properly belong there. After all, what is Derrida ultimately satisfied with in life? Because he claims that everything is contextual («*il n'y a pas de hors-texte*» or, "there nothing outside-the-text"), Derrida says that he has ". . . never believed that there were *metaphysical* concepts *in and of themselves*. No concept is by itself, and consequently in and of itself, metaphysical, outside all the textual work in which it is inscribed."[28]

On the other hand, even if we grant the proposition that everything is within some context, where within a context does Derrida textually describe God? The philosophical posit of a metaphysical place called Khôra, within a context, actually denies the Truth of its own metaphysics—that this particular place has an Ultimate quality about it which is above or beyond or determinative of the contextual. Is philosophy P exclusively the text of P, and nothing of the atmosphere of the place where we say we *feel* P? If so, it is hard to tell why millions have died in thousands of wars unless some philosophy of living in wars has been felt and felt successfully such that the wars have been fought and endured through fighting. Monks live in monasteries, not because of the compelling nature of a philosophy of monastery-living, but because of their philosophical *treatment* (yes, a feeling) of the issues of their lives *as a whole*. Likewise, Frenchmen live in France, not because of the compelling nature of a philosophy of *la vie française,* but because of their philosophical *treatment* (yes, a feeling) of the issues of their *whole* lives, especially if a multi-national corporation pays them well to live it outside of France. But Derrida describes an atmosphere to the Khôra without divulging *the underpinning of his feelings* beneath the text of it. He insists, repeatedly, that we set it apart intellectually from *Logos* or *Mythos*. As an end result for one set of transcendental concepts of *différance,* he supposes that Khôra determines the character of *Logos* (read: Reason) and *Mythos* (read: Subjectivity) Ultimately. The resulting description (in the words of another author) is as follows:

> "[Khôra] is a place in the "interior of philosophy" where it anachronizes space and calls forth atemporality. . . . It is an infinite space. Yet, it is not like the infinite space that is occupied by philosophy[;] it is not an infinity whose origin is induced in the shape of linear progression. It is rather a space whose infinity is given as philosophy's [A]bsolute [O]ther."[29]

Isn't this description similar to a function which I assigned to Beth-El? What is the embarrassment of a philosopher if he overlooks the foundations of his own personal experiences and refuses to explain or to justify what may be actually said about them? This is the large embarrassment of the German philosopher, Martin Heidegger (1889 to 1976), about his personal tolerance of life in Nazi Germany. What is the accomplishment of a philosopher in dealing with Greek metaphors when ancient Greek existence had gods, but the philosopher would take the metaphor while declining to discuss even one of the gods contextually? This is the small embarrassment of Derrida regarding the Khôra. As a work of intellect, Khôra is fair analysis but, for any reader yearning for synthesis or unity, an unedifying philosophy of existence. To be Real, in

---

[27]Martin C. Srajek, *In the Margins of Deconstruction* (Dordrecht, Kluwer Academic Publishers, 1998), p. 208.

[28]Jacques Derrida, "Interview etc.," in *Positions, op. cit.* (English ed.), p. 57 (original italics).

[29]Srajek, *op. cit.,* p. 246; see Jacques Derrida, *Khôra* (Paris, Galilée, 1993) pp. 35, 36.

my black ink, the exposition of any philosophy of existence must surmount the author's own Scholasticism, even as that author labors under Scheler's principle of linguistic sketching, and even when that Scholasticism is an otherwise unavoidable enterprise for every other part of the exposition, and that exposition is consciously intended to destroy the *relèvement* inherent in the Scholasticism to begin with. For even *différance* has Scholastic components which do not relate to experience, or to that sort of experience which I live in, even by living in the United States rather than by living in France. Derrida does not describe his concept of the Khôra vacuously, but it is nonetheless a description of puffing and flatness, even as a Scholastic puffs at air, because Derrida has consciously abandoned his search to find certainly that singular, all-encompassing theory of Reality in which he actually believes and lives his thinking life.

The Enjoyment of the Designs of Thinking and Feeling

We said that we have consciously searched and pursued an all-encompassing theory called quasi-Realism. Have we arrived at better results than the asphaltic road of Beacon Street or Derrida's Khôra? Well, we have approached answers to this question in different ways: Kantian intellect transcending over the world, Cartesian thinking within the self, *Gestalt* and Freudian reductions of these thoughts further and, finally, by allowing for mysticism and the self-Revelation of $G_X d$ in Love. The rest of this discussion recapitulates them one by one.

If experience is weighed carefully enough by objectifying interpretations of the human consciousness and the world, and the interpretations of themselves *(an sich)* are objectifying enough about both, there is a massive predicate of "content" that, of itself, may be enough for transcendental form, even if we accept Kant's restriction of transcendence to forms only. It is easy to name such a base of transcendental "content" as an essence of God, because of the quality of the "content" or because of the transcendental form which that quality "acquires." A massive predicate (quantity) of meanings and objects under the proposition that "some G exists" might amount to a meaningfulness (quality of justification) for the proposition of G. The shift from quantity to quality is not a Truth-destroying, fallacious shift of logic if, but only if, there is something in the massive predicate of transcendental content which keys it for a subsequent cross-reference—that is to say, something in the content which acts like a pronoun and "binds" the quantification so that it can be used again.[30] It is for you to judge whether there is any such of a "binding pronoun" from the *Gestalten* which I hope that I have developed.

In the famous Third Meditation (1641), written in clear, interesting and readable sentences, Descartes refrained from presupposing God in existence before *(a priori)* Man. Instead, his supposition was rather the reverse *(a posteriori)*. Descartes said: "God exists because He is the cause of my idea of Him." This supposes that God exists in order to constitute this cause, such that God is *causa sui*, the cause of his own cause. What is difficult about accepting this supposition? God *qua* (as) God does anything He wants. He *may be* the cause of a cause or the cause of multiple causes. The difficulty, however, is with the *sui* (itself) component of the *causa,* for we return by it to the lasting

---

[30]Willard V. O. Quine, "Logic and the Reification of Universals," in *From a Logical Point of View* (Cambridge, Mass., Harvard University Press, 1953, 1961, 1980), pp. 102, 103.

dilemma of our tautology of a self-identity. Exactly what Truth does a tautology (self-referring statement) show? Alternatively, Descartes's proof of God supposes that I exist in order to constitute the idea of the saying of what Descartes said. In other words, I must exist beforehand in order for God to be in my idea of Him. Descartes's famous proof, therefore, rests upon the premise of either my existence or of the tautological existence of God. It does not, strictly, "prove" God's existence. It is tempting to apply to the tautology of God in Descartes's Third Meditation the same surmounting of it we tried to apply to show the justification of a single human ego in the previous discussion. By defining God with absolutely more universal characteristics than a human ego has, performing the task of this justification is doubtlessly easier. But we have already done it, even twice, in the cases of the natural self, and of psychic, transcendental self. To perform it a third time for a purely metaphysical object is essentially a task for a Scholastic.

It is for you to judge whether the effect of God in me is, after the manner of Descartes's thinking in The Third Meditation, a morph (form) of God. If so, is such a morph equal to a morpheme (a linguistic device which contains no smaller meaningful parts)? Is it necessary that this morph amount to Immanuel Kant's million-dollar word, entantiomorph—the duplication in "real space" of something whose molecular structure has the relationship of a mirror image? (Your two hands are enantiomorphs unless one of them has artificially implanted bone substitutes.) The morphemized nature of a morph is ultimate reality in several theories of the meaningfulness of language, because it means that Reality has been de-constructed to the extent of reducing it to no further component parts of explanations. On the other hand, the enantiomorph is ultimate reality in several theories of the factual nature of science, because it means that Reality has been constructed to the extent of duplicating it physically, exactly and at least once. Morphs (forms) are another vocabulary for *Gestalten*. Does *Gestalt* psychology show *Gestalt* patterns of religion repeat themselves in each normally undefective replica of our species, "after the physics," *meta ta physika*, every time there is the birth of a new one? We already know that cortical activity is well advanced in a fetus even before it leaves the womb and breathes air.[31] In any event of a human birth, it is for you to say whether another morph or "binding pronoun" for the existence of God is in generalized psychological conditions. In particular, does an inevitable natural condition of bewilderment and perplexity arise among all replicas each time the complex of epistemology, which I hope that I have developed here, is respectively known by them as they exist? If you say so and judge this, the quantifier-shift fallacy from "some G" to "all G," which Quine noted would otherwise apply to the foregoing propositions of meaning about G, can be unwound.

Wait! We use the signifier G without a theory of the meaning of our doing so. A few thinkers of linguistic and metaphysical deconstructionism say that this theory of our Real meaning involves three steps. First, we must perceive of a G object in physical existence (but, how do we know it is a G object except by a metaphysical notion of G-ness?); second, we must identify the G object of, say, a greyhound (which we see physically) as a linguistic G; and third, we must ascertain that our signifier of G works

---

[31]James E. Loder, *The Logic of the Spirit: Human Development in Theological Perspective* (San Franscisco, Jossey-Bass Publishers, 1998), p. 83.

properly in signifying the greyhound as G. To translate the absurdities of this philosophy into some of our previous discussion, we say that, since the mental life of a greyhound before starting a greyhound race is only a postulation, we may suppose it is the dog's version of a generalized psychological condition of fear and anxiety—such that we could suppose it is a morph or "binding pronoun" by which "some G-ness" is Really "all of G-ness." The quantifier-shift fallacy about the characteristics of greyhounds is, then, logically surmounted for G-ness. But this still means that it is G-ness (the meaning of G), and not the existence of G, which we have discovered. For what we say is G is Really only the meaning of G since actual G must be translated and related back to that part of the transcendental content whence G originated. For example, what Really constitutes a greyhound is the ability of his species to run faster than any other dog. We do not care about any of his other dog-like attributes. Even so, G's origin is still a presupposition about G. (Some greyhounds in existence are actually slower than mongrel hounds.)

This school of linguistic philosophy is based on the theory of the Reality of Pan-Scientism. Future historians of intellectual history may characterize this school of linguistics with as much scorn as they have characterized the distinctions of Scholasticism for the last two centuries. By our review of Scholasticism, the definitions and distinctions about God which would be required for Him to escape from Descartes's tautology of self-identity of a cause with an effect amount to a puff of wind. Scholasticism lives,[32] but I Believe in God, even with the baggage of puritanism about living an empirical life. We said we would be empirical and take what we can only relate to experience, though logic allows possibilities otherwise.

Thoreau tells us to "[s]implify. Simplify." He said, "It is not worth the while to go round the world to count the cats in Zanzibar."[33] Was this because of the trouble of traveling the distance involved, or because of the mundaneness of numerous animal essences at an exotic location once you arrived? Has our journey in this discussion been of a comparable bother? Isn't the House of Beth-El a mundane location for an exotic essence? Does any reversal in Thoreau's metaphor mean its meaning changes at all? On the other hand, Paul the Apostle wrote: "Brethren, do not be children in your thinking; be babes in evil, *but in thinking be mature.*"[34] Mature thinking implies complexity which implies the opposite of a simple Belief. Please remember that Quine said: *a pure existential is valid if and only if we get a truth-functional schema by taking the alternation of results by substituting the free variables for the existential ones in the matrix.* This discussion is a matrix of propositions yielding a Truth-functional schema about God if *we assume* that the *only* remaining free variables of it are you and me, that you and I are substituted for the existential ones—*viz.,* all of the discussion here

---

[32] For example, see Dick T. Cole, "Against the Integration of Psychology and Christianity: A Bold Proposal for an Alternative Paradigm," *Journal of Psychology and Christianity,* Vol. 17, No. 3, p. 210 (Fall, 1998). The author's suppositions about the creation of the natural world are completely and validly contradicted by the empiricism of the natural sciences. Likewise, his supposition about a "sphere" for psychology is not shown in the natural world as matter of psychological experience in actual human beings. It is only a sphere the author holds Scholastically in his own head.

[33] Thoreau, *op. cit.,* pp. 91, 322.

[34] Saint Paul, *First Letter to the Corinthians* ch. 14, v. 20 (italics added).

regarding your and my existences—and that you and I Believe in God *already*. Are you the only free variable left? On the other hand, the meanings and objects which I have built up in this discussion, under condition of those strict circumstances where there is no alternation of results from them, may be our elusive Y, a massive predicate of much stuff which is Y but also roughly equal to G. If so, we think that this Y is, indeed, a "middle term" from Aristotelian logic regarding attributes which accounts for G. Does Reality show that G and Y are the same but different? If True, this is an important paradox. The resolution of it shows whether God exists as a matter of our logical form—a fact of no special significance for *experience* generally—but emotionally important to the feeling of whether we should be simpler about it. Tillich thinks the mature thinking of the direction of Saint Paul to think maturely means even an allowance for "divine foolishness." Tillich says that "[t]here is no maturity where an awareness of the divine foolishness is lacking."[35] Is this, under the philosophy of Husserl, an adequate perception of Reality or too clever by half? Do we allow that the meaning of God meant to mess the world by death (Auschwitz), divorce (Platonic philosophy), drug addictions (the heresy of Arius about a Platonic Christ), lying *gourmets* (the delicious natural-ness of Pelagius about a tasty Christ), or the ambiguously determinable perceptions we have to some determinable stimuli? Or, do we only know that the meaning of God saved the world and us and every other human soul by Jesus the Christ? Where is the balance between "mature thinking" and simplification?

We say the analysis of this discussion may be complicated, but it is positive. I have not, so far,[36] discussed the problem of showing a negative, the non-existence of God—what cannot be shown because He was never there. (This is the so-called school of negative theology. It tries to show God affirmatively by negating what He is not and never was.)[37] On the other hand, we show God here for what He is or is not—not for what He never was. You must say if the paradoxical conclusions of this discussion about God's existence are more pertinent than the unresolved alternatives they may logically (but not empirically) be compared to. These alternatives of negativity must remain unresolved for us. As issues of both our actual and hypothetical experience (the hypothesis of Husserl's thought-experiment), the experiences of those negative

---

[35]Tillich, *The Eternal Now, op. cit.*, p. 160. Tillich asserts "divine foolishness of thought and divine foolishness of life are united in the symbol of Christmas: God in the infant, God as infant, ..." *Ibid.*, p. 162.

[36]For example, if God *were* burned up on Beacon Street, destroyed or dead, and the non-existence of God existed, how would we know of this non-existence? What do you prove to prove the non-existence of X? X's very non-existence? But isn't this tautological? Important to science and to scientific minds is verification by an ability to know—that is, by epistemology. There's no verification of God's non-existence scientifically; logic does validate, however, the wager of the French mathematician, Blaise Pascal. Pascal wagered: "Why not Believe in Christianity because you lose nothing by doing so and may win everything?" To a gambler Pascal's famous wager is either "God is dead" or "Does existing God have the attribute of love, the attribute of grace, the attribute of mercy and so forth?" But isn't this another game and so much sport by taking, as Quine puts it, "unfair advantage" of a negative?

[37]For example, see Moses Maimonides, *Guide for the Perplexed* trans. Shlomo Pines (Chicago, Universitry of Chicago Press, 1963) Vol. I, § 58, p. 134; Jacques Derrida, "Comment ne pas parler: Dénégations," in *Psyché: Inventions de l'autre* (Paris, Galilée, 1987) trans. Ken Frieden as "How to avoid Speaking: Denials," in *Languages of the Unsayable: The Play of Negativity in Literature and Literary Theory* (Budick & Iser eds., New York, Columbia University Press, 1989).

alternatives cannot be compared to the Reality theorized in this discussion, except by a further theory. But this theory amounts to a theory of our theory of Reality and is an excess of theory to the theory of a Realist. I am Cartesian thinking thing, who thinks of the difficulty of saying what never was is not and what is not never was, though both may be said tautologically in a philosophical tract. All I know is what there is for me today. Is this an unfair Cartesian restriction upon that alternation of results which, Quine said, would be required for the existence of an existential entity?

Geography and maps have always compelled me since childhood. I show you my roads to Truth here. They do not allow for changes upon a landscape unless there are natural causes for the changes. The title of this book, for the essence of God as an unmovable, natural boundary stone, is an essence of that psychology about me. Do spatial metaphors of this fact of my *Gestalt* pattern of Belief mean my House of Beth-El rests in Truth better than Derrida's Khôra does? Derrida does not show how his concepts relate to his life. Lest you conclude that my pique is a simple repetition of Romantic thinking which Western civilization heard in the first parts of the 19th century, you must consider at least one Freudian analysis, among other possibilities, that says my father's design for God in his essay of 1953 compels me to take it further while I kill it Oedipally. Another Freudian analysis says that "[t]he origin of religious feeling can be traced back in clear outlines as far as the feeling of infantile helplessness."[38] But how far does the reduction of my psychology go? I hope that I have traced the origin of religious feelings much further in this discussion than to the simple helplessness of an infant, or even my infancy. I hope that I have shown how—for the latter case, at least—the reduction of my psychology of religion, by Freudian analysis of it into infancy, itself may be reduced from infancy into wombs, memes, memory, *Gestalt* patterns, Good Tricks, Chomsky's language innateness, Jung's collective consciousness and so forth.

Besides unbounded reductionism to Freudian psychology or to anywhere else, we know that we have a sacred, upright stone where the reductions may live satisfactorily. In any case of a reduction, we ask: how is the thing, or a thing-i-fication being reduced thereby, actually diminished when the parts of whole are reduced? We are tempted by our witless minds to hold this supposition, but where does it exist for *things?* The technique of *reductio ad absurdum* in traditional philosophy meant reasoning, most often inductively, through a series of propositions to a case of absurdity shown by them, so that the single case, which had been arrived at as a matter of logical necessity, would refute the necessity of either the propositions or the premises of the propositions on which the case had been founded. The technique did *not* mean that the propositions or the premises supporting the one absurd case were *themselves* absurd; it meant just that they were not *necessary* logically as a result of that case. Yet, today, the thinking of the world is that, if there is one absurd case shown by a given analysis of experience, the analysis itself is absurd. This may be a roughly true characterization about a false analysis of objects under observation or experiment scientifically on the "facts," but it cannot be a true characterization for a "state of affairs;" that is to say, for any level of existence where any level of doubt about the chain of inductive reasoning has been

---

[38]Sigmund Freud, *Civilization and its Discontents* (1930) in *The Freud Reader* (Gay ed., New York, W. W. North & Co., 1989), p.725 at 727.

introduced. Yet, today, the thinking of the world, so besotted by science and the mental set of the scientific method, is willing, nay cavalier, about imputing absurdity into cases where it is not logically absurd to think so. This is a stupefaction of most minds by the rigor of the scientific method of inquiry. Science insists on a complete re-think for each case which is anomalous, or "absurd." But, in psychology or religion, most anomalies are often made normal as a matter of readjustment, and not of reconstruction. It is the readjustment, not the complete re-thinking, of a reductionist analysis which is the sublime end of reductionism, considered properly. This "proper consideration" is another *Ding an sich,* deserving of a home in God where it is welcomed.

The French author and Minister of Cultural Affairs, André Malraux (1901 to 1976), playing the politics of anxiety, declared that "the 21st century will be religious, or it won't be at all."[39] But the scientist whose accomplishments were the most heralded of all in the 20th century, the Swiss-American physicist, Albert Einstein (1879 to 1955), Believed in God and wrote that he could not "imagine a God who rewards and punishes the objects of his creation, *whose purposes are modeled after our own* [viz., to make the 21st century religious]—a God, in short, who is but a reflection of human frailty. . . . It is enough for me to contemplate the mystery of conscious life . . . to reflect upon the marvelous structure of the universe . . . and to try humbly to comprehend even an infinitesimal part of the intelligence . . ."[40] These declarations by Einstein and Malraux imply a large intellectual, philosophical and cultural task, but one tinged with ulterior motives from politics and the human intellect. In any event, the task mentioned by Malraux and Einstein is a more beguiling pursuit for intellectuals than a simple, if abrupt, acknowledgment of God emotionally. No thinker wishes to acknowledge he should not think. No Socrates wishes to acknowledge that he is unable to emerge, by himself, from himself, out of psychic, religious or philosophical dreaming. In the event of a surprising admission along these lines, what is the compulsion of psychology and religion to surpass the dreaming? Do God and the psychology of God affect at all the mythopoetic dream of life, given by Derrida as a text, or transcend over this text with content as well as with the form of transcendence? Where is Truth in religion required finally to show that the Center of Man is not a mythopoetic dream but a Real Place? On the other hand, we have seen the conditional nature of Truth of all kinds, such that *some* truth is reached by all thinkers mentioned in this discussion, even the characteristically Atheist or absurd ones. But, for truth to be True, why is there any "some-ness" about it? Do we only dream further by saying that Truth exists Absolutely for us? If so, our dreaming, the mythopoeia of the Khôra and apodictic Truth may still repose in God Terminally. This is so because, if we do not repose them Divinely, experience amounts to an earthly hell of contradiction and unresolved paradox, even if some part of their combination is truthful and relativity relates well to reality insofar as it goes. How can we live on this Earth in any existence which stands apodictic Truth together with experience? This is the return of the same question we asked at the beginning. At the

---

[39]See Jacques Ellul, *La Foi Au Prix Du Doute* (Paris, 1980) trans. Peter Heinegg as *Living Faith* (New York, 1st English ed., 1983), p. 128.

[40]Albert Einstein, "Credo," in *Living Philosophies: a Series of Intimate Credos* (Leach ed., New York, Simon & Schuster, 1931), pp. 6, 7.

least, a framework or structure has been suggested here for answering it, even if that essentially characteristic content of it, what is fully *necessary* about necessary existence, is still not answered to your satisfaction.

The Enjoyment of Emotions

The English Christian mystic, Lady Juliana of Norwich (c. 1342 to c. 1415), dreamed and said: "No man can see God and live after, that is to say, in this mortal life."[41] If the Reality of this mysticism is in Juliana's Ultimate need to continue to be mystical, one might suppose that she should have "seen" God and died before even saying it in comprehensible English vocabulary. On the other hand, if the Reality of Juliana's mystical saying is not Ultimately founded in her continued need to practice mysticism, or the phenomenal silence of it, a Cartesian rationalist might suppose that it is based in her desire to live, and not to die. The desire to live life is a teleology (ending goal) of both the Reality of Science (apprehended by Descartes) and the Reality of Subjectivity (apprehended by mystics such as Juliana). I visit my ophthalmologist and submit to the science of eyesight-thinking because I want to live. On the other hand, I Believe in God because I want to live also. To live is to avoid Auschwitz, premature blindness, ignorance of the Ultimate meaning of my ophthalmologist in my life, and the potential grip of death upon all aspects of me, including even the most elevated thoughts which I hold about life-thinking. By thinking about God in this discussion, we either cut at Reality Really, or we nonetheless slice it as a dreamer sleeps it, in dreams, fantasies, fragments and hallucinations. Does Juliana Really want to live (the rationality which is an analogue to her existence) or does she want to hold what she does mystically in the first place (the innate subjectivity of the soul)? Her justification seems to be more tied to her subjective self than rationality is to any analogue of life about her, or is it just the opposite? Much is discussed whether or not the analogues of life and living, by rational Truth-claims and speech-acts, overwhelm Husserl's psychic, existing, transcendental I. But is it even edifying (desirable) to ask these conflicting questions? If so, when is the edification itself eaten by a larger Reality of Pan-Scientism? Didn't we contend in the first place that Husserlian analysis of consciousness was empirically and, therefore, "scientifically" based? If so, Pan-Scientism reaches to the extent of validating even some hypotheses behind Husserl's existing, psychic, transcendental ego.

On the other hand, if we are, in any sense, Real, we foreswear from Ultimate (intellectually conceived) Scholastic distinctions. To say that there is one Reality (whether it be Subjectivity or Science) on top of another Reality in a Chain of Reality is an Unreal Chain of Meaning fully similar to the Chains of Being and Meaning about which we previously bound ourselves in this discussion. Multi-layered Reality is Unreal, dependent completely upon the first layer, and even more removed from the point at which, in that first layer, all analysis begins. We said we began this discussion with quasi-Realism. Does the pureness of this quality of the first-ness, which we have ordained to quasi-Realism, save it from being re-cut in our butcher shop of perceptions about what would be logically possible from it? Is a point of beginning about an argument determinative of the whole argument, or only what it appears to be, one point

---

[41]Juliana of Norwich, "They Shall See His Face," in P. Franklin Chambers, *Juliana of Norwich* (New York, Harper & Brothers, 1955), p. 135.

and a premise still within it? In the latter case, then, of different and changing premises, we are inevitably bound to Meaning and Being Chains and, therefore, to the possibilities of ever further intellectual constructions about Reality. But, on the other hand, doesn't the declaration of this last sentence contain the adverb "inevitably," consist of the only Cartesian Way (yes, the word "way" has a double sense) to look at it and, therefore, amount to apodictic Truth? If so, this is the crucial turn. The "only-ness" of the manner of this looking invalidates everything else in a visual field because it means that the theory of the Reality of quasi-Realism is the only way to look at it. If this is so, Husserl's psychic, existing, transcendental I prevails.[42] It wins the war of Reality between itself and everything else. With its own conquered Truth-claims and speech-acts, it says that of which it is its own Reality.

But, in conquering speech-acts and claims on Truth, how do we determine the spoils of victory? In other words, how do we know which Truth-claims and speech-acts have been conquered and, therefore, permanently appropriated by an ego? How does an ego Really know them? Real conquering of speech-acts and Truth-claims by an existing, psychic, transcendental, human ego is done emotionally. This conquest is what one does when he reads, for example, the following lines of poetry:

> "Why, if the Soul can fling the Dust aside,
> And naked on the Air of Heaven ride,
> Wer't not a Shame—wer't not a Shame for him
> In this clay carcass crippled to abide?"[43]

Furthermore, the emotional content of lyrics set to music often substitute for verbal expressions of my consciously held emotions, and there are many emotions which I am likely to hold unconsciously. Within me is a large warehouse of emotional behavior which I store for use as daily life demands, so that I wheel the behavior out in pallets to a loading-dock, one package at a time, as life itself calls for them for delivery. For example, in the act of wheeling out my behavior and loading packages of it into conscious states, I write this but do not sleep while writing—because my consciousness is quite unable to do both activities together. You own the same warehouse. As you consult with your own version of Juliana inside of your consciousness, you may hold that most of this discussion has been, indeed, the act of a sorry manufacturer with poorly packaged products at some dilapidated warehouse in the Inner City of the soul. You may contend, moreover, that this discussion proves that I dream and even sleep-walk. As you contend your cut at Reality and hold these things, please know that both your slice and the content of it, which, as one whole self, you must eat tonight at dinner, is emotionally based. The concept of "Juliana" is the depository within personhood or soul of all those things the blazing Reality of which the soul or person does not wish to see because the person or soul believes that such a perception causes death. Accordingly, as we noted,[44]

---

[42]But see, to the contrary, Jürgen Habermas, *Postmetaphysical Thinking* trans. William Mark Hohengarten (Cambridge, Mass., Massachusetts Institute of Technology Press, 1992), p. 40, quoted in Thomas Guarino, "Postmodernity and Five Fundamental Theological Issues," *Theological Studies* Vol. 57, No. 4, p. 654 at p. 663 (December, 1996).

[43]Omar Khayyam, *The Rubaiyat of Omar Khayyam,* trans. Edward Fitzgerald (New York, Scott Foresman, 1955), p. 419.

[44]See Chapter Three, footnote 79 and accompanying text.

Love caused death for the people of the tribe of Aszra, not only because they were of such peculiar male chastity that they had no sexual love, but because of their fear that if they did Love, they would die. "Juliana" is, therefore, that particularly stored package of behavior within a human warehouse which may burn it down. You say that you do not hold any such of an inherently dangerous thing. But this very saying about your warehouse is the most dangerous inventory in it of all. It means that, if it is True, you have opened all of your stored packages of behavior and looked inside of them to see what's there. If you have done so, the packages are no longer packed, and your inventory is no longer able to be counted. You have nothing left to store. Nothing in existence does a warehouseman fear more than not being able to tell the inventory of the warehoused boxes and packages inside of it. Please ask yourself: What is the concept of "Juliana" inside of me? What do I not see because I believe that seeing it means death? Does a powerful person see death when he sees the Real prospect that he might lose his *characteristic* power? If your *characteristic* power is one of mysticism, you may perceive that, like Juliana of Norwich, if you do see God, you will either die or He asks you for a perilous mission which likely causes death. If your *characteristic* power is one of stochastic rationalism, you may perceive that, like the former United States Secretary of the Treasury, Robert E. Rubin (b. 1938), if you do see a principle of Certainty, you will either die by adhering to it or that Certainty, except to the extent that it is in any way uncertain, will certainly cause suffering. The concept of "Juliana" is in everyone's Central Bank.

The House of Beth-El is another name for the depository of feelings which the fear of existence in learning, knowing and dying causes for existence. Jean-Luc Marion's G_Xd, Christian *Terminus* and even the strictly "unproven" God of Descartes all live there. The Holy Trinity of Scholastic distinctions from orthodox Christianity sometimes lives there also, if the Christians who say so transform their distinctions about the Trinity from texts and puffs of air into packaged content which a warehouse of behavior may store for use as life calls it at a loading-dock. To conquer even these last mentioned Truth-claims and speech-acts, which surround around our death-prone existence, *not our texts of the learning and knowing of it,* emotion is required in all cases. From their texts and within their contexts, scientists and philosophers who do not think of the necessity for satisfaction and emotion about them are Truly ignorant. Even schemes of *différance,* which philosophers pose for the purpose of limiting, interrupting or destroying reality, have no Reality unless this scheme can also can grasp it, and do so as humans, like humans, always grasp Reality—by gripping it with *feelings*. The first principle of edifying philosophy is that it is a place of *felt enjoyment;* and the second principle is that, if there is an immanance of this felt enjoyment with everything else in the world, including the processes by which the enjoyment originated, edifying philosophy eats Pan-Scientism and everything else in its path.

The lyrics of a vast quantity of harmonious sound say that life itself is the fact and act of feeling vibrations in the air and of seeing visions of all sorts by a *mental* eye. If you cannot cope with *all* of musical and visual perceptions inside your mind, as it shows your consciousness how fully you *feel* them irrationally, you do not Really live and probably even die. Is this the innate concept of "Juliana" which is not seen by the reasoning of Cartesian thinking things? I am a thinking thing of Cartesian philosophy, see an emotional whole-ness to my musical and visual perceptions, and live gloriously—all because I see and live with God, *that which does not exist.*

Certain lyrics from a solo in the popular theatrical production, *Les Misérables,* put in poetry some prose of the last many pages.[45] Although I sought permission from the owner of their copyright to reprint them here, it is an altogether fitting and proper commentary upon the overwhelming contextual and commercial nature of our civilization that the owner would refuse it. The context of love and war of *Les Misérables,* or the context of whatever representation to society the owner of certain entertainment chooses to present (remember the words of Sinatra?), is where we often put our faith and truth. Can we ever peer beyond? It is no surprise that certain lyrics, often of love or war, describe whatever context of life we choose to place them into, even as we hear them in traffic on car radio. But it is also no surprise that even the most mundane of words and places—the voices of actors on a stage in *Les Misérables* or the voices from a radio—may, if we choose a different context, describe the inspired walk of soul with God. You do it "on your own" and by yourself, even if there are moments of pretending, because you Feel, you Love. The solitude, the darkness and the Love are emotional and, therefore, for the rhapsody I have been reciting—as the ancient Greeks recited epic poems in recitations called rhapsodies, a telling, emotional conclusion about logical Reality in this day and age and the subjective Belief in God I hold arising *now.*

---

[45]See Herbert Kretzmer *et al.,* "On My Own" in *Les Misérables* by Alain Boubil and Claude-Michel Schönberg, Concert Performance, Royal Albert Hall, October 8, 1995. © 1986 Alain Boubil Music Ltd. All Rights Reserved. Compare Arthur Schopenhauer, *The World As Will and Representation* (1883-86) trans. Haldane & Kemp (New York, Dover Publications, Inc., 1958, 1969) Vol. I, pp. 257-67 (recognizing the connection between self-understanding and the understanding of music).

Index of Names

A

Achilles, 10, 35
Adam, 155
Alston, William P., 23-25, 30
Anaximander of Miletus, 79, 80
Anselm of Canterbury, 94-96, 99, 158
Apel, Karl-Otto, viii
Aquinas, Thomas, 8, 80, 82, 83, 118
Aristotle, 88, 89, 92, 131, 132, 134, 137, 158, 160
Archbishop of Canterbury, 41
Archbishop of Cologne, 81
Arius, 59, 60, 158, 169
Athanasius of Alexandria, 59
Athena, xii
Auden, W. H., 138
Augustine (Saint) of Hippo, 34, 37, 80-82, 85, 89, 93, 94, 99, 103, 114, 155, 158
Avicenna, 81, 131, 134

B

Bacchus, 157
Barth, Karl, 154
Bistami, Abu Yazid, 81, 85
Bogart, Humphrey deF., 153
Brinton, Crane, 159
Browning, Robert, 65
Bruckner, Anton, 22
Bruner, Jerome S., 37
Brunner, Émil, 143
Buber, Martin, 92

Buonarotti, Michelangelo, 58, 68, 70
Buswell, J. Oliver, Jr., 8, 13

C

Caesar, Julius, 45
Celsus, 71
Châteaubriand, Vicomte François R., 110
Chomsky, Noam A., 55, 56, 170
Clement of Alexandria, 118
Clinton, William J., 73, 74, 117, 154
Cole, Dick T., 168
Confucius, 60
Constantine the Great, 59
Cooper, Prentice, 62, 65, 79, 170
Cyclops, 68

D

Daniel, 98, 99
Darwin, Charles, R., 52, 80
Davidson, Donald, viii
Dawkins, C. Richard, 52
de Biran, Maine, 124, 129
de Chardin, Pierre T., 79, 80
(see Teilhard de Chardin, Pierre)
de Châteaubriand, Vicomte F. R., 110
Dennett, Daniel C., 15-21, 32, 52, 62, 128, 144
Derrida, Jacques, xv, 145, 146, 164-166, 170, 171
Descartes, René, 1-5, 15-17, 22, 24-26, 30, 38, 39, 42, 46, 57, 71, 72, 85, 132, 135, 153, 166-168, 172, 174

Dionysus, 157
Donne, John, 77
Duns Scotus, Johannes, 73, 126, 127, 129, 137, 145, 146, 155, 158
Durkheim, Émile, 61

E

Eckhart, Meister, 81, 85
Egidio of Viterbo, 32
Einstein, Albert, viii, ix, 15, 17, 41, 102, 158, 171
Eisenhower, Dwight D., 68
Eliot, T. S., 88
Ellul, Jacques, 142
Ellwood, Charles A., 68, 159
Emerson, Ralph W., 103, 104, 137
Euclid, viii, ix
Eve, 101, 155

F

Faust, 10
Field, Hartry H., 46, 128
Findlay, John N., 56
Fodor, Jerry A., 37
Frege, Gottlob, 86
Freud, Sigmund, 48, 49, 55, 91, 94, 139, 140, 170
Friedrich Wilhelm II, of Prussia, 116, 154

G

Gabriel, 98
Gamaliel, 115, 116
Geyser, Joseph, 17, 128
Gödel, Kurt Friedrich, 41, 44, 46, 102, 158
Goethe, 10
Gregory of Nyssa, 22
GXd, xiv, 76, 84-86, 88, 91, 166, 174

H

Hajala, Ibn Abi, 95

Hegel, G. W. F., 164
Heidegger, Martin, 2, 42-44, 47, 73, 85, 126, 149, 166
Heisenberg, Werner, 9, 10, 17
Hilary of Poitiers, 109
Hume, David, 7, 26, 28, 29, 40
Husserl, Edmund G. A., 18, 32, 42-44, 47, 52, 67, 124, 129-136, 145-149, 156-158, 161-163, 169, 172, 173

I

Ibn Sina, Abu Ali, 82, 131, 134
(see Avicenna)
Isaiah, 149

J

Jacob, xiv, 100, 151
James, William, 13, 16, 17, 61, 90, 93
Jesus of Nazareth, x, 54, 59, 71, 77, 85, 89, 92, 95, 97-106, 108-121, 123, 137, 154, 157, 158, 162, 169
Job, 85, 110
John (Saint) of Damascus, 114
John (Saint) the Apostle, 104
Judas, 119
Juliana of Norwich, xv, 172-174
Juliet, 96
Jung, Karl G., 55, 170
Jupiter Optimus Maximus, 76
Justin (the) Martyr, 105

K

Kähler, Martin, 119
Kant, Immanuel, 30, 31, 80, 107-109, 116, 117, 154, 166, 167
Kierkegaard, Soren, 103, 113, 114, 116-121, 134, 138, 142, 143, 157, 158, 162
King, Archbishop William, 79, 80

L

Lady of Fatima, 67
Leuba, James H., 75

Liebnitz, Baron G. W. von, 73, 84, 85, 126
Locke, John, 26-30
Luke (Saint), 95, 104
Luther, Martin, 45, 154

M

Maimonides, Moses, 169
Malraux, André, 171
Marion, Jean Luc, xiv, 76, 84, 85, 88, 91, 174
Mary Magdalene, 99
Mather, Cotton, 159
Mather, Increase, 159
May, Rollo R., 95, 153
McKinley, William, 87, 88
Merleau-Ponty, Maurice, 10, 18-22, 29, 42-44, 47, 56, 120, 136
Mill, J. S., 6-8, 18, 74, 87, 115
Moses, 60
Muhammed, 60
Murdoch, Iris, xv, 93, 155, 156

N

Nelkin, Norton, 38, 133
Nicholas of Cusa, 124, 125, 152
Nicodemus, 115
Nietzsche, Friedrich Wilhelm, 54, 126, 137, 158
Nixon, Richard M., 70
Nozick, Robert, xi, 2, 58

O

Odysseus, 62
Oedipus, 120
Oken, Lorenz, 84
Otto, Rudolf, 152, 158, 163

P

Pandora, 101
Parker, Theodore, 104, 109, 110, 156, 158
Parmenides, 125
Pascal, Blaise, 95, 114, 139, 169
Paul (Saint) the Apostle, 71, 76, 81, 84, 85, 102, 104, 106-108, 116, 141, 168, 169
Pelagius, 140, 155, 158, 169
Peter (Saint)the Apostle, 98, 104, 119
Phillips, Abigail, 159
Phillips, Stephen, ix
Pinnock, Clark H., 7, 8, 13
Pius, IX, Pope, 109
Plantinga, Alvin C., 31, 46
Plato, 53, 59, 60, 62, 65, 93, 132, 137, 164
Pontius Pilate, 115
Pope, Alexander, 125
Powell, Margaret H., 15
Psalmist, 54
Pseudo-Dionysius the Areopagite, xiv, 84, 134
Putnam, Hilary, viii, 73

Q

Quine, Willard V. O., viii, ix, xiv, 2, 9, 27, 33, 48, 73, 86, 91, 146, 158, 160, 161, 164, 167, 168

R

Rachmaninoff, Sergei W., viii
Rolland, Romain, 48
Romeo, 96
Roosevelt, Theodore, 74
Rorty, Richard MacK., 34, 47, 50, 146
Rousseau, Jean Jacques, 48
Rubin, E., 10
Rubin, Robert E., 82, 174
Russell, Bertrand A. W., 3, 71, 72, 158

S

Sahid, 95
Santa Claus 130, 131

Santayana, George, 94
Sartre, Jean Paul, 29, 152
Schaeffer, Francis A., 141
Scheler, Max F., 21, 47, 92, 125, 134, 166
Schleiermacher, F. D. E., 50, 70, 157
Schopenhauer, Arthur, 34, 124, 129, 145
Schweitzer, Albert, 98, 99, 119, 121
Scruton, Roger, 61, 83, 159
Shakespeare, William, x, 96, 118, 153
Sinatra, Frank, 123, 153, 175
Socrates, xv, 60, 65, 171
Strawson, Peter F., viii

T

Teilhard de Chardin, Pierre, 79, 80
(see de Chardin, Pierre T.)
Terminus, xiv, 76, 78, 101, 102, 152, 158, 174
Tertullian, 78, 116, 158
Thomas (Saint) the Apostle, 115
Thoreau, Henry David, 104, 145, 158, 168
Tillich, Paul, x, xi, xii, 30, 34, 50, 81, 91, 99, 105, 106, 124, 143, 155, 169

V

Van Til, Cornelius, 28, 154, 155
Verbeke, Gerard, 38, 39
Virgin Mary, 78
Voltaire, 68

W

Weil, Simone, 32
Weizsäcker, Carl F. von, 17
Wertheimer, Max, 144
Whitehead, Alfred N., 56, 108-110, 158
Wittgenstein, Ludwig, xi, xii, xiv, 24, 25, 30-32, 38, 40-42, 44-48, 71, 72, 76, 83, 89, 90, 142, 158
Wolf, Alfred Peter, 14

Z

Zarathustra, 54, 99